Reap the Whirlwind

Book Two of the
At the Edge of Promises Series

Chris Burgess

Copyright © 2024 Chris Burgess

The moral right of the author has been asserted.

Apart from any fair dealing for the purposes of research or private study, or criticism or review, as permitted under the Copyright, Designs and Patents Act 1988, this publication may only be reproduced, stored or transmitted, in any form or by any means, with the prior permission in writing of the publishers, or in the case of reprographic reproduction in accordance with the terms of licences issued by the Copyright Licensing Agency. Enquiries concerning reproduction outside those terms should be sent to the publishers.

This is a work of fiction. Names, characters, businesses, places, events and incidents are either the products of the author's imagination or used in a fictitious manner. Any resemblance to actual persons, living or dead, or actual events is purely coincidental.

Troubador Publishing Ltd
Unit E2 Airfield Business Park,
Harrison Road, Market Harborough,
Leicestershire. LE16 7UL
Tel: 0116 2792299
Email: books@troubador.co.uk
Web: www.troubador.co.uk

ISBN 978 1805143 277

British Library Cataloguing in Publication Data.
A catalogue record for this book is available from the British Library.

Printed and bound in Great Britain by 4edge Limited
Typeset in 12pt Adobe Jenson Pro by Troubador Publishing Ltd, Leicester, UK

For my father

"You are as like the forming of God as ever people were…
you are at the edge of promises and prophecies."

Oliver Cromwell

"For they have sown the wind, and they shall
reap the whirlwind."
Hosea 8:7

1

WILL FLETCHER

(London, 8 May 1644)

They strode along the street towards Westminster. Will had polished the steel of his breastplate to an impressive shine, and thought it went well with the red of his coat. His sword clanked at his side, swinging in the black leather baldrick. His pikeman's helmet was tucked under his left arm.

At his side, half a pace ahead, was Sir Philip Skippon. If freeborn John Lilburne was Will's political hero, then Skippon was the military equivalent. Will had come to Skippon's attention through his enrolment in the Honorary Artillery Company, where he was, at that time, a captain-general. Then, as a member of one of the regiments of the London Trained Bands, Will had the opportunity to meet with Skippon who was, by then, commander of all the Trained Bands, appointed by Parliament.

Will had received lavish praise for his part in training the men and, along with others of merit, had been invited to lunch with the commander. As they spoke about the state of the regiments, it had become clear that, despite his youth, Will's experience of combat was more extensive than all but a few of those gathered. His experience of fighting on the continent, and particularly the fact that both he and Skippon had performed heroically at Breda, albeit ten years apart, helped to create a bond between them. In addition, Skippon was from Norfolk, and they knew many of the same towns and villages. Will had acquired another mentor.

They had served together ever since, as Skippon recruited Will into the regiment of foot that he had raised two years previously. This new regiment contained many of the survivors from Denzil Hollies' regiment, the Red Coats, who had fought so bravely against Prince Rupert at Brentford. That day they had fought alongside Lord Brooke's regiment where Lilburne was serving as a captain. As the Red Coats were being overrun by superior Royalist numbers, Lilburne had acted to rally Brooke's wavering troops and the combination had just managed to hold Rupert at bay. In the end, John Hampden's Green Coats had enabled the battered remnants to retreat to safety. But not Lilburne. The news of his capture had stunned Will, and much of London. No one could imagine the King looking kindly on this notorious rebel. However, fate had smiled on Lilburne and, earlier in the year, almost at the point of his execution being carried out, he had been reprieved to be exchanged for high-ranking Royalist prisoners. He had received another hero's welcome from the people of London, but all the credit for his narrow escape lay with his wife, Elizabeth, who flogged up and down the dangerous roads between London and Oxford to secure his release while heavily pregnant.

Will had been present at the standoff with the King's army at Turnham Green, where it seemed all of London had turned out in its defence. All the Trained Bands and other regiments were there, and this time the King was outnumbered. The show of defiance had meant it was the last time the King threatened his capital. Will had considered it a victory for

(London, 8 May 1644)

the ordinary people, as the Trained Bands were packed with former 'prentices, and they had been kept fed and watered by gangs of women and children ferrying food and ale to the front lines. Although a farmer by heart and upbringing, he had never felt so proud of his fellow citizens.

The regiment had gone on to perform admirably at the siege of Reading the previous April, and then, as the army returned from its successful relief of Gloucester, it had been blocked by the King, this time at Newbury. Skippon had commanded the centre and kept most of the Trained Band troops as the reserve. He had taken the central high ground quickly and then sat there determinedly holding off waves of Royalist attack, deploying the reserve to great effect to reinforce the more vulnerable wings. Will had been amazed at how the militia units had performed, doggedly holding off their more experienced opponents, and Sir Philip had been fulsome in his praise of their training. In any case, they had held their own sufficiently to have limped back to London intact.

Will had been promoted to captain, and was popular with the men he commanded, although he also had a broader role in supervising training. He knew there were sometimes sneers behind his back, usually from gentleman officers who resented the rise of this uneducated bumpkin, but this just reinforced his growing conviction of the change that was needed in England. Radical change, where the simplest working man could stand proudly alongside the privileged, and all would be made equal, as they were in God's eyes. At present, Will reflected, this only happened in death – the Great Leveller. He knew his life's work was to make this change happen.

Sir Philip strode on. Dressed all in black, save for a large white lace collar, he too wore a sword in his belt. He kept his hair shoulder length and sported an impressive moustache above his tidy goatee. He kept half turning to talk to Will on the narrow pavement as people stepped aside to let them pass. Some because they recognised an illustrious soldier and saviour of London. Most because they were intimidated by the sheer size of the fair-haired giant looming behind him.

They made their way through the Great Hall until Skippon paused and turned to Will. "So, Fletcher, you are resolved to pursue this? I know this was my recommendation, but now I wonder if I am not shooting myself in the foot."

"Sir, if you think this is how I can best serve the country, then I am content. I trust your judgement in these matters."

"And you have met some of these gentlemen previously? Is there anything more you would know before we enter?" He indicated a heavy oak door to his left.

"I have met Sir Thomas Myddelton, albeit briefly, but that was prior to coming to this understanding. I have not met Sir William, although of course I know of his reputation, and his standing within the cause."

"Indeed. 'T'was almost like a Roman triumph of old when he entered London with his prisoners from the battle at Nantwich." He smiled at Will. "We must not forget that some of the credit for that famous victory also belongs to my Lord Fairfax, but I do not begrudge him the people's favour. 'T'was well done, and it must be difficult to maintain communication that distance from Parliament." He smiled again. "Although Sir William is not backward at putting quill to paper."

"I have to admit, sir, that the sight of Colonel Monck amongst those sorry men was upsetting. I met him just before the assault at Breda, and he impressed me with his manner and bravery. He was astonishing that day as he led the charge."

"It is true, Fletcher. Many worthy men have fallen onto the King's side of this affair. I hope George Monck does not fair too ill in the Tower. He is indeed a brave man, and one I might

(London, 8 May 1644)

otherwise call 'friend'. But a note of caution for you. He is also a mysterious fellow, and keeps his own counsel, and keeps it secret. It would not surprise me if he did not turn his coat at some point and fight against the King. If he does, step wary. I have no real grounds for suspicion, but George Monck runs deep, if you know what I mean. An ambitious man but despite his bravery in battle, one who himself treads carefully through the politics of the day."

Will nodded. He too had felt a little of that reserve on his meeting with Monck. Skippon was altogether more affable, although himself never an open book.

"Think on this as an interview then, Fletcher. Sir William may have ideas for you himself if you do a good job whipping Myddelton's new regiment into shape. From what I have seen you do with the Trained Bands, and my own men, I don't think they will ever let you go, Captain Fletcher."

Will blushed and looked at his feet.

"Right, Fletcher! Let us go and meet these illustrious men from the North." He knocked and pushed the door open.

Four men were seated around a long table. Will recognised Myddelton, a man of nearly sixty, with a grey moustache and beard framed by long dark hair, only just showing signs of the same grey. Despite his age he was a vigorous man, although Will knew he felt the humiliation of having lost his ancestral home, Chirk Castle, to the Royalists in January of the previous year. Myddelton, who was sitting opposite the door, stood and walked around to greet them both, shaking hands.

The man with his back to them also stood and turned. Will did not recognise him, but Myddelton introduced him as Colonel Henry Brooke. Will knew of his reputation, gained largely from the stout defence of his house, Norton Priory, from a large body of Royalist troops, but he had never met him previously.

The man at the head of the table also stood, but made no immediate move towards them. Instead, Skippon strode over and, taking his hand, slapped him on the shoulder. "Sir William! It is good to meet again. I hope we are not interrupting? This is the young captain I was telling you about. Let me introduce Captain William Fletcher, formerly of Godmanchester, and veteran of Breda, Newbury and Turnham Green, not to mention the fight with the Covenanters."

"Perhaps best not to mention that indeed, sir, as they are now our allies." Brereton's response seemed terse and there was a slightly awkward moment before his face creased into a slight smile. "But then these are strange times. Welcome, Sir Philip, you are not interrupting." He nodded at Will. "Please, gentlemen. Be seated. And may I also introduce my ally here in London?" The fourth man came around the table and shook hands. "This, gentlemen, is William Ashurst, MP. He also sits on the Lancashire committee, and generally helps us to keep an eye on events here in the South so that we are not, ah, disadvantaged in any way." He smiled slightly.

When they were all settled, Brereton spread his hands on the table top. "In fact, we were just giving thanks. We have had some good news. As you know, we have been forced to remain here in London, away from our troops, to beg for aid in building our forces."

Leaning forward, Skippon interjected, "Ah! You have heard about your award of monies?"

"We have. In March and April we were awarded funds in excess of 5,000 pounds for arms, powder, match and so forth, but had not had any word of when these items would be delivered. Now we have a date for the shipments, and it should be within a few days, or maybe a week. Furthermore, just yesterday, as you rightly conclude, we were awarded more than 2,000 pounds of additional support, and Colonel Brooke here, a sum of 1,000 pounds for the completion of his own regiment of foot, and troop of horse."

"Congratulations, Sir William. That is good news. And to you, Colonel." He nodded to Henry Brooke, who looked as happy as a young lad who had just been given his first pony for Christmas.

"Yes, with this we can equip perhaps another 1,500 foot and 500 horse. We will be a force to be reckoned with."

Skippon relaxed back into his chair. "Indeed. You will be, sir. My congratulations again. Now perhaps we can cut the link between the King and Wales and, if we can but take Chester, put an end to the threat of more troops coming from Ireland to support him."

Brereton frowned. "Chester will be a hard nut to crack, I think. They are determined, well supplied and, generally, well led. Certainly, we will take it if we can but, if not, then we must keep the Cavaliers bottled up in there."

"I have the fullest confidence in you, sir! And to aid you in bringing your new forces up to fighting readiness, I have one of the best soldiers in England and, more to the point, one of the best for training raw recruits it has been my pleasure to command. I have discussed this with Captain Fletcher and he is in agreement that I will loan him to you for the next six months. If, of course, this is still of interest to you, Colonel?" He looked across at Myddelton.

"Most assuredly, Sir Philip. We need all the assistance we can get. The men are willing, but as you say, somewhat raw. I cannot imagine any of them giving lip to a man of Captain Fletcher's dimensions." They all laughed, Will blushing again.

"Do you have any reservations about this, Captain?" Brereton looked sideways at him. Will noted he used as few words as he could, and his gestures were contained and controlled. He had a reputation as a superb organiser and a master of spies and intelligence. Perhaps less of a reputation for leading a charge, but his results were impressive.

"I am content, sir. I have discussed this with my wife and she is as passionate for the cause as any man. In truth, she has seen precious little of me in any case. It is the same for us all. I have no reservations and I am keen to do my duty."

Again Skippon leaned forward, speaking conspiratorially, one eyebrow raised. "Captain Fletcher has married into the Chidley family, gentlemen. He is an admirer of freeborn John Lilburne."

Myddelton looked blank. "I am not aware of the Chidleys, although of course we all know about Lilburne. Even," he added, "in the wilds of the border country."

"Ah. If you stay long enough in London, sir, it will be almost impossible for you to miss one of their pamphlets. Katherine Chidley, poor Fletcher's mother-in-law, is a remarkable woman. A woman of very strong views and eloquent phrasing. Woe betide you if you start an argument of nonconformism with her!" He clapped Will on the shoulder, then theatrically shook his hand, feigning injury.

They all laughed.

Brereton turned his gaze on Will. "You admire Lilburne?"

Will immediately sensed a loaded question but was not going to shy away from his views just because he was surrounded by knights and baronets. "I do, sir. None can doubt his courage or his determination. None can doubt his steadfastness to the cause. None can doubt his support for the ordinary man. As a man of very ordinary background myself, I appreciate his sentiments. I believe he is now commissioned a major with Lieutenant-General Cromwell and the Eastern Association."

Brereton regarded him coolly. "Indeed. You are aware that Lilburne himself is no peasant farmer? He is of the minor gentry, albeit a third son."

(LONDON, 8 MAY 1644)

"I am aware, sir. My father is what you would call a peasant farmer, and so I am very aware of the distinction." But Will added nothing further, sensing this may not be a good time to pursue the conversation.

Brereton's gaze hardened slightly. "I see."

Perhaps regretting he had raised the topic, Skippon attempted to move the conversation on. "So, gentlemen, with your affairs in order, you must be straining to return to the saddle and to head north? What are your plans?"

"We have a few matters to attend to. The money is one thing, but we must secure a supplier and plan for delivery. Everywhere there is shortage. But soon, yes, you are right, we must head for Cheshire and the borders again."

Myddelton sighed. "Indeed we must. Even the newspapers are calling for our return. These writers must think war is all about gallant charges, roaring guns and heroic blocks of pikemen repelling the enemy. They never stop to think about where the saddles, powder and breastplates come from. The world of shillings and contracts! Without it, we would have to throw mud at the enemy and hope for the best."

A sudden thought occurred to Will. "If I may, gentlemen, if you need assistance with this procurement, I might seek out an old friend of mine. We have lost touch somewhat, but he also fought at Breda, and then became involved in the supply of arms. In fact, now I think on it, he was supervising the delivery of arms to Chester even before the war began. He may be available for consultation on such matters."

Now Brereton leant forward, a curious look on his face. Here was something of use to him. "The name, Captain? What is your colleague's name?"

"Farrell, sir. Richard Farrell. He had previously worked for an arms supply business, in Amsterdam."

"The Marcelis company. Yes, I know of them. And, in fact,

I know Farrell. He worked for me for a while. Unfortunately, Captain, he is unavailable. I looked him up here in London with the same thought, but he is also enlisted with Cromwell, although he has not risen as you have, it seems."

Will nodded. The matter seemed closed, although that was not what he would have expected to hear of Richard.

Skippon slapped the table with his palm. "Well, gentlemen, we will take our leave and delay you no longer. Captain Fletcher is at your disposal. You can reach him through my office." He stood and shook hands all round. Will stood and saluted.

Outside, Skippon walked a few yards and then stopped him. "I apologise, Captain. I should not have mentioned your personal connections. It created some awkwardness that I had not intended. But perhaps it serves well. Remember, when you head north, and deal with folk from those parts, it is not London. They will not have been exposed to the ideas and passions that run through the streets here. I would not seek to sway you on your views, but I counsel you to be careful what you say, and to whom. Not all, as you have seen, are necessarily admirers of Master Lilburne."

"Thank you, sir. In fact, thank you for everything. I sincerely hope to return to your command before too long. And I shall be careful. Although I doubt the common man in Cheshire fares any better than the common man in Cambridgeshire, or London. And yet they fight for their Parliament and hold hope in their hearts for a more just world. A hope that this war may yet turn many things upside down."

"Maybe, Captain. Maybe."

"Farewell, sir. I must now make my peace with Sarah. And remember to pack ink and paper, or she will never forgive me."

2

MARLEIGH HUME

(Macclesfield, June 1644)

She sensed, rather than heard, the bundle of energy that called itself Maggie Walker tearing along the corridor above her head. Then came the voice, rising in volume and pitch, as she made her feelings known to the house, and possibly the rest of the town as well.

"I will NOT have HIM here! He is NOT Daddy! It's not fair! I want my daddy!" Marleigh could hear the rest of the monologue dissolve into a mixture of shouts and sobs as she hurled herself up the stairs to the second floor and the sanctuary of her bedroom. She knew Eliza was there already, quietly removing her funeral clothing, and so Marleigh did not rush to follow. She could feel the calmness of Eliza slowly enveloping the burning hatred raging from Maggie, but like some kind of alchemic reaction, even as she slowly gained more composure, the turbulence she had brought also disturbed Eliza's carefully constructed tranquillity, and soon the embrace reached an equilibrium where both girls cried quietly in each other's arms. She would leave them alone for now, but she quietly monitored the mood from two floors below as she helped Cook prepare food for their expected, but unwelcome, guests.

To Marleigh it was neither fair nor unfair, it was just the way of things. Perhaps unlucky was nearer the truth. They had only shortly returned from burying Samuel Walker, her employer, and the girls' father. Master Samuel had been as good as his word and he had not only supported Sir William Brereton in his campaigns across the county, he had joined his small army and fought. In the first months of the war, Macclesfield had been seized and occupied by Royalists, under the leadership of Sir Thomas Aston. His motley collection of militia and professional soldiers had marched up the Chestergate into the marketplace, and the burgesses of the town, including Samuel Walker, were powerless to stop them. Known as a town loyal to Parliament, Walker and all his prominent friends were monitored by Aston's agents and, as always, there was no shortage of townsfolk with grievances who would happily trade tales and lies about them for gold. There was little opportunity to plot the overthrow of the enemy. They needed help from outside the town and the only Parliamentarians in the region were with Brereton. But he had had other goals.

Everyone knew the importance of Chester, not just as a formidably fortified city but as a gateway to Ireland. Brereton had to bottle it up. If troops were to be shipped back over the sea to aid the King, Brereton would have to try to contain them. He needed to distract its leaders and prevent it acting as a base for the Royalists in the North-West of England, and as a critical link with the largely sympathetic population of North Wales. His first objective had been to take the market town of Nantwich, and to use this as his own headquarters in the county, from where he could strike the enemy. Once established there he could hope to liberate the towns he knew were loyal to Parliament.

And so, more than a year before, Brereton had passed close to Macclesfield with a small company of horse and some

(MACCLESFIELD, JUNE 1644)

raw infantry recruits, travelling down from the Pennines and making for Nantwich. They had halted a few miles away near Congleton and were joined by some further small troops of horse. Sympathetic gentry and citizens had also found their way to him, to be met with the iron discipline of his new right-hand man, Major Lothian, a Scotsman and a professional soldier, recruited precisely with the aim of licking the untrained but enthusiastic into shape. Samuel Walker had joined Brereton on the march and had witnessed the barely controlled chaos in the lanes and fields of Nantwich that had, somehow, seen him emerge as an unlikely victor and in possession of the town. In truth, men like Walker represented a conundrum for Brereton. Important men in a political sense, and loyal and enthusiastic. But only adequate on a horse, with most scarcely having fired a musket or pistol and never handled a pike with any real intent. They may have attended drill sessions as honorary members of Trained Bands, but it was seldom taken seriously. The gulf between their experience and that of Major Lothian was vast. What to do with them?

After Nantwich, once he had been reinforced by a number of local squires and their followers, Brereton had set about dispatching units to capture Royalist houses in south Cheshire. Samuel Walker, entrusted to lead a small troop of raw musketeers, had been attached to the force commanded by Henry Mainwaring, and in February of the previous year, had had the pleasure of helping to retake his hometown as the Parliamentarians had driven out the Royalist forces, now under the command of Colonel Leigh, of nearby Adlington. Mainwaring's force had risen to 5,000 after reinforcements arrived from Manchester, and Marleigh recalled the crowds cheering the marching men as they too strode up the Chestergate and into the marketplace. The girls had been so proud, cheering their father as if he had taken the town single-handed.

Having secured the town, Mainwaring had marched them off to take Adlington Hall and from then on they had received no further word of their father for some time. He had come home to see them as the previous year had drawn on and had complimented Marleigh on the way his daughters were progressing with their studies. She knew he was impressed but also sensed his disquiet that they were becoming increasingly fond of her, more than might be expected with a cut-price governess. She had hastened to reassure him that she would never try to take their mother's place, but nonetheless he had departed in conflict, trying to balance their happiness and progress in their learning, with the strangeness that he continued to see in Marleigh, and with the rumours about her that occasionally surfaced in conversation around the taverns of the town.

The end of October was to be the last time his daughters would see him alive. They knew of the risk; they had seen fathers, husbands and sons of other Macclesfield families return dead or horribly injured, but somehow never believed it could happen to them. Then, in January, word came of a determined Royalist attempt to take back Nantwich under the command of Lord Byron. The Cavaliers had stormed the earthen walls and broken through one part of the defensive ring, gaining access to the town. Only courageous resistance from the garrison thrust them back but, in that action, their father had taken a wound to the stomach.

For months, he had clung on to life as the wound failed to heal. The musket ball had never left his body and there were none with the skill to go in after it. Gradually Samuel became weaker and weaker until his letters home to his daughters stopped completely. They feared the worst. In early June, another letter came. This one from Brereton himself. It told them that Samuel had finally lost his fight but was now surely with God and would be waiting for them in paradise.

(MACCLESFIELD, JUNE 1644)

He also told them that one of Walker's fellow burgesses from Macclesfield had informed him of their status – motherless and now fatherless – and that he had taken the liberty of writing to Samuel's sister, their aunt Mary, in order to ensure that the family of such a loyal servant of the people and of God would not want.

This news had crushed the girls' spirit almost as much as the news of their father's death. They liked their aunt. She was quiet, intelligent, and while there was no doubt she was a godly woman, she could have the sisters in stitches with the stories she would tell them of the goings-on of her neighbours in Rainow, the nearby village where she and her husband lived. While she did not radiate the smugness of the saved, or the hostility toward those of other views on faith, Jeremiah Smale presented a mirror of his wife's thoughtfulness. In Eliza's opinion, there was not a more pompous, self-righteous and unpleasant man in the country. Maggie, although she was now of an age to have a more sophisticated view, still referred to him by the name she had given him when she was only just walking. Uncle Fat.

How the marriage between Uncle Fat and Aunt Mary had ever been engineered was a mystery to Eliza, and she had always wondered what sin her aunt was being punished for. She knew it was the hypocrisy that stoked her disgust the most. He would stand in their drawing room and preach at them on the virtues of a simple, godly life – devoid of pleasure, of meagre needs, and filled with the love of the Lord. Smale railed against the foppishness of local gentry, especially those from the South, against women of doubtful morals and anything that could possibly hint at popery. And yet this godly man had a reputation for gluttony, which he seemed desperate to live up to whenever he dined with them, and for meanness to his employees, who scarcely met the breadline on what he paid for their labour.

Whenever Eliza had tried to talk to him about her heroines taking on the established Church, he mocked her for ever thinking a woman could match a man's debating skills, "... for didn't a woman's sin lead to Adam's expulsion from Eden? What more evidence do you need that a woman can only glimpse the thought of God through a man's interpretation?" Aunt Mary would pull a face behind his back, which would set Maggie off laughing, which inevitably caused a scene. Maggie backed down to no one.

Now, with the letter from Brereton, Marleigh could see that Eliza feared the worst. They would be dragged off to live in the dark, forbidding house folded into the hillside with only a distant view of Macclesfield to be glimpsed from an upstairs window. Although he had studied and practised the law, Smale had changed profession when he saw a greater opportunity for profit. He became one of the increasingly wealthy 'button-barons', an industry for which the town was becoming moderately famous. Smale's success came not from the beauty of his designs, or the quality of the craftsmanship, but from his use of arcane contract law to buy his way into ownership of a successful business and then to pay poverty wages to the workers he employed. Yet, little or none of this man's wealth found its way back to the community, it being spent purely to advance his own standing. While his home was modest and austere, he was generous with donations to the causes of other godly men, building his position with those he hoped would consider him their peer. And of course, if God noticed his generosity, then all to the good. And if God didn't notice the balance he was accumulating with the bank, then that was also fine with Jeremiah Smale.

He was never the first to accuse someone of immorality. He would observe carefully to see which way the wind blew, but then, if the tide of opinion was against the accused, he

(MACCLESFIELD, JUNE 1644)

was the loudest and most extreme in his denunciation. None were more righteous than Smale. None pursued the severest of punishments, whether legal or reputational, as strongly as Smale. Marleigh had never seen a grain of compassion in the man and she wondered how Aunt Mary could live her life as calmly as she seemed to.

Marleigh had little doubt that he would already be considering how best to profit from the girls' father's death. Samuel Walker left a substantial townhouse, a successful legal practice and certain investments in local businesses. He also owned a number of properties in the town, which delivered a good rental income. Eliza and Maggie were well provided for, but Marleigh wondered how much of their inheritance they would ever see. The Will was to be read once the Smales had arrived, which was expected later in the afternoon. Samuel's partner in the law practice, Joseph Brough, was to make the reading, and having met the man, albeit briefly, she at least had some hope that he would protect the girls' interests as she could see he adored them, being in a childless marriage himself.

Marleigh reached out briefly and sensed little Eva dozing in her cot. She touched her mind gently and promised that she would be coming to her shortly. Eva smiled quietly, eyes closed, tucked under her blanket, and radiated happiness. Marleigh knew she would need to make herself scarce once the visitors arrived and this would give her an opportunity to spend time with Eva, her beautiful child. The first being to ever elicit such a passion within her. The centre of her universe, the key to her vision, the solver of her puzzle.

Although they visited infrequently, she avoided Smale as much as possible and had had only brief conversations with Mary. She was aware that she was precisely the type of person Smale would not wish to be associated with. A doubtful reputation hung around her, she knew that, although thankfully her position with Walker, a much-admired man, had calmed her fears over the last years.

It was near five in the afternoon when Jeremiah and Mary arrived. Marleigh loitered on the stairs out of sight but within earshot of the greetings in the hallway. Profuse apologies for missing the funeral and confidence in Samuel's position with God. In truth, Smale had known Samuel's distaste for him and the feeling was mutual. He considered Samuel to be a long way from devout, and despite being a childless man himself, felt he could have told Samuel a few things about how to raise children in a godlier manner. In fact, he had told Samuel so on a few occasions and had been outraged by the rudeness of response he had received. On one occasion, back at home, he had lost his temper with Mary when she had criticised him for his intervention. He had beat her with much righteousness for the affrontery and had not let her out of her room until she had prayed for forgiveness for a day and a night. And when her bruises no longer showed.

Mary embraced both girls, although she now had to look up to Eliza, being slight in build herself. A few tears were shed. Smale shook hands with the girls, stiffly and formally, and there in the hall, led them in a short prayer.

A few moments later, Maggie came running up the stairs and bumped into Marleigh, sitting around the corner. She hushed Maggie, who whispered fiercely into her ear, "There! I was polite to Uncle Fat! I have done as I promised. I will be in my room and don't wish to be disturbed." She walked off up the stairs, and Marleigh followed. At the doorway she called on Maggie to wait.

"Maggie. Thank you for doing as we asked. It was well done. When you have sat in your room for a while can I ask you to do something more?"

(MACCLESFIELD, JUNE 1644)

"What? I have done as was asked. I shook Uncle Fat's hand and smiled. I did not shout at him or embarrass Father."

"That is all true and I thank you again. What I ask you now is that after a little while, when you have thought about how you are feeling, you then think about your sister, and how she is feeling. Maggie, you are a good girl, even if you drive me mad sometimes." She smiled at her. "You loved your father. You are sad and angry. Everyone understands that. But remember that Eliza is feeling the same. And Eliza has to sit and represent your family now. She has a heavy responsibility – you know what that means – which she must bear while all she wants to do is shout and cry. You love your sister too, I know."

Maggie's eyes brimmed with tears as she nodded.

"Do you think perhaps she needs your help today? Can you help her with this burden? When your anger has cooled a little, do you think you can return to the drawing room? You do not need to say anything. Just being there will help Eliza cope with what is expected of her. I just ask you to think on it, Maggie."

She left her there and carried on up to the top floor to Eva. After a few minutes she heard Maggie's door close and quiet footsteps heading slowly back down the stairs. She smiled to herself and scooped a sleepy Eva out of the cot. They looked into each other's eyes and the connection deepened. She lowered herself onto the oak chair in the corner of her small attic room where she could see out onto the sunlit hillside and sat Eva on her knee, so they faced each other.

"I am pleased to see you, Mama. I have missed you."

"And I you, my little one. I have brought you some warm milk and bread. Are you hungry?"

The faerie eyes, one grey and one brown, sparkled back at her. "Very!" and she shared the sensation with Marleigh.

"Oh yes, you are! I am sorry for keeping you waiting. I had to help the girls. It is a difficult time for them. I hope you understand."

"Of course, Mama. I love them too."

As Eva started to dunk her crusts of bread into the mug, Marleigh let her awareness rise and the world lit up with the energy of life. She saw the myriad of flows and connections between herself and Eva, and the life around them, near and far. She closed her eyes to dim the brilliance again and let herself float away.

*

It was after the guests had dined that Marleigh crept down to the girls' room and softly knocked. Over the time she had spent with Eliza and Maggie their relationship had deepened. She liked both girls in different ways, especially the independence of spirit and the challenge they always brought to any discussion. They were intelligent and curious and passionate about accumulating knowledge. She knew that they both adored her and saw her as somewhere between mother, big sister and best friend. Marleigh could not return the same depth of feeling, only Eva had ever managed to wring a true feeling of love from her, but she cared deeply for their welfare. She also was desperate to understand how events might impact on her own future. And Eva's.

Eliza opened the door a crack and Marleigh saw an intense blue eye peer at her. An eye red-ringed with exhaustion and sorrow. She opened the door further and Marleigh slipped inside. These midsummer days were long and the room was illuminated with the ruddy glow cast by the lowering sun. The grey, leaden skies had temporarily departed and the drizzle-coated roof slates of the cottages behind the house were glinting.

(MACCLESFIELD, JUNE 1644)

"How are you, Eliza? Maggie? What has occurred?"

Maggie was already in her bed, leaning against the headboard, knees drawn up under the covers. Eliza sat down wearily on the end of the same bed and pushed her blonde curls back from her face.

"Well. We are saved. For now." She managed a watery smile and wiped at a tear track down her cheek. "Father selected his executor well. Master Brough has saved us all this afternoon."

Marleigh walked around the bed and climbed on next to Maggie. She put her arm around her. Maggie seemed suddenly older, as if she had aged several years since Marleigh had last seen her. She felt proud and gave her shoulder a squeeze. Maggie smiled faintly up at her. "How so? Tell all, Eliza."

"I am not learned in law yet..." Marleigh smiled to herself, "...but from what I understood, Aunt and Uncle have no claim upon Daddy's estate. At least not a direct claim. All is to be held in a kind of trust for us, until we are both of age. When we are eighteen we will then have full control of the, hmm, the assets?"

Marleigh nodded.

"When I am eighteen I will have a say in the management of affairs, and when Margaret reaches that age, all control will pass to us."

Marleigh noticed that Maggie had become Margaret. Perhaps Eliza had also noticed a change in her sister, or perhaps she herself had decided it was time to move on from childhood. "So, if that is the case, why were your uncle and aunt asked to attend the reading of the Will?"

Eliza sighed and hung her head again. "That is the less positive outcome. Uncle Jeremiah is to be a joint trustee with Master Brough. Neither can do anything with the properties, or this house, without the agreement of t'other. Uncle cannot sell anything out from beneath us, and anything that both do agree to sell, the proceeds can only be held in trust for me and Margaret."

"That sounds quite normal, Eliza. Your father was a lawyer. It is all good news for you both, I think, but I would have expected such an arrangement. What about where you both will live? Who will run the household? What of your education? You are nearly a woman grown and into your inheritance, Eliza, but Margaret still has some growing to do." She nudged Maggie and smiled at her. Maggie stuck her tongue out but then seemed to check herself and frowned in what she thought was an altogether more grown-up response.

"From what I understood, Father has left Uncle and Aunt in charge of our spiritual and moral education, and upbringing. At least until I am eighteen when I become responsible for both myself and Margaret. We are yet to learn what this will mean for us. He cannot force us to leave this house, but he would have the right to live here until I am of age."

"And what has your uncle decided? Did he give any response on this?"

"They are thinking on it. They will pray to God this night and our uncle will reveal His will to us in the morning. I know I shall not sleep this night." A tear slid down her cheek again. "I do not think I can live with that terrible man in charge of my life. And, oh, Marleigh, what would become of you and little Eva? I could not bear it if you were to go!"

What indeed? she thought to herself. Although she had been thinking primarily about the girls, which immediately surprised her, she did wonder how Jeremiah Smale would take to Marleigh Hume and her little faerie-eyed, bastard girl.

Maggie answered for her. "Don't worry, sister. If he tries to do anything to hurt you, or Marleigh, or darling Eva, I shall cut his fat throat while he sleeps."

3

WILL FLETCHER

(Oswestry, June 1644)

He slumped down onto the earth. Nearby, some of the men were trying to get a fire going with little success. The drizzle of the last few days had left everything damp and he didn't fancy their chances. Even for Will, it had been a hard few days, but he knew there would be no rest until nightfall. *Just a few moments, then I will get up.* He closed his eyes. And opened them again immediately. *No! Not a great example, is it?* he chided himself. Gripping the long ash handle of his pike, he levered himself up again.

He could see long lines of men, horses and wagons making their way through some scrubby trees and onto the heathland. Although the day had seen a great victory, heads were down from sheer exhaustion. He called across to one of those trying to build the fire. A man he recognised from training drills. "Hey! Any idea where we are?"

"Not me, Captain. I'm from Putney. Might as well be in Barbary."

Another voice called out, "Felton, Captain. Or thereabouts. About part way 'tween Oswestry and Shrewsbury."

The first man looked at Will and winked. "Like I said. Might as well be Barbary."

Will grinned back at him, and then started to wander around to try to gather up his company. The new red coats of Myddelton's regiment at least made sorting them from the three regiments of Cheshire foot a little easier. As more wagons started to enter the encampment, the groans of the injured and dying started to reach him. Knots of walking wounded were also starting to appear, slowly making their way towards the fires and the smells of cooking that started to drift on the breeze.

He directed men from Myddelton's regiment towards the western side of the camp, reserving an encouraging word or sharing a joke with men he recognised. Some of these were members of the company he commanded, some from the drill sessions he had been running throughout the long march up from London into Cheshire, and while they were encamped at Knutsford, waiting for the push north. But that push had never come. A few days earlier, Myddelton had received word that the newly captured town of Oswestry was under siege again, this time from a Royalist force drawn from Cheshire and Shropshire garrisons.

The Earl of Denbigh, who had overall command of the north-western forces for Parliament, dithered. *There is a man not born to lead!* With Prince Rupert arcing through Lancashire and heading for the relief of York, he was receiving daily encouragement from Parliament to send support there. Equally, his local regimental commanders were concerned about the trouble brewing in their own backyards, and the letter from Oswestry was such a case in point. If Oswestry fell, the Royalists had a corridor from their strongholds in the Midlands, right across to loyalists in Wales. What to do?

After frantic lobbying from Myddelton, he had agreed to dispatch his regiment, together with three Cheshire foot regiments and a good force of cavalry, immediately. They had set off on Sunday, marched thirty-five miles south-west in just two days and camped at Whitchurch. This morning they had set off for Oswestry, a near twenty-mile march.

Will had not even heard of the town before the briefing Myddelton had given to his captains. It was walled and protected by a castle, occupying a strategic position in the Welsh Marches. Capturing it had been a welcome boost to parliamentary objectives. Losing it would be disastrous, potentially cutting off the North-West from London.

The column of foot had wound its way along country lanes and through fields of grain and cattle, screened all the time by the troops of horse. After a long morning trudging through the humid air, the men were flagging, and regimental colonels called a stop for rest and food. However, just as the columns were starting to relax, word came down the line that the enemy had been sighted and were formed just a few miles up the road. Regiments re-formed, this time in battle order, and stepped off at a fast pace. Will had been pleased with the noticeable increase in discipline among Myddelton's men who, while not at the same pitch as the more experienced Cheshire foot, were nevertheless showing up well.

After an hour, the sounds of battle could be heard ahead, and a trickle of wounded horsemen started to appear, heading for the rear. The word was that the enemy had dispatched its horse to hold up their advance and protect the besieging Royalist troops. They held the River Perry at Whittington up ahead, and had launched a series of ferocious charges at the Parliamentarian horse. Their cavalry was holding, just, but needed urgent support.

He could hear the commands echoing up and down the lines and blocks and columns of men. Men, already tired from the march, picked up the pace again, almost jogging through the fields. Will marched at the right-hand front corner of Myddelton's main pike block. Constantly shouting and waving to keep the men together. They were flanked by lines of musketeers, blowing on their matches to keep them glowing. If the enemy horse broke through, the pike block would become a refuge for these men. Few horses would charge into a wall of pikes.

The trickle of horse started to turn into a stream as it became clear they were arriving at the front line. A furious melee could be heard. Ringing clashes of steel on steel and the occasional pistol shot, and the shouts of men and screams of their mounts.

Myddelton's regiment came up the left side of the cavalry and the musketeers started to extend their line to pour a volley into the Royalist flank, the smoke from their muskets soon obscuring the scene. Will shouted for pikes to be lowered and the call was taken up by sergeants through the unit. Will's company made up the front ranks of the block and the pikes came down in some semblance of order, creating a hedge of steel. Supporting the musketeers who were now reloading as fast as possible, the red-coated pikemen slowly advanced on the Royalist flank. Will could see the urgency of the moment. After a long period of battling against a numerically superior opponent, their cavalry was breaking. But driven forward through the smoke by the steady drum beat, Will could see the enemy horse becoming aware of the foot soldiers lapping around both flanks. He could just make out Myddelton's horse filtering back between the blocks of infantry coming up behind them, and the Cavaliers' confidence turned to fear, as instead of chasing a broken formation, they encountered fresh troops. Will winced involuntarily as a withering volley of musket fire crashed around him, men falling, and wounded horses screaming and plunging. He smiled grimly as he led the thick hedge of pikes towards them.

Now it was the Royalists who broke, frantically turning exhausted mounts in the scrum and trying to force their way out of the trap. Some fell, and some could not escape in time, throwing down weapons and calling for quarter.

Heartened by the turning tide, Myddelton's own horse rallied, re-formed and set off in pursuit, with the foot regiments jogging along behind, cheering wildly. They kept up the pursuit for as long as the exhausted men could manage, chasing the Royalists across the fertile farmland south, towards Shrewsbury.

Now, they were preparing food and grumbling over cuts and bruises, sore and blistered feet and the availability of water, sack and ale. There were terse disagreements over the best places for sleep, and latrines. Always the youngest, rawest recruits got the job of digging those. Will's mind always went back to Breda, and Rich and himself endlessly digging latrines and trenches in the heat of that summer. He wondered where Rich was. He wondered where Roger was. He wondered if they were both still breathing.

After an hour so, he heard his name being called. Captain Swift was walking in the direction of Myddelton's command position and hailed him. "Fletcher! Captain Fletcher sir! We are required to attend the colonel. He will brief us for the morrow."

Will raised a hand in response and buttoned his coat. "I am following, Thomas!" He noticed Swift wince slightly at the familiarity, but he managed a thin smile and nod in response. He was still feeling his way in the regiment. It was a strange mix. Some officers had been with Myddelton throughout the campaign and were local men. Others, like himself, had been part of the recruitment in London and were regarded with a mixture of suspicion and disdain. He felt relatively relaxed about this, partly because he knew his own experience was inferior to no one's in the regiment, partly because he no longer felt intimidated by those who would consider themselves his 'betters', and partly because he was, generally, of an easy-going disposition.

Myddelton's men had already erected a large tent in the centre of the growing encampment, and as Will approached, he could see a number of officers converging on the location from different directions. Some of these were from Myddelton's own regiment, Will's regiment, but others were from the Cheshire foot regiments temporarily under Myddelton's command, led by Colonels George Booth, Mainwaring and Croxton. As he ducked and entered the tent, he saw these other colonels conferring with Myddelton behind a long trestle table draped with maps and other papers. Myddelton looked tired and harassed, and Will had to remind himself of the man's age. It must be painful for him to ride around this countryside, just a few miles from his home, but to not be able to visit. The Royalist garrison there would be unlikely to welcome him in.

A crowd of fifteen to twenty officers from Myddelton's regiment were packed into the space on the other side of the table. A handful of more senior officers from the other regiments had also shuffled into the cramped space. Will assumed they would carry out their own briefings.

Once everyone was as comfortable as they were going to be, Myddelton started by congratulating the assembled on the conduct and valour of the men, with particular reference being made to the commander of the cavalry, and to the determination of the foot regiments to engage after the long march.

"Gentlemen. That was the good news. We have carried the day with acceptable losses, God be praised!" Will saw glances exchanged. "Now the bad news. We have heard that the enemy has carried the siege and are now in possession of the town and castle. We but drove off their screening troops, albeit a noble deed, professionally executed."

There was muttering and not a little whispered cursing. Myddelton banged the table sharply to regain attention. "Gentlemen. Please. God is testing our resolve. He wishes us to remain humble in his presence and does so by laying challenges in front of us. We still have an enemy to defeat, it is just that we must now evict him from Oswestry."

Now the colonel next to Myddelton banged the table. "And we are just the men to do it!" he shouted, seemingly nonplussed by the low-key oration of his commander. This brought a rousing cheer from the assembled men and immediately the mood lifted. Will thought this must be George Booth, a man building a reputation as a courageous leader of his regiment.

"Thank you, Colonel. Almighty God, we beseech you that it is so."

There were mumbled 'Amens' around Will. *Hurrah for George*, he thought.

Myddelton continued, "Gentlemen, we have been conferring and it is our belief that we cannot undertake a full attack on the town tomorrow. The men are tired and in any case we must reconnoitre the ground."

Some voices were raised again, calling for the assault, but Myddelton dampened this down, making palm-down gestures. "However, neither can we let the Cavaliers think they can settle in and put their feet up. We do not want them happily digging more trenches and repairing defences that they so recently demolished themselves. No, gentlemen. We mean to distract them. We mean to keep them otherwise occupied whilst the bulk of the army gets some rest."

He paused, and took a mouthful of wine, wiping his full beard with the back of his gauntleted hand. "Oh, yes. And I forgot to mention," he smiled mischievously at the other colonels, "the Earl of Denbigh will also arrive tomorrow with substantial reinforcements! No escape for the enemy!"

The cheering broke out again, this time with an edge of relief and a greater feeling of confidence.

Again, Myddelton held up his hands for silence. "Gentlemen. On the morrow, we will bring the army to the walls. Your colonels know where to place you. We will also be attempting St Oswald's church. The importance of this will be clear to you when we arrive. It is fortified, but lies outside the town's walls. If we do not take it, the enemy will be able to deliver flanking fire on our assault. If we deny it to him, it damages his morale and provides us with a staging post to attack the walls. Above all, as I have said, it will distract him. It will keep him guessing and it will prevent him from strengthening the defences before the main assault which will follow."

Murmurs of approval around the tent.

"Gentlemen. We will allocate no more than 200 to this task and I intend the honour of this to fall on men of mine own regiment." He held up his hands again as there were both protests and cheers from the assembly. "Do not fear! On the following day I will expect all to do their duty most valiantly and fall upon the occupiers of Oswestry like lions. On that day, my regiment will lie in reserve and will cheer you on to victory. Now, gentlemen. If you are not in my regiment, you are dismissed. Thank you for your patience. Away to your men. Rest and prepare them as necessary for what is to come. My officers, please remain so I may give you the orders for tomorrow."

An hour later, with the evening turning to the light dusk of midsummer, Will walked from Myddelton's tent with Major Lothian, the Scot who had helped Brereton to raise the quality of his troops so dramatically. He had not been too surprised to learn that Lothian had met Captain Browne, who had commanded Will at Breda, but was frankly astonished that he also knew Roger DeLacey.

"Don't let the swagger and foul mouth fool you, Fletcher. I have seldom seen anyone better with a blade. He can aggravate the hell out of you, but I would want him on my side in a fight!"

They found a quiet part of the camp to sit and discuss the assault. Myddelton was leaning on Lothian's expertise, and the old man had been sharp enough to remember that Will had taken part in more than a few sieges on the continent, although not at the rank of captain in those days. They had scarcely begun to plan, when they were approached by another man. He was not in uniform but wore a broad-brimmed hat and long brown leather coat. He looked like he made a habit of sleeping in hedgerows, and his odour, even in the midst of the camp of an army that had been marching for days, took Will's breath away.

"Aye, I know! I'm a bit ripe, gentlemen. But so would you be if you'd been crawling around the ditches of Oswestry for days. You don't know me, but I report to Captain Walker, Brereton's scoutmaster. I won't give you my name, but here is my pass if you want some proof of this."

Lothian took the paper carefully between the tips of two fingers and examined it. "Alright. Sit. Now, why have you followed us here and what do you want?"

"Myddelton sent me, Major. You be plottin' the assault on St Oswald's tomorrow, ain't ye? He thought I could provide you with some intelligence. As to what I want? Well, now. That's a question with a long answer that I won't bore you with, but suffice to say it involves hot water, hot food and a hot w…"

"That is quite enough!" Lothian snapped.

Will looked down to hide his smile as Lothian blushed. Not something he had thought the hard-bitten mercenary capable of.

"Whatever you say, Major."

For the next half-hour, using a stick to draw in the damp soil and gravel, the spy indicated the position of the church, its lines of fire, his estimate of the garrison size and competence, and the possible routes of attack. It was enormously helpful for their planning, and Will could see Lothian's respect for the man increasing as he laid out his knowledge.

"I have to say, sir, your help has been invaluable. I wish we could have this before every engagement."

"Well, whilst Colonel Myddelton is not overly keen on spies, or scouts as he likes to call 'em, Brereton will take every chance he has to outwit the enemy. He is not one for the brave charge and death or glory and all that. He prefers to think and plan his way to victory. Saving his men's lives as far as possible. You know, why blunder around in the dark, so to speak, when you can use the ground, the time o' day or some trick to push the odds to your favour? Colonel Myddelton thinks that may not be very honourable."

Will sighed. "I have seen that very often," he said. "Commanding officers put their own honour and glory first, and spend the lives of the common man to achieve it without a second thought. Perhaps, once the King is defeated, we can create a new England where the lowborn count as more than fodder for the fight."

Lothian looked hard at him. "Sir, keep those thoughts to yourself. You should not disrespect your colonel, particularly as you are new in his service."

"I mean no disrespect, sir. Men like Myddelton know no other way. I do not blame him. But we must show people there is another way. Otherwise, what is all this for?" He gestured around him at the thousands of men. "If the King is defeated, do we raise another in his place? This is not like the wars we have fought on the continent. Wars for territory. Wars of conquest. We are all English," he looked at Lothian, "or Scots. There is no foreign invader. This is about what kind of country we want to be."

The spy grinned at him. "Well, good luck wi' that, friend. If you think them that 'as the power is going to 'and it to the likes of you or me, then I think you 'ave 'ad too many blows to the 'ead!"

Lothian was altogether less jovial. "Don't let me hear talk like that from you again, Fletcher. Maybe that passes muster in London – God knows they are strange people down there – but here? Here, that is borderline sedition. Now, go and pick your men for tomorrow. We must be away from here before dawn if we are to offer any kind of surprise."

Will shook his head. "Alright, Major. I hear you. We will be ready." He slapped the spy on the back and thanked him, and wandered off back to his men. Lothian was right in that he had to be more careful. Hadn't Skippon also warned him? He had to be more sure of his audience before speaking. He had to be clever, like Lilburne.

Quietly, he spoke to the men of his company who would take part in the assault tomorrow and warned them to be awake and ready to march in a few hours. He dare not try to sleep himself, so he settled to write a letter to Sarah. A letter which told of his frustrations at his ability to persuade others to his views, his love for her and his thoughts about the battle to come. Even though his writing was much improved, he was only just finishing when it was time to rouse the men.

4

MARLEIGH

(Macclesfield, 22 June 1644)

As usual, she had woken just before dawn. Immediately she felt the warmth of Eva's mind reaching out to her. *I have been awake for an hour, Mama. Why do you sleep so long when I am hungry? So hungry!*

But no crying. Just patience, love and understanding of her need to sleep. Eva was a miracle. For the thousandth time she asked herself, why? Why had she taken so long, so many long years to take this step? Eva had opened her eyes to such marvels and opened her mind to an understanding of the true nature of the world. She extended her remade mind slightly, feeling for energy flowing around the house. Nothing was stirring, just a couple of sparrows splashing in the gutter outside her window.

She swung her feet out of the bed to the cool floorboards. Two steps and she swept Eva out of the cot and into her arms. Her faerie eyes glittered back at her, catching the light sifting through the thin curtain. Eva smiled and gurgled, her black hair now encroaching on her forehead, already a little tanned from the long walks Marleigh had taken her on when she was not working. Up into the hills, or along the river.

(MACCLESFIELD, 22 JUNE 1644)

"Very well, my love. You are too old for me to feed you, so don't get any ideas. We will find some bread and milk in the kitchen."

Now, Marleigh thought, *what to do today?* She had lessons with the girls until midday, but after that she was free. Eliza and Maggie were going with their uncle and aunt Smale to visit cousins who were in the area, displaced by the war. A mission of God's mercy, Smale called it. An opportunity to spy and gloat, she thought more likely. She could do a few chores for Cook, and then perhaps have some time to herself to play with Eva.

Eva looked up at her. *That's a good plan, Mama.* Eva didn't need to speak; the words just came into her mind. Marleigh had found that her new awareness enabled her to reach into the minds of others with greater ease than before. Previously, in extreme situations, she had managed to use her talent to escape, conquering lesser minds, bludgeoning them into submission when the power released by death surged through her and enhanced her raw natural gift. Now, it was all more precise and unaided. She felt she was getting closer to the time when she would perhaps be able to influence the thoughts of others without their knowledge. Riding along the flows and interactions of energy that she had only half glimpsed before Eva came. She was excited, but knew she had to be cautious.

Today was the solstice. The longest day of the year. She longed to celebrate her rite. Up in the hills with just the rocks, soil, plants and animals for company. To reconnect and return to them. To become part of the whole again and to feel that community for just a few hours. But now she had other responsibilities and that was a sacred duty. Without Eva she might never have known. Never have gained her insight and her new powers. She might have remained cursed to hover on the brink of truth across the years, without ever quite grasping the whole. It was worth missing out on her midsummer celebration. Now she knew she could rejoin at any time, without the need for any physical communion. She could not remember, in all her long years, feeling so happy and fulfilled.

"Right, little Eva, what on this earth can we teach those two girls today?"

*

Marleigh sensed the buzz in the town that always came with market day. She had stepped out from the side door of the house a little after two in the afternoon, her work done but with a list from Cook of what she should buy for the household. A cake was being made to celebrate Eliza's sixteenth birthday and she had a list of items to secure. Now, with most of her list completed, she sat with Eva perched on her left thigh, propped against her, viewing the comings and goings of the marketplace from the steps of St Michael's parish church. It was warm enough – a pale watery sun tried to pierce some stubborn low cloud – but she felt that the atmosphere was still austere and restrained. The war had taken its toll, and fear, suspicion and resentment were always just under the surface of exchanges between shoppers and stallholders, and friends, relatives and neighbours who happened to meet in the square.

She was painfully aware she had something of a reputation for being different. It wasn't good to be viewed that way at any time in these more rural parts of the country, but this time of civil conflict made it even more dangerous. Her employment by the highly respected Walker family, and her connection through that to the less respected Jeremiah Smale, protected her to some degree, but nevertheless she generally tried to keep a low profile in the town. At last month's market day, she had seen old Alice Mellor, the cunning woman she had met in Alderley Edge woods, but she had managed to avoid her. It would do her no good to be seen with one such as Old Mother Edge, harmless though she was.

But now and again, she needed to get out. Walks in the hills and valleys refuelled her spirit as she soaked up the glories of her newly enhanced talents and understanding, but it was only here, in the town and among the people, that she could truly attempt an application of that knowledge. Sitting quietly, she could commune effortlessly with Eva, manipulating the flow of energy to transmit thoughts and messages. With a crowd of people, their forms seemed like a hive of bees, and it was seemingly impossible to pick out individuals and their minds. She had to concentrate, to focus her mind and try to discern the patterns of thought in a stranger. She searched the crowd for someone who was relatively stationary. This would make it easier for her to try to connect. It would have to be subtle of course, but her new skills enabled this precision. Her target would not have to suspect anything, just a light caress. Stimulate an action she could then observe to test the process.

She lighted upon a stallholder standing not too close, but close enough. Her stall was at the top of Church Wallgate, a narrow street which wound up from the valley below and into the south-east corner of the marketplace. The woman had her back to her so would not see her concentrating gaze. She was selling eggs, cheeses and a few poor-looking vegetables. She had no customers and so no distractions. *Well, Eva, let us see if we can get the goodwife to drop just one of her eggs.*

After a few minutes of study, Marleigh felt she had a good picture of the woman's mind. How she thought, how she moved her body, her character. It was all there for her to see, a simple interpretation of the streams and eddies, the tides and waves of energy. All she needed to do was nudge. To extend her own self, her own well of energy-driven thought, to find the way in and to push. Gently. Softly. A feathered whisper of suggestion.

Oh, Mama! This is fun! Go on! Do it now! Unbidden, Eva flowed powerfully into her own mind like a sluice gate had been suddenly released and, to her horror, before she could exert any control over the process, the woman had grabbed a tray of eggs and flung them up into the air.

Eva! No!

The eggs rose and fell, making satisfying squelching thuds as they hit cobbles and compacted earth. All might have ended harmlessly there, but suddenly the woman screamed, looking wildly around her, the palms of her hands pressed to her temples. As she turned she locked eyes with Marleigh, and then Eva, her eyes rolled skyward and she collapsed, fainting in a heap. The scream frightened a horse just entering the marketplace, a young man on its back. It whinnied, rearing up onto its back legs, its eyes rolling in apparent mimicry of the collapsed stallholder. The man managed to cling on and slowly calmed the horse. Others ran towards the collapsed woman; some helped hold the skittish horse's bridle, to allow the man to dismount.

Eva! Bad girl! Marleigh surveyed the scene with anguish. *You must not do that!* She rose slowly, trying to remain inconspicuous. As long as the woman was out cold, she could slip away. Everyone was too distracted by the nervous horse to see her as she started down the steps, aiming to slip into the crowd of people craning their necks to see what had happened. From there it was just a short walk to the house and to safety.

Calming a distressed-looking Eva, she had made it onto the bottom step, when a hand gripped the arm that was holding her sack of shopping like a vice. Marleigh whirled around, looking up into a pinched, weather-beaten face.

(MACCLESFIELD, 22 JUNE 1644)

"Did you think no one had seen you, Hume?" Mary Brassey's pale blue eyes bored into her. "You did that." She was speaking softly, but her voice was full of menace. "I was watching you and you never took your eyes off that poor woman. You bewitched her and I bet you did the same to the horse. I am a witness to it."

Marleigh tried to pull away without making a scene, but Mary Brassey was not letting go. As they struggled on the steps, Marleigh not able to fight effectively with Eva cradled in one arm, Brassey finally glanced down and caught sight of Eva. "That your whore's brat, is it? So much for 'Oh woe is me. Me 'usband is in the wars and I know not when I will see 'im again.' Just a common whore after all!"

Eva stared back, and Marleigh feared she was going to try to attack Brassey in some way, feeling energy build within her. But now Brassey locked eyes with Eva and took in the mismatched eyes, and sensed the disturbing intelligence behind them.

She dropped Marleigh's arm as if she had been stung, raising a hand to her mouth with a look of horror. "Not just a whore," she hissed. "The Devil's whore!" Her voice had risen, and Marleigh sensed rather than saw heads in the marketplace turning to this new entertainment. She took a smart step away from Brassey so she could not grab her again easily.

She pushed her way through the people, head down and sheltering Eva under her shawl. Behind her, from the steps, voice carrying over the heads of the shoppers and traders, she heard, "Witch! I accuse you, Marleigh Hume! Witch! Witch with the Devil's child on your hip! No escape for you this time! Whore!"

She made it around the corner and into the Mill Street. Half running with the sack of shopping in one hand, Eva clamped to her chest with the other. Looking for the safety of the house but knowing that safety could not last.

5

WILL FLETCHER

(Oswestry, 22 June 1644)

The sky was just turning to a heavy grey as the hidden sun started to dawn on the longest day of the year. There would be no spectacular sunrise to mark the solstice, as thick cloud had ensured a warm but pitch-black night.

This had been both a blessing and a curse for Will and the men crouched along the hedgerow behind him. The darkness had masked their movements, and the close, humid atmosphere had helped to muffle the sound of their passage through the countryside, but they had resembled a troop of the blind, walking hand on the shoulder of the man in front. They had followed Brereton's spy in a long, snaking line, with only the man's keen night eyes and his knowledge of the countryside to guide them. Even so, the quiet of their progress was marked with whispered curses and exclamations of pain as toes were stubbed, heads collided with low branches and abrupt halts resulted in pile-ups, as men walked into the back of the one in front.

But now they were here. Crouched down in a shallow ditch that ran along both sides of the hedge. They were ankle deep in last year's beechnuts and acorns, trying to arrange themselves between clumps of stinging nettles and a few thistles, and gain a few moments of rest and comfort. Men were stretching and yawning, some from a lack of sleep, but Will knew that most of this was from fear. Fear of the unknown, as many had not been in a skirmish before. Fear of a horrible, painful death, or mutilating injury; they had all seen the bloated corpses of friend and foe, and the makeshift surgeons' tents. Or fear of fear itself. When the order came, would they stand and fight with their friends, would they turn and run, or would they freeze like a rabbit in the gaze of a weasel? He knew how they felt. Despite his years of experience, he still felt the same. There was little he could say to help them now, even had he the opportunity. No stirring speech would change anything, they all had to find out for themselves what kind of man they were. What fate awaited them when the time came to cross the field on the far side of the hedge.

Suddenly, in the oak above Will's head a robin launched into song. The fluid notes rose and fell – a challenge to its rivals that, in this tree, along this hedge, he was King. There was a pause, as if the birds of the air had a collective intake of breath, and then the full chorus of the dawn erupted around them. As a conducted choir, a hundred voices rose into the murky sky. Announcing, each to their own kind, that they were there. They had survived the night, and they were going to defend their mate and their territory from all comers. Woe betide any that ignored this warning.

Will rose, and gradually, sequentially, the whole line rose with him. Musketeers blew on their matches and loaded their weapons. Pikemen, having left their pikes behind, checked pistols, or drew swords. Will stood where they could all see him, at the angle where their hedge met another at a right angle. At the far side of this second hedge, a grassy field, perhaps 200 yards wide, separated them from the church, the graveyard surrounded by a low wall. A few cattle were lying in the lush, damp grass, brown hide glistening damp. He gestured with a chopping motion, and the fifteen men immediately behind him, together with the spy, started to push their way through the hedge they had followed to this point and to make their way to the right, along the second hedge. Lothian started to lead the rest to the left, lining the rest of the hedge with men, concentrated at the point closest to St Oswald's. He would lead the left end of the line, Will the right.

It was a simple plan, but these were usually the best. The small group would get to a point at the extreme right and then start to fire and make as much noise as possible. They would fake advances and generally try to convince those defending the church that that was the point of the attack. Way over to the left, the main body of the army would be seen deploying around the area of the main gates to the town. With the defenders so distracted, and his own men well hidden, they hoped to be able to storm across the field with minimal casualties and arrive with enough weight to carry the doors of the church itself. What they didn't want was to turn the meadow into a morgue.

They settled again into position and waited for the main body to start their deployment. They were more than an hour behind Will and his men, but even so, their arrival so early in the day should panic the Royalists. Panicking men don't make good decisions. Or that was the idea. Some started, as quietly as possible, to make or enlarge holes in the hedge, so they would get a quick and unimpeded start to their charge across the open grass. Many men prayed. Some sipped water or chewed on a hunk of stale bread. They waited.

The sky lightened to a steely grey and the birdsong quietened. Some of the men had fallen asleep in the ditch while others peered through the hedge. They waited. Will sat watching the position where Lothian was crouched, waiting for the signal. A messenger from the main army would contact Lothian who would then signal Will. Will would signal to the spy and his small detachment of men, and the feint would commence. And there it was; Lothian half stood, and waved, repeatedly crossing his arms over his head. Will raised a hand to confirm he had seen it. He then burrowed through the beech twigs, squeezing his massive frame through the gap. He pulled leaves and sticks from his full beard and long hair, and waved his own arms at a point along the intersecting hedge, away to his right. He saw the answering wave and retreated back to his side.

He crept along the line, shaking men awake, mumbling some words of encouragement, reminding them of their objective. Getting them all in to a starting crouch, checking and rechecking weapons, muttering final prayers. He was halfway along the line when he met Lothian coming the other way. Just as they shook hands, there was a crash of musketry from the right, and the cries of men. Someone had taken a drum and started to beat this violently, sounding the charge. A few moments later a second volley sounded, further to the right as the group tried to make their line seem longer than it was. Powder smoke would soon mask the hedge in any case, but they were doing a good job, fifteen sounding like a hundred.

Peering through the hedge he could now see activity behind the wall. Figures scurried about and a small flag was being waved silently. He could faintly hear shouting as officers tried to organise their men. Away over to the left, there was the unmistakable sound of a large body of men on the move. Drums, feet, the rattle of equipment, shouted orders. There would be no attack, although this would be held as an option depending on the progress Will and his men made.

They waited. Waited to give the enemy plenty of time to move men to the left and to the right. Hopefully when the time came, when they made the dash across the grass, there would be fewer men opposite them. Fewer muskets aimed their way. When the time came, it should be easy.

And now the time had come. Will and Major Lothian returned to their respective ends of the line. With all eyes on them, they motioned for the men to rise, and with no shouts, no drums, the nearly 200 men started to run, as fast as they could, across the field. They started in bunches, driven by the need to push their way through the gaps in the hedge, but then started to spread out into more of a line. As Will looked to his left he could see they were in good shape. To his right, there was continuous firing, as the defenders were trying to target the spy's detachment. To his front, at that moment, silence.

They were halfway to the wall when a cry suddenly went up. This was followed almost immediately by a single shot. They were less than a hundred yards from the wall, and now he could see figures rising up and swinging muskets round in their direction. "Come on!" he bellowed and waved his sword in a circle above his head as he ran, holding his pistol in the other. The pace picked up slightly.

The wall in front of him now seemed to erupt in flame and smoke. The crash came a moment later. He pounded on, not daring to look how many were down. Just got to close that distance before the reload. He sensed the feverish activity behind the wall, and decisions that were being made by the individual soldiers. *Is there time to reload and get in another shot? Do I draw my sword? Do I run? There is always that one*, thought Will grimly. *Had that thought many times myself.* They would all have half an eye on what their fellows were doing. No one wanted to hold back the enemy by themselves, nor did they want to be the first to turn and run. Agony of indecision in the blink of an eye. A life-saving or a life-ending choice.

Enough stood their ground. Enough had reloaded. The second volley came through the drifting smoke. Enough had kept their nerve. Will thought perhaps there were twenty in front of him. Perhaps enough when you are defending a wall.

This time, at the extreme close range, it was difficult for the enemy to miss. He heard the thud of bullets finding flesh, punching through thin steel breastplates. He heard the screams. But they were so close, even the men who were already dead on their feet crashed into the low stonework. With his height, Will did not even need to slow down, and he leapt the wall straight into a Royalist whose eyes were so wide they almost seemed to pop from his head. He flattened the man, and hit the ground himself, trying to roll, to speed up the time in which he could regain his feet. He slammed into a gravestone and winded himself. Gasping for air, he raised up on one elbow, looking around him. The man he jumped into was lying on his back in the grass just behind the wall. He seemed to be unconscious. He saw more of his men scrambling over the stones amidst one or two hand-to-hand fights. He looked behind him, up the shallow rise of the churchyard to the church itself. Royalists were running back up the hill and the defenders were preparing a firing line in place across the width of the front of the building.

"Take cover!" he called out, gesturing for his men to keep low. Some ducked behind the wall again, while others dived for cover behind the gravestones or just flattened themselves to the ground as best they could. Another volley fire raked across them, smacking into stone, yew trees and flesh, and masking the enemy with smoke. "Now, boys! Up and after them."

A cheer slowly built as his tired men pulled themselves to their feet and charged up the slope. The laggards vaulted the wall and formed a second wave as they swept forward. He raised his pistol in his left hand and fired into the smoke. He saw some of his own men drop to one knee, steady their muskets and fire. On the other side of the churchyard, Lothian was leading another group forward and they were all converging on the church door.

He shouted as loudly as he could towards Lothian, "Round the back, round the back!", but he had no idea if he had been heard. The Royalists were not retreating but held their line, waiting with swords and pistols. Muskets were grasped by the barrel to be used as clubs, as there was no time for reloading this time. As the smoke was clearing, Will's men hit home, the numbers seemingly evenly matched.

Weapons rose and fell, and pistols cracked. The screams and moans started, and the fighting dissolved into brawls. They were not breaking, and now Will glimpsed muskets being pointed at them from windows, and from the bell tower that overlooked them.

"Come on, boys! One more push!" He swung his sword like a cleaver, powered by his strong arm, and used his spent pistol as a club. He had two down in front of him, but elsewhere they were being pushed back as the covering fire started to take a toll.

He could then hear Lothian's frantic voice shouting for them to disengage. *Easier said than done*, he thought. He started to shout himself, "Pull back!", and slowly tried to back away from the fight. He sensed his men doing the same, some just turning to run. When they had opened a distance of some yards, there was a massive crash as Lothian's men poured their volley into the defenders. Men dropped like corn to the scythe as the point-blank firing of over fifty muskets from the line he had formed ripped through the press of bodies. As the powder smoke cleared, the surviving

(OSWESTRY, 22 JUNE 1644)

Royalists could be seen retreating into the church, leaving a twitching heap of bodies behind.

The fire from the windows and tower intensified, and Lothian signalled for the men to take cover around the gravestones.

Shit! He had hoped they would carry the doors in the first rush. He didn't want to start some kind of siege of the building. He could see the Royalists were struggling to get the great metal-studded doors shut as bodies and equipment lay in the way. *It has to be now!* He called to a knot of men making their way to the first line of gravestones. "You! Come on. With me to the doors!"

He sprinted to cover the yards to the doors before a marksman above could take him down. He hoped the men were following, but he had no time to check. If they got the doors shut it was going to be a long, painful day. The doors opened inwards and were almost shut. He launched his shoulder at one of them. It gave beneath his weight but didn't fully open. He could hear shouts from inside and a pistol barrel appeared in the gap. He hacked at it with his sword, keeping his weight straining against the door. Now two more of his men joined him, leaning against the push coming from inside. The musketeers above could not get an angle to shoot at them due to the angle of the stonework.

It was only now that he noticed blood seeping down the front of his thigh. He couldn't feel any pain yet, but that would come. The other men put their shoulders to the other door. Something, someone, had to break the deadlock.

Looking back to the churchyard, he could see the men taking potshots at the church windows and trying to pick off the snipers in the tower, but there was no attempt to take advantage of the efforts they were making. The strain was telling on his men as muscles heaved. Their breathing was getting more ragged, veins stood out on their foreheads. He must look the same. The end was coming soon.

Suddenly, he thought of Sarah. Miles away back in London. Probably staying with her parents with him gone. He thought of her receiving the news of his death and this gave him renewed strength. He gritted his teeth and drove the heels of his boots into the gravel to get better purchase. His legs ached, his shoulder ached and now his wound was starting to throb.

There was a sudden uproar from inside the church. Shots were fired and he could hear the sound of steel on steel. There were shouts and curses from behind the doors, and he felt them give slightly. He looked at the two other men and they both nodded, understanding immediately what he meant. He turned, and looked back at the churchyard, at the men hiding behind the gravestones, loading and firing.

"Come on!" he shouted, for what seemed the hundredth time that morning. "C'mon, boys! We've got them!" With some uncertain looks, a number of them, perhaps twenty or so, rose and ran across the open space to the doors. Clearly there was heavy fighting now inside the church. He shouted for some of them to set up a firing line, and others to help them push. With the last of his strength, he leant his weight to the task again. This time the doors gave slightly, and then crashed in with a rush. The sudden lack of resistance meant Will's momentum carried him in and he fell flat on his face.

A crash behind him, and lead balls hurtled over his head and into the darkness of the building. He heard the sound of running boots sweep past him, as the rest of the men outside the church rushed up to secure the doors. He staggered to his feet and followed them in. He could see a knot of men fighting down near the altar. He saw Lothian and, frantically loading a pistol, Brereton's spy hiding in the choir stall. He was trying

(OSWESTRY, 22 JUNE 1644)

to work out why the spy would be inside the church, when something heavy hit him a glancing blow on the helmet. He collapsed to his knees and blood sheeted across his eyes. He saw Sarah's face again as he slowly toppled forward and hit the stone floor, face first. He could still hear the noise around him, but everything was dark. *Oh dear God, I am blinded,* was his last thought as he lost consciousness.

6

WILLIAM BRERETON

(Nantwich, 24 June 1644)

He watched the bustling activity of the town from the window of his office. After a period of grey weather and drizzle, a warm June sun illuminated the Nantwich streets, and the mood of townsfolk and soldiers alike seemed lifted by its return. *As well as the good news from Oswestry,* he thought, *and we could do with some!*

He had entered the town, accompanied by his personal guard and Colonel Myddelton, around midday, and he was now engrossed again in his correspondence. Never in his life had he written and read as many communications as he had in the last six months. Never had he received so many contradictory messages. The Committee of Both Kingdoms was trying to run the campaigns from London, but they were always days behind actual events in the northern part of the country. They tried their best, but with his network of scouts and agents, Brereton knew he was in a far better position to take quick, effective decisions.

He didn't like being subordinate to the Earl of Denbigh. People said he, Brereton, was sometimes too cautious, but Denbigh! The man was such a ditherer! Brereton tried to ensure everything was set to give his men the maximum

(NANTWICH, 24 JUNE 1644)

advantage. He assembled all the intelligence he could. He favoured attacks in the early hours before the enemy was fully prepared. He had seen too many men lost to satisfy reckless heroism, some vision of honour, when a little caution and planning could deliver a completely different result, for the loss of fewer men, horses and precious equipment. It just took a little more effort and a thicker skin.

However, he had to admit, grudgingly, that the news from Oswestry perhaps signalled a change in the man. The reaction to word of the siege there had been swift and decisive, although he had made sure his scoutmaster, Captain Walker, had provided local men to assist the relief. A good result had ensued. A dawn assault had secured the church at St Oswald's, a place he knew well, thanks to the determination and skill of the picked companies of men. He had heard that the fellow Captain Fletcher, the tall captain, the farmer's boy, had played a key role. He drummed his fingers idly on the desk. *He is one to watch*, he thought, *but not just for his competence and bravery.*

In his time in London, Brereton had seen the pamphlets circulating and listened to some of the tub-thumping preaching in the streets. He found he could agree with much of what was said. The arguments were articulate and appealed to his views on the nature of God, and his hatred for popery. But, as with his brief conversation with Fletcher, he felt there were undertones to this agenda. Subtly communicated but there, nonetheless. A sense of disrespect among the mob for their betters. A disdain for title and property. These ideas were disturbing and threatened the backbone of the country. Even more worrying was that some of the texts that were printed and distributed had been written by women! Here was a clear sign that the world was turning to anarchy.

While the King was in the wrong, and had fallen victim to the influence of his Catholic queen, the traditions and structures of the country were sound. The foundations were there, the people just needed to embrace a more godly attitude.

Fletcher – with his long fair hair and beard, and massive physique, just how Brereton imagined some pagan warrior to have looked – was carrying that defiant message out of London and into the shires. He needed watching. He would write to Myddelton on this when he had a moment.

The day after the church had been taken, Denbigh had arrived with his reinforcements and battered down the doors to the town with his field gun. The Royalists had retreated through the town and taken refuge in the castle, and no saker was going to breach those doors or walls. Assaulting the castle would have been a costly affair, but they had been saved that ordeal as the women of Oswestry had begged Denbigh to stay his hand, and then persuaded the garrison to surrender. The Royalists had marched out of the town leaving it to Denbigh with no further shots fired or lives lost. The messenger had arrived just as Brereton got to Nantwich and it had lifted the mood of the whole town.

This was very welcome, given the news reaching him from both London and sources across the North. Prince Rupert, recently appointed to command the King's forces in the North-West and border area, had gathered troops and set off into Lancashire, meeting little resistance from Parliamentarian forces. Given the run of victories the King had been experiencing in the previous year, this looked bleak for the cause. Fairfax's army had been routed at Adwalton Moor and Parliament had been driven out of the county, or forced to hide in the fortress and armoury at Hull. The King was ascendant and morale was the lowest he had seen it.

But then, in January, the Scots under Lord Leven had appeared at Berwick with 20,000 foot and horse, and a hundred cannon, and threatened the North of England. The

(NANTWICH, 24 JUNE 1644)

King's supporter, the Marquis of Newcastle, had hurried north to face them, but had failed to bring the cautious Leven to battle, only registering a stalemate in freezing weather at the Bowden Hills. This had been followed by the slaughter at Hilton, losses the marquis was less able to bear.

The tide now appeared to be turning as, encouraged by the Scots' march south, in March, Thomas Fairfax's Cheshire army had returned to Yorkshire and recaptured Bradford. The town was known to favour Parliament, and Fairfax now used it as a base for his Yorkshire campaigning. On 11 April, further disaster struck the Royalists. The Governor of York, John Belasyse, was wounded in the glorious victory at Selby, and had been taken prisoner to Hull. His scouts told him that the word in York was that their governor had been betrayed by the coward George Porter. While fierce fighting raged through Selby, Porter sulked in Nottinghamshire, refusing Belasyse's desperate plea for aid.

As a result, the Marquis of Newcastle had evacuated garrisons at Durham and Lumley Castle and raced back to York, which was only lightly guarded. He had arrived without many of his veteran infantry – depleted by battle, cold, disease and desertion. Some cavalry trickled back in through April and May, but the rumour was that most of the Northern Horse had been sent under the command of George Goring, to join Prince Rupert in Lancashire. *How strange*, he thought, *not so long ago I was dining with Goring and his wife in The Hague, and Lady Goring had taken me to meet Elizabeth, Queen of Bohemia, and elder sister of my King. We talked of witches…*

Shortly after, the armies of Leven and Lord Fairfax had come together at Wetherby and then appeared at the walls of York and started the siege. The grip tightened when first Cromwell arrived, and shortly after, toward the end of May, the rest of Manchester's Eastern Association army had joined the besiegers. Cannon started bombardment of the walls, and rubble and bodies started to accumulate.

But this turned out to be the high watermark of the campaign. While Brereton fretted in London, trying to recruit men and procure arms, the allies had probed for weaknesses in the defences in vain, with men falling in droves on both sides. The pendulum of success had reached its zenith and started to swing back. Hope of a swift victory in the North slowly turned to despair. Rupert had joined with Lord Byron and had sacked Bolton, with a terrible slaughter of innocent civilians. Goring with his 5,000 horse and nearly 1,000 foot had then joined Rupert at Bury. It seemed clear that Rupert was heading to relieve York and it was now a case of whether the city would hold until he arrived.

Brereton had sensed a decisive moment was approaching. After Edge Hill, there had not been a large-scale pitched battle. There were skirmishes, sieges and counter-marches. Certainly battles had occurred, but nothing that could ever have dealt a knockout to the other side. Cat and mouse, surge and stalemate. Parliament had gained territory in one part of the country only to lose it in another. Back and forth, a weary attrition leading nowhere. This was starting to look different and the pace was quickening.

The townspeople of Wigan had thrown flowers before the hooves of Prince Rupert's guard as they captured that town. The Scots captured two forts on the western side of York, as Rupert arrived at Liverpool. As the Marquis of Newcastle had opened negotiations for the surrender of York, word had come that Liverpool had fallen to Rupert, giving the King another route through which to bring in troops from Ireland. Its governor had fled by sea.

The terms for the surrender of York had been rejected by the allies, but Prince Rupert had reached Skipton, a foothold in Yorkshire. Brereton became convinced that the biggest confrontation of the war was upon them, when Rupert's meteor arc across the Pennines smashed into the armies of Fairfax, the Eastern Association and the Scots. He was also convinced that the forces in Cheshire would play some part, and he had instructions to join the assembly that Denbigh had ordered at Knutsford. Surely some of them would be dispatched to race across the hills to support the allies. He hoped more than anything that it would be him, that he could help to strike the blow that would end this war.

He had found himself thinking more and more about Cecily, and his son, Thomas. He managed to snatch some days to see them, but his duties were all encompassing. He scarcely found time to pray! To properly pray. *Tonight, I must do so. Once I have written to my commanders, written to Denbigh and to the Committee of Both Kingdoms. Oh, yes, and written to Myddelton about that Fletcher. And I must review my men – it has been so long since I have been amongst them. After that, I will pray, and I will write to Cecily and Thomas.*

There was a knock at the door. He sighed and put down his quill.

"Come in."

The lean face of his scoutmaster, Captain Walker, appeared around the door. "Sir William, I have much news to share, sir. Do you have a moment for me?"

7

MARLEIGH

(Macclesfield, 26 June 1644)

It did not take long for the axe to fall. She had known it would ever since Cook had told her that she had seen Smale deep in conversation with a pinched-faced woman in the street. It had to be Mary Brassey. She knew Smale would not want the taint of suspicion on his household – and he certainly already considered it *his* household.

She was helping in the kitchen when the knock came at the door. Smale and his wife had stayed the night, as they had returned late from visiting their cousins, and he opened the door. Marleigh peered down the hallway from the kitchen, trying to stay out of sight. There were three standing in the street, but Smale's bulk hid them to the extent she could not clearly see who was there. But she picked out one voice she recognised. Brassey.

She thought briefly about a rapid exit through the back door, and escape into the town and then the countryside. But Eva was upstairs sleeping, and she would not make it up the stairs without walking in plain view through the hall. She heard Smale say, "Well, Constable, this is most worrying. And these are serious accusations." Her hopes that the incident would fade from memory, and that Brassey would think twice

(MACCLESFIELD, 26 JUNE 1644)

about making a second serious accusation after the way it had been dismissed the first time, were dashed.

In the days since the market, she had considered her options, weighing the clear possibility of slipping away with Eva, against the happiness she had found in her lodging, and the affection she had for Eliza and Maggie. In the past she had always run. Always found a way to preserve and extend. Her work was too important to risk. But now she felt differently. Having Eva had changed everything and her long search for understanding was over. Now she would risk. She would face Brassey's charges. She would win. She would continue.

She slipped back into the kitchen and leaned back against the wall, straining to hear the conversation in the hallway. Cook eyed her curiously. "I 'ope you ain't in trouble with th' master. He's a wicked temper that'un."

Footsteps thumped towards her down the hall. Smale stomped into the room, not seeing Marleigh at first, and hissed at Cook, "Where is she? Where is that viper of a governess?"

"I am here, master." Her voice was quiet, but Smale still leapt six inches into the air. *Rather dainty for such a fat man.*

Recovering, he whirled towards her and slammed the palm of his hand against the wall just next to her head. "Don't play the innocent with me!" he snarled, spittle spraying the front of her dress. "You have brought shame on this house and on me. Never have I trusted you and now God has vindicated me. Witch, or no, you will not remain here! Corrupting my nieces and defiling the virtue of this family." She knew his raised voice was for the benefit of the audience by the front door.

"Master Smale, will you not hear me?" She remained calm. "Perhaps if we can sit quietly, I can exp…"

Again, Smale slammed his hand to the wall, inches from her face. "No!" he bellowed. "You will not sit in this house ever again. You will not speak in this house, ever again. The constable will take you now and I pray that God's swift judgement will follow! Go!"

He stepped back, allowing her to leave the kitchen, Cook's eyes so wide they seemed to fill her whole face. Smale followed her, and made a great show of shoving her along the hall.

The constable, a solid man in his forties, balding and sweating in his cloak in the June sunshine, held up a hand. "Now, Master Smale, careful now. Nothing is proven, only accused." He looked over his shoulder with some apparent distaste into the thin but triumphant face of Mary Brassey. "We must investigate before we form any conclusions."

"Of course, Constable. Of course." But Smale could not hide his disgust and embarrassment at this occurring on his doorstep.

"Mistress Marleigh Hume. Will you come with me?" The constable smiled warily at her, torn between the desire to avoid conflict and fear of the unknown.

At that moment Eliza came hurtling down the stairs, face horrified. "No! Uncle! What are you doing! You cannot take Marleigh. We won't let you." Maggie followed her down, and Mary Smale appeared at the top of the stairs behind them, looking shocked and distressed.

Eliza dodged around Smale's considerable girth and grabbed Marleigh's arm. "No! You cannot take her! She has done nothing!"

"See," shouted Brassey. "She has witched the children already. Wicked! Take her, Constable, or I will drag her to the gaol by the hair if you do not!"

Smale had grabbed Eliza around the waist, trying to ignore Maggie's repeated kicking of his ankles. The constable gently peeled Eliza's fingers from Marleigh, trying to maintain his calm. "Come now, Mistress Walker. I am sure this is all just

(MACCLESFIELD, 26 JUNE 1644)

a misunderstanding. 'T'will be sorted out very soon and your governess will return."

"Not to this house," growled Smale. "Over my dead body!"

"I'm working on that," panted Maggie as she swapped kicking for punching.

"Ladies, please!" Finally losing his patience, the constable bellowed. Eliza dropped her grip. And Maggie shrank back, tears forming in her eyes. Mary Smale had appeared behind her and, crouching down, wrapped her, gently but firmly, in a tight embrace.

"But, Constable." Eliza's voice was shaking with anger and fear. "What can she have done? She is the best person I know!"

"I am sorry, Mistress Walker. There has been a serious accusation against your governess. This lady," he jerked his thumb over his shoulder at Mary Brassey, "has accused Mistress Hume of witchcraft. She claims witnesses. The magistrate will hear this when he is next here. In the meantime, I have no choice but to take her and hold her. There will be a chance of bail. This will be discussed once I have her secured in Dog Lane. She will be comfortable and cared for. She is no common drunk."

"No, she's a whore!" shouted Brassey. "She is a witch and a whore! And she will beguile you too, you foolish, foolish man!"

"Enough!" shouted the constable again. He gently took Marleigh's hand and tried to lead her down the few steps to the street. Marleigh resisted. "What about Eva? What about my little girl?"

"The Devil's child, more like!" spat Brassey. "She has the Devil's mark. Just look at her eyes!"

The constable looked at Marleigh. "The gaol is no place for a child."

"She will be safer there with me than left here." She looked up at Smale and back to the constable. "Please? Can I take her with me?"

"Then I suppose you must," he replied doubtfully. "I am sure this will be sorted out soon in any case."

Marleigh looked up at Eliza, part hidden behind Smale's bulk. "Please, Eliza. Will you fetch Eva, and a few things for me and her?"

"Of course." She disappeared. Several minutes later and she was back, cradling Eva, and with a bag over her arm. She carefully handed both to Marleigh, and leaning up on tiptoes, kissed her on the cheek. "Do not worry," she whispered, "we will get you out. Both of you."

"Enough!" Smale grabbed Eliza roughly by the arm and half dragged her back up the stairs. "You girls have had too much freedom it seems to me, against my better judgement. That stops now. Inside!"

The door slammed on the Smales and Walkers. Marleigh adjusted her hold on Eva, and passed the bag to the constable who had held out a hand to take it. She turned her back on the house and followed him up the street, back across the marketplace and into Dog Lane. Walking through the door of the gaol sent a chill through her, and she shivered, the only relief being that the closed door smothered the stream of abuse and accusation from Mary Brassey that had followed her every step of the way.

8

WILL FLETCHER

(Oswestry, 27 June 1644)

In the days since the fall of the town, he had been lying in a barn which had been put aside for care of the injured. Some of these included Royalist defenders of the town who had turned their coats for Parliament and were being cared for alongside his own men. They had removed the thick bandage from around his head and told him that the gash would heal soon enough and the lump, which felt like half of an iron ball from Denbigh's saker, would reduce in time.

When he had regained consciousness, lying on a straw mattress on the floor of the barn, he had not dared to open his eyes for several anguished minutes. He had tried to imagine a world without vision, and what he might do in such a world. He had not found any answers. When he had started to detect weak sunshine through his eyelids, and opened his eyes to the sight of light entering the building through a high window in the hayloft, the relief was visceral. Tears had streamed down his face, and for the first time in days he had prayed and thanked God.

He sat with his back to the stone wall watching swallows flitting in through the opening to their nests in the angles of the stonework. A steady flow of insects fed the chittering babies that seemed to have insatiable appetites. He marvelled at the energy and determination of the birds and wondered if this was how his own parents had thought about him. Judging by his memories of their exhausted, weather-beaten faces, he thought perhaps it was. Scuttling noises from the straw heaped around him, across the floor and into the loft, told of a thriving population of rats. Always rats where there were men and their food, he thought.

A few soldiers were busy forking piles of straw onto a wagon, no doubt destined for the cavalry which were now camped in large numbers around the town. Feeding men and horses was a continuous job, and it exacted a toll on the ordinary along the line of the march. Theoretically folk should be paid for their produce, but generally all they got was a slip of paper with some scribbles on it, with instructions to claim the money once the war was over. The local troops were usually better than most at foraging – there was a good chance they may be known to the villagers and farmers – but the ones from outside the area, particularly if they were considered to be the 'enemy', couldn't care less if they left them with nothing.

A number of the men, those with relatively minor injuries, sat around in a rough circle, sharing a meal of bread and cheese. Some were local men from Cheshire and Shropshire, while others had joined the regiment through the recruitment in London. The mix of accents made communication surprisingly difficult.

Will had been trying to introduce them to the ideas that so excited him. Ideas discussed at meetings or set out in pamphlets circulating surreptitiously through districts of London and among the 'prentices. Radical ideas, to be sure, but so logical and just so morally *right*. He was careful, so he thought, trying to draw out opinions from the men rather

(OSWESTRY, 27 JUNE 1644)

than preaching at them. This was how he had been encouraged to spread the word by his friends at the Windmill. He was finding the practice more difficult than the theory, or maybe he just wasn't an orator like Lilburne and others.

"At least taking a cut for Myddelton means I get to sit on me arse for a few days and get a decent meal. Wouldn't mind garrisoning this place. Beats marching back 'n' forth across the county." The man was older than most here. Possibly nearly in his forties. He nursed his left arm, which was wrapped in cloth from the elbow down. "Sword cut," he responded as Will raised an eyebrow in enquiry.

There was some mumbling agreement to this. In the background, the moans of others not as fortunate provided miserable accompaniment. Will had seen this mood before. Worry about whether they would recover or maybe take a fever, but balanced against relief that the fighting was over and they had survived.

"Is that who you took your wound for? For Myddelton?" He kept his voice even, trying not to load it with opinion.

The man thought a moment. "Aye, well. Maybe not for 'im. Not that he's a bad'un like some. He's not the best I fought for, but there's plenty worse."

"Then who? Maybe it's for your family? For the money?"

"Ha! When did ye last see a shilling o' pay? Maybe it's different in London, but we ain't seen silver for months." He rubbed his bristled chin with a hand with grime ingrained in every line. "But they say him 'n' Brereton came back from Parliament with cash, so maybe times are changin'. Have to wait and see."

"What about you others? What do you fight for if not for Myddelton, and not for the money? Do you fight *against* the King, or *for* Parliament?"

Another man, red-haired, bandaged around the top of

his left leg, spat on the floor. "Well, I suppose if you put it like that, the King ain't never done me no harm…" he paused, shifting position to try to get his leg more comfortable, "…but then he never done me no good either." As he moved, Will picked up the sickly smell of wound-rot. He would not keep that leg much longer. He caught the eye of the older soldier. They both knew.

Another voice: "I suppose we fight for them as tells us to. Simple as that. My family has farmed around Chirk for generations. We are his men, you could say. He asked, and we came. Simple as that."

"And what about the Parliament?" Will asked. "Don't that seem important to you?"

The same farmer spoke up again. "Aye, but it is a long way off. Ain't never seen it. Never will see it."

A much younger man, from London, Will thought, judging by his accent, piped up, "I see all o' that. But for me, and I think for many o' the men, it is a question of the Church. About how God demands to be worshipped. The King 'as fallen into popery. He has been blinded by his Catholic queen and the corrupt bishops. All good godly men must fight that!" There were murmurings of support. "If the King would just see reason, we could unite again, aye, even with the Scots, with a good Puritan heart."

Will nodded. "And Parliament? You think the men you send to Parliament support you? Men like Brereton and Venables, do they have your wellbeing at heart?"

The men looked at each other. Some shrugged.

London lad again: "I don't know those men, but I know that Parliament stood by us 'prentices when we was defending Lilburne and others 'gainst the papist bishops! They are closer to the ordinary man than the King could be, with 'is crown and silks and shit like that."

The old soldier raised an eyebrow. "Aye, I guess that's right, youngster. I guess we don't all get so excited about the Pope as about the price of bread on most days, though."

They all laughed at that. Will tried to take it on further. "So the Parliament men, who do you think they look after?"

Another man, one of the Royalist turncoats, spoke quietly. "Well, it's like everything, isn't it? You do this for me, I'll do that for you. They looks after them as votes for 'em. Those that can do most for them on things like tax, and land, and titles and stuff."

One or two shot him a look. Distrust still lingered.

Will smiled encouragingly. "I don't know what it's like in this part of the country, but where I'm from, people like me don't get to vote for 'em. My family are tenant farmers, for generations. Feet in the soil. Hand to mouth. We never had any say in anything. Do any of you have a vote?"

The farmer, a lad with probably a very similar upbringing to Will: "'Course not! Don't talk daft. Same all over, isn't it." He realised what he had said to whom, and clasped a hand over his mouth.

Will laughed. "Don't you worry, mate, I am not a captain when we talk like this. Say it how you feel. Because you're right. None of us vote men into Parliament. Who cares about us? The ordinary man. But here we are, fighting for it."

There was a long silence. The Royalist turncoat was watching him carefully. The others largely looked at the ground. He said, "So what's your thinking, Captain?"

Will leaned forward, his large frame looming over the circle. "Do any of you think that the gentry, them as owns property, work any harder than you do?"

There was silence, but a few shook their heads.

"Do any of you think that more of the gentry are dying in these battles than the likes of you? Or your families?"

A few heads came up, staring at him.

"Do any of you think that your life, or the lives of your wives and children, are worth less in the eyes of God than them as has the vote?"

The young farmer said, "I don't. I guess none of us could think that."

The older man seemed to be losing patience with all the talking. "But there's nowt to be done, is there?" His voice raised. "This is but hot air!"

The 'prentice cut across him "No, mate. It is more than talk. The captain's right. If we are ever goin' to change things, this war 'as to be the time. We are not fightin' some foreign army. Here we are, family fighting family. Brother fighting brother. Look at this 'un here." He gestured at the turncoat. "He's no different from you or me. Just ended up on the losin' side for a time. But if we don't change things while there is a chance, then whoever wins, we are all still on the losin' side anyway."

Will looked at him in amazement. He could not have said it better, or with more passion, himself.

The man went on, and Will was not about to interrupt him. "There are men – it is true, they are mainly in London – that are saying things must change. Saying that the highest born and lowest are all equal in the sight o' God and must be treated so. Every man has a right to vote on who represents him in the Parliament. And every man is equal before the law."

The old soldier glanced across at Will, and then back at the 'prentice. "I doubt not what you say is right and true. But it remains a fact that it can't be changed. How can it?" He looked squarely at Will, and he noticed several other men now leaned into the circle, waiting for a response. "How can it, Captain?"

Will, lowering his voice, began, "Well, once the war is won, and it has to be won by Parliament, 'cos if anything *is* certain, it is that nothing will change under the King, then is the time.

Parliament will owe the army such a debt that it must listen to the voices of the ordinary men who fought for it. They cannot argue against the rightness of what men like John Lilburne have said." He saw the 'prentice nodding along vigorously. "We must…"

At that moment, he was hailed from the doorway of the barn. "Captain? Captain Fletcher?"

They all looked up. Some looked alarmed, others guilty. Will had no idea the man had been standing there, or if he could have heard anything of their conversation. He stood up, then had to grab on to the wall as a wave of dizziness and nausea swept over him. The 'prentice grabbed his other arm to steady him.

Will now recognised the new man as a sergeant in Myddelton's regiment. As Will regained his balance, the sergeant wandered across and had a few words with the old soldier, asking him about his wound. "Captain, are you well enough to come with me? The colonel will have a word."

"Of course, Sergeant." He grabbed his pike, which was standing in the corner of the barn, and leant on this as he followed the man outside.

"Any idea what this is about?"

"No, sir. He has heard about the part you played in the capture of the church. Maybe he wants to thank you personally? There are lots of men who would. I reckon your action saved a few lives that day, God be praised."

They wound their way into the town and headed towards the castle gates. Will already felt weary and his head was throbbing again. He was thankful for the pike to lean on. There was activity all around him. Walls were being rebuilt and the gates were having timbers replaced. The sergeant told Will that first Denbigh had tried to blow it down with the saker, as he had done with the town gates, but to no avail. Then there had been a half-hearted attempt to burn it down with pitch, but this had also failed. It had been the intervention of some women of the town, those married to members of the garrison, that had persuaded Denbigh to push for a surrender. The lobbying of the women had been the excuse they were waiting for, and it had come to a peaceful, if humiliating, conclusion for the Royalists.

From the slightly elevated height that the castle provided, Will could see lines of marching men, columns of horse and an endless baggage train disappearing north. "The Cheshire boys are going back to join Brereton at Knutsford. They are needed for the fight against Prince Rupert. Praise be to God that that devil is headed for York, and not for us!"

Myddelton was conferring with his other officers around a long table in the main banqueting hall of the castle. He looked up as they entered, his whole manner seemingly lifted by the victory, and the atmosphere was jubilant. Maps and papers littered the table, and the colonel had been scratching out some letter for a waiting messenger.

As Will approached, the sergeant peeled off with a cheerful word and headed back out into the town. The officers around the table started to applaud, and even a few cheers went up. Will, leaning heavily on the staff, hobbled over to the table, managing a weak smile and holding up his free hand in an attempt to stifle the greeting.

"Fletcher! Good to see you up!" Myddelton called to him. A broad smile lit up his face, but Will thought there was some other emotion behind his eyes, and that troubled him. Careful slaps on the back from the others, and shouted demands for Will to tell his story of the attack. He was steered towards one of the great oak chairs spread around the table and sank gratefully onto it. As briefly as he could he recounted the events from the moment of the charge across the field. He

(Oswestry, 27 June 1644)

praised the courage and discipline of the men, and how they had seen the opportunity to force the doors of the church.

He learned that one of the two with him had taken a fatal musket shot but that the second man had survived unscathed and was to be promoted. "But after that, gentlemen, I have little memory." He gently touched the great lump on the side of his head. "I seem to have taken a bang. I have no idea how we managed to gain entry."

"I can tell you that." Major Lothian had been standing quietly at the back of the group. "It was Brereton's scout. After he had led the decoy party, and the main attack started, he led them through the field, hidden by the powder smoke. Apparently, the Royalists were holding the rear door to the church open, in case they needed to retreat that way, but only had a couple of men guarding it. The detachment managed to surprise and overpower them. At that stage, some of them appeared at the side of the church and signalled the rest of us to follow them round the back. You were keeping them occupied, and some thirty of us swept in and surprised them from the rear."

"Praise God! That was some quick thinking! I had better find the man and thank him, for he surely saved our lives."

"I fear not. He has already left with the main force, but I feel I owe him an apology. I did not speak kindly to him of his type of work, but you are right, he saved many lives." He smiled. "I did, however, arrive in time to see what happened to you. There were snipers in the gallery above the door, shooting out through the window into the graveyard. As you burst in, they swivelled around and had you in their sights. We brought them down with a timely volley, and one of them, as he fell, dropped his musket right onto your head." He looked around at his audience. "Of course, the musket shattered into a thousand pieces on your skull!"

There was laughter all round, more handshakes and congratulations but, after a few moments, Myddelton held up his hands for silence. "Gentlemen, there is much still to do, but I need some moments with Captain Fletcher before we resume. Can you please leave us for a while?" They trailed out, leaving him sitting opposite Myddelton, who was leaning on the table, a letter lying between his gloved hands, the seal broken.

When they were alone, Myddelton's demeanour quickly changed. "I meant what I said earlier, Fletcher. You showed bravery and intelligence in taking the action you did. You are to be commended for that. However, I have heard other things about you that are less commendable. Indeed, I have a letter from an esteemed colleague," he nodded at the paper in front of him, "which says I should be wary of your sort."

Will was surprised, and not a little angry. He stood, leaning heavily on the pike until he found his footing. "My sort? What can you mean, Colonel?" He towered above the elderly man but, to his credit, Myddelton did not flinch.

"Captain Fletcher, you have been accused of spreading unrest amongst the troops and trading in dangerous ideas. I have heard this from some of my own men. It seems you have been training them in more than just soldiering since we left London."

Will could feel the colour rising in his cheeks. "Colonel, I have engaged the men in conversation, that is only natural when we must get them battle-ready. All I have done is understand to what degree they have been following some of the exciting ideas washing through London. You must know of what I speak of? Nothing that is not in support of Parliament's cause. Nothing that is treasonous or in support of the King!"

"Nevertheless, Fletcher, this will not stand. Our focus must be on doing God's work, not the ravings of fanatics like Lilburne. He causes trouble wherever he goes."

(OSWESTRY, 27 JUNE 1644)

"Trouble for the King, sir. Not trouble for the cause. Freeborn John merely speaks to the morality of a new settlement after the war is won. No more."

"So you say, but there are many who consider his thinking dangerous and, more importantly, a distraction." He jabbed the page with his finger. "We cannot afford this. It is my decision that you will leave the regiment and return to London forthwith. I will not discipline you beyond this, not after your contribution to the training of our men, and your obvious courage in action, for which I remain grateful. But I will not have you corrupting the minds of the men with these… ideas. I will not. There will be no mention of why you have been dismissed, I will merely report that your work in training the men is complete. I sincerely hope and believe you will find a place with Skippon again. He seems more inclined to these new… ideas." He curled his lip with distaste as he repeated the word. "Be gone in the morning and I will hear no more on the subject. Nor will you speak to the men about this. You are dismissed!"

9

MARLEIGH

(Macclesfield, 28 June 1644)

The parish constable had been as good as his word. With the limited options available, he had fitted out the cell with a serviceable pallet, bucket and a tin dish, and white pottery jug for water. There were blankets, although the room was hot. It was set mainly below street level but had a barred, unglazed window at the top of the wall, which gave her a view of stonework and the ankles of an occasional passing citizen.

The constable clearly admired Samuel Walker. "A fine man. A man of sound judgement. If he was minded to give you a job, that is a strong mark in your favour, mistress. Don't you worry. This is just procedure. We ain't had a witch trial in Macc' for I don't know how long. Probably never."

"I thought I heard about two women in Rainow? Thought they were hanged?" Marleigh had asked.

"Aye. That's true. But they weren't tried here. They were sent to Chester Assizes, and everyone knows folk are strange over that way. Getting their comeuppance now, though, ain't they. Our man Brereton's got 'em bottled up tight. Sir William will take the city for the Parliament before the year is out. You'll see."

(MACCLESFIELD, 28 JUNE 1644)

"So there will be a trial? Where will that be if it can't be Chester?" Above everything else she was worried about being separated from Eva. No one knew how special Eva was. No one would be able to look after her. To protect her.

"Not sure, mistress. I believe the burgesses of the parish are discussing this today with the mayor, Alderman Booth. No doubt we will both find out soon enough. In the meantime, please be patient. Is there anything you miss?"

"Apart from my freedom, no, sir. Wait!" She looked up at him from under her eyelashes, radiating charm and innocence. "Is there a bible for prisoners? Perhaps if not, someone might fetch one from the house. Miss Eliza will know where I keep mine."

The constable smiled. "Of course. I will send instructions."

*

Marleigh was used to hardship and rough sleeping, but she had to acknowledge, the time spent in the Walker household had softened her. The pallet had been uncomfortable and that, coupled with Eva's restlessness in the strange surroundings, had left her with little sleep.

She had completed her toilet, and the constable's wife had emptied her bucket and brought her bread, and clean water for washing and for breakfast. She had been friendly enough, but Marleigh could sense she was nervous of her, and didn't want to look at, or hold, Eva. She had obviously heard all of Brassey's accusations. She had no news on a trial and counselled Marleigh to pray, and wait for the constable.

The morning passed slowly. She practised conversation with Eva, strengthening their mental bond and trying to teach Eva greater awareness and control over her skill. Her mind wandered over options and schemes. She had faced tighter scrapes before, and had used her unique skills to find a way out, but this time she had Eva. For the first time in many years, she had something she could call a home and a family. She must remain calm and, as the constable said, remain patient. But always plan. Always keep a few steps ahead. Because as she knew, although there was no real evidence against her, jealousy, envy, fear and discrimination can go a long way.

Top of her list was to keep friendly with the constable. Daniel Roe was his name and she gradually took to calling him Dan. He didn't seem to mind. She wanted his trust because if the worst came to the worst, he was not a very careful man, and probably not immune to her charms. He carried the keys in his pocket. He carried a stout wooden truncheon in a loose loop at his belt. She had no doubts she could outrun him if need be, perhaps also carrying Eva. But this was a last resort. Her main hope lay in her ability to influence the magistrate. She would make him see the flimsy nature of the accusation. Brassey would not be a good witness.

Sometime in the afternoon, the cell door grated open and admitted the constable and the frowning figure of Jeremiah Smale. Dan smiled encouragingly at her, ensuring he stood between the two. Marleigh rose from the pallet, doing her best to look tired and pathetic, which to be fair was how she was starting to allow herself to feel. Eva's quiet questioning tugged at her thoughts. *Hush. I must concentrate now.* "Please! Tell me. How are Miss Eliza and Miss Margaret? Are they well?"

"That is none of your business! Do not dare to speak their names to me again!" snapped Smale.

"I had hoped, Master Smale, you were here to meet my bail. You cannot set any store by such ridiculous charges. You have known me long enough to see this is just petty jealousy and falsehood." In a further play for Roe's sympathies she

(MACCLESFIELD, 28 JUNE 1644)

continued, "Master Samuel Walker certainly trusted me. Can you not do the same?"

"I can see how you must have beguiled Walker. Well, he and I are different men!" Marleigh caught the constable's eye. "Long have I suspected something was not right about you, Hume. The thought that I might lay down good money for you to go free and abscond," he raised a hand to stop her protest, "is what is ridiculous. No one will meet your bail, even if it had been granted. Believe me, I will see to it that it won't be."

Roe broke his silence. "We have some news, mistress. The mayor and the parish have reached a decision on how to deal with this matter."

"About time too," growled Smale. "Open and shut, this seems to me."

"Now, sir. The good men of the town have provided a process to follow. Like it or not." He addressed Marleigh again. "A date has been set for a trial." He held up his hand as Marleigh started to speak. "Please. Hear me first. There has been correspondence with the magistrate. Normally he would be competent to hear minor matters but, as you know, proper process would require the Chester Assizes for a trial of witchcraft. But…" he sighed, "…these are not normal times and that is not a possibility open to us. The magistrate is stretched thin. So many good men of the law are fighting for the cause." He looked sideways at Smale, his meaning clear. "He cannot agree to delaying matters until Chester be taken for God, and so he has agreed to conducting the trial here, in the town. Knowing this is an exceptional accusation he will only do this if two other men of distinction sit with him as judges. He will be here on 13 July. That is the date of the trial."

"And a swift execution to follow. I am instructing the carpenters to draw plans for a scaffold, my dear." Smale smiled in satisfaction.

"No, sir. This is no private prosecution for you to command. This is the law of the land. We will look after any such arrangements, but only if required. What the magistrate has demanded as a condition to this trial, unusual as it is, is that the examination is completed in advance. He cannot delay here more than two days."

"Examination?" asked Marleigh, knowing the answer only too well. "What does this mean?"

Smale leered at her. "Well, my dear, some of us have been advising the learned magistrate on the process for convicting a witch. The more devout amongst us have been following the remarkable events guided by the godly men of Essex and Suffolk in these last years. In that part of the world, they know how to treat witches, and…" he eyed Eva with distaste, "…their imps. Firstly, whilst we gather witnesses, and take statements, you will be examined."

"Examined?"

"Yes. Examined. Learned men know the signs of a witch. All witches seal their pact with the Devil through the acceptance of imps from him. Their familiars. And through… fornication. These imps come to the witch to feed, to suckle on teats in secret places."

Marleigh rolled her eyes and glanced at Roe. "Teats. And imps. Are you mad, sir? This is to be your proof?"

"I have no doubt. Don't act as if this is unknown to you! Three good ladies of the town will examine your body in detail. They will go over every square inch of your skin and note all and every blemish and mark where the imps come to suckle. When this is done, you will sit, for three days and three nights, and we will observe. And when your imps come to you, as they will, you are done for. And you will confess to us! I will be there to supervise it all." Smale seemed to be in something of a trance. He even licked his lips.

(MACCLESFIELD, 28 JUNE 1644)

"You will be there whilst these good women search my body?" She raised an eyebrow and glanced again at the constable.

"No, mistress. He will not be present for the examination. Because that would not be proper." Roe fixed Smale with a hard look.

Smale collected himself, shaking off his reverie. "Maybe not. But Mary Brassey will be there to watch your every move." He smiled triumphantly.

"No," said Roe again. "She will not. If she is the accuser and a witness for the prosecution, then she cannot participate in the examination. I will gather the women together and my own wife will supervise. None of us have done this type of thing before, and I hope to God we do not need to again, but we must make a professional job of this or the magistrate will not be pleased."

Smale actually stamped his foot in frustration. "Be that as it may," he spat. "It matters not. Because you will confess, Marleigh Hume. Because witches always damn themselves from their own mouths."

"Why are you here at all, sir? I did not think you would wish to be in my company any more than you had to? Think of your reputation."

"You think you are so clever, Hume. Can you not guess?" Smale's smile was back. She thought he looked like a fat, satisfied toad. "I am to prosecute the case. I will make sure you do not escape God's justice. It is coming for you. Swift and sure. Ha! This will not damage my reputation. On the contrary, a conviction and execution will cement my reputation as the most godly man in the county. Have no fear, my dear, you are a dead woman."

He span on his heel, almost colliding with the door frame, and she could hear his boots ringing on the stone steps up to the street. She looked at Roe. "Did you see the girls? Did they pass you the bible?"

"Ah yes! I almost forgot." He reached into the pocket of his coat and brought out the book. "They were anxious, and I would say perhaps have had limited sleep. But they are well, mistress. Sarah will bring your supper later. Farewell."

"Thank you, Dan. Thank you." She pursed her lips. "When will this abomination start?"

"Not for a few days yet. Perhaps in about a week? We have a little time before trial, but we must press on. Sooner done, sooner over. I am sure they will find nothing and the magistrate may well just throw the accusation out then. If he does, there will be repercussions for our friend Mary Brassey. Patience, as ever."

After he had stepped out, she flipped through the bible. As she had hoped, about halfway through, a small piece of paper dropped out onto the pallet. Making sure she could not be observed from the door, she quietly opened it out. Eliza's careful handwriting.

Dearest Marleigh,

We have sent letters to friends. Help may be on its way already. God be with you and Eva.

Eliza and Maggie

Maggie had scrawled her name next to Eliza's. Marleigh felt a tear form. She looked down at Eva, now sleeping. *Help may be on the way, although what help that may be, I do not know.*

Time drifted. She lay on the pallet imagining how events might unfold. Imagination became dreams as she too slept. Dreams of old crones picking and prodding and poking at her

(MACCLESFIELD, 28 JUNE 1644)

body with the face of Smale, glistening with sweat and lust, gawping down at her from behind the women, reaching over and between them with his own grasping fingers. There was no sign of help in her dreams…

10

RICHARD FARRELL

(West of York, 2 July 1644)

To the east, the sky was lightening, and he could now discern the lacework pattern of the leaves and twigs of the hawthorn that supported one corner of the canvas. He had already been awake for some time, in fact he wondered if he had been to sleep at all. He guessed it was sometime around four o'clock and assumed it would not be long before the first stirrings in the camp were heard.

He lay with five others under the canvas sheet; soft snoring from his companions, echoed by the hundreds of other sleepers within earshot, provided a background murmur which he had long since learned to filter out.

Some people were moving about – soldiers on watch, cooks, people tending to the sick and wounded – but they felt distant and unreal. Shades of grey against the dim pre-dawn.

He felt numbly pleased with the spot they had found for their camp. After all, they had been farting about all day on this bloody hillside while the great and good, and not-so-good, decided their fate. To fight or not to fight? To stand or retreat? Of course, they would never call it retreat. The soldiers of God

(West of York, 2 July 1644)

never retreat. It would be a pragmatic, tactical repositioning. Securing the better ground. Making the strategic withdrawal.

Leven, the ever-cautious Scot, was for heading south towards Tadcaster. The Earl of Manchester would waver and bluster. The younger Fairfax would want to fight, and his own commander, Cromwell, well, at least on this point Richard and he would agree. Cromwell, always a reasonable and moderate man, would want to sow the valley with Royalist dead and water the crop with their blood. They came at this from different starting points, he knew, but on an opportunity for a good honest slaughter, here they walked shoulder to shoulder.

A slim white arm, hanging awkwardly out of an upstairs wardrobe. A pair of blank, dead eyes regarding him from the shadows as an apocalyptic storm doused the fires that had burned down half of his home. The casual execution of his oldest brother and the burning alive of many of the ordinary people who worked the land. This was what fired Richard's strategy. He cared nothing that the men who might soon be facing them across the valley were not the men responsible. They were all of a kind. They had the same allegiance and followed the same colours. And he had found that they all looked the same with their guts around their knees.

In the days after the fire and murder, he had found his brother Lionel. A small mercy from Lionel's God had spared him from being included in the inferno. Called to the far side of his parish, he had not received the news of the attack until a day later, when Richard himself had found him returning to his house. The news had crushed Lionel. He blamed himself at first, convinced that his sharp language when preaching had so incensed the authorities that they had visited this vengeance upon him. When Richard convinced him that this was a vendetta personal to himself, this almost seemed worse. Lionel had found he could not look his brother in the eye. Deprived of the release of self-hate, he had struggled not to reassign that hate to his younger brother. Surely here was God's punishment for Richard's life of violence and ungodly morals. Lionel shared Richard's short temper, the death of John and Angelica seemingly robbing the family line of any patience and balance, and he had raged uncontrollably in his grief.

This high emotion seemed to have the opposite effect on Richard. Still in shock after what he had witnessed, and how he had witnessed it, his brother's fierce attack caused him to retreat within himself. He balanced Lionel's fire with ice. He became cold, numb, uncaring. In the end, it was the agonising heartbreak of the double funeral of their siblings, and mass burial of the farm workers and their families, that had extinguished the enmity. They had wept together and vowed that evil such as had been visited upon them would not split what remained of the Farrell family.

They had parted calmly, but Richard wondered if words said could ever be unsaid. Or forgiven. He had pleaded with Lionel to leave with Anne and flee to London where they would be safer. He had agreed to think on it and that was the last he had seen of him.

In the days that followed, he took a room at the Blue Boar and made what remained of the house safe. He had gathered the remaining farm workers left on and around the small estate and told them that he would be leaving and that the harvest and remaining livestock were theirs to do with as they wished, at least until he returned. He had thought this approach would have delighted Will, with his new ideas.

He felt remarkably calm, almost matter-of-fact, about the preparations he was making to leave, although he was quietly relentless in his search for any news of Cobb's raiding party. There were many witnesses to the path of destruction that Cobb had carved through the district, but none knew of his whereabouts or his destination after the raid. Locals described a man Richard would not have recognised. He was powerfully built and apparently had lost his belly. He was hard-faced and rather gaunt, bearded still, but now balding. If he was not convinced of his identity by the simple fact that he sought Richard and his family out, he would have sworn this was some distant relative. Clearly the death of his son had changed him. Richard supposed it must do. After all, was he himself not changed?

He wondered at the departure of his fiery temper. Almost from a distance, he observed himself dealing with the smallholders and the few surviving workers from the house. He was quiet and courteous. He helped with money where it was needed, with an arm around a shoulder where it was welcomed. But the calmness came from the cold void that had consumed his spirit. He had no energy to waste on anger. All his effort was channelled towards revenge. No outbursts. No tears. No distractions.

After a week of enquiry and following false trails, it was clear that Cobb and his men had disappeared from the area and Richard assumed they had gone to join the King's army. Word had spread rapidly. The King had declared war on his own people – at least that was the message in this part of England. It was the not-so-secret Papist sympathisers against the true family of God. Men flocked to fight, joining the local militia and the regiments that local gentlemen were trying to form. Some even asked Richard to lead them, seeking him out as a known military man, but that was too long and uncertain a process for Richard. He needed a faster road to vengeance.

He had sought out Thomas Wolfe and found him pleased to welcome a man with his experience. He helped Wolfe to train the growing number of local men who had stepped forward to join their troop, and within a few weeks their twenty had grown to fifty. They worked the men hard, for very few had any idea of how to fight. They admitted none that didn't provide his own horse, or that they couldn't find a horse for, and any who could not master riding in a week were sent to the militia who needed musketeers and pikemen.

They were short of firearms of any quality and even swords were hard to come by. Richard knew only too well how such things were supplied, but they were too small a unit to register with any quartermaster. They needed a battle, because after a battle there were weapons a-plenty to be had, either for sale or picked from the dead.

In the meantime, the men drilled on horseback. Holding a line, changing formation, practising swordplay with sticks, or sharing the handful of muskets and pistols to improve their aim. Wolfe led them, and Richard concentrated on one-to-one skill training. Day by day they improved, and he and Wolfe sorted the lions from the sheep. The better their skills and discipline, the better his own chances of survival, and he had concluded that the longer he could stay alive in the war, the more likely he was to find Cobb. And in the meantime, if the army of King Charles the First welcomed a man such as Cobb, well he would happily cut his way through all of them for a chance to face him again.

Abruptly, in the stunted tree above him, a blackbird decided it was time to start its day and the lilting, bubbling song brought him back to the present. It conveyed a sense of wonder and optimism in the new day that he couldn't find in himself. He rolled quietly out from under his blanket and knelt facing the growing smudge of a paler grey where the sun was rising behind the bank of cloud.

He rose carefully, favouring a right knee he had twisted a day or so before, and rolled his shoulders to loosen the hard ground from his muscles. He buttoned his jacket. For all that it was summer, there was a chill in the morning air

(West of York, 2 July 1644)

and he fancied rain would make an appearance again before too long.

Quiet movement behind him and the sound of a short prayer, spoken quietly in the gloom. A hand on his shoulder. Richard saw the blackbird shoot away, hugging the ground but having to rise and fall over unfamiliar humps of sleeping men and baggage that had invaded its territory.

"Gonna rain, I reckon. Mornin', Captain."

"I'm not your captain." He said it automatically, because he wasn't a captain. Trouble was that all the men in the troop called him Captain, much to the actual captain's irritation.

"This it, d'you reckon? Will it be the end today, or are they movin' us again?" Trooper Henson hawked and spat. "That's better."

"Dunno, Abel. We got the ground. It's good ground, but who knows. Maybe Rupert won't come. Maybe he'll slip away."

"Doubt that. He's not gonna let us back at York, is he? Nah. If we stay 'ere, he'll fight."

"Hope so. It'll be a proper battle if he does. They say he's brought around 14,000. And what, another five or so from York garrison. We got the numbers on him, but them Scots are a bit mixed."

"Aye, Captain, but then so are some of our own. Some of them lot from Lancashire are as green as they come. We will need God on our side to beat Prince Rupert. I should pray again."

"Again? You'll wear out his ears, man."

"I know you don't mean it, Captain, but please, don't mock our Lord. He can yet be your salvation." Henson's hand was back on his shoulder, and he patted it.

"Best if I keep my mouth shut then, Abel."

"Well, you're not exactly the talking type. That's the most I've had out of you for weeks. You know Mason's dead?"

Richard shook his head, not turning to look at Henson.

"Fever, they said. Took a scratch from something a week ago. Don't know what. Two days later it were all red and angry-looking. Two days after that he keeled over. Two days after that fever took him back to the ground, and his soul to Jesus."

Richard kicked gently at the turf with the toe of his boot. He could think of nothing to say. Not that he didn't like Mason, he had never really spoken much to him. He didn't really speak much to anyone if he could help it. He just didn't really feel anything these days.

"You know what that means, Captain? That means it's just you and me now from the start. All of the others are gone."

It dawned on Richard that he was right. A few had quietly deserted when the reality of war had become too much – the first musket ball flying past their head, or the first bloated corpse by the roadside.

Some had been transferred to other regiments to make up numbers.

But mostly, they were dead. Shot, stabbed, clubbed, trampled or, most frequently, sickness or pure bad luck.

They had lost Wolfe in their first engagement, even before their first real battle. It had been dawn then too. Birds just waking in the trees which concealed them. All lined up on the edge of the copse watching the column of Royalist horse wend its way back to Oxford. It had been perfect. Rising sun behind them. Element of surprise. Nice, clear gentle slope down to the track to gain momentum. They even had the numbers. Around thirty of them to, what, twenty or so?

Months of training, begging horses and equipment, and Wolfe was proud of his men. Wanted to give them the chance to prove themselves. Disciplined, godly (apart from Richard of course) and increasingly competent. With no flourish or trumpet, just the raising of an arm, they had started down the hill. A perfect line, swords vertical, pistols primed. Wolfe had let himself gain a few yards on the rest to look back at them. Just as he did, they were spotted by the column below and a shot fired. It had spooked his horse, just slightly, but enough. A small change of direction, a slight slowing, but enough. Wolfe, looking over his shoulder in pride, had fallen. A twenty-year veteran, survivor of battles, sieges and skirmishes just like this one, and he fell from his horse and broke his neck without delivering a shot or a blow in the war.

Things never work out quite how you plan them.

"Just you and me, Captain. The left and right hand of God to bring His justice down on His enemies. See! The sun's breakin' through. Always shines on the righteous, eh, Captain."

"I'm not your captain," he muttered. They watched the moorland starting to fill with the pale gold of the sunrise and the long shadows of enemy horse. *Can't wait*, thought Richard. *I really can't wait.*

*

Richard waited. The sun had certainly taken the chill off the day, and now he and all the other poor sods on that hillside were cooking in their buff coats and steel. The stink of tens of thousands of men and horses, shitting, sweating, smoking under the July sun was becoming unbearable, even to a nose hardened by years of campaigning.

It must be around lunchtime already, he thought. Like water filling up a dam, continuous lines of horse and foot slowly made their way onto the moor, covering the green with the sprawl of units at the end of hard marching. Anxious Parliamentarian foot were being shepherded into position in the centre with little order to it, just plugging into the lines where there were spaces. Some had almost reached Tadcaster before being pivoted back towards York. Seasoned English troops alongside largely untried Scots and green levies from Lancashire. Concerned that the Royalists might attack and take them in a column of march, the cautious commanders had finally decided this was the place for battle, and they had raced back to regain the best ground.

Opposite him, the bulk of Rupert's horse had appeared by nine o'clock, with his foot gradually trudging in and occupying the ground behind a long ditch and hedge in the centre. Not many of them. If they attacked now they could sweep them away, but he knew their cautious commanders were miles away, somewhere towards Tadcaster. He looked down the incline, and this same barrier was between him and the enemy. He had been looking at it all morning and considering how it would break up their lines if they were to attack. It was by no means certain they would be the ones to attack but, as they had the numbers, it seemed likely. He hated that hedge. In his mind he could hear the order to line that ditch and hedge with muskets, and maybe cannon. If they did manage to get through, their disordered mass would be vulnerable to the counter-charge.

He looked up the opposite slope. He could see the banners of Lord Byron and his horse. With him would be Urry and Vaughan. Behind them, and slightly masked, were more units. Reserves. *Maybe Molyneux?* All competent commanders, although Byron was a hothead and could be a liability.

Where is Rupert and his lifeguard? That could be a crucial intervention. He brought a formidable reputation and raised the morale of his men wherever he appeared. *Let us hope his attention is drawn elsewhere today.*

Richard was to the far left of the Parliament line. The only units to his left, to the west, were some Scottish dragoons. *Good men*, Richard thought, practical and business-like, doing

(WEST OF YORK, 2 JULY 1644)

the clean-up jobs and scouting that some, who liked to think of themselves as gentlemen, would consider beneath them. He was glad they were there. *Maybe they can clear that fucking ditch.*

He had been moving to the left all morning. Firstly they had the brief excitement of forcing some advance units of Rupert's cavalry off a rise on the left wing. The Bilton Bream or some such name. Manmade hills and lumps to serve as a rabbit warren. Slightly higher than the surrounds, it was good ground to hold, and they had had to show strength and determination to win it for the left wing of the army. A brief encounter, largely shots at range, but ultimately successful. The dragoons had again been useful, and both his unit and theirs now watched the pioneers clearing the brush, filling holes and flattening the ground as best they could to allow for the movement of the 5,000 horsemen that made up the left wing.

He checked his horse was staked and gave it some water. He asked Henson to keep an eye on it and went to find what passed as a latrine. He wanted to be absolutely empty when the time came, and if that meant several trips to the foul pits, then so be it. He didn't hurry. Nothing was going to happen for some time yet.

*

Nothing much happened for some time. He sat on his horse, with all around him similarly mounted. He was in the second line of his regiment, towards the left end. Henson just to his right, as they both liked it. Here and there the lines of horse were broken by groups of musketeers, matches still unlit. They were there to disrupt an incoming charge, although Byron would have to be a madman to charge uphill, over the ditch, into their superior numbers. Still, maybe Henson was right. It was their day, and God would make it so.

A few hours ago, the cannon had started to exchange fire across the moor. This was not the intense barrage that might indicate they were on the move. It seemed just to be range-finding and giving the men something to relieve the tension. It was half-hearted and stopped on more than one occasion when brief showers of drizzle threatened to dampen the powder and matches.

He had been watching it in a detached, bored way, leaning forward to whisper to his horse and keep it calm.

It was a new horse to him, and they were getting used to each other. A bay with black mane and tail, it was a little wild, but he didn't mind that. He had lost so many over the last few years that he had learned not to get too attached. He used to give them names, but he had stopped after he had a fine white mare shot from under him. It had taken a long time to die, and lying next to it with a twisted ankle, he had no means of putting it out of its misery. So this horse was called Seven. At least he didn't have to think about what to call the next one when the time came.

The sun had become hazy as the afternoon turned to early evening, but he was soaking under the layers of leather and steel. His helmet sat on the pommel of his saddle, and he wiped the sweat from his forehead and batted away the flies that were plaguing them all. The horses were becoming distinctly fatigued, even though the men were stood down from time to time to give them relief from the weight of man and armour.

He had been here so many times in the last few years. Waiting, waiting, waiting. Waiting for the call, the shot, the flag that sent him forward. But merciful Jesus! Never had he waited so long.

(WEST OF YORK, 2 JULY 1644)

Always the nerves. His icy exterior belying the turmoil within. His furious desperation for revenge like a lake of lava surging back and forth beneath a snowy volcano. It was not fear. Not really. Only a fear of missing his opportunity. The right to justice for the wrong done to his family. If he lived long enough to collect payment for the injustices, then everything else was trivial.

He knew the men around him were wary of him in the fight. Those that knew him, anyway. *The others will soon learn*, he thought to himself grimly. Only Henson seemed to understand the rage that drove him to hack and slash seemingly beyond the capability of a normal man. But even he didn't really know the truth. To Henson, it was God speaking through the steel in Richard's right hand. Henson just marvelled at why Richard wouldn't accept it.

Richard knew it wasn't this. He thought back time and again to the encounter he had with the mysterious Marleigh. She had sensed something in him. She had tried to talk to him about it. She knew something. Somehow. The taking of life lent him a terrible power. He couldn't control it, but in the middle of a battle, the energy washing through him from the dead and the dying blinded him to pain, to caution, to fatigue. To restraint or mercy. He knew men thought of him as a butcher. But at least he was their butcher. 'Cromwell's berserker', he was called. Better to have Richard Farrell with you than against you. An uneasy situation for all concerned.

He had accepted it. Embraced it. So be it; that is who he had become. He was fighting his way along a dark road, and the light that lit the way was the pale corpse of John Cobb swinging from a rope. And in a sudden flash of vision, Angelica's cold white arm hanging through the wardrobe door. The back of his brother's head blown out. The smouldering barn with its smouldering dead.

He jumped in his saddle, startled, as Henson elbowed him and said softly, "Look, Captain. All of York has come." He pointed away to the right. From their height on the Bream, he could see a long line of foot snaking down the opposite slope to join what had been the painfully thin centre of the Royalist line. "Must be some thousands. So do you suppose we let them settle themselves in, or will some bright spark at the top of our hill give the order?"

*

Another hour had passed, and the lacklustre exchange of cannon had fallen silent with another shower. As relative silence fell, voices could be heard among the allies. Carried on the light breeze, the sound grew until it was picked up by those around Richard. Thousands of English and Scots joining together in song, the words of psalms rising and falling. Even to Richard's godless ears it was beautiful, at once familiar but somehow strange and unworldly as it drifted across a field staked out for slaughter. He felt the hairs rise on the back of his neck.

Looking across the moor, he could see the Royalist centre in the distance. A few final stragglers were still arriving to bolster their numbers and there was some awkward reshuffling of his pack by Rupert. But everywhere, among those close to him, and across on the Royalist side, men were starting to realise that there would be no fight today. Some enemy units appeared to be standing down. As the day finally seemed to be cooling, Richard felt himself doze, leaning forward in his saddle.

Abruptly, his apathy was shattered when he realised that the enemy's range-finding was directed at his regiment. The Royalists had brought up a small battery and sited it on a raised spur of ground behind the ditch but in front of the mass of Byron's horse. The intention was clear as they lined up their guns at Cromwell's regiments.

In the distance they saw a few puffs of smoke, with the harsh crack following a second later. Moments later there was a thin screaming as a shell whooshed over their heads, men ducking instinctively even though the iron ball was already well past them. A few horses had plunged around, but this was by now an experienced unit, and most had been under fire before.

Still, it was not a comfortable thing to be sitting in the middle of such a large target. A mass of flesh formed of 5,000 men and 5,000 horses, waiting to receive the impact. With the first shell going high, the next one pitched into the tuft twenty paces short of the frontline and some seventy paces to his right. He saw it throw up soil and skip over the heads of the front ranks to plough into the Scots horse at the rear. He couldn't see the outcome, but he could soon hear it. The screaming, piercing noise of a horse, in harmony with the wail of the unlucky rider.

With no warning, another shell tore a bloody furrow through the front rank not thirty paces to his right, decapitating a horse in a fountain of blood, and taking the rider through his midriff, near splitting him in two. Both crashed to the ground, dead before they hit the churned earth. The horse behind was similarly slaughtered and collapsed as its legs were shot away by the same iron ball. The rider emerged from the wreckage of his mount, spattered with the blood of his own horse and his comrade from the rank in front.

Rearing, terrified horses span away from the carnage, riders desperately trying to regain control as a further shell screamed overhead, the gunners now overexcited at their success and missing their aim. The regiments were peppered with shot for another ten minutes, each minute seeming a year, but, thankfully, as the guns started to bog in the earth and cannon smoke started to obscure the view, the accuracy of the shelling decreased.

Cromwell was not idle and Richard saw guns brought forward to return fire. Protected by some battalions of foot, hurrying to positions, these managed to suppress, if not entirely halt, the Royalist fire. They too came under a sharp and damaging fire from the musketeers lining the ditch, reminding Richard of their presence in a very unwelcome way. He had thought that this skirmish was an isolated incident that would bookend the day, but he sensed a rising excitement around him. Orders were shouted. Flags were being waved. Men taking their ease and resting their horses hastily remounted. He stood in his stirrups, as did many around him.

"My God, Henson! We are on the move. I think we are attacking!"

A colonel arrived on a sweating black horse, reining to a halt in front of the mass of the regiment. "God be praised!" he bellowed. He held his sword aloft and waved it in a circle over his head. "We will sweep them from the field. Hold now, brothers. Keep your line. Maintain discipline. No looting! We stay together whatever happens. You know Cromwell's command – we leave the baggage train 'til the battle is done and God has given us victory."

He could only hear a few words given the rising noise around him and his distance from the man, but he knew the message. They all did. It was hammered home in training. They may not be gentlemen, but by God they had iron discipline. They had seen how the fucking Cavaliers were in battle. A quick skirmish then into the baggage train to loot and murder the defenceless camp followers. Cromwell's men had learned to turn this to their advantage and they held together.

He checked his pistols were secure in their holsters. He loosened his sword in its scabbard and gripped the reins.

"By God!" a man just in front of him shouted. "By God! Here they come, boys!"

They all strained to see and the colonel whirled around on his mount to observe. "Praise God! He is right. God has delivered the arrogant fools into our hands. Let us make a good harvest today, brothers!"

Richard strained to see. On the far side of the moor, Byron was leading his horse forward. He was attacking. Already the Royalist cannon had fallen silent, as they could not risk hitting their own horse. Pretty soon, the musketeers in the ditch would be in the same position. "The stupid fucker," Richard said under his breath.

"Please, Captain. Don't blaspheme at a time like this. Not when His Spirit is with us." An anguished-looking Henson looked at him with pleading eyes.

Richard laughed and clapped him on the back, feeling the heavy steel plate. "Not blasphemy, Henson, just a little ripe language to express an unarguable truth! You must admit, he is a stupid fucker!"

He pulled his helmet's visor down. Loosened his sword one more time, and waited for the order.

*

They watched as the front ranks encountered the ditch and the hedge. Orderly advance became chaos. Lines struggled to keep formation. As the first horsemen emerged and waited for their comrades, the order was given and the whole of the Eastern Association horse, backed by Leslie's Scots, started to walk down the hill to meet them.

Richard could almost feel the mass of men and horses like

a physical weight on his back pressing him forward. Bottled-up tension released, momentum starting to gain a hold, and thousands of tonnes of flesh and steel gathered pace from a walk to a trot. He glanced along the line, seeing others doing the same. Superb order was being maintained. All the training, the drilling and previous battles had forged this. Always one who preferred to fight on his own terms, with his own motivations, Richard nevertheless felt a swelling pride at the sheer competence.

Trot became canter and swords were swept out, or pistols gripped as men called out to their God. Richard left his weapons in place; he had seen too many men accidentally skewered by a careless blade, or shot through as a nervous rider battled a skittish horse. Plenty of time for that.

It was wonderful to finally feel some breeze on his face, cooling his skin. Just the release from the waiting, his frustration at being kept from the enemy, the build-up of anxiety now swamped with the adrenaline of his thirst for slaughter. They were off the Bream, and away from coney warren. The bands of musketeers had jogged along with the cavalry for a while but were now trailing, toiling, sweating far behind in the close evening.

All the front rank now had pistols raised. He could see over heads and between shoulders the extreme right wing of Byron's men. He could see the panic, eyes wide as they tried to bully their mounts into a semblance of a formation, spurring hard, and pulling tossing heads with rolling eyes this way and that. They were caught between trying to generate some forward momentum and maintaining contact with their fellows, and Cromwell's men were almost upon them.

He could feel the fear and apprehension growing around him too. The euphoria of disbelief at Byron's catastrophic blunder, and the elation of the charge, giving way to the practical realisation that for all of their advantages in the collision just seconds away, it did not guarantee their personal survival. Pleas for God's protection were whispered, muttered, shouted. *For lo we are in the valley of the shadow of death, and no mistake*, thought Richard, lips drawing back into a grimace. *God give them strength, and whatever it is that I draw upon, let it not desert me today.* He glanced at Henson, to acknowledge him for what might be the last time, but Henson was too intent on the enemy, quietly mouthing some prayer or psalm. He couldn't catch his eye.

A strange silence seemed to envelope them all for a moment. Not a real silence, but almost like a split second stop in time – a collective deep breath before immersion in the icy water of some deep, black lake. A plunge they could no longer pull out of. They had leapt from the rock and were inches from the surface. Final thoughts and exhortations of those who knew they were about to depart the world, and were praying to open their eyes in paradise. Some with confidence, some less so.

Richard recalled, in the blink of an eye, his years with Roger DeLacey. Conversations about how to stay alive on campaign. How to avoid the front rank. How to avoid the dangerous night patrols. How to avoid heroism at all costs, unless it was low on risk and high on chances of being observed by those with the power to reward. Now, with a heart bent on bloody vengeance overruling a cool head bent on survival, all of that was forgotten. A cold white arm hanging from black shadow. A bloody, bunched dress. Lightning and flame. He was ready. He was always ready.

A ragged volley of pistol. Horses screamed. One in the front rank to his right collapsed, pitching onto its knees, its rider arcing over its head. The crackling Parliamentarian response rippled along the front rank and suddenly he was riding through the smoke of their volley. Those in front hastily holstered pistols; those fumbling with wood and leather simply dropped them. Heavy cavalry swords were swept out. Richard took this chance to do the same. Henson was shouting next to him. *Any second!*

Abruptly the riders in front slowed and swerved. No horse could be persuaded to charge flat out into a wall, even if the wall was constructed of flesh, blood and bone. Arms raised and fell, a few flashes of hazy sun on drawn steel. Along the line, through the gaps created between them, other horses surged. Some riderless, some carrying wide-eyed, screaming men. Richard gripped Seven as tightly as he could with his knees and pointed the tip of his sword like a lance. A face, long hair flying, feathers in a black hat, appeared through the pistol smoke, screaming with terror or rage. Richard didn't care which, and with his left hand gripping the front of his saddle, he stood in his stirrups and leaned forward to catch his enemy full in that screaming face. The man's own momentum skewered him through the cheek, and Richard pulled his blade back and free quickly to avoid losing it as the corpse rode past him and into the mass of men behind.

And here it came. With the thrust had come the feeling of fire coursing through him. The death of his opponent, and others around him, fed him like kindling thrown into the furnace. He felt his rage building, and his strength with it. So much he almost lost consciousness, fighting the feeling like a drunk trying to stay on his feet.

Confusion reigned. Shouts, curses, screams and the unending clash of steel on steel as those packed tightly together hacked at each other. He felt the weight of ranks behind driving him forward and then he sensed almost immediately that the disorganised Royalist horse was on the point of breaking already. The front ranks had disappeared and all was disorganised melee. Knots of riders from both sides straining for advantage, using their horses to push and shove while they struck overarm at helmets or those foolish enough to be wearing no more than a feathered hat.

He swallowed hard and tried to focus. He saw a gap in front and pushed Seven towards it, seeing so far unfought enemy beyond. White faces, wide eyes, open, shouting mouths. He spurred hard and burst through into a small space. He opened his body and cut hard to the right, felt the parry, and heard the gasp as his opponent felt the weight of the attack. His arm went limp and Richard's backhand slash swept through the unprotected neck, spraying bright red over those behind. Wedged in by the dead man's horse he swivelled left just in time to block a vicious swing aimed at his head. Black hair and beard framed as the arm was raised again for a second strike. But faster than that, instead of bracing for the parry, Richard used the massive strength lent to him to cut hard from the wrist, with no real backswing, chopping at the upraised elbow and almost severing the arm. The bearded man screamed and instinctively grabbed at the wound with his left hand. Richard's thrust caught him in the throat and the surge of energy told him everything he needed to know.

Blocked now on both sides he tried to force Seven forward to the next victim. Both horses were panicking as they sensed the lifeless state of their riders. He shoved at them, pushing their heads and flanks. He succeeded in unseating the headless rider, who flopped to the turf covering his mount with more blood. Eyes rolling, the horse started to back out of the crowd and Richard spurred to follow it. Another was trying to slash at him, leaning over the back of a riderless horse, but they couldn't reach each other. After a few seconds of frustrated sword waving, Richard dropped the reins and grabbed the right holstered pistol with his left hand. The Royalist's eyes widened, and he struggled for his own weapon. *Too slow, bastard.* The ball punched through the breastplate, and he rolled slowly backward and into the mud, his own horse finishing the job as it danced its back hooves over his head, driving the steel helmet into the surface.

Again, Richard spurred on, and this time he broke free of the mass and into clear ground. He sensed, and then turned to see, a half-dozen of his regiment following him through the gap, Henson among them. He looked up and saw they were close to the ditch; more enemy horse was coming down the slope but plenty more were fleeing back up towards them, breaking away from the rear of the melee and forcing their way back across the ditch. He shouted to those that followed and they fell upon the rear of those still engaged in the fight. He snatched a glance along the line and could see other breakthroughs, and the sheer weight of the Eastern Association horse driving the shredded Royalist units backwards.

In the midst of death and despair, he was full of strength and power, not even blowing. No more than a few more minutes of slaughter, hacking at the enemy from behind, men already on the point of breaking from the weight of enemies in front of them, and it was done. The Royalist horse, wheeling away as best they could, headed for the ditch, or for the edge of the field, anywhere to get away from the relentless press and whirling steel.

The shout started up almost immediately – "Re-form! Re-form!" He struggled to bring Seven around and into the forming line. He was among men of a different regiment, all mixed together now. Grim nods. The hard grins of those amazed to find themselves still alive. Even some prayers.

"C'mon, men! Over we go!" and now it was their turn to force their way through the hedge and across that fucking ditch.

(WEST OF YORK, 2 JULY 1644)

*

An hour later, and he sat on an exhausted horse at the top of the slope. He patted Seven on the neck, white with drying sweat. All around him were dead and dying men and horses. Groans and screams ate at his mind. The men around him were dead tired, slumped over in the saddle. For himself, even though his whole right arm, from gauntlet to shoulder, was caked in drying blood, he felt full of energy. Even though there were lines and splatters of gore across the steel of his breastplate, and blood dripped off the tip of his sword, he could scarcely contain the bloodlust coursing through his body. All the death around him had pumped him almost to bursting point with power. He wanted more. It was like an opium addiction.

Other members of the Eastern Association were around him, still in impressive numbers, and he could see Leslie's lancers making their way up the slope too, having picked off the small bodies of Byron's wing that had escaped Cromwell's attention. As they halted, he learned that the great man had been injured early in the fight and only rejoined them when they had charged into the second body of horse on their wing, commanded by the bloody Molyneux brothers, the butchers of Rupert's Lancashire campaign.

For all the tales of their killing prisoners in cold blood they had put up a sterner fight than Byron's first wave. But the weight of numbers told against them in the end, and the wave of their panicked retreat had carried away Rupert and his reinforcements too.

Even from this vantage point it was not possible to see what was happening elsewhere on the field. Everywhere the smoke battle hung in the close, still air. The noise of clashes, close and further away, carried to them, but it was difficult to make any sense of it. Surely, after their spectacular routing of the whole of Rupert's right wing, they must be on the verge of victory, but there was a sense that they were somehow isolated from the rest of the conflict, in their own, small, personal war, removed from a bigger, more important event.

They milled around, some dismounting, gasping for air and water, awaiting orders. The evening was drawing on and the light was slowly beginning to fade, the gloom intensified by the smoke, all hemmed in by the low cloud. Richard slipped off Seven and started to examine him for cuts and scratches, whispering in his ear praise and encouragement. He looked around for Henson; in the press of men he recognised a few faces, but Henson was not one of them.

Back in the saddle, standing in his stirrups he could now make out the mass of Cromwell's horse behind him and the Scottish lancers making their way up the shallow slope they had so recently fought over. The ground was becoming a quagmire, churned by countless hooves while still wet from the rain, and now resoaked with blood and piss. Even further back he could see more fighting – fresh powder flashes, rolling gunsmoke, and the harsh cries and sound of steel on steel of hand-to-hand conflict. He strained to make out what was happening and concluded it must be Fraser's Dragoons trying to clear the ditch of the Royalist musketeers.

No cheery blackbirds now, he thought, *just crows and kites and flies.*

Purposeful hoof beats penetrated his wandering thoughts. Cromwell, surrounded by some of his officers, was riding along the rough formation, urging men back into their saddles. Rough bandage around his neck. He was shouting, but Richard could not make out much of what was said. He was pointing in different directions and talking urgently with his commanders, who now peeled off and rode off to re-form the line.

(West of York, 2 July 1644)

He was still on the extreme left of the wing, and he now looked north and east. An officer he recognised reined in, frantically scanning faces to find someone he knew. He met Richard's eyes and gestured for him to approach. He walked Seven around the end of the line and trotted over.

"Farrell. Good to see you alive. God has been merciful and granted us victory, but there is still much to do. The lieutenant-general has seen the course of the battle and all is in balance. It seems our success on the left is matched only by the enemy's on the right. The centre holds by a thread. He marches us around the rear of their army to find the place to deliver the hammer blow. He seeks Goring's horse to neutralise them and God knows where they are in this murk."

Richard just nodded, wondering why he was being singled out for this information.

"But he doesn't want to expose our own flank and rear as we manoeuvre, and he does not like the look of yonder trees and what they might conceal. So he wants them scouted."

"And he wants me to scout?"

"Yes. And scouted, Farrell. Not an excuse for looting the baggage." He caught a look from Richard. "Not that you would, I know. Too keen on slicing more Royalist necks."

"The bastards showed no mercy to my family. Damned if I can see why I should not return the kindness."

The officer frowned. "God does not favour butchers of civilians or camp followers, whatever their allegiances."

"They have no allegiance when they are dead. How many shall I take?"

"Four others. And find me or another who can take a message to Cromwell once you are done. Remember, the message is more important than engaging the enemy. Now quickly, man! Get about it."

They had passed a few abandoned carts, animal feed sacks, and a scattering of dead horses and men who had only made a half-mile from the slaughter before collapsing. They entered the wood from the south-west, and once in the trees, they moved quietly, the din of the battle growing more distant and muted. It seemed the wood had not long since seen much clearance, for there were pockets of open space with the signs of timber having been dragged out, and piles of decaying brush left behind by those responsible. Richard led the line of five in single file, initially walking their horses to reduce the noise of their passing but now in a loping trot, concerned that it was taking too long and thinking Cromwell might be waiting.

He sensed they were not far from the north-east edge, and he intended then following the edge of the trees south down the eastern side to try to find the Eastern Association horse again. As the light faded further under the thin canopy, he urged them into a canter, hammering along the faint trail they had found. Rounding a small rise in the ground they suddenly burst into a broad clearing, which narrowed at the far side but then opened out under the eaves, framing a view of rolling moorland.

He reined quickly to a halt, his companions spilling past him into the open space to form a rough line. Opposite, tucked in under the trees, was a large wagon pulled by two fine black horses. A man sat holding the reins, but he was no soldier. Three horsemen seemed to be accompanying him, one talking to the wagon driver, the other two peering down the short open track to the moorland. All four were taken completely by surprise by the appearance of Richard's party, the not-too-distant sounds of battle masking their approach. Both sets of men froze momentarily as they eyed each other.

At the same instant Richard shouted, "Weapons down!", the rider nearest the cart grabbed the pistol from the holster on his saddle. Richard, knowing both his own pistols had been discharged, and cursing himself for not reloading when he had the chance, dug his spurs into Seven who launched himself forward. In slow motion, he saw the other cock the pistol and aim while the other two cavalrymen spurred off down the track to the open ground. He sensed some of his companions start off in pursuit.

He swept out his sword and screamed as the distance closed, willing his shout to deflect the inevitable pistol ball. He had no time to attend to the man on the wagon and had to trust in his companions to deal with him. The rider was taking an eternity fiddling with the firing mechanism. Richard was almost there, and his arm lifted the heavy blade high above his head for a decisive strike. Seven slid to a stop and half reared, giving him more height and momentum for the blow. But finally the pistol cracked, the flare from the barrel almost touching him, and he felt a massive impact in his sword arm along with the burning of the discharge. The ball smacked into his raised arm, flinging it backwards and twisting him round in the saddle. The sword flew from his grip as he lost all feeling below the elbow.

Seven reared again, shocked by the proximity of the shot. This time his descending front hooves caught the other rider's mount on the shoulder, driving it to the ground. Richard rolled off backwards, blood sheeting down his arm, and staggered to his feet. His opponent rose groggily from the wreckage of his horse, which thrashed around, and started dragging at the sword in his scabbard as he tried to avoid the flailing legs. Richard could not immediately see his own sword but didn't want to give his opponent time to draw his blade. He dodged the rolling horse and leapt at the man. His right arm useless, he swung with his left, trying to get close enough to stop him drawing the blade. Pain shrieked at him from his shoulder to his elbow, but with his opponent intent on his struggle to extract the sword, Richard grasped the opportunity and punched him full on his windpipe.

The man collapsed, sword forgotten, grabbing at his neck, trying vainly to draw in great breaths. He lay helpless on his back. Richard, breathing heavily, placed one boot on his chest, while the man's contorted face went redder and redder, eyes wide and desperate. Richard bent and pulled the man's sword from its scabbard.

"See? Not so difficult was it, friend? The secret is not to panic. Panic makes you clumsy, and this is your reward." He hefted the sword in his left hand to gauge the weight and balance.

"Seems you have a problem with your throat? Can't get your breath?" He leaned in but no reply came, just a slow, tortured wheezing, eyes wide, desperate. "Perhaps I can help with that?" Richard whispered, feeling both relieved and pleased with his narrow escape. "After all, I think it might have been my fault."

The man closed his eyes now. Face scarlet, chest hardly moving. "It's a kindness really," he said out loud, but really it was a conversation with himself. With a swift movement, he raised the blade, and with a slightly awkward backhanded left-hand swing, crashed it down across the man's neck. It took the fingers of both clutching hands before it bit into the gasping flesh, almost twisting it from his hand. A crimson wave flooded the ground and Richard stepped smartly backward, feeling at the same time the familiar surge of energy that violent death had released. All his tiredness fled; the pain in his arm subsided. He wanted more.

Only now did he look up and notice the silence around

him. Three of his companions had disappeared, presumably in pursuit of the fleeing enemy.

To his left was set a strange tableau, a still life it seemed, almost frozen in time. Still mounted, one of his party sat staring at him in disbelief. At the same time his arm was extended with his pistol pointing vaguely in the direction of the wagon. On the bench seat, the driver was half crouched, his hands held high. Richard could see no other weapons.

Pumped with adrenaline, bursting with the borrowed energy and power of a dead man and covered with blood, Richard vaulted onto the back of the wagon and moved slowly past the canvas-covered mass behind the driver. Awkwardly, with the sword still in his left-hand, he advanced on the man.

"And what the fuck are you doing hiding in the woods, my good man, no more than a spit behind the biggest battle of the war?"

The man didn't answer. He seemed entirely lost, horrified by the position he found himself in and hypnotised by the bloody, otherworldly apparition in front of him. He raised his hands higher, shifting round to face Richard rather than the pistol. He could see where the true threat lay.

"Captain." Richard blinked, and looked to his left. His companion was still staring at him. "Captain, your arm!"

The man had called him 'Captain', so he must know him. Only those in his regiment, in his troop, called him that. He looked down at his useless right arm, a bloody sleeve from the midpoint of his bicep, droplets dripping from his fingers.

He laughed. "A bit of a mess, eh, boy?" He couldn't place the man's face, but he was barely containing his rage as the berserker within him grew, feeding his fury with a lust for more blood, more death and more power like this. To use it before it faded. It was only when he was possessed in this way that he felt alive these days. When he truly felt like he could drown his bitter loss in a sea of blood.

He turned back to the driver. "Please, sir. Please. I am no soldier. Please. Let me go." The voice was soft, but steady. The man was scared, but not yet in despair.

Richard said nothing but shuffled further up the cart until he placed the point of the cavalry sword against the driver's chest.

"Please," the driver said again, looking Richard in the eye and slowly bringing down his hands until they lightly gripped the blade. "Let me go. I am no threat to you. God be my witness."

"Perhaps we should let him go, Captain. You know the orders on looting."

Richard turned to his companion, realising there was no chance of the driver jumping him, but left the sword tip gently grinding against the man's sternum, a small red stain marking the shirt. "Who said anything about looting? He's got nothing that I need, have you, friend? Well, perhaps one thing."

The blue eyes gazed back at him. "Sir. Captain? Let me return to my family. I am no soldier. You can see that. I am unarmed. Please." He gently tried to move the blade to the side.

"Captain! Please. Let 'im go. 'Tis clear there is no harm in this one. God is with us today. Let us not stain our honour with this!"

Richard, who had been enjoying his moment of grim wit, lost patience with the trooper. "If you can't stomach it, lad, then piss off back to camp. God has watched us slaughter thousands today! Do you think he cares any more for this one? Now fuck off if you can't bear to watch, and help your mates cut down the two bastards who rode off. Perhaps they don't deserve to die on a battlefield either!"

(WEST OF YORK, 2 JULY 1644)

The trooper, shocked out of his horror, scowled. "Don't mock me or the Almighty, Farrell!" *No 'Captain' now*, Richard thought. "I will go indeed, and I shall report you on my return. I won't be surprised if you will swing for this!"

Richard, half drunk on blood and death, had already lost interest in him and waved him away. He didn't even register the hoof beats gathering speed across the clearing and disappearing down the narrow track to the moorland. The sounds of war, no more than half a mile distant, also faded into the background as he returned his focus to the man in front of him.

"My brother John," he said quietly. "He was unarmed when they came to his door. The men and women of the estate who they herded into our barn? They too were unarmed. And, friend," his voice lowered to almost a whisper, "my sister was unarmed and hiding in a wardrobe when they found her. And yet, they showed no mercy. They shot. They burned. They raped. And they stabbed." On the last word, he leant his weight forward and slid the blade through the man's despairing grip and between his ribs.

He expected another delivery of berserker energy to flow down the steel into his body. But nothing. The cart driver slowly crumpled, dropping to his knees with a sigh, and folding forward. Richard quickly pulled the blade free to avoid losing his grip on it. *Not enough*, he thought and raised his arm for a killing strike. Instead, an enormous fatigue rolled over him, and he suddenly became acutely aware of the dead weight and screaming agony of his right arm.

He swayed, lightheaded, and slowly tilted, fighting for consciousness. His left calf was wedged against the edge of the cart, and as his centre of gravity passed the point of no return, he fell, unconscious, before he crashed into the earth of the clearing.

11

RICHARD

(Marston Moor, 3 July 1644)

He did not know how long he was out, but when he opened his eyes, it was almost completely dark. Faint moonlight showed him patches of varying degrees of blackness and he sensed, rather than saw, the large presence of Seven standing almost on top of him.

He also became aware again of the dull aching throb of his right arm and he gingerly tried to move his fingers. To his relief, the feeling had returned and he could gently clench and unclench his hand into a weak fist. He tried to sit up, and immediately the pain grated at him and he had to let the useless limb dangle, keeping it as still as possible. He patted Seven on the foreleg, whispering to him, thanking him for staying with him. He could not hear sounds of battle any longer, just the faint melody of aftermath. Screams and moans of men and horses. Occasional shots as wounded animals were dispatched.

He knew he had to get back. Find his regiment and get his arm looked at. He assumed he would not have it for much longer and wondered why he didn't feel a terror at that thought. He wriggled along the ground on his arse and, groping in the dark, found the stirrup. Slowly, biting down in his pain, he hauled himself first to his knees, and then to his feet. He stroked Seven's nose and gathered the reins. As he did so, he trod on something long and thin. A branch or a tree root? But the thing moved slightly, and he heard the low grunt of another horse. The one Seven had maimed. A hint of moonlight glinted off the breastplate of the cold corpse he had so recently made. In the dark he could see the rough outline of the cart and its covered load, but he couldn't see the driver.

He saw no risk. The man was done for, as surely as Richard's own right arm, and the ghosts of the dead had never bothered him. Anyway, this Royalist soldier would be at the back of a long queue for vengeance. Richard hauled himself into the saddle. A feat of balance rather than strength, and mercifully Seven stood still.

His original mission was now overdue. Whatever had happened on the battlefield had happened hours ago and without him. He did not know if he was to ride into a victorious camp, or imprisonment, or worse. He gently nudged Seven through the blackness, aiming broadly for the gap in the trees, trusting the horse's nose and night vision to deliver him down the short path from the woods and out onto the open moor.

He felt no relief. Nor fear, really. He searched for the word to describe the strange, unaccustomed feeling washing over him. He felt nauseous, but that could be the wound. Now congealed, but he didn't doubt he had lost a lot of blood. He still felt faint and had to concentrate to stay balanced on Seven's swaying back. But underneath all of this physical challenge, there was an emotion he had not felt for years. No longer anger. No longer the nagging ache for revenge. Now he knew what it was, and it surprised him. It was shame.

He wondered if the fall from the cart, the blood loss, the narrow escape from death had left him no longer thinking straight, but he didn't think so. He felt shame at what he had done in the clearing, away from battle, faced with an unarmed man. A wave of exhaustion and self-pity washed over him. What had he become? How far had he fallen from his childhood ideals of heroism? Where was the life he had seen for himself? A successful merchant with a beautiful wife, a loving family and a prosperous life ahead. Now all taken from him by betrayal and outrageous twists of fate.

He waited for the familiar rage at the unfairness of it all, but nothing came. No rising heat, no fury. Just coldness. Tiredness. Shame. He expected he would die from the wound to his arm. Either he would die as the surgeon hacked it off, or from the inevitable fever to follow. No more than he deserved. He was now as low as the men who had raped his sister. What was the point of it all?

As he rounded the corner of the wood, he started to see a little more. Fires had been lit here and there across the field, and Seven started stepping over bodies and making his way around mounds of equipment. He had re-found the battlefield. He could see right across the moorland, almost back to where he had started the day. It was a vision of hell. The flames lit men moving around in the dark. Piles of corpses being dragged into lines. Struggling horses, missing legs or leaking their innards into the soil. Moaning, cursing, screaming.

From the direction of the trail of dead, Richard could see that his own side had had the victory. *Hurrah*, he thought. *God was indeed with us, for he hath overseen the massacre of more of them than of us. Praise be.* Troops of cavalry were jogging wearily back to the field from the direction of York. Pursuers of the fleeing Royalists. Harvesters of the craven in the name of the Lord.

He slowly picked his way across the field, aiming broadly for where his regiment had billeted the previous night, hoping to find rest, food and perhaps a surgeon to take off his arm or put him out of his misery. He found he had to take a wide berth around a large mass of men, hemmed in by a few Parliamentarian infantry with muskets held ready and pikes lowered. Fires lit in a broad circle to light the scene. Royalist prisoners, he assumed. Weary, many with wounds. Some recent dead. Drained faces looked up at him as he walked Seven past them. Looked towards the guards. Pleas for water and wine. It would have been an easy task for them to overwhelm their guard and slink off into the night, but they seemed resigned. Perhaps even relieved. They waited in the dark to see what dawn would bring as the efficient Parliamentarian staff officers started to process them, dividing the gentry out for ransom, the commoners to some other fate.

He was leaving them behind when a shout cut through to him. "Richard Farrell! Richard fucking Farrell or I'm a blind man! Hey! Rich! Don't you fuckin' dare ride away!"

He pulled Seven to a halt with little difficulty; they were scarcely moving anyway. He didn't twist around and didn't turn the horse. He just sat there in the semi-darkness, shivering and swaying in his saddle.

"Oi! I'm talking to you, Roundhead! Tell your mates here they have the wrong man! Tell them Roger DeLacey has always been a…"

"Shut your mouth, you old shit!" A second voice cut across the shouting of the first and there was the sound of a scuffle starting up. More men's voices were raised, some cheering but most just trying to get the combatants to stop.

With a long sigh and a wince of pain, Richard swung Seven around and walked him back to the sound of the commotion.

There was a knot of Royalists in a scrum at the edge of the group. A couple of guards were trying to pull them apart, but it was a pretty half-hearted effort. Richard drew one of his pistols from his saddle holster and fired it into the air.

After a day of battle the effect was not immediate, but it was enough to give the guards the opportunity to drag a bloodstained, grey-bearded, leather-coated Roger out of the crowd. One of them backhanded him across the face with the butt of his pistol, knocking him to the ground and leaving a cut across his cheek, adding more blood to his soaked shirt.

"Stay down. Haven't you had enough for one day, you old fool?"

Richard halted right next to them and stared down at the man on the ground. Long grey hair and a full beard obscured the face as the man flailed in vain at his oppressor, but the language that accompanied the feeble effort could only have come from one man.

"Roger? Is it really you?" Richard was surprised at his own voice. It was no better than a hoarse whisper, and he had to clear his throat and try again. DeLacey pulled his hair back from his forehead and peered up from the mud.

"No, it's King fuckin' Charlie. Who do you think it is?"

Even the guards laughed at that and backed off a few paces to give him space to stagger to his feet. He grabbed at Seven's bridle to steady himself and he looked slightly sheepish.

"Seems I am on the wrong side o' things. We almost had you before... Rich? Rich?!"

Richard felt himself starting to slide off the saddle as fatigue, blood loss and the surprise of seeing Roger hit him.

Roger shouted at the nearest guard for help as he propped Richard in place. "This one needs a surgeon! Help me, damn you!"

*

He woke to find himself on a blanket, staring up at a sheet of canvas. It took him a few moments to remember who he was and where he was. *Not good on either point*, he thought. His arm throbbed and his first thought was to check if it was really still there. He didn't want to look, so just carefully felt with his left hand. The forearm was still there, so that was a good sign. As he gingerly felt higher, he encountered a bandage and as he turned to examine it for himself, he found Roger peering at him from a low wooden stool.

He leant forward and gently pulled Richard's hand away. "Leave it. They did a good job on you. The lad on the blanket next to you recognised you and told them to save you at all costs. How you was the best fighter in the regiment or some other fuckin' nonsense. Trooper called Henson?"

Richard rolled to look, but Roger placed a hand on his shoulder. "He's dead. I'm sorry. Shot in the guts. They took him away about half an hour ago. They think you'll make it. Ball missed the bone and when they dug it out it had all the cloth wrapped around it. Good sign. I gave 'em the last of my brandy to clean it out. So don't die and waste it."

Richard swallowed, trying to take it all in. "What time is it?" he croaked.

"It's late afternoon, I reckon. You have slept for some hours."

"How are you even here?"

"Ah. Yes. Well, when you tried to fall off your horse, one of the guards led you over here to be looked at. They needed someone to hold you onto the horse and couldn't spare two guards. So when I said I was your friend, and I added in a silver piece, well, things just kind of fell into place. When the first guard handed you over and headed back to the rest of the prisoners, I was able to invent my own version of events." He smiled.

"Oh yes. And how did that go?"

"Well. It seems I'm something of a hero now, seeing as

how I saved you from several of my former comrades who had caught you alone as they fled the battle. Me. Recognising you for an honourable former colleague when we were fighting papists, rescued you, at great risk to myself, I might add." The same smile. "And here I am, detailed to keep an eye on you. One hero to another like…"

"With all the things in this madness of a war that have surprised me, finding you the same dishonest, slippery, self-centred bastard is a huge relief. At least some things are constant. What brings you to this field in the first place?"

"Bad luck and poor planning. I came with Browne – remember him? Been in England a few months. Spent a while in Ireland on the way. Too dangerous. Too wet. So we came here. Been following Rupert across the North and so there was no way to avoid this disaster."

He paused. "Browne's gone too. Had had the shits for days and was struggling to even stand up. Some horse rode over us and that was that. Crushed into the fuckin' mud. No way for a man like him to go. How did you get here?"

"Now that's a long story."

"Don't reckon you're going anywhere for a while. And neither am I. But only if you're up to it, of course."

Silence.

"Only it is pretty boring sitting here watching someone trying and failing to die. Just sayin' you might feel obligated to tell me after I saved your life again."

Richard looked at him, expression somewhere between contempt and amusement. "Can't say it's very entertaining, Roger. You might regret asking."

"Try me. And then I may have some news for you too." He said this quietly, almost gently.

"You're talking about Neelie?"

A nod.

(MARSTON MOOR, 3 JULY 1644)

"Not sure I want to hear. She's one of the reasons I've turned into this charming, outgoing bastard you see before you."

"You first, then me."

Through the early evening, accompanied by the hellish sounds of the dying and wounded in the butcher's yard around him, he told his story. His missions for Parliament and for Brereton. The loss of his family. All of it. He left one piece to the end. He concluded that as both of them were likely to be dead within the year he owed it to his friend to tell him the truth. To tell Roger what he had learned about his wife and son. The wife who had disappeared and pretended to be dead of the plague. Who had despaired of Roger ever coming home and being a father. Who had taken their son and found a new life.

He had expected rage. Anger. But got none of it. There was a long silence as Roger contemplated the mud between his boots. He had shed tears over Richard's family who he had never met, but the loss of his own family provoked no more than an eventual grudging nod of the head. "You may know," he said looking at Richard from under his eyebrows, "that I am not a particularly God-fearing man."

Richard coughed politely.

"But I thank Him now that she was born with a brain and wits. More than I ever had. I thank Him that they are both alive and free of me, and I wish her all the luck in the world. Strike me down if that is not the truth."

They both paused, but there was no thunder. No column of flame.

"So good luck to 'em. And if I ever see 'em again..."

"I am not sure that's a good idea, Rog."

"...if I ever see 'em again, I will make sure they don't see me. I don't wish to cause her any more grief. She has had enough of me for a lifetime. I am just happy beyond words that they ain't lyin' in a plague pit. Thank you, Rich," he said softly. "Thank you for telling me. For trusting me."

"I was wrong earlier, Roger. You have changed. It seems you've discovered what it means to be a decent person. A bit late in life, but definitely a change for the better." Richard managed a faint smile. He was exhausted with the battle and the blood loss, but he finished his story to the end. To the encounter in the woods behind the battle and his latest cold-blooded killing.

"It seems we have both changed, Richard. I hardly recognise the man you describe and would not believe it if your man Henson had not told some of it before he passed. I have no words for the loss of your sister and brother."

Again he paused and looked at the ground.

"Neelie?"

"Neelie. It is clear from what you have told me that you did not receive my letter? Or from Hudde?"

Richard shook his head. "I have not really been home and when I did… well, I haven't been back. And there was the fire. Any letter was likely burnt."

"So, I will tell you now what I wrote in the letter. The man? The man you saw her with?"

"How can I forget? I picture that scene, that kiss, that look, every day." He shook his head. "No. That's not true. After… you know, my sister… I haven't thought of her as much. But now I do, it is all very clear to me." He could feel the bitter taste of betrayal like bile in his throat.

"I was going to marry her, Roger. That was why I was back in Amsterdam. I was going to marry her. And she took it all away. I cannot be as generous as you are with your wife. I had done nothing wrong and she betrayed me. I don't understand. I never understood why. I know I kept her waiting, but we were past that." An angry tear welled.

(MARSTON MOOR, 3 JULY 1644)

Roger bent down from the stool and patted him on the shoulder. "Well, my friend, perhaps you are not as clear on events as you might think? The man you took to be her lover? You couldn't be more wrong. It was her brother. Not her lover. Her brother."

12

GABRIEL

(3 July 1644)

He shifted his position slightly, trying to get more comfortable. He had seen this sky before somewhere. He was sure of it. He thought it must have been in some kind of dream, but then it struck him. He knew where it had been. It had been the minster. Somewhere in that place he had seen a painting. A marvellous, ethereal, spellbinding painting of an ancient scene. Figures, nymphs, he thought, around a pool in the foreground, and men hunting stags with hounds in the near distance. Stone columns and ruined temples in the background. But the sky was the thing. Turquoise and pink, orange and vermillion. A creation of such transcendent beauty and artistry that he had felt it was from another world. A world of nymphs and wonders.

Now, as he looked out towards the coming dawn, the sun just hidden below the eastern horizon, he felt part of that painting. He had been transmuted through time and place to that world of wonders, an observer existing in the observed. How strange a feeling. He felt he was in the presence of God.

And he was no stranger to that feeling. Oh, but he was

blessed. All his life he had felt God's blessing upon him. Time and again God had rewarded his hard work and devotion. He knew he was blessed. This sky was just one more sign that bound him to a paradise he knew would be his.

His memory drifted back to a time more than five years previously. It was April. He remembered it well. How could he forget such a blessed day?

It had dawned bright. It had been a remarkable run of warm, sunny weather after the weeks of cold and rain. He had stood in the stone-flagged kitchen of his soon-to-be father-in-law's house, in one of the newer suburbs. A stone's throw from the city walls, and the spring sunshine streamed in through the newly cleaned windows.

The patch of sunlight illuminated a table, although table seemed an inadequate word for it. His soon-to-be father-in-law, Master Joshua Ormskirk, was walking slowly around it, trailing his fingers across its smooth, beautifully grained and patterned surface. He paused at one of the corners, crouching to run his rough palms over the flowing form of the leg, which seemed far too slim to support such a weight of oak, but that he knew was solid as granite. There were drawers built expertly into the sides, shallow so as not to destroy the perfect proportions, but deep enough to hold cutlery and other items. It was oak, robust and yet delicate and refined, and it glowed a honey colour in the sun's spotlight.

Ormskirk straightened and took a few steps back. His eyes were moist and when he opened his mouth to speak, he could not find any words. He suddenly strode forward, threw his arms around Gabriel, and crushed him to his chest, the surprise knocking all the air from his lungs. "My boy! My boy."

Ormskirk released him, grasped him by the shoulders and looked him in the eye. "My boy. God has worked through you in this, for surely only the blessed can produce such a wonder.

I have never seen the like. I cannot thank you enough. We..." he gestured to where his wife, Mary, stood, equally aghast, "... thank you."

"Oh, Gabriel." Mary wiped a tear from her eye. "'Tis wonderful. All that time apart has been worth the wait. I am so happy. I am so happy for all of us."

Gabriel too was now struggling to keep his emotions under control. "Master. Mistress. It is but only part of what I owe to both you. Never has anyone seen such kindness as you have bestowed on me. I could labour making such things for a lifetime and still be in your debt. Everything I have, everything I am and everything to come, I owe to you."

"Let us praise God, for such happiness can only come from Him." Ormskirk knelt, holding out his arms for Mary and Gabriel to join hands with him, and they prayed together, on the stone flags of their kitchen, while Agnes prepared herself upstairs.

Gabriel had returned north to York a week previously, journeying to the city along with hundreds of would-be soldiers. Trained Bands and other militia led by minor nobility, answering the King's call to confront the traitorous Scots. But Gabriel did not travel to fight. The politics and the fury passed him by. He was headed back to his home, the five-year-long 'prenticeship with Master Smythe completed, with acceptance into the glorious Carpenters' Company a formality when his judges had examined examples of his workmanship, particularly his masterpiece, the oak table now illuminating the Ormskirk kitchen.

Master Smythe was a devout Puritan, and he could see with certainty that Gabriel worshipped God not only with the words of his mouth but with the love of his heart, his eye and his hand. He had implored Gabriel to stay in London, to work with him, build his skills further and perhaps join him in partnership one day. But Gabriel only ever had one intention. He had to repay not only the considerable amount of money that Ormskirk had put up to pay for this apprenticeship, but he had to return to Agnes, his love, his life, his best friend. Because despite all the unfathomable kindness that the Ormskirks had shown to him and his widowed mother, the greatest gift they had given him was Agnes. As far as Gabriel was concerned, this was a debt he intended to spend a lifetime repaying. And was happy to do so.

And now the day was here. They were to hold a simple service at the church where the Ormskirks worshipped, and then they would feast with friends and family in the water meadows by the river. Agnes wanted no smoky tavern room, or austere meeting hall. She wanted God's blue vault above her head, the sound of the river and the spring birds for her music, and the yellow, white, blue and purple spring meadow flowers for a living bouquet. He could not believe the fortune that God had bestowed on him, and as Agnes appeared at the top of the stairs in her wedding gown, the sun streaming from behind her like an aura, again his eyes filled with tears of joy.

The miracle of that day had not ended with the wedding. As the wedding party were leaving the city, occasionally stepping to the side to allow the steady trickle of military men their passage, Gabriel could hear, and then see, an altogether more solid mass of men and horses bearing down upon them. Their party hurried to leave the road, standing back in the grass. They could see the tall, feathered hats of horsemen at the front of the column, some with brightly polished breast and backplates, followed by more soldiers, with matchlocks over their shoulders and swords at their sides. And then a coach drawn by six beautiful grey and white horses, with long manes flowing in the breeze.

Agnes had grabbed Gabriel's hand in excitement. "Do you think? Could it be? All the talk has been that he is coming to York."

The horsemen passed, paying them no heed. The foot soldiers followed, shooting Agnes some leering, knowing looks, and Gabriel some winks and descriptive hand gestures, but apparently none daring to call out. The coach, resplendent with gold inlay, was drawing past, and they strained to peer in. There was a thumping sound from within and, to their delight and horror, the liveried coachman reined in his team.

Two footmen riding on the rear of the coach, and the coachman's mate, all jumped quickly down and surrounded the door. After some conferring with the occupants, a footman had swung the door open and another pulled out steps that were folded ingeniously under the frame. From the deep shadow of the interior, a figure in bright blue satin stepped out onto the second step, remaining carefully above the mud of the road. Cascades of black curls framed the sharp face, prominent nose and immaculately trimmed beard. Calm and solemn eyes looked down upon the couple and other Ormskirks, who stood immediately behind them.

"Well met on this fine day. 'Tis your wedding?" The voice slightly higher pitched than Gabriel had somehow anticipated.

As if suddenly waking from a dream, the entire wedding party dropped as one onto their knees, the women doing their best to produce low curtseys. There were mutterings of "Your Majesty", and even a "God save the King" from somewhere behind Gabriel.

"Please, good people. Do not soil your wedding clothes for me. Please arise. We are not on ceremony here." Perfectly choreographed, they had all risen together. Gabriel, struggling to bring himself to raise his eyes to meet those of the King, felt himself incapable of answering. To his relief, his new father-in-law broke the silence. "If it please Your Majesty, today my daughter Agnes has been wed to my ward, Gabriel. Never has there been a couple more fortunate, as their love for each other and for God has now been blessed by your words and your presence."

All the party had bowed, and there were more shouts of "God save the King!"

"You speak like one of my courtiers, sir. Perhaps you are wasted up here in the North?" and Charles smiled down on them. "But you are quite correct. On such an important day, as I arrive in your fair city to uphold the sovereignty of our nation and stand in defence of our religion, I cannot drive past such a clear and happy expression of God's love without adding my own blessing. Gabriel and Agnes..." and he lifted both arms out straight in front of him, palms facing down, "...I do give your marriage my blessing and wish you God's peace all your days."

The King now raised one hand as a farewell and stepped back into the darkness of the carriage. One of the footmen approached Gabriel and placed a single, large, golden coin into his hand, and remounted the rear of the coach. The horses moved on, providing just a brief, regal profile before the column of military had obscured their view again.

There was a period of nearly an hour where the whole wedding party was in a state of collective shock. The celebration in the meadow was muted, and he had to show the coin to all in turn. He tried to give it to Ormskirk, but he would not take it. But then someone broke the trance with the sound of a fiddle. Smiles reappeared, and he and Agnes had danced their joy across the wild flowers of the Yorkshire spring.

*

Their joy had lasted for some time, but soon enough the dark tide of the war had engulfed them, like so many ordinary people across the country. Just days ago he had been in his workshop just after dawn, sweeping wood shavings from around his feet. He had been planing the seats of a set of chairs and thin curls of pale oak lay around his feet, like Mercy's blonde baby curls after Agnes had cut her hair. The thunder of the bombardment had been a constant backdrop to the siege of the city and had only stopped in the early hours as the children had cried inconsolably with fear.

But word had come with the rising sun. The siege was lifting. The armies were withdrawing, packing tents, lowering flags and burying dead. The Scots, and the Parliamentarians. All pulling back in the face of the King's avenging angel. Prince Rupert, like a flaming meteor, arcing across the Pennines to bring relief to York. Lighting up the darkness of their misery with hope. None could withstand him. Surely now they would see the error of their ways and cease their persecution of King Charles.

If only they could have met him, as he had done. Then they would see the true man. A good man. As only a man, made King by God, could be. Gabriel cared little for politics. He knew only God and his work. He trusted in his God, and if God made Charles their King, only God could unmake him.

He had no hate for the Roundheads. He could not even bring himself to call them that. They too were godly men, just tragically misguided. Somewhere they had lost their direction and the true path to bliss. They complicated things that were simple. God. King. And honest labour. Working for God's glory and loving his fellow men. And if he put his family above his fellow men, then he recognised this as sin, and prayed for forgiveness.

Agnes was already up and out. She had left the children at home as she had headed for the infirmary. Here she worked daily to tend the wounded and dying. Ever since her father had been smashed to a bloody pulp by the solid iron ball that

(3 JULY 1644)

skipped down the muddy street, its trajectory unaltered by its momentary acquaintance with Joshua Ormskirk, she had dedicated herself to the task. She too must have heard the news by now.

An end to the siege also meant he could get back to work and he had a contract to fulfil – a most prestigious commission. A set of dining chairs for the Marquis of Newcastle. Not for his residence, but for his tireless campaigning.

The marquis had been rescued by Rupert, and they were now able to unite their own armies. Gabriel hoped this might be the end of it. That the allies would crumble, the killing would stop and that his life with his family could resume.

Gabriel had raised his mug of nettle tea in a toast to the King, to Prince Rupert and to peace. At that moment, the door was thrown open and Agnes almost fell through it. She beamed at him, a bright sun returning to light the room. "You have heard?" She was breathless with excitement and the run from the infirmary. "Gabriel! Have you heard the news?"

He threw his arms around her and buried his face in her neck. "Yes," he mumbled into her skin, damp from the light drizzle that was framed in the still-open doorway. "I have heard. They are gone."

"Aye. Gone! And Rupert will be with us in the morning. They had tried to block his path, but he fooled them, Gabriel. They thought he would cross at Boroughbridge but he kept north of the river and now he hastens to the city. A captain of infantry came to see his wounded and brought the news. Even though some are almost with God, they cheered the King and the Prince. Oh, Gabriel! There were so many times I lost faith. I thought of you and the children dead. I thought we would be at the mercy of the Puritans and the dirty Scottish. I had heard so many terrible things about what happens when a city is taken."

"Maybe this is the end of the killing, Agnes. Maybe now we can get back to our lives. Perhaps God has heard our prayers and has brought Rupert to York to bring us peace."

They knelt and prayed, and Gabriel was deeply ashamed that, as they petitioned God for the safety of their fellow men, he couldn't help wondering if the Marquis of Newcastle would still want his set of dining chairs.

The sun was now nearly up and the colour of the sky edged towards blue. Again, he shifted position, but he couldn't quite get comfortable. He had the nagging feeling he should be going somewhere. The rough bark of the oak dug into his back and threatened to disturb his reverie. He tried to hold on to his memories, but they faded like a dream.

How apt that it is an oak, he thought. *Always my favourite. It is trying to remind me of it*, he smiled to himself. *And I can never turn a deaf ear*. Perhaps he could mark this tree and return to harvest it. After all, he had so much work to complete. He started to plan how this oak might help him with all the commissions he had accepted, but the beauty of the sky kept distracting him. He waited for the sun's warmth to ease the chill that had set in.

He settled to thinking of all the work he had waiting for him once he got home to his workshop. He could almost see the fine oak shavings climbing in little waves from his plane, like surf in front of a ship's prow. He could smell the perfume of the heartwood and sense the wood dust hanging like a galaxy in the sunlight streaming into the workshop. He could... think no more as he drifted back to sleep.

*

He woke with a start. *Someone is coming.* Odd. Somehow, he had thought himself alone. That this day, this place, was his and no one else's. How could another exist in his dream of God? He felt cold and wondered how long he had slept. The sunrise was long gone, but now it seemed the sky was toning for sunset. Could he really have slept for so long? What about his work?

The sound of a horse walking slowly. He looked to his right. He felt strangely stiff and had difficulty turning to see the horse.

There! It emerged from a light mist, which was gathering around the trunks of the copse, illuminated by the late sun's fading rays. A dream-horse. It snorted, and steam erupted from its nostrils in the cooling air. A man was riding although swaying slightly in the saddle, as if exhausted, or even asleep. He couldn't yet see his face.

As they cleared the patch of mist, the man and horse stopped. The man stared at him, as if he were also peering to establish some kind of recognition, a connection. He slipped slowly from the saddle, whispered into the horse's ear and slowly trudged towards him.

Gabriel heard himself call out, "Hey, friend. Come and sit." His voice sounded strange to himself – rough and a little croaky. "Come share in God's own glory." He waved a hand at the view, suddenly wincing at an unexpected pain. "It is truly the strangest day I have witnessed, outside of a dream. If we *are* outside of a dream. Do you know, sir? Do we dream?"

By now the man was standing next to him, looking down. He knew him. He was sure. But from where? A customer? A relative of his wife's?

The man spoke. "I have been looking for you. You have travelled further than I expected. I did not think… I did not think I would get the chance to speak to you again."

This was puzzling. "Why have you been seeking me? Do I know you? I feel that I do." He coughed and struggled to clear phlegm from his throat. "I believe I have caught a chill. Agnes will scold me for my foolishness. Please sit and share the sunset. It is a wondrous sight, do you not think? I had no one to share the sun's rising with, so 'tis a happy chance. Indeed, a pleasure to share it with someone." And it was. Now he had company, he was pleased that others could share his good fortune. He felt blessed.

The man looked towards the west, a frown on his face. He turned back, wiping drops of a light drizzle from his forehead. He sank down next to him, on his knees, facing him. "Do you recognise me now, friend?" the man said in a soft, low voice. "I have not come to sit and talk, but to kneel and ask forgiveness."

He peered at the man. "I do not think I place you yet, but by my faith, if Jesus our Lord could forgive those who crucified him, I can surely forgive you for whatever your imagined sin." He smiled, lifted his hand from his lap and touched the man gently on his cheek. *Odd.* He stared at the red print he had left on the damp flesh. He stared at his hand. It was sheathed in blood. He moved it from side to side to check it was his hand. *Odd.*

He looked down to his lap and pulled apart the leather coat. His whole lower body was awash with blood. Some looked old, and black, and crusted at the edges. In the centre, though, it was still fresh, and he stared in fascination at a small pulsing motion where new blood welled to the surface.

He looked up again and peered at his red hand. The sunset was gone, and the world was cold and grey and damp. So cold now. He turned to the man, who now sat on his heels observing him quietly. Now. Now he recognised him. A cold hand gripped his heart. He shivered. Now he remembered. The battle. The clearing in the woods. The brief and terrible violence. The man before him had stabbed him. Had done... *this*... to him. Like he was nothing. Just a minor inconvenience. The man who had killed mercilessly. Like a clockwork automaton he had once seen, wound up with a key and become a terrible engine of wrath.

But today he looked different. Was this truly the same man? Sad eyes regarded him. "I... did this to you. I am sorry. I would take it back if I was able. This, and all the other terrible things I have done in the name of hate and revenge. I looked for your companions of last night, but it was too late. I had thought you dead also, but you are here. With your dream of a sunrise." He looked back to the east, understanding, it seemed. "Today, I think a different sun rose for me. Too late for you. Maybe too late for me, but my first step was to try to find forgiveness from at least one I have wronged. I cannot ask them all. All the men I have set upon your path."

He bowed his head. "I am Richard Farrell, and I have killed you. I have taken from you everything you have, and I do not even know your name. I have done evil things. From today I will strive to do no more."

The man called Richard looked up, pain in his eyes. "Please. Forgive me if you can. Tell me what I can do for you." He bowed his head again.

Looking at that pain, his heart broke. He strained forward slightly, now feeling the pain of the effort that he had previously been spared. He again placed his bloody right hand on Richard's head.

"I am Gabriel. Of the city of York. I make furniture." He coughed a short laugh. "I should not brag, so close to God's presence, but I am good at it. The cart I was driving was for the Marquis of Newcastle. He had ordered a set of chairs for the campaign to come. I have a beautiful wife and beautiful children." He coughed again, fighting a rising tide in his throat. He could hear the strain in his voice now. "I love my work. I love my life. But, friend, I love Jesus Christ more than all. If you have hastened me to his side, then how can I bear you ill will? I forgive you. How can I not?"

He stopped, and leaned back against the tree. One oak among twenty along the edge of the wood. "If you will, take my body home, Richard Farrell. That is all I ask of you. Take me home." Through his eyelids, the sunrise was back. The light quickly became blinding, and it warmed his chill body. He felt himself sliding…

*

He drove the cart down the hill, the body laid out in the back, among the chairs. He was exhausted and the effort to lift Gabriel into position had near finished him. His arm throbbed 'til he thought it would drop off. He tied Seven to the rear and gripped the reins with his good left arm.

He crossed the plain outside the walls, avoiding the pits, latrines and earthworks thrown up by those sieging, and the besieged. He joined the small river of sorry souls wending their way to the gates. He had tied a piece of white cloth from the wagon to a pole at the front, but none stopped him. He drove through the gates, parting the sea of wounded and retreating soldiers in front, and asked several the way to Gabriel's workshop. Eventually, he found someone who could tell him.

He couldn't get the cart down the narrow street to the house. He dragged Gabriel's body on to his shoulders and slowly staggered the final twenty yards to the door. It stood open, and he could see into the kitchen, a beautiful table almost glowing in the dim light. With the last of his strength, he swivelled sideways and crouched through the doorway and half flung the body onto the table. He laid Gabriel out, folded his hands on his chest and tightened the belt around

(3 July 1644)

the bandages, made from the same wagon cloth that he had stuffed into and around the terrible wound he had made.

As he stumbled out of the house, he heard footsteps coming down the stairs.

As he mounted Seven and abandoned the wagon, the beautifully crafted chairs were already being liberated by the people of York.

13

RICHARD

(Marston Moor camp, 4 July 1644)

At camp it took him some time to find the remains of his regiment, and then a long conversation with his commanding officer about the merits of recruiting Roger. He collapsed from pain and exhaustion before a decision was taken, but this seemed to have been conclusive, as he woke hours later on a blanket on the ground, with Roger again sitting by his side.

"Job done?"

Richard nodded. He had little energy to speak.

"Well, not quite yet, Rich. I'm sorry to have to wake you – you still look like shit – but you have to go."

Richard summoned just enough effort to raise an eyebrow. He noticed Roger had shed all evidence of Royalist trappings and had found the buff coat and steel breastplate and helmet of Cromwell's horse. He saw Richard eyeing his transformed uniform and gestured towards the battlefield. "Well, it's not like there wasn't a lot of stuff lying around out there."

The noise of ravens, kites and crows carried to him as the feasting was well underway. Here and there men had been

(Marston Moor camp, 4 July 1644)

detailed to dig great pits, and bodies, some stripped, some not, were being dragged and thrown in. *Different field, different men, but always the same song,* Richard thought.

"Go where?" he finally managed.

"Cromwell."

"What?" Richard managed to raise himself onto his left elbow. "Cromwell?"

"Apparently. He asked for you. Well. When I say 'asked'..."

"Fuck."

"Yes. Probably. Or perhaps field promotion? You have to look on the positive side."

"I'm a realist, Roger."

"Alright. Fucked it is then."

*

Cromwell sat behind a trestle table. He was pale and looked as exhausted as Richard felt, swaying in the doorway of his tent, leaning on Roger's shoulder. He had a bandage wound around his neck, red on one side below his ear.

"Farrell? You look... Well, you probably look like I do." His mouth twitched momentarily at the corners, which was the equivalent of a belly laugh for a normal person. "God be praised for our victory. I am glad you have survived."

Richard nodded in agreement. "So am I, General."

"And this is?" He nodded at Roger.

"DeLacey, General. A new recruit to the regiment. A fine soldier. Vast experience of fighting papists in Flanders."

"Ah. You remember when we last met, Farrell?"

"I do, General. My father's funeral. A lot has happened since then."

"Some things have. Yet despite your background, you have not risen in the ranks." Richard could see the pleasantries were over. "I understand the men call you 'Captain', yet you are not a captain. I hear you are a fine soldier – in many respects – yet you are but a common trooper. Why is this?"

"Promotion." Roger spoke as quietly as he could. "Told you."

"I am not sure, General. Only strive to fight for the cause. I have no ambition to command."

Roger groaned, quietly.

"Is that what you think? I have heard otherwise, Farrell. I have heard that you view your role not as supporting the cause, as you put it, but as fighting your own private war of revenge." He held up his hand as Richard started to interject. "No sir. Be silent."

"Not promotion then," Roger whispered. "The other thing."

"I have heard stories of the cold-blooded killer in your regiment, but I refused to believe it could be you, sir. But I also heard what happened to your family, and so I thought that maybe it was true. And then I thought that the tragedy that has befallen you has probably visited half the men in this army, but they do not react as you did. Now I have a report that you were murdering civilians in the baggage train, against my express orders. Please, tell me this isn't true."

There was a silence that seemed to go on for hours. Richard swallowed, looked at Roger and then back at Cromwell.

"It is true, General."

Roger groaned again.

"In fact, all you have said is true. The events of last night have shown me to myself as if in a mirror. I have asked for forgiveness."

Cromwell eyed him quizzically. "Really? Have you? I wonder." His expression hardened as he went on, "I cannot grant you forgiveness. Only Almighty God can do so. I can only deliver a sentence. Please understand, Farrell, if it were

(Marston Moor camp, 4 July 1644)

not for the respect I held for your father and mother, or my recognition of your brother Lionel's good work in our community, you would already be swinging from a tree as an example to others."

Richard swayed, but Roger held him up. He could feel the beads of sweat on his forehead running down into his eyes. He didn't know if this was fever or fear.

"Can you swing a sword?" He nodded at Richard's bandaged arm.

"Honestly, General? I doubt it. At least not for some time."

"You can ride?"

"Aye. I can."

"And is what I hear correct? That prior to hostilities, you were in the employ of Sir William Brereton, in Cheshire?"

This was unexpected and it took Richard's feverish mind a moment to refocus after the abrupt change in direction. "Er, yes, General. I did. I supervised delivery of arms for Ireland. I worked for Parliament and for Sir William in this matter. Later, I also acted as his liaison with supportive gentry across that county."

"He trusted you? Answer truthfully, Farrell. God has seen fit to give me strength to detect a lie."

"I believe he did. Yes, he trusted me." He looked Cromwell in the eye, trying to determine where this was headed.

"You can't fight. You can ride. You know Brereton and, quite frankly, I don't want you serving in my regiments any longer. An accurate summary?"

"I believe so, General." *Where is this going?*

"Well then, Captain Farrell, I have a job for you."

"General, I am not a captain."

"I am not used to being contradicted, Captain. Is that understood?"

"Sir."

"You will act as my liaison with Brereton. This victory must have fatally weakened the King, or so I believe. We must take full advantage of this opportunity and strike decisively. Brereton has so far failed to take Chester. He must take it, Farrell. He must. You will stay with Brereton and observe the movements of his army and the rigour with which he pursues his objective. You will advise him and support him in his decision-making. You will also report back to me. Take a man from the regiment with you to ride between us with messages."

Richard glanced at Roger.

"Yes, if you wish. Although he looks a bigger rogue than Prince Rupert. It may surprise you to know that Brereton is here."

Richard was puzzled and he could feel his energy flowing away. He was going to collapse. "Here? At the battle?" He swayed and grabbed at Roger's shoulder for support.

Cromwell did a poor impression of a man smiling. "No, not at the battle. Unfortunately, Sir William arrived a little late, but he is here now. By the look of you, you should seek him out tomorrow. Go and rest, and think on God's mercy and your, hmm… forgiveness."

"Yes, General. Thank you, General."

"Thank your family's good name and thank God. For surely this is His intervention. Be thankful, but not to me."

14

BRERETON

(5 July 1644)

The table top was good thick oak, smoothed and polished by countless elbows and forearms. Stains and rings left by a hundred years of dedicated drinkers competed for attention with the knots and lines of the tree itself, interrupting the flow of the deep amber-coloured wood, but not detracting from its beauty. Brereton felt he could have shared hours with it, tracing waves and ripples with his fingers. Seeing shapes, objects, even faces, emerging from the random patterns formed by the growth of the oak. It was solid, reassuringly steady and fulfilling its purpose with calm authority. All the things he wanted to be.

He shifted in his chair and reached for his mug of small beer. He nudged his bible away lest a clumsy elbow should lead to a disastrous spillage. But his attention was on neither of these things. Across the table from him sat Captain Jerome Zankey, his most trusted commander. A man equally adept with a sword in his hand, or with a bible, preaching to the men. Next to him was a man he had not expected to see again, Richard Farrell. Farrell looked pale and slightly feverish but had the same 'old man in a young man's body' eyes he remembered. His upper right arm was heavily bandaged, a wound from the great battle, no doubt. *He had been but a day late!* With his body of horse, perhaps he could have played a decisive part in the victory, but the Earl of Denbigh's dithering had delayed him. Damn that man!

Brereton knew he had grown from the man he had been just a few years ago. No longer was he the slightly nervous Parliamentarian, in awe of men like Pym and Hampden and intimidated by the austere Cromwell. He had found in himself reserves of courage and yes, even cunning, that he had thought impossible. He knew he was a competent administrator and businessman. He was well educated and could debate with any man. But it was his prayer to God to grant him a task that had opened this well of confidence that had carried him through the conflict. He had seen setbacks, of course, but on the whole he had enjoyed much success against the enemy.

He had consolidated his hold in the North-West and built an army, small though it was, that had discipline, fortitude, valour and no little skill. Above all, he worked to spend the lives of his men as dearly as possible. They were the children of God and how could he deprive the Lord of his servants on earth through recklessness or poor planning? No, he would ensure he was always as informed as possible on the movements of the enemy and its agents. He would work patiently to develop the right opportunities to surprise the foe or turn the landscape to his advantage. He had become renowned for dawn attacks, daring certainly, but planned and coordinated for the greatest result with lowest possible risk.

He had responded willingly to the call to support the allied armies outside York and, once agreed with Denbigh, had raced troops of cavalry from Knutsford east. But now, here he sat, late for the battle, in the middle of a county where he had no responsibilities, marooned.

Between the three men, on the table, were three letters, opened but folded. *What a polite and orderly torture this is,* he thought. *Pulled apart by correspondence!*

He pushed the central letter with his finger, shunting it towards Zankey and Farrell. "In the absence of all else, this is my duty, gentlemen. I know this just as clearly as Oliver, my friend in God. I give thanks for the victory in front of York. I have prayed for a decisive stroke every day and now God has rewarded us." Unconsciously he placed a hand on his bible. He looked at Farrell. "You should see my surgeon. When we are done, I will take you to him myself. You know the contents of this letter?"

Farrell nodded. "I can guess, sir. If you had not arrived here, I think it would have been me delivering it to you in Cheshire."

"Chester. Cromwell urges me to turn again towards Chester. I agree with all my heart. There is strategic importance in this. It is the northern gateway to Ireland. A gateway for supplies, arms and men. It is a Royalist thorn in our side and a peril at our backs whenever we seek to intervene in Wales, or further north where Rupert's Cavaliers cut a bloody path through Lancashire. All the damnable papists in that county have taken heart. Liverpool is no longer ours. There is much to accomplish."

Zankey gently bumped his fist onto the wood. "Then that way you should go. You have said to me more than once that you have felt it is God's plan for you to take Chester for him. It is the trial you prayed for and, through the godly men in Parliament, your friends and allies, this task was laid upon you." He spoke softly, but there was fire in his eyes.

"This is true, Jerome. And so should I think too. But then there is this." He nudged the right-hand letter a few inches across the table. "From many of the same godly men. Forget Chester, they say." He leant forward and picked up the page, and read, "*We have certain intelligence that the Scottish, the Earl of Manchester's and Lord Fairfax's armies fought upon Tuesday last with Prince Rupert and the Earl of Newcastle's forces, and had a great victory. It is of great importance that this victory be improved...*" He looked up. "This is from the Committee of Both Kingdoms, to myself and the Earl of Denbigh. There can be no mistake, they expect Rupert to retreat back across the Pennines and reinforce Lancashire. There he can recover and rebuild his army. There are many sympathisers in that most papist of counties. I am to correspond with the allies before York and to seek resolutions '*you shall find most advantageous for the total suppressing of the enemy*'. They want me to stay and assist in the final capture of York. I am to forget Chester. At least for now."

Farrell, leaning back in his chair, eyes half closed, almost whispered, "So what will you do? And what bearing on this matter does the third letter bring? Does it clarify?" The man looked exhausted.

Yes. The third letter. From nowhere. Unexpected and unlooked for. At the worst possible time. *Oh my God, help me to decide what I am to do?*

"That is a personal matter. It has no relevance to this discussion and it is for me to pray for resolution." He met curious looks from both men. *Do they think I have no other life than this? Politics and war?*

"Is it your family, sir? Your wife and son are safe and well?" Zankey leaned forward anxiously.

"No, Captain. It is another matter. My family are well. Do not be concerned. It is a matter only I can resolve. Now, I will ponder an hour on this and weigh all things in the balance. No longer. There are diverse issues that those far away in London will not be aware of and I must be sure I lay the right plans.

"But, before that..." he glanced at Farrell, "...I promised to walk this gentleman to my surgeon. So he can be competently examined and his wound re-dressed. Jerome, alert my commanders. Bring them back to this room in an hour and I will issue orders."

Zankey stood, nodded at Farrell. "Farewell, Captain Farrell. May God be with you."

Farrell wobbled to his feet and, leaning on the table, reached to shake Zankey's hand. "And you, Captain. But remember, I am now attached to Sir William as liaison officer. I am sure you will be seeing a lot more of me."

After Zankey had left, Brereton held out an arm for Farrell to steady himself on and he nodded his thanks. *Do I dare? Can I trust this man?*

"Come. My surgeon is just a few minutes' walk away. John Chadwick. He is a good man."

*

After the dim light of the inn, the grey light of an overcast sky made them both blink. Brereton had camped his men around a small hamlet on the edge of the moor, close enough for communication with the allied commanders, but far enough away from the carnage of the battle. "What are your plans now, Farrell? How does Cromwell see your role working?" He smiled. "Are you to spy on me?"

Farrell kept his eyes down, but had dropped Brereton's arm. After a slight pause he said, "I am sure the general would not use that term, sir. I believe I am to carry messages between you, to better coordinate our efforts."

"That was carefully put." *This man is something of a diplomat then. More than just a competent soldier.*

"I hope so." Farrell smiled weakly. "Also, I hope I can be useful to you in other ways."

"How so?"

"Well, I have practical experience of sieges and it is clear that one way or another, you plan to lay siege to Chester. I was at Breda when it fell. Perhaps I can help? And whilst it may be a week or so until I can fight effectively, I have no little experience of killing Royalists."

"Indeed? Well, perhaps we can make good use of you." He smiled at Farrell. "But the siege must wait. In truth, I have made up my mind. I must walk a diplomatic line here. I do not think that the fine gentlemen that seized victory here have much need of me or my men. I will play a part for a few days until York is fully secured, but then we will head for the armoury at Hull. It is too good an opportunity to miss. We have already harvested some 500 or so muskets from the battle, and at Hull I aim to procure carbines and pistols. With your background, I am sure you appreciate the need to re-equip?"

He could see that Farrell was surprised that he had remembered the man's former trade in the shadowy world of the arms supply business.

"And then we will rejoin the main body of the army back in Cheshire. We must prepare to welcome Prince Rupert and again turn our attention to Chester. I have word from one of my most trusted agents that the King will not, or cannot, reinforce the garrison there. We may have a free hand to lay siege. God is preparing the way." Almost at the moment he said this, an idea exploded into his mind. *Yes! Here is the answer to my dilemma.*

"Farrell. Here is what I want you to do. You are clearly in no current state to fight…" he nodded at Farrell's arm, "…but can you ride?"

The man nodded, a curious look growing on his face.

"Good. I need the agent I refer to, to monitor this situation in relation to Chester. I need up-to-the-minute information. This meets my purpose and also that of our friend Master

Cromwell. I will write a letter that must be delivered to her as soon as possible."

Farrell looked startled. "Her? Your agent is a woman?"

"Correct. Does that surprise you? Are women incapable of godliness and passion for the cause? I think not."

"No. Of course. It is just… unusual."

"We have to use the best tools at our disposal to serve the will of God, Farrell. The lady in question is staying at the residence of the alderman and mayor of Macclesfield. His name is Captain Anthony Booth, he commands a company in Colonel Duckinfield's regiment. I will write the letter now, please return to collect it immediately you have seen the surgeon Chadwick. It needs to be delivered as soon as possible."

"Of course, Sir William. I know my way around Macclesfield. You may recall that I spent time there securing support for your cause before the hostilities started."

So he did! This may work out better than I hoped.

"Ah yes. Well, as it happens, you can also help me with a minor additional matter. It relates to the third letter – I had almost forgotten it."

Farrell raised an eyebrow. *Too shrewd by far, this one.*

"Whatever you command, sir."

"'Tis less an order. More a favour in this case. I have correspondence from a Miss Eliza Walker, daughter of the late Samuel Walker."

"I have met them both, sir. A fine family, although I am very sorry to hear of Master Walker's death. Was it as part of the war?"

"Indeed. He took a wound which failed to heal and passed on to God. He was truly a strong supporter of the cause and his two daughters are left orphaned, although Eliza must be close to coming into her estate. In any case, she has written to me in great distress. It seems her governess has been accused of witchcraft, and they are preparing a trial of sorts. She asks for my help."

He was disturbed to hear Farrell laugh out loud. "Witchcraft? Really, sir? Surely there can be no merit to this? I know there has been some history of this in certain parts, but surely in this more enlightened age no one would consider accusation of witchcraft to be more than playing out of petty jealousies!"

He felt uncomfortable in the face of this mirth and scepticism. Who was this man to mock? "No, Farrell. The accusation is being taken seriously. *I* take it seriously. I have seen and experienced these phenomena myself. Admittedly on the continent, not on these shores, but why should that make a difference? Why, in your part of the world, there are stories of witches that seem as if an infestation is occurring."

Farrell stayed silent. His face now betraying no emotion.

"I want you to visit Eliza and investigate what is happening. Write to me confidentially. Send your repenting Cavalier with the letter if you must, but do it quickly. I do not know the date set for the trial."

"Of course, sir. That is all clear." Farrell paused. Now he seemed cautious. Watchful. "The name, sir? Of the governess?"

He tried to act with nonchalance, but he feared he was not a good enough actor to fool the man he faced. "Oh. Her name. Hmm." He took out the letter again and made to reread it. When he felt sufficiently composed, he looked up. "Hume. Mistress Marleigh Hume."

"Certainly, Sir William. Leave it with me. We will be on our way as soon as we have your letter. Must we deliver it to your agent's hand, or is it sufficient to hand it to Captain Booth?"

"What?" He had almost forgotten the letter. It was, after all, merely an excuse to get the report on the trial. "Ah yes.

(5 July 1644)

Deliver it to Booth. He will see she gets it. Better that only a few know of her name and her appearance."

"Very good, sir."

"And, Farrell? I must ask you now to keep this second matter between us. In fact, I must ask for your promise on this with God Almighty as our witness…"

15

RICHARD

(6 July 1644)

Richard and Roger rode from the camp, heading west for the Pennines and the dangerous road to Cheshire.

"Just like old times!" Roger leant in the saddle and slapped Richard on the back. "Oops! Sorry, old mate. Forgot about the arm." He chuckled, partly from embarrassment. "How is it anyway?" He tried and failed to look sympathetic.

"Oh fuck off. How do you think it feels? It's going to go black, stink to high heaven and then fall off, I expect."

Roger rolled his eyes. "Not your cock, I meant your arm! How is your arm?"

This brought a smile from Richard. "Just like old times. Sure."

But it felt nothing like old times. If he searched his memory for old times, he found nothing but a mess. Lurching from one poor decision to another. Failure after failure. Every time he found something good, he contrived to find a way to fuck it up. In all honesty, he could not lay it all at his own door. Sheer bad luck had played a part, as had the evil of others, but his response had been to drop all sense of a moral life, and to wallow in self-pity and cold-blooded slaughter. That could carry you some distance in a war, but his narrow escape from Cromwell's rope just served to show its limitations.

Against the bleakness of the last year, the events of the last two days felt miraculous. He had avoided death in battle and a deserved death for his callous murders. He could not call them anything else. And now this new assignment, and a promotion. This truly felt like a turning point. He would strive to deserve it. To deserve the forgiveness, not from God, but from a carpenter from York.

When Brereton had given him his assignment, he had scarcely concealed his surprise. To go to Macclesfield, of all places. Despite Brereton's rather poor effort at nonchalance, Richard had seen immediately that his primary motivation in sending them to the town was not the letter to the mysterious spy, but to investigate the circumstances surrounding the mysterious governess. *Oh goodness, now what was her name? Ah yes, Marleigh Hume.* That would not have fooled a six-year-old. Given Brereton's godly reputation, he doubted he had bedded her. His vanity prompted him to hope she was not in the habit of sleeping with just anyone, even baronets. But there was some hold she had over him. *What would Cromwell make of that?*

He was excited to see her again. He shifted in his saddle as he felt his excitement growing. *That was welcome!* He hadn't had a response like that for months.

He looked across at Roger, picking his nose and having his first swig of sack, and he wondered if this was the very best or the very worst travelling companion he needed if he was going to leave his bitter past behind him. The man certainly lightened the mood and seemed to have taken the news about his wife and son in his stride. *Could he really let them be?* He didn't think he could be so, well, forgiving, in Roger's position.

He thought about the road ahead. Still a lot of Royalists

in the area. Scattered units of horse, militia, ragtag battalions trying to find their way to some measure of safety. They needed to be careful. For the third time he checked his saddlebag for Brereton's letter.

"Will you relax! It's not gone anywhere. It's not grown legs and run off into the trees. Jesus Christ, you used to be a lot more fun than this!"

"Alright. Give it a rest. I can only take so much Roger in one day." He rolled his eyes at Roger's smirk. "Oh, stop it!"

"Sorry. You were saying?"

"Nothing. Have you ever come across Brereton before?"

"No. Not in any sense of the phrase."

"For God's sake!"

"No. Heard his reputation amongst the King's men. Cautious. Efficient. Good organiser. Always seemed a step ahead somehow. And, of course, a fucking zealot! But only bagged a few small victories and as Cromwell said, he hasn't taken the big one. Chester is still for the King."

Richard pondered on that. It did sound very much like the man he had known and had served. He thought again about his time in Macclesfield. About Marleigh Hume. Just as he was starting to drift again into his warm daydream, Neelie's face flashed into his brain. He had hardly had time to think about Roger's revelation. What did it mean for him now? He was not even sure how he felt for her now. Could he find her even if he wanted to? He doubted she would want him if he did. But there was nothing he could do about it now.

He owed Marleigh a debt too, did he not? He should see if she was safe. Neelie was too hard a thing to think about at the moment. He had to focus on the achievable. On his mission.

*

(6 July 1644)

They were in the saddle again after a break for midday. He had passed a miserable morning. His wound throbbed and had deprived him of the sleep he badly needed. A slight fever also preyed on his mind, convincing him that Brereton's surgeon had missed some poison and that he was slowly rotting and would die in torment as wounded soldiers had done since time began.

He swayed slightly and had to cling to Eight's neck to steady himself. Eight was a solid grey mare, and her placid nature was just what he needed. They had swung north of the Royalist stronghold at Pontefract, aiming to cross the Pennines and head down towards more friendly country around Manchester, before passing south to Macclesfield. The area was solidly for Parliament. The rolling green country was behind them and they were starting to climb, following a well-established road between high stone walls.

As they had lunched on bread and some stale cheese, Roger had looked at him from under the brim of his hat. "I saw him, you know," he said quietly. "I don't think he saw me, but on a couple of occasions outside York, he was there."

"Who? Rupert?"

"No. Montague. Remember him? Your friend and mine. Going quietly about his business. No doubt he would have considered me a sinner returning to the fold. DeLacey has finally realised his true duty and the divine right of kings to fuck things up and still command your loyalty. That kind of thing."

A coldness settled on Richard. He shivered, not knowing if it was a trace of fever, or the name of his adversary. "I have no proof, Roger, but I am certain he is behind the death of my family. He may not have pulled the trigger, but I would wager he aimed Cobb and his mob like a musket and let him do the rest."

"Maybe. Sounds like him, doesn't it? Manipulate others to do his dirty work. Mind you, he showed us in Scotland how dangerous he can be when he does roll his sleeves up. You can respect the man's abilities whilst damning his soul to hell. Still, it would be nice to get him alone in a small room and, you know, put the question to him."

Richard didn't reply. He didn't trust his voice not to waver. His encounter with Gabriel had seemingly cured him of the madness of his bloodlust; the focus of his anger and need for revenge may have narrowed, but it had deepened. Despite his words to Roger, he had no doubts who was responsible, and that a day of reckoning would come.

After a couple of hours of riding, Roger called a halt. "Nature calls, my friend. And I must answer, right smartish!" He slid from his horse, handing the reins to Richard. There was a gate in the wall and he slipped through, and Richard could just see the plume in his hat heading purposefully for a patch of scrubby bushes. Richard stretched and surveyed the surroundings. Ahead, the lane continued its climb towards a saddle in the ridge, the fields rising on either side, the grass cropped low by the sheep. *Lucky not to have been foraged for the army's belly*, he thought.

Ahead, to the right, a rowan tree hung over the stone wall. It was alive with small birds, fluttering and twittering, flying away, then streaming back. He saw tiny round bodies, marked with subtle pink and cream, highlighted with a long black tail. Like little balls of fluff on a stick. He remembered his father pointing them out to him when he was a child. What was it he called them? *Bumbarrels!* Richard laughed out loud. Memories of long summers around the farm. Playing with his siblings, helping with the harvest, enjoying the life all around him. With the sun starting to break through a flat grey sky, he started to feel better.

(6 July 1644)

Off to the right, up the slope, a sudden movement caught his eye. Something dropped from the branches of a solitary oak and came skimming over the contours, slight adjustments of wings lifting its sleek form over clumps of reeds and tussocks of grass and wildflowers, a slate-grey shape arrowed towards the wall. Oblivious of the approaching menace, the little birds continued their chat and flutter. Richard watched, stock still, as the sparrowhawk tilted its wings at the last moment and rose in a blur of speed to clear the wall and sweep in what seemed an impossibly tight circle around the back of the rowan tree. Too late the tits exploded away in all directions, but the hawk was already in their midst and emerged grasping a small body in its left talon. Encumbered, it lumbered awkwardly back to the wall and flopped onto the stones. Richard's shoulders slumped and his movement attracted the bird's attention. Its head rotated and it fixed him with a stare sharp enough to cut through steel plate. Cold disdain. The face of Montague formed in his mind, and he swallowed down a wave of anger and nausea. Slowly the hawk turned back to its stricken prey. Its foot clenched and he saw blood well up around a talon. It sunk the hook of its beak into the plump breast and ripped. But the next moment it suddenly looked up the lane and then launched itself back up the slope, flapping slowly back towards the oak, no doubt to feed its young.

As he followed its gaze, he could now see a stationary mounted figure on the horizon, framed by the stone walls. It sat there a moment more and Richard also remained motionless, watching. Roger's horse was grazing on grass at the edge of the track and Eight was trying to do the same, but he pulled her head up.

From the outline he could see this was no farmer. The figure started to walk his horse slowly down towards him. He called, "Roger", trying to pitch the sound loud enough for

Roger to hear but not loud enough to carry to the advancing figure. No response. He slowly pulled a pistol from its saddle holster and laid it on his lap, out of sight. He called again. "We have company." Nothing.

The mounted man was now only a little more than fifty yards away. He was definitely a military man, but Richard struggled to recognise any affiliations from the man's appearance, dress or weaponry. The face was shaded by his hat.

Richard dropped the reins of Roger's horse and moved the pistol so that it was now in plain sight. The man, for his part, reined his mount to a halt, now raising both his hands to show they were empty, managing his horse with his knees.

They stared at each other for what seemed like minutes. There was something about the man. *Had he seen him somewhere before?*

The spell was broken as a loud grunt carried over the stone wall, followed by a distinctly agricultural sound. A slight pause, another grunt and a long stream of flatulence, punctuated by even more worrying and unsavoury noises which held the newcomer in a state of almost hypnotised disbelief. As he turned his head, Richard could now see his face more clearly and, in an instant, knew where he had seen him before. He had been with Montague, at the Blue Boar near his home, but even that degree of recognition couldn't answer the same question he had had in the tavern. He knew this face! Why couldn't he put a name to it?

The man looked back towards Richard. His look of shocked disgust at the noises emanating from beyond the stone wall turned to horror, as it seemed he too now made an identification of his own. He grabbed at the reins and swung his horse around.

"Hey! Hold, sir!" Richard brought up his pistol, but the man was already driving his horse towards a gallop. Richard found he couldn't shoot the man in the back. *Well, that's a different experience.* He couldn't ride off after the man and leave Roger, literally with his trousers down.

Richard could now see the hat plume returning behind the high wall. Roger appeared, adjusting his breeches with a happy smile on his face. "Do you know, that's the best shit I've had in days, possibly in weeks." It was only as he stepped into the lane to retrieve his horse that he noticed Richard's pistol and, swinging around, the now-distant shape of the fleeing horseman.

"Did you do that, or was it me?" he asked.

"It's the damnedest thing," Richard replied, ignoring the question. "I know that man. He was with Montague. Some time ago now. Even then I couldn't shake the feeling that I knew him. He seems so familiar, but I just can't put a name to it."

"One of your tenant farmers maybe? Someone from the village?"

"Maybe. But that doesn't feel right. Why would he be up here?"

"Well, you can't feel too strongly about it 'cos you let him get away," Roger remarked, looking pointedly at the pistol. "Bit of a mistake there, d'yer think? If it is one of Montague's boys."

Richard sighed. "Yes, probably one more to add to the list. But I couldn't do it, Roger. It was an easy shot, but I couldn't shoot him with his back to me."

"Lucky for him it wasn't you havin' the shit then, 'cos I haven't got those... what-do-you-call-'ems? Morals."

Richard raised an eyebrow. "Not what you told me at Breda when you punched me in the face and broke my nose."

"Those were principles, lad. Big difference to morals. Do you want to go after him?"

Richard shook his head. "No. Let's push on. But we must be vigilant if Montague is around. Why would he be here anyway?"

"Well, this is a bit of an obvious route from west to east. Could be any number of reasons. Trying to find Prince Rupert? Rounding up stray Royalist units to bring 'em back to the fold? Or just doin' a bit o' spyin' – looking for fools like us."

Richard nodded.

"And anyway," Roger continued, "how long have you been using words like *vigilant?*"

16

7 July 1644

Richard and Roger jogged along a leafy lane, partly shielded from the drizzle by the beech and elm that lined the hedgerows on either side. Although it was no more than mid-morning, it felt like evening was gathering, the heavy grey sky promising more than just this light shower. His horse was happy enough, but Richard felt conflicting emotions.

His dreams had been filled with Neelie. For the most part this had been an overwhelmingly good thing. He desperately tried to hang on to the images and feelings of the dream, but they gradually faded and now he ached with the hole that had been left. A hole that gradually filled with guilt. Guilt for assuming she would betray him. Guilt for not abandoning the war and racing for the nearest port and ship to Amsterdam. Guilt for not thinking about her more often. Guilt for the fact that he was riding to the aid of a woman with whom he *had* betrayed Neelie. And a woman who still held a fascination for him. He couldn't deny it. An exotic mystery who had woven a spell of wonder around him that night. He started to feel appreciative all over again. He couldn't help himself.

And here was an added confusion. There was perhaps a surprising coincidence that he should appear before Cromwell just as the general needed a liaison officer to communicate with Brereton, but the content of the letter that Brereton had shown him had almost floored him. Luckily, Brereton had assumed his reaction was a symptom of his fever, or difficult questions might have followed. Richard had kept hold of his wits and kept his mouth shut, but as he read and Brereton had spoken, his mind had been reeling.

His shock and surprise at the letter's revelation had been matched by Sir William's awkwardness and embarrassment. He had struggled to explain why the letter was important to him. Of course, he had some connection with the Walker family. Samuel Walker had been a prominent supporter and had become a capable soldier. Brereton had been saddened by his death, but he must have been saddened by the deaths of numerous men under his command, and beyond. The impact of this letter, sent by Eliza Walker just a few days ago, should have been minimal. *"Our governess, Mistress Marleigh Hume, is falsely accused of witchcraft and has been arrested. Please, in God's name, help us to free her."*

So why was Brereton so focused on this issue? Why was this seemingly as important as taking the city of Chester, or tracking down the remnants of Rupert's army? Brereton talked of his regard for Walker, and there was passing mention of an encounter with Marleigh. Richard could sense the lie, or if not a lie, an omission. It was there in Brereton's eyes as he said her name.

Richard knew the impact Marleigh Hume could have. Perhaps as well as anyone did. He did not doubt that at some time, in some place, Sir William Brereton, for all his godly devotion, had fallen into the bear trap and was struggling to find a way out.

7 July 1644

So here he was, making his way through the lush green of the east Cheshire countryside, to call upon the Walker family and see how he could aid his ex-lover and, who knows, the secret lover of the commander of the parliamentary army in the North-West of England. It would be nice to see the Walkers again. He had memories of happy, bright, engaging girls. He hoped their father's death had not scarred them too much and he wondered what effect being tutored by Marleigh might have had on them. But most of all, he wondered what reception he would get from the lady herself. He could not deny he was keen to renew acquaintances.

The rain had stopped. Time was getting on. He called to Roger and coaxed Eight into a trot.

*

It was early afternoon. Marleigh had been waiting hour after tedious hour for her ordeal to begin. The constable had been in a few times, as had his wife. There was nothing to share, only that arrangements were still being made and that they would tell her as soon as they knew something. Jeremiah Smale was trying to drum up a case against her, and had been seen questioning people around the town, in the inns, in the few shops. The Walker girls seemed to be confined to the house. None had seen them out.

Her biggest concern was how Smale's vanity and conceit would drive his behaviour. Having reacted swiftly to try to cover his embarrassment, he now had his reputation on the line. Only a conviction could salvage this now. An acquittal, and he would appear no more than a petty gossip. Vindictive and shallow, and above all, not a man among God's Chosen. He must put his all into this and it could drive him to do many things.

With a snoozing Eva on her lap, she watched the small patch of light from the high window slowly inch across the packed dirt of the cell floor, marking the slow passage of the day. The rain of the morning had eased, and a watery sunshine added at least some brightness to the gloom of the cell. Through the stone of the walls, she could 'see' the small bundles of energy and piece together the lines of the runs that the rodents were using all around her. She tried touching their minds, but they were too alien to her. Small, fragile, elusive. She could not grip them without crushing them, and she didn't want to do that. Not even to evaluate the mechanism. This in itself surprised her. A year or so ago and she had no compunction in taking things apart to see how they worked. Now, since Eva and the revelation that had brought, she viewed these things differently. The rats were, in some strange way, an extension of herself. *We are all part of the same thing. Perhaps that makes us brothers and sisters? At least we are comrades on some level.*

She was musing on this when she heard footsteps. More than one pair. She could sense two bodies coming down the narrow stairs outside the door. *This is it,* she thought. *Although I expected more of them.* She swallowed hard and prepared herself for the ordeal. *Trial by pinching, probing finger.*

The key turned and the door grated open. Constable Roe pushed the door open. "You have a visitor, mistress. He will not be denied and has paperwork which overreaches any authority that I have to refuse him."

He stepped to one side and the second figure entered, stooping under the doorframe. Once in the room, the man straightened and removed his brimmed hat.

It was not what she was expecting. She was not usually surprised by much, but this took her completely off guard. She was lost for words.

7 July 1644

"Good day, Mistress Hume. I had hoped to meet you again under rather better circumstances." Eva's father bowed and turned to the constable. "Please. Can you leave us? I need to confer privately with your prisoner."

*

As evening fell, Marleigh reflected on a day like no other. The shock of seeing Richard again was profound. Once the constable had left them, he turned to her, and smiled. He, at least, seemed genuinely pleased to see her and this was not something she had often experienced.

The smile also reminded her of the night they had spent together. Although it was some time previous, the uniqueness of the purpose, to create a child, meant that the details stayed with her. She felt herself blush slightly. Again, not something she was used to happening. She felt that unfamiliar feeling spread through her body. Her memories were warm and a welcome distraction from her predicament. If Eva had not been sitting up on the pallet, she might have felt like exploring those memories further. She made herself stand, and she bowed slightly.

She took in his weathered face and scruffy beard, his lean physique and the traces of a past fever haunting his eyes. "Master Farrell, is it not? Or should I now address you by some military title?"

"It seems I am now a captain. Although that is a story which is too long for the time we have."

"My congratulations, Captain. I am very pleased to see you. Things have not been going as well for us."

"Well, my own fortunes have only recently taken a turn for the better. As I said, 'tis a long story." He paused, and the smile faded. "You should know that I have come from the Walker household."

"The girls! Are they alright? Have they been mistreated?" She had not realised how anxious she was for their safety.

"They seemed fine when I left, although it took some effort to get to see them. It was Eliza who summoned help for you. She is a very resourceful young woman."

"But how? She said she was writing to friends, but how did Eliza find you? You met but the once, how can she have got a letter to you?"

"Not to me," he smiled, "I do not flatter myself that I left such a positive impression on any in this town." He seemed to search her face for some reaction to this and she rewarded him with a smile.

"Captain Farrell. You left a big impression on an impressionable girl. You also left a considerable impression on me. Is that what you wanted to hear?"

Now it was Farrell's turn to blush. She looked down to hide her expression. "But you left me something else as well."

The blush of pleasure had turned to puzzlement. Then shock. "My God! I am sorry." He paused. "Wait! But I didn't have the clap." He straightened, and clearly attempted to project a dignified air. "I have never had the disease. You must have got that from someone else!"

She looked up from examining the floor. "What? No, you fool!" She stepped to the side. "You left me with Eva."

Eva looked at Farrell from the mattress. Her faerie eyes dancing with excitement. *Really, Mama? Is this he? He is handsome! A bit battered, but handsome!*

Farrell was saying nothing because his jaw was on his chest. He stared at Eva, then at Marleigh, then back to Eva. "Your daughter, Captain Farrell. Richard."

He doesn't say much, Mama. Doesn't he like me?

Marleigh scooped her up off the bed and took a step towards Farrell. Instinctively he put out his arms and she lifted

Eva to him. Marleigh smiled shyly. Eva grinned at Farrell, and he shifted his grip, one hand under each armpit as he raised her up to be eye to eye with him. He seemed to be slowly recovering his composure.

Without taking his eyes off Eva he said, "I... I think I need to sit down." He slumped onto the pallet, Eva still held out at arm's length. "My God, Marleigh, she is beautiful." He cleared his throat, suddenly struggling to get his words out. "In fact, I think she is the most beautiful thing I think I have ever seen." Eva's grin turned to a delighted laugh. *I like him a lot, Mama. Can we keep him?*

"Are you sure? I mean, are you sure she is mine? It was just one night."

"I am sure." She looked at him reprovingly. "And I am not insulted. It was a strange time for me, and I suppose I did seduce you."

"I'm sorry! I didn't mean it how it sounded. This is something of a shock. I did not anticipate... a child."

"You mean you didn't anticipate a child with me at least."

"No. You are right. But it would be untrue to say that I haven't thought about you many, many times since that night. But also, what really shocks me? I never thought I could make something quite so beautiful." He was rewarded with more beaming smiles from Eva.

You are such a flirt, daughter! Behave yourself. He is your father!

Farrell was now bouncing Eva on his knee. "But, Marleigh, regardless of Eliza's letter, I was on my way to see you. It seems fate has been working towards this moment."

Eva was now playing with his hat. Marleigh sat as well. She looked at him with a more serious expression. "You haven't answered my question. How did Eliza find you?"

"Not me. She told me she wrote to several people. Her father's partner, Brough, is it?" Marleigh nodded. *That's good.*

"But the letter that brought me here was to Sir William Brereton. I am attached to his command. It is another long story, but he sent me here to Macclesfield to find out what had happened with you." He was watching her carefully, seeing how she reacted to this news.

Thinking, thinking, thinking. "Of course! Sir William wrote to the family after her father's death."

Farrell nodded. "Yes. That is the connection. What I don't understand is why such a letter grabbed his attention. I admit, a witchcraft trial is not an everyday thing, but it seems to me there is some other reason he asked me to come here to investigate. Is that true?"

And she had told him. In fact, really there was not much to tell but the story of her evening encounter with Brereton that then led on to the incident the following day with Mary Brassey and her family, and the first accusation of witchcraft. How Brereton had dismissed it out of hand. About the suicide and the bitterness that followed.

Farrell seemed to understand, nodding as if this confirmed something he had already considered. She had then questioned him about his visit to the house.

"You met him? Smale?"

"I did. Not exactly a welcoming soul. At first, he tried to slam the door in my face when I asked to see Eliza. When I threatened to cut his balls off, he seemed to calm down a little. When I showed him my pass, and my instructions from the parliamentary commander, signed by Sir William Brereton himself, proclaimed protector of the godly and hero of the Battle of Nantwich, he became much more hospitable. I saw Eliza and Maggie. They were well, but I do not think Smale will ever forgive them for their letter writing."

He went on to say that the family solicitor, Brough, had called before him. As a trustee for the girls, Smale could not refuse him an audience either, but Farrell did not know what passed between them all.

He had left and sought out Brough at his offices. Unsurprisingly, as it was the Sabbath, he was not there and so Farrell had gone to find lodging at the Bate Hall inn in the Chestergate. "I will try to find him again tomorrow and I will write to Brereton to update him on how things are progressing. I am sure it will come to nothing."

In turn, she told him of the coming ordeals. The examination of her body, and the vigil. He had shaken his head at the madness of it all.

He stood, and after kissing her on the cheek, he handed Eva back to Marleigh. She suddenly did not want him to go and grabbed his hand. "Please, Richard. Please return tomorrow. You have already done much by coming, but there is something more I would ask of you. Please come again in the morning."

He swallowed, and nodded, ducked under the doorway, and was gone.

It was an hour after he had gone that the constable had returned with his wife and two other women. He had left them to their task, and they performed it with diligence. Every inch of her body was examined, discussed, and some note taken. She knew her own body intimately and that there was nothing to find. They were quiet, serious and business-like. It felt like she was a prize animal being judged at the country fair. Limbs were lifted and rotated. One went through her hair and looked in her mouth, raising a candle for a better view. One, who had clearly drawn the short straw, muttered an apology and investigated her private areas, front and back. In the end, their discussions confirmed what she had hoped for, and expected. There was nothing. Nothing at all. Not a blemish. Not a mark. Not a growth or a lump.

The constable's wife thanked her for her patience and she, in turn, thanked them for their gentleness and dignity. She asked them, "Will it be yourselves who sit with me? You know, to watch for the Devil's imps?" She tried to keep her face blank.

"Not me," replied Mistress Roe. "Not us. He that prosecutes you. He will be there. There will be two others, but I know not who they will be. They will come tomorrow. Get your rest now, dear, for I fear you will not get much in the next few days."

After they were gone, she collapsed, exhausted. She was awash with emotion. She had never considered she might see Richard Farrell again. She had not hoped for it but, now she had seen him, she had a feeling of family. The first time she had felt such a feeling in so long. She had made her decision on a whim but did not regret it. It was for Eva. That was all that mattered.

17

RICHARD

(8 July 1644)

"Shit!" He stood at the grimy window of his room at the tavern, thumping a clenched fist slowly, softly and repeatedly against the plasterwork. It wasn't anything he could see in the street that caused his disquiet. He had had a disturbed night – *What is it about this place?* he thought, remembering his previous stay at the Bate Hall. Certainly not haunted by the tavern's ghosts, or the terrifying dreams he had experienced here previously. This was wrestling with a problem all too real.

He was a father. He had, in some respects, a family. This was… amazing.

On the other hand, it wasn't the family he pictured. He had been playing out a future in his mind, where he found and reconciled with Neelie. They came to live in England. Maybe, if he could stomach it, they would rebuild the old house and take their place in local society. Children would come. He would die old, fat and happy surrounded by his family and friends.

His new reality was somewhat different. A bastard girl with mismatched eyes, born of a night of passion with a woman, the like of whom he had never met before or since. A woman who was about to be tried as a witch. How had *that* happened? What he couldn't work out was how he felt about it.

He had felt an immediate connection with the girl. With Eva. He had no doubt she was his. It was almost like she was in his head. Perhaps that was how it was with children? He knew he could not walk away from Eva. Marleigh was a different matter. It was clear she had never intended to tell him he had a daughter. For someone who passed herself off as an ordinary, respectable woman, fallen on hard times, she had a depth he had never encountered before. Never. Alright, she said her father had been a teacher, but she had such knowledge!

And she knew about '*it*'. About the effect that washed over him if a violent death occurred close to him. The energy. The strength. Not in so many words perhaps, but she knew something, for all her innocent questions. *How* did she know? Unless of course, she felt it herself? *That is something I had not considered…*

Oh God! What did it all mean? Why did he feel like he would do anything for her, while at the same time being more than a little afraid of her? What should he do?

What he did was sit and write a letter to Brereton. He set out the position as he saw it. The date for the trial and his thoughts on the procedure the magistrate had laid down. He wrote of Marleigh Hume's state of mind. He promised to write again. He also noted his own improved health. His fever seemed to have passed. His wound remained clean, and he was starting to get some strength and grip back in his hand.

He determined to seek out Brough, the lawyer. Perhaps he could help Richard understand the local politics. That was his next step.

He found Roger in the tavern room below. No big surprise there. He had his feet up on a wooden bench and was layering

(8 July 1644)

jam onto a hunk of buttered bread. A cup of ale sat on the table in front of him.

Richard slipped into a chair opposite and slid the sealed envelope across to him. "This must get to Brereton as soon as possible. Will you take it?"

Roger eyed him with an amused smile. "I wasn't aware there was a choice in these matters, Captain?"

Richard rolled his eyes. "Will you take it? And will you leave now?"

The bread disappeared into Roger's mouth, leaving jam sticking in his beard. "Of course," he muttered around the obstruction, spraying Richard and the table with breadcrumbs. He gestured at his plate. "Just as soon as..."

"Of course. Start with the camp at York, but he also talked of going to the armoury in Hull. Please, Roger, find him and bring his response back to me as soon as you can."

He had relayed the news from Marleigh to him the previous evening and Roger had taken the announcement of Richard's fatherhood in his stride. This made Richard wonder just how many children Roger had left in his wake across the continent and the towns and villages of England. Still, he had welcomed the lack of judgement. He reached over and put a hand on his shoulder. "Be careful, those roads will be full of spies and enemies. Don't get yourself killed. Not just yet anyway."

Roger winked. "The day someone gets the better of Roger DeLacey will be the day he dies! That's Shakespeare, that is. With some of the words changed around a bit."

"Quite a few words, I expect."

"Probably."

"And a few added, here and there?"

"Oh yes. Of course."

As Richard left the tavern, a low voice hailed him from the passageway down the side of the building. At first, he could see nothing, but then a small, hooded figure detached itself from the shadow of the narrow lane and beckoned him to follow. With a look over his shoulder and a hand on the pommel of his sword, he slowly walked into the gloom.

To the rear of the Bate Hall, in a heavily shaded yard, he found himself looking down on an old woman. She looked like she had just wandered in from the woods, a little scruffy with seeds and bits of vegetation here and there on a moth-eaten cloak. Richard could see she was vigorous, despite her age, and the grip she placed on his forearm was impressive. She had bright eyes like a small bird, and these moved constantly from his face to the passageway. He resisted the temptation to brush her off, caught between unease, curiosity and the rather odd smell she gave off.

"You been to see 'er, then?" Her voice surprisingly low and he only just caught her words as she spoke just above a whisper.

"I don't know what you mean. Who are you?"

"That don't matter. You seen 'er. In the gaol. Mistress Hume." Statements, not questions. The bright eyes burned into him.

"Why is that your business? I ask again, who are you? And it *does* matter to me."

The woman sighed, and peered again round Richard, back up the passageway. "M'Alice. Alice Mellor. I know Mistress Hume. I would get a message to 'er. It's important."

She was agitated, clearly not wanting a prolonged conversation.

"And why would you trust me with it? Assuming you are a friend of hers, why would you trust me? And why should I trust you?"

"I saw you yesterday. Went to visit the Walker house, didn't yer? I saw how you dealt with that Smale on 'is own doorstep. That made you her friend as well, I reckon. And anyway, you're the father, ain't yer?"

Richard stepped back, shocked. "What? How do you…? What…?"

"Keep yer voice down!" she hissed. "Look. I got some insights." She tapped the side of her head. "I can see things in you that are in her as well. They's just not nearly so strong in you. Stands to reason she would pick you as the father. Got to keep up the bloodline, eh?" She leered at him and winked.

He was speechless, mouth open.

"Anyway, I've seen the child, and she's got yer looks. Not too hard to see. Don't need any magic for that." She spat, expertly. "Calm down. Will yer pass on me message? This is serious."

Richard was still trying to keep up with Alice. How many more people knew his secret? "Yes. I mean, what is it?"

She put a hand on his shoulder and stood on tiptoes. He bent down so she could whisper into his ear. He expected her breath to be rank, but it smelt of mint. "I told 'er when I met 'er before. You got to watch out for that strip of a girl. She's been summoned. She's coming for the trial. Smale sent for her, and she be comin'. Tell 'er that."

Richard stood back, confused. "I don't understand. What girl?" He was now convinced the woman was either mad, a malicious timewaster, or both.

She sighed again and rolled her eyes, apparently frustrated by his slowness. "The Maid! The Maid o' Rainow. The one got them two girls hanged in Chester. She's comin' to make her judgement, and like enough Smale has 'er in his pocket already. Or at least her connivin' fuck of a brother. Tell 'er. So as she can be prepared."

He looked at her blankly. He had no idea what she was talking about.

"Just tell 'er what I said. You don't need to understand it. Just tell 'er, if ye can keep yer mind above the waist that is." She winked and leered again. "You's playin' wi' fire there, boy. Hope yer up to it." One last look up the alley and she was gone through a gap in the yard wall.

18

ROGER

(9 July 1644)

It had been, he thought, an interesting few days. He had rejoiced at being back where he belonged. In an army among other fighting men where he had a purpose. Enjoying the thrill of the adventure and the opportunity to exercise his modest skills. And earning pay again. As a veteran, his views had been sought and respected. He had been placed in command of a detachment of musketeers and had found himself marching with Rupert's army through Lancashire, over the Pennines and the relief of York.

Those had been good days. He found the civilian life in Amsterdam difficult, as he always had. Making money with Hudde had been easy but dull for the most part. It was the boredom that got to him. Yes, there had been a few adventures, but these were few and far between. With Richard's departure for England, and Neelie's disavowal of him, he had lost his closest friends and the bottle had largely taken their places.

He felt no particular allegiance to Rupert and the King but, as always, it was good to be on the winning side. Fewer corpses. Greater chance of being paid on time. He had had to admire

Rupert's skill as a commander and the confidence this had given his men. After the fall of Bolton, some had questioned the army's morals. A massacre was never a pleasant thing to witness, but he told those around him that this was nothing compared to some of the butchery he had witnessed in the foreign wars.

Roger had certainly let off some steam when the gates of York had opened to them, and suffered for it the following day. His hopes of a few relaxing days with the grateful goodwives of the city had been dashed when they had received orders to march. The allies were waiting for battle and Rupert had decided to give it to them. He could understand the reasoning. Even if outnumbered to some degree, they had the momentum, the confidence, the – what did the French call it? – élan!

It had seemed very hopeful. Yes, they had been hampered by the late arrival of the garrison of York. Yes, they had been taken by surprise by the sudden assault as the day seemed to be slipping into cautious stalemate. But the centre had more than held. They were pushing the allies backwards. But then that killjoy Cromwell had swept around behind them and finished off Goring's horse, leaving them vulnerable and unprotected.

But he had escaped death, again, and while there was the uncertainty of being a prisoner, he knew he might have the option of turning his coat. His skills and knowledge were useful to both sides. All it required was the right monetary reward and the opportunity to make a transaction. He could be patient.

When he had seen Richard Farrell coming by on his horse, looking more than half dead, well, here was the opportunity he was looking for. It had just arrived a little sooner than he expected. If he had been a godly man, he might have seen this as a sign from heaven. But he wasn't. So he didn't. This was just another turn of fate, and it had fallen right into his lap. So much the better that it was Richard. He liked him. Even, grudgingly, admired him. He had been good to him when he was at his lowest point, or at least as good as Roger had allowed him to be.

And things just kept getting better with the cushy assignment from Cromwell. Every opportunity for a bit of rest and relaxation, and some 'foraging' along the way.

But then had come something entirely unexpected. How he had maintained his calm, dignified exterior he would never know. His wife. His son. Alive. His world turned upside down. It tasted like redemption. It tasted of a new opportunity. He wasn't sure if Richard had bought his "I will not pursue them. They have chosen a different life, and I respect it" sentiment. Nothing could be further from his mind. He had to find them. He had never stopped loving them. Of course, he understood why she had done it. But he was different now. He could re-enlist down in London. He would make a home for them. He *was* different now. A few weeks with Richard and then he was off, with or without his blessing. This was family. Richard would understand.

But first, he had a little tricky issue to resolve. It was the second day since he had left Macclesfield and he was now convinced he was being followed. As he had camped the previous night, in the shelter of an old, ruined barn in some godforsaken piece of wilderness in the Pennines, he was certain he had heard voices. He had doused his fire and crept away from his tethered horse, pistol gripped in his right hand. He moved slowly in the near darkness, edging up the rise to try to get a better view of his surroundings. Mainly, he was looking for another campfire, but it seemed they were cleverer than that. Nothing further disturbed the night and in the end, he managed a few hours' sleep before dawn.

Under a grey sky that threatened a downpour, he had moved off the track and was making his way across country. He tried to keep the track in sight so as not to lose his way, but made use of woods, hedgerows and the natural folds of the land to try to see if any did follow, while not being seen himself. Having passed an edgy morning, he found a place to stop to rest and for his horse to feed and water. He broke out some bread and cheese and an apple from his bag. He sat with his back to a lump of limestone in the middle of a hollow, which masked him from view. A small pool lay in the middle, where rainwater collected in the bowl-shaped depression. Some gorse bushes were scattered here and there, flowers now faded and dropping small brown petals.

He looked warily at the sky. Surely it couldn't hold its heavy burden much longer and he was going to get very wet, very quickly. Oh. And here it was. The first few heavy spots spattered onto the rock and created ripples in the water. *Shit!* He put down the pistol he had been cradling, brushed breadcrumbs off his jacket and tossed the apple core over his shoulder. He rolled towards his saddlebag for his oiled canvas cape. At least that would keep some of it off him. He coughed violently and grabbed for the rag inside his coat. He wiped his mouth, staring at the bloody smear. Another cough. More blood. He looked at the cloth in his hand for a moment, and then carefully folded it and put it away again.

His horse, grazing just yards away and likely hoping for the apple, suddenly started, and raised its head. Suddenly Roger was showered, not with rain but with blood as his horse came crashing down beside him. A split second later came the crash of the ignited powder. Crimson sheeted down its neck and sprayed from a gaping slash just below its head. It lay on its side, eyes rolling and feebly kicking a front leg.

He rolled again, grabbing the pistol, and not stopping until he tucked in behind the outcrop. He could roughly work out where the shot must have come from and, sure enough, he saw a figure break cover on the opposite side of the grassy bowl and come running down the slope, pistol in hand. Panting heavily, Roger squeezed in behind the rock and, as he looked up the slope behind him, saw a second man rise up from the shelter of the lip, musket aimed. He could not have been more than twenty yards away and the musket was lined up steadily on his chest. The man advanced slowly towards him.

"Drop it! Put your pistol down and you can live to tell your grandchildren about this, old man!"

The steady plinking of rain droplets was turning into a torrent.

The gap was ten yards. "All we want is your messages. Letters or such like you are carrying for Cromwell? We know where you are bound. We have been following you. Put down your pistol, give us the letters and you can ride on."

Roger, with his arms held wide, pistol in his right hand, slowly rose. Looking over that shoulder, he could now see the man who had fired the first shot was a similar distance away. His hat had come off as he had charged down the slope and Roger could see the rain bouncing off his bald head. He was squinting through the slanting deluge.

"I ain't got any grandchildren, on account of not having any children. And I ain't riding anywhere, friend, 'cos this stupid fucker shot my horse. You should explain to him that horses have more legs than a man and tend to be bigger. That's how you can tell the difference. Only thing we got similar in size is in my breeches and I ain't showin' him that. Don't know how 'e'll take it, in a manner o' speaking. Perhaps 'e won't get the two confused next time. Not that there will be a next time."

Behind, baldy now spoke. "Sorry 'bout your 'orse. But it's not far for you to walk. Put the pistol down and hand over yer bag. Then you can leave. That's a promise. One soldier to another." The man walked forward a few yards, pistol raised and pointing at Roger's head. The other man, older, the one with the musket and the calm nerves, stayed where he was.

Slowly, and with exaggerated care, Roger squatted down again, keeping his arms extended. He placed the pistol on the increasingly sodden earth. Keeping his hand hovering over it, he almost had to shout over the noise of the rain, "Cromwell's letter is not in my bag. Don't trust myself not to lose that. It's in my coat. I'm going to stand and reach inside for it. I trust you gentlemen can relax your trigger fingers." He slowly rose and half turned to address the bald man, now just three yards behind him.

He reached into his leather coat and sensed the man lower his pistol and take a half-pace towards him, hand extended. In a smooth, flowing movement, Roger's dagger was out of its sheath. He swung fully round, taking a long stride forward into a classic lunge position. Left arm batted the pistol hand away and right arm extended, and not knowing if the man had a steel breastplate under his coat, he drove the point of the dagger into the man's groin.

The bald man doubled over, and Roger swung round behind him, all the time expecting the musket ball in his back. He reached around and with his crooked left arm around the throat, pulled the man back vertical. He was bleeding copiously down the inside of his leg and was growing heavier in Roger's grip as his life ebbed. The man with the musket remained where he had been, face impassive. His aim never wavered.

"Don't want to take the chance on a moving target," he growled, "but you're standing still now."

"Yes. And I have yer friend here. Had you noticed? You goin' to finish 'im off for me?"

"No friend o' mine. And he's dead anyway. You seen to that. I reckon this will put a ball through both of you. Shall we try?" He raised the musket a little higher, sighting carefully.

(9 JULY 1644)

But this had been Roger's gamble. He shoved the bald man away and he collapsed to the ground into the pool of his own blood, moaning faintly, the pounding rain creating meandering streams of it across the hollow. He swept his sword out, metal grating, and walked purposefully forward, dagger now in his left hand.

The other man grinned, hair plastered to his head. "Be my pleasure!" he laughed. "Go on, just one more step…"

Roger broke into a run, sword arm high. Even with the rain lashing in his face, he saw the finger tighten on the trigger, barrel pointed straight at the middle of his chest. A click. The hammer fell. But no spark, and no flash and crash of igniting powder. No heavy lead ball smashing its way through his sternum.

Roger's sword came chopping in from high to the man's left, angling towards his neck. He recovered quickly from the shock of the misfire and swung up the musket to block the vicious cut. As he contorted his body to take the shock of the impact, Roger's boot stamped hard on his knee and he collapsed to the ground howling in agony. Roger moved carefully around the rolling body, until he could safely draw out the man's own sword and toss it away. He couldn't see any other weapons. He placed his boot on the man's throat and leant forward to look into the frantic grey eyes. The downpour was easing slightly, and Roger's body sheltered the fallen man.

"Right then. Who would have thought all this rain might dampen your powder, eh? At the end of the day, better to trust a simple length of sharpened steel. Very reliable."

Wide-eyed panic, smeared with pain, looked back at him.

"So let's get the basics done. How many of you are there out there?"

"Just the two of us. I swear it!"

"Ah! A London boy like myself. It has been a while since I heard that accent. All these dour northerners and bloody

Scots. No sense of fun. I like a bit of fun m'self." He stepped back and kicked the man's damaged knee. He howled and rolled around, trying to cradle it. "Now come on. You know how this goes. I keep kicking you until you give me the answers I need." He kicked him again, this time in the back of the head. "What's your name, friend?"

"Cooper," he hissed through teeth clenched in pain. "Please. Don't kill me." Roger wiped the other man's blood off his knife onto Cooper's coat. He held the tip an inch in front of the man's left eyeball.

"Now, you focus your attention on that, whilst I ask a few questions. A cripple might be able to beg a livin'. War has made lots of them. But a blind cripple? So, mate, let's get to know each other better and you can tell me all about what you are doing and who you are doing it for, for I know you are no regular soldier."

The rain had stopped, and a surprisingly warm sun started to raise steam from the grass around them.

19

BRERETON

(10 July 1644)

He pounded the table in frustration. *Why now? Why me? Why do you test me so?*

The letter from Farrell lay in front of him, delivered by a bloodstained rogue who claimed to be his subordinate. One of a heap of notes received, and those being written. All those were focused on the coming campaign. Orders from London. Messages to his highest-ranking officers. Complaints from locals about overenthusiastic 'foraging' by his men. All but two.

One, from his wife. Full of cheerful news. The garden was looking lovely, helped by the recent rain. Roses were blooming and the apples were starting to appear in the trees of their small orchard. Their son was thriving and wanted to come and help Daddy fight his enemies. They prayed all the time. Prayed for his safety and for God to reveal his plan for them all.

I could certainly do with that now! He grabbed the other letter, the one from Farrell. He read it again and then slowly and deliberately tore it and burnt it over the candle, the only source of light in his tent. *How can I discern your plan? What should I do? Oh Lord, grant me wisdom to see your righteous path.*

He shifted off the stool and knelt on the earth to pray. His horsemen were on the move. They had broken camp outside of the armoury at Hull and were set to move back west, to join the forces trying to intercept Rupert. He was painfully aware of the need for intelligence on the whereabouts of the remains of the Royalist army and the kind of numbers they might have to face. He did not want to rush into battle and risk losing all the recent gains, so bloodily won. And so he had sent out a tide of scouting parties and spies, to probe and watch and report back. But so far? Nothing. Nothing useful. So, he had to blunder on. And hope.

But the second letter arrived laden with doubt and distraction.

...trial on the thirteenth of this month. The magistrate is looking for a bench of three honourable gentlemen of standing, in lieu of the proper assizes in Chester. Mistress Hume has precious few friends in the town, although the same could be said for her accuser. Perhaps here is an opportunity for you to kill this accusation now and forever. You could preside with the magistrate, who by all accounts is a sensible gentleman who is angered at the waste of time this trial promises to be. With two of three then certain to acquit, this can be dealt with quickly and we can all move on to things more important...

He read of the ordeal that Marleigh Hume would be subjected to. He could see Farrell's contempt even for the idea of a trial, but for himself, this all felt a little more real. He thought back to his travels in the Low Countries and his strange meeting with the Princess of Portugal, and his conversations with the Winter Queen. His natural curiosity had been replaced with a more ominous feeling. On the continent, witches were much more at the front of people's minds. Terrible stories of accusation, murder and mass execution. Here, they seemed a fading legacy of the religious turmoil of a former time. It was true, King James had been something of a zealot on the subject, but there had been few trials in England, and even fewer executions.

Here he was weighing one woman's fate against the needs of the country. But he was deluding himself if he thought this was an ordinary woman. She was a remarkable, unique woman. He wondered at that for the thousandth time. What, truly, was his motivation for even thinking of attending? There could be only one answer. Her significance must be a divine message from God. A symbol. A question that needed addressing. Why else would the thought of her have this hold on him?

Farrell was right. Here was an opportunity to prove his worth, and move on. God had placed the opportunity of this trial before him. While the cavalry returned to Nantwich, he could divert to Macclesfield, make his judgement, and then rejoin. The timing would just about allow it. He would tell his officers he needed to see the sequestrators who were based in the town. He also wanted to meet with Captain Booth, the town alderman, and to speak with his most valuable of agents. A most remarkable and versatile woman, who lodged with the captain. His officers would know where he was if need arose.

He felt the decision click into place like a key turning in a well-oiled lock. The door opened, light flooded in and he saw the rightness in it. He picked up his quill and fresh paper and shouted for Farrell's man to attend him.

20

MARLEIGH

(12 July 1644)

"What is the time, sir?" she whispered. Constable Roe stood in the cell doorway, shaking his head in disbelief.

Marleigh sat in the middle of the room, on a small, ill-balanced stool. Against the three walls, which didn't include the cell doorway, leaned three others, also seated on stools. Smale, Mary Brassey and another woman – Marleigh thought she was called Margaret. All of them asleep, Smale snoring lightly.

"'Tis a little after noon. I was coming to inform this... gentleman... that the vigil is over, but I see they have already decided to call a halt to proceedings."

She was sure the stool was starting to become part of her. She had been sitting still on the hard circle of wood for most of the three days of the vigil and she was convinced that if she stood up, the stool would come with her. Every small movement seemed to grind her pelvic bones against the unyielding surface and her thighs felt numb to her knees. Her lower back ached and she could feel it slowly extending to grip her shoulders in tense, cramping knots.

(12 July 1644)

Marleigh smiled despite her exhaustion. She swayed as she stood and the constable grabbed her arm to keep her upright. But she had drawn on reserves of strength and fortitude that her three watchers could only dream of. Smale and Brassey had been with her since the start, not wanting to miss anything. Only the third watcher had been changed, Margaret swapping her seat with two other women over the course of the three days. Smale and Brassey had tried to ensure that one of them was awake at all times, but at about five o'clock that morning all three had succumbed and she had passed a boring morning, trying to remain on the stool and keep little Eva amused as she had tottered about the cell.

Eva had made friends with the other women who had watched her. Once they had got over her unusual appearance, she had charmed them all. Marleigh knew Eva's skill in reading people and their emotions, and she had put on a virtuoso performance. She had avoided Smale, and after being pushed away by Brassey's boot, had also kept her distance there. Brassey had made a great show of claiming protection from the Lord whenever Eva was nearby, and Marleigh was sure she would have been making signs to ward off the evil eye if she did not think it would be equally heretical in the eyes of Smale.

Smale and Brassey both brought charcoal and paper with them to record any events of note. This, of course, was primarily to write down the names and forms of Marleigh's demons and imps. Her gifts from Satan. By the second day, these materials were largely forgotten, and the quiet vigil had turned into a contest to see which of the two could bait or browbeat her into some kind of incriminating response or confession. As the hours went by, and both could see that there would be no weakness shown, and no confession to be had, they lapsed into boredom, just throwing out the occasional insult. The poor women who had to witness the ordeal quickly became withdrawn and were clearly overjoyed when they were relieved of their duties.

Marleigh, cradling a now-sleeping Eva, carefully laid her down on the mattress. Roe quietly picked up the papers under the stools of the watchers, folded them and placed them in his pocket.

"It seems they have nothing to report," she said. "What happens now, Constable?"

"So it would seem. I think now, you have earned the right to rest. The trial will start in the morning. You need to sleep, mistress. I will get these out of your way."

He gently shook Margaret awake. She was startled, wide-eyed and for a moment trying to work out where she was. "Don't fret, dear. Your ordeal is over. You can go now."

Margaret looked around for the paper, although Marleigh was not convinced she knew how to write. "I have it here, Margaret." He patted his jacket. "Don't worry. You can go." He nodded towards the open door and she scurried towards it, shedding anxiety as she went.

"Oh," he said, "and you have a visitor, mistress. The same military gentleman as before. Captain Farrell. Do you wish to see him?"

Her heart leapt. *That's not happened for some time.* "Yes. Please. Send him in."

He called back through the door. "Captain Farrell? Mistress Hume will see you."

His raised voice woke both Brassey and Smale. Smale stretched and rubbed his eyes, looking quickly around the room. He spoke accusingly at Roe. "What is the meaning of this interruption? And where is Mistress Smith? There should be three of us here at all times!"

"I told her to go. The vigil is ended. Your time is up." He brought out the papers from his pocket. "And I have collected these. Your evidence." He looked contemptuously at Smale. "You have no need of these any longer. I am to give them to the magistrate who has recently arrived in the town."

"What? No! You must return them to me. They are a vital part of my case. How dare you!"

"No, Master Smale. My orders are from the magistrate. He wishes to prepare for the trial and wants to see the record of the vigil whilst it is, er, fresh, shall we say. You understand? So no one can cast any doubt on the authenticity." He looked pleased at his use of the word. No doubt straight from the magistrate's mouth, thought Marleigh.

Footsteps down the stairs outside the cell. A slight dimming of the light as Richard walked in. He surveyed the scene, wrinkling his nose at the stale smell of sweat and other odours. Smale backed against the wall. "Keep him away from me, Constable. He is a violent man. He threatened me in my own home!"

"Not your home, I think." Richard stepped towards him. "Not yet. Although I have few doubts that is what motivates you in this matter."

Smale stepped warily around Richard. "Come, Mistress Brassey. It is clear that the godly are not to be treated with the respect they deserve in this place." He extended a hand to help her from the stool. Her body was stiff from the endless hours of sitting.

"Ah. You are Brassey!" said Richard, rubbing the knuckles of his left hand. Marleigh could now see they were red raw. "Please give my regards to your husband and his friends. They did not seem inclined for conversation when we met, but I think we understand each other better now."

"What have you done, you thug! I will have you charged! Constable! Do your duty. He has assaulted my husband!"

"Mistress Brassey. Enough. All I heard was talk of a

discussion. If there has been any assault I need to hear that from your husband himself. And I need witnesses. Clearly, emotions are running high. We should all try to calm down." Nevertheless, he raised an eyebrow at Richard, who ignored him.

Eva, wide awake now, was watching from the bed. Her bright eyes followed the exchanges. She hopped down and wobbled across to Marleigh, who swept her up, before herself sitting down on the thin mattress.

"I think we have all had enough. Please, sir," Roe looked again at Richard, "do not detain our guest for long. She needs sleep before the trial." He looked at Smale and Brassey. "I am not sure in the end which of those in the room were maintaining the vigil, and which were not. So, Master Smale, do I need to drag any imps away to custody? Under the bed, are they?"

Smale just scowled, and he and Brassey edged towards the door.

"I will not be long, Constable," Richard said. "I wanted to give Mistress Hume the news about the magistrate, and the appointment of the two others who will sit with him in judgement."

"I was just about to tell her myself. And you too, Smale. Are you not curious who will be on the bench?"

"Surely it is Edward Savage? Is he not magistrate?"

"It is, Master Smale. Sir Edward has arrived and he has good news. By good fortune we hope to have another fine gentleman agree to preside. Perhaps the finest gentleman in the North."

"And who is that, man? For goodness' sake, spit it out!"

"Why, sir, it is Sir William Brereton himself! Sir William is returning from York, and is passing close to the town. Letters have been sent to Sir William to ask for his participation as he always held Samuel Walker, God rest his soul, in high regard. Sir Edward was most pleased to learn of the request."

Richard turned to Marleigh, careful that none but she could see his face, and slowly winked. As he turned again, Marleigh could see Mary Brassey had turned as white as a sheet. After days of insult and threat, she could not resist it. "Oh, Mary! What luck! Perhaps you will be able to renew your acquaintance with Sir William. Imagine his surprise when he sees who my accuser is!"

Roe and Smale both looked confused. Brassey grabbed Smale by the arm and started to drag him out. "It means nothing!" she hissed at him. "Come. We need to talk. Let us leave this nest of Devil worshippers and footpads." Marleigh could hear them arguing all the way up the steps, and then along Dog Lane past her window.

Roe went to follow them out. "Five minutes, please, sir. No longer." The door closed behind him.

"Truth be told, I have no news of Brereton. He seems keen to bring this to a swift conclusion and I am a little surprised, given the weight on his shoulders. He must think highly of you indeed. But I await his reply to my letter. My colleague is riding between us. I hope for his return any minute." He raised an eyebrow.

"I think he feels an obligation to the Walker girls, or so I would guess." She looked down, feeling awkward. Not wanting to explain again what she thought had been put to bed. He seemed to decide not to press the issue.

"Whatever the reason, if Brereton does consent to act as judge, this means Sir Edward Savage is the key. I understand Smale has dug up some member of his parish, some other Puritan zealot, as the third to sit in judgement. No doubt he owes Smale money or something, but we must assume he is Smale's creature. With Sir William in your corner, Savage is then the key that opens your cell door. Everyone I speak to says he is fair and reasonable. Something of a rarity, a champion of the ordinary folk. I must try to meet him, although I think Sir William will be a more effective champion for you than I."

She had to agree, although she was less sure that Brereton would ride to her aid.

"Anyway, at least it wiped the smirk from Mary Brassey's face. For a short time if nothing more. Maybe she will decide to withdraw her charges now."

"There is that chance, but I think Smale is now too committed to withdraw. He will be balancing which would cause him the biggest embarrassment. But he will be angry with Brassey. Perhaps there is an angle there to exploit. I will think on it."

Marleigh suddenly remembered something. "What was that about her husband? Did you meet him?"

Richard laughed. "Ha! Yes, on the way here. Further down the lane. Looked like a farmer, with a couple of his labourers. The oaf stepped in front of me to have a quiet word, but things got a little noisy. He said things about you. And Eva. I didn't like what he said and made a point of letting him know. His friends legged it when they saw steel."

She felt a lump in her throat. "You don't need to do that for me." She looked at Eva. "For us. You don't have to do any of this for us. There is no obligation on you. You can just ride away, back to the war. I ask nothing of you." She looked down at the floor, partly to hide the tears welling in her eyes. What was wrong with her? She could not remember ever feeling like this before. Never, in her long memory. Why this moment to develop feelings like this?

He leaned towards her and gently cupped the side of her face with his bruised hand, slowly raising it until he looked her in the eyes. "I know," he said softly, "I take the obligation on myself." He paused, seemingly contemplating his next words carefully. "I do not know exactly what I feel for you. I am still confused. I am trying to take all this in." He turned slightly and placed his other hand against Eva's cheek. She smiled up at him. "But, if you will let me help you further, I would be honoured to do so." He leant forward and gently steered her face towards his. He kissed her lightly, looking into her eyes all the while. He sat back.

There was a long silence. "Thank you," she said. "Thank you."

"Yes, thank you," said Eva. Marleigh and Richard both laughed. She dashed a tear from her eye.

"I know you need your rest, but there is another gentleman I would like you to see. I will bring him in before I leave. He waits in the street."

She looked at him, puzzled, but he pressed on. "I have some other news." He looked less happy. "I met a friend of yours."

More surprise. She had no friends in the town outside the Walker household. "Oh." A sudden realisation dawned on her. "You mean Master Brough. You went to his office?"

"Well, I did. But that's not who I meant. Brough is supportive, by the way, but does not think he is the right man to defend you. Some of that was professional. He did not think himself qualified for this type of matter. But I also think he was concerned about his reputation." He raised a hand to stop her objection. "I do not think he is worried you are guilty, or even worried for himself. I think it is out of concern for Eliza and Maggie. He is their representative, and perhaps the only person preventing Smale from taking control of their assets. He is concerned that if things do go against you, or even if they don't, and he is representing you, it might strengthen Smale's hand. I can see his point."

She nodded. So could she. "If not him, who did you meet?"

"I think I met a real witch this time." He grinned. "Some old crone called Alice stopped me outside the tavern a few days ago. Said she knew you and you knew her. From Alderley, I think she said."

"Old Mother Edge!" Eva called out from her lap.

"Yes. Probably," Marleigh said, ruffling her dark hair. She looked up at him. "I am surprised she risked being seen in town. Some might consider her one step from a noose herself. What did she want?"

His grin disappeared and he sat down next to her, taking her free hand. "She wanted to warn you. I am not sure I understand this, but she told me to tell you that the Maid of Rainow was attending the trial. That this would mean something to you. Does it?"

"Does it, Mama?" Eva looked worried, her forehead crinkled with lines.

She looked down and sighed. "It does. I had hoped this would not happen. Smale is leaving no stone unturned."

"Who is this woman? This Maid?"

"Some kind of holy person. She claims to speak directly to God, and God tells her who is a witch and who isn't. It is rubbish. A fraud. It is said by some that her brother is her pimp and collects the money for her appearances. But it is true that she was the reason two girls from Rainow were hanged at Chester some years ago. It made her reputation. It may be nothing, the magistrate may not even let her speak, but it will make things very uncomfortable if she can incite some kind of mob. Particularly if Smale and Brassey are supporting her too."

"Mama? What's a pimp?"

"Later, Eva."

"Look. Don't worry about it. We will think of some plan. And the constable is right. You need to sleep. I am going to try to see Sir Edward, and I'll see Brereton when he arrives. He is expecting to be here late this evening. There is just one more thing. Let me call in the gentleman who awaits us."

He rose and headed for the door.

She lay down, cuddling Eva to her side. It was true. She was exhausted. This latest news had dented the growing confidence she had felt. All Smale's scheming had brought him nothing. Nothing. No one could convict her on the evidence he had assembled, because there was none. But a combination of superstition and religious hysteria might work on the townsfolk. And then, how might that influence the magistrate?

But more than this, she could not get another thought out of her mind. What was it that she felt about Richard? Each time she thought of him, it was like her insides turned over. Like jumping off a high rock into deep water. A combination of floating, helplessness and a slight tinge of nausea. Excitement and fear. It was a little how she felt about Eva but not the same. She knew the word for it but couldn't even say it to herself. Not now. She must bottle it. Preserve it and keep it for a time when it could be safely opened.

She heard the returning footsteps. The door opening. The man accompanying Farrell and the constable was not one she had expected. Suddenly, the world seemed full of surprises.

21

RICHARD

(12 July 1644)

Richard left the gaol in a state of confusion. He leant against the wall, heel of his boot against the brickwork, head in his hands. He felt like he too had been awake for three days. With elements of his fever still trailing through his mind he just didn't feel equipped for what he must do. The effort of maintaining his air of confidence for Marleigh was draining. All he wanted to do was drag her and Eva out of the cell, sit them both on the back of his horse and ride away. Anywhere. He was not known for his patience.

He had lost one family to war. He had lost the love of his life to his own jealousy and stupidity. He couldn't explain his feelings for Marleigh. What had been curiosity, mystery and some kind of erotic adventure had changed. He had been coming to the town hoping to rediscover what he had experienced with her before. Instead, with the mission from Brereton, and discovering Eva, he had fallen into something deeper and now he couldn't see the bottom. With each meeting he was sinking further. He was helpless in the current pulling him down and he wasn't struggling. He wasn't striking for the surface to grab a lungful of air.

Because Marleigh and Eva were relying on him.

He straightened, pushing off from the wall. He walked down the lane towards the marketplace, and as he turned the corner, heard raised voices from a small crowd of twenty or thirty people moving slowly across the open space towards him. As they progressed, a gap in the mob revealed a young couple, male and female. He was holding her hand, but at chest level, as if they were a married couple coming back down the aisle.

The man looked ordinary. Nondescript. Bareheaded with black curly hair and trimmed beard. His expression was serious, with a hint of... what? Arrogance? As if he carried a great responsibility that lesser folk could never understand. He studiously ignored the adulation aimed at his companion. She was in no way ordinary. She was dressed all in white. Her skin was almost as pale, and her long hair was a pale gold. She was skinny, a slender beam of pale light illuminating a dreary world. And she was barefoot. She reminded Richard of a painting of an angel he had once seen in a private collection of a wealthy merchant in Amsterdam. He had heard Marleigh described as 'unearthly' but had never agreed. To him, she was the opposite. As if the earth, rivers, trees and mountains had been made into a person. She was entirely of the earth, just more so than anyone else he had met. This woman was truly unearthly. Cold, distant, out of reach. A creature of awe.

As they walked past, the girl half turned and fixed her gaze on Richard. She looked like a recent survivor of some wasting disease. Gaunt, barely alive. Her eyes were the darkest he had ever seen, as if her pupils had devoured her irises. Stark, like pieces of coal in snow. She did not pause, did not blink, but her eyes never left his until she disappeared again, his view blocked by the crowd. They were on their way to the gaol. The Maid of Rainow was to meet with Marleigh and Eva.

He shivered and gulped in air, realising he had been

holding his breath. He shook himself out of what seemed like a waking dream and then nearly jumped out of his skin as a voice spoke right behind him.

"Who the fuck was that then? Is that her? Didn't think that was your type."

A heavy hand slapped him on the back and an odour of sweat drifted around him.

He recovered his composure and turned. "And where the fuck have you been? Did you decide to walk back from York?"

"It's funny you should say that. Buy me a drink and a bath and I'll tell you. Make it a big drink and a long bath as I have much to tell. You'll need a drink too, but I'm not sharing the bath."

*

"You're sure about this?"

Roger had filled him in on the conversation with Brereton when he had handed over Richard's letter, and had given him the letter Brereton had written in response. Richard had told the tavernkeeper to send word both to the gaol and to the magistrate.

"The poor fucker lost a few parts of his anatomy before he told me. Nothing 'e won't miss too much. He thought he was going to die. I didn't prompt him; he came up with the name. All by himself. It's the truth."

Roger was deep into his second cup of wine. He smelt and felt much better after a bath and an hour's sleep. "And if I had known he would ride off on the only horse left I would have killed him."

"I have waited for information like this for a long time. I have done… terrible things trying to find this man. And now, it seems, he is coming to me."

"That is my thinking. When he said he was with Cobb's

(12 July 1644)

merry band of butchers, I thought it better to let him go and drop some hints as to where you were."

"You're cleverer than you look."

"Fuck off. It wasn't that long ago you were begging me, in fact paying me, to teach you to be just like me. Remember those days? And I'm not sure you ever paid up, come to think of it."

"Different people. Different lives."

"Huh. So Cobb and his men have been haunting the main passes over the Pennines looking for poor sods like me, carrying messages back and forth. Or vulnerable detachments of troops to ambush. They looked a professional lot. They have been carrying out this campaign all over the country. Like Old Queen Bess used her privateers to harass the Spanish shipping. Cobb is just a licensed bandit. Got a taste for it after torching estates across East Anglia. Yes. He mentioned that too. I didn't ask. A whole new career opened up for him and he has been busy ever since."

"And it seems he hasn't forgotten me."

"Not forgotten. Not forgiven. This fucker knew your name too. Knew you would be travelling to and from Brereton. 'Just luck it was Farrell,' he said. They had a man in Cromwell's camp and as part of 'is spying, he passed on the name of the officer who would be travelling west. Your name. Cobb just assumed it was you."

"So we can go looking for him. Cobb. When this business here is over. We will go looking for him and finish it. Will you come with me?"

"And what about your new responsibilities, Captain? What about Cromwell and Brereton?"

"Fuck them both. I don't owe them anything, but there is a debt outstanding between me and John Cobb. That takes precedence. After that, if I survive it, I will pick it up again. It's war. Who is to say what happened when, and with whom?"

Roger shrugged. It clearly didn't bother him either way.

He could feel the familiar tide of hate rising. His heart quickening and his mouth drying. But he stemmed it. He had to. There were other things he had to do first.

"Anyway," Roger said, "I'm glad your urgent need to visit this shithole of a town wasn't because of that woman you were gawping at earlier. That would have been a real disappointment and I would have had to revise my opinion of you. I've seen more meat on a butcher's apron. And those eyes! They would haunt you for days after – and not in a good way!"

"That was she as they call 'the Maid of Rainow'. And she spells trouble for us."

"Oh? What's a 'Rainow'?"

"What? It's a village. A few miles north-east. In the hills." He sighed. "Apparently, she can speak to God. Or God speaks to her. Gives her special insights into witches. He tells her who and where, and she points the finger. Got two girls hanged not so long ago. Now she is a local miracle, and everyone is shit-scared of her."

"Sounds more like she is the witch. Certainly looks the part…"

"I reckon the magistrate will see through her. I didn't see him for long but he seemed a practical man. A practical man keen to be gone from here. But Marleigh is worried this Maid may incite enough hystericals and fanatics that he opts for an easy life to keep them happy. Seems just like a fraud to me. The man with her? Her brother? He handles the coin apparently. Like a freak show, but with a bit more resting on the outcome."

"So we just ignore it? If Brereton is judging too, then it can't matter. Surely?"

"I don't know. I tell you, Roger, the thought of losing her, after... all that has happened. I don't want to take any chances, but I don't know what to do about it. How do you fight that kind of thing? People believe this stuff and believe it deeply enough to burn people alive for it."

Roger scratched absentmindedly at the table top with the point of his dagger. "I see your point. It is a shock to find out you are a father. You, for the first time. Me, to find out all over again. Knocks you back a bit."

"Jesus, Roger. I'm sorry! You have hardly spoken of it since I gave you the news, and I had forgotten in my own selfishness. Have you changed your mind? What will you do?"

"I don't know. I am still thinking on it, and I will think on it some more. Listening to you talk about Eva... It was Eva, your daughter? I can't help but think about my son. What age would he be? What would he be doing now? What sort of man would I be if my child came back from the dead and I just shrugged and went on my way?"

Not really knowing what to say, Richard just nodded.

"Leave Her Maidship to me, Rich. I'll think of something. We will get your family free. We'll settle the account with Cobb. Then perhaps you can help me find my wife and son."

"You have my word." He paused. "You are not going to murder her, are you?"

"Best you don't know, don't you think?"

"Aye. Probably so. And actually, now I think of it, I don't really care. Not if it gets Marleigh and Eva free."

Roger nodded and sheathed the dagger. To Richard, more than ever, it seemed that Roger was one of the most complex people he knew. Cynical yet sentimental. Self-centred but loyal. Full of humour one moment, and a cold-hearted killer the next. He was glad he knew him, and glad he wasn't the enemy.

"I need to go and prepare for tomorrow," he said. "The other thing Sir Edward said to me was that someone needed to speak for Marleigh in the trial. Seems like there is no one but me. I haven't much of a clue where to start. I guess I just aim to annoy the shit out of Smale, the prosecutor, and smile winningly at the magistrate. And I need to try to speak to Brereton before the morning."

"Is that a good idea? Is there no one who is more detached from this than yourself? Losing your cool and punching someone in the middle of the trial will not endear you to the magistrate, even if you are making doe eyes at him."

"I know, but I can't see anyone else stepping forward. I am a different man, Roger, since Marston field. Maybe this is, in a way, some kind of trial for me as well. I will see you in the guildhall tomorrow. Be careful."

"Always. It's why I have lived so long."

A sudden idea came to him. "Look, Roger, I don't know if this will do any good, but I know someone who might be able to help you with your plan for the Maid…"

22

THE TRIAL

(13 July 1644)

He had arrived early and had found his seat behind a long table which ran down one side of the hall. They had thrown white linen over it, probably to disguise that it was normally a banqueting table. To William, it looked like the table from a painting he had seen of Christ's last supper. He wondered which disciple the position of his seat matched him with. Thomas? Paul? Judas?

Behind him, windows looked west, down onto the north end of the marketplace. The glass had been polished, and as he peered out, he could see people making their way across the open space, or east along the Chestergate, or south from Titherington. The guildhall would be packed. It was not every day a woman was on trial for her life, accused of making a pact with the Devil. He hoped the constable could control the numbers. He had offered the services of his small military escort, and Constable Roe had gratefully accepted.

The guildhall was a stone building, about fifty years old. The hall itself was on the upper floor, above an arcade of shops. Two of his men were positioned at the main door, at the bottom of the stairs, standing with Roe to cast an eye over those looking to attend the trial. The other four were in the hall with him. Two by the entrance and two in the opposite corners. In front of him, rows of benches, chairs and stools were laid out in motley rows, some clearly borrowed from the parish church, just a hundred yards away. In front of him to the left and right were the smaller tables behind which the accused and those prosecuting would sit. As yet, these were empty.

It had been late when he had ridden into the town. The sky had been clear and full of stars, but chilly for midsummer. He had passed the ruins of the castle as he climbed the Mill Street into the marketplace. The central turret and the porch were still standing, but the other walls were rubble, gradually being pilfered for house building elsewhere in the town. It had been too late to find accommodation, and so he had woken the constable and he had found the means to open the guildhall. Brereton had written letters for an hour or so and then dozed in a chair until the dawn had woken him. He felt little rested and irritable, and was impatient for the trial to start and to rejoin the men marching north in search of Rupert.

The smell of the bakery next door had drawn him out onto the street and he had breakfasted on warm, fresh bread, the remains of which clung to the white cloth, defying his attempts to brush them away as they stuck in the weave. He kept returning to the table to try to rid himself of the mess he had created, and it had done nothing to improve his mood.

He heard bootsteps coming up the stone stairs, and he turned from the window. He caught a brief conversation outside the hall with his men, and Farrell entered, looking slightly flustered and out of breath. He noticed the man was not in uniform but carried a cavalry sword – an ornate and expensive-looking rapier. *Prepared for trouble? The constable did not see fit to confiscate the weapon?*

(13 July 1644)

"Good morning, Sir William!" Farrell hurried across to him, sweeping off his hat. "I tried to see you last night, but you must have arrived very late."

"I did indeed. And have barely slept. It seems things have escalated rather more than I had hoped."

"Yes. They have. Despite my efforts."

"Captain, quickly, tell me what has occurred here. What do you expect to see today?"

For the next fifteen minutes, Farrell provided him with the story. The accusation and the accuser. The identity of the prosecutor. The vigil and the examination. The coming of the Maid and what that implied. He also admitted that he had stepped forward to represent Marleigh Hume, as no others had volunteered.

Brereton sat through it all in silence. As Farrell finished, others were now filing into the hall. He took a step closer to Farrell and lowered his voice. "I have heard, vaguely, of this Smale. An insignificant man in many ways perhaps, but he has a reputation as a godly man. What is your impression of him?"

Farrell raised a hand to shield his mouth as he replied. "Sir William, I have seen nothing to suggest that. He has the words, and can strike a pose, but he is, above all, a coward. He can bully women, but I think met his match with Marle... Mistress Hume."

"Hmm. And this... what is her name? This Maid of Rainow? I have not heard of her, but I recall the hangings you mention."

"Apparently that was her doing. She backed up the accuser of the women. I have my doubts about her, General. We have seen her brother seemingly taking coin for her to appear."

"That is a serious accusation. Men and women have been burnt for acting as if God spoke through them. Those not of the Church, of course. Well, I suppose we will soon have an opportunity to make our own judgement." He tried to sound nonchalant as he came to the question he most wanted to ask. "And you say she has a child? The letter from Mistress Eliza Walker did not mention a child."

"Yes, General. She has a daughter. I would guess at a little over two years old? A very bright little thing. But this could be a problem. Unfortunately, she is odd-eyed. Mismatched. I am sure you have seen it in dogs. I had a horse once with the same thing. The problem is, some are saying it is a sign the child is unnatural."

"I see. Most unusual." Quietly, Brereton was horrified. He had heard tales on his travels on the continent of this. It was true. People there had called it the evil eye. Such children were lucky to make it to teenage years. But it was not what he really wanted to know. He tried again. "And, Farrell, do you know who the father is? It may have an important bearing."

Farrell immediately looked awkward. *Hmm. Some local noble frightened of a scandal no doubt and refusing to come forward*, he thought. He struggled to keep his emotions under control. *A child! Why does this churn my stomach? All we ever did was exchange words. Why does a child, born of a common woman, cause me such anguish?*

"Farrell? If you know, I need to know."

Farrell was about to answer when he felt a hand on his upper arm. He turned. An elderly man, with shoulder-length white hair and grey eyes, all in black with a large white lace collar, stood with his hand out. "Ah, Sir Edward! It is good to see you again. I trust you are well, sir. And your lady wife? I am sorry we have to meet again in such terrible circumstances."

With a surprisingly strong voice for someone of his age, Sir Edward Savage cut an impressive figure. "Thank you, Sir William. Yes, I am well, and all the better for seeing you here. I was so very pleased and grateful that you have offered to share the bench with me. These are extraordinary times and it seems God has sent me an extraordinary solution to my problem. I thank you, sir. And I thank you also for your dashing captain here." He nodded at Farrell who now stood behind Brereton's left shoulder. "He has kindly offered to stand as representative for the accused. I know he has no legal experience, but I cannot see this being a complicated case. Indeed, I am as anxious as you to see this over with as soon as possible."

Brereton half glanced back over his shoulder. "Farrell is Cromwell's man, not mine. He is only temporarily attached to my staff. I hope he can acquit himself honourably today."

Savage seemed slightly taken aback. "I am sure he will. I am sure he will."

"What is the timetable for the trial, Sir Edward? It is some time since I acted as magistrate and certainly I have never been involved in a trial relating accusations of witchcraft."

"Well, come to that, neither have I. However, I thought it best to start with the prosecution case. Jeremiah Smale acts for the accuser and there is certain procedural evidence to review first. The examination and the vigil for, erm, imps. I am sure you are aware of these procedures?"

"I am aware, sir, but only dimly. It seems that the East Anglian counties have seen more of these trials than most. I have heard and read a few reports of these events."

"Well, I think it will be largely self-evident. After this, I feel we should hear from the accuser, a local woman. Farming family. After this, any other witnesses called by the prosecution. This should take us to lunch. We can discuss and review at that point. We can hear the defence in the afternoon and I hope we can get to a verdict this evening."

"Agreed. It would serve me well to be gone from this place tonight. I have other important meetings before I rejoin the army. This takes up too much time already."

"Indeed, Sir William. But justice must be served. I am sure you will agree. Now. Where is our colleague? I am expecting Thomas Elcock to join us at the bench. He was nominated by Master Smale, which is irregular, but I can find no bad reports of him. He is a rising force amongst the godly, I hear. The local minister – Stringer? He tells me the man is honest and, erm, extremely diligent in rooting out sinners. Have you met the minister?"

Brereton shook his head, but Farrell nodded. "Yes, I met with him recently. He helped me with a matter."

Brereton looked sideways at Farrell and raised an eyebrow in enquiry. Farrell seemed keen to respond, but the presence of Savage clearly inhibited him for some reason.

At that moment, there was a small commotion at the doorway to the hall. A man, all in black and wearing a wide-brimmed black hat, strode purposefully across to meet them. He was young, perhaps in his early thirties, and carried a bible in his right hand. But in the background, Brereton also couldn't help notice that Farrell's man – who was it? DeLacey? – was following the newcomer towards their group. As he heard Savage greet the man as Elcock, he noticed DeLacey slip a small note into Farrell's hand and move off to a seat at the back of the hall.

"Sir William? I was just saying, this is Thomas Elcock. As I mentioned, he has kindly agreed to join us on the bench in judgement of this case. Master Elcock, let me introduce the commander of the parliamentary forces in the North-West, Sir William Brereton."

Brereton could feel himself going through the motions with Elcock. The man seemed competent enough, and he had had some legal training prior to devoting himself to joining the Church. The truth was, his mind was engaged elsewhere, trying to map out a way through this mess. A way that would

(13 July 1644)

allow him to leave as soon as possible while conducting the important business he had with the sequesters and Alderman Booth. All the while his guts churned at the thought of seeing Marleigh Hume again. He had held a picture of her in his mind all these years and the prospect of seeing her again, in the flesh, was a small torture to him. He gathered himself together. He would do what had to be done and then he would ride to his men. God's great command to him remained unfulfilled. He had work to do.

The pleasantries over, he made his excuses and made his way to his seat behind the long table. He leant on his elbows, chin cupped between his hands. He saw that Farrell was now also sitting behind the table prepared for the defender of Marleigh Hume. He looked even more nervous than he himself felt, going through various pieces of paper and glancing anxiously towards a second door at the rear of the hall. Brereton watched as a well-dressed man entered through the main door and sought out Farrell. He handed him a sheet of paper and watched as Farrell signed it. He then also signed it and left it with Farrell. Farrell stood, and they shook hands. Curious. He leaned towards Savage who had now joined him behind the table. "Who is that?" He nodded towards the man who was now taking a seat a few rows behind Farrell.

Savage peered. "Ah! I think that is, erm, Brough. Yes, that is him. Brough. He is a lawyer acting for the Walker family. He has some say in the estate of the late Samuel Walker. A trustee, I believe. He and Smale, the other trustee, are at loggerheads apparently."

Brereton nodded. Some procedural issue, no doubt. More people were now entering the hall. A fat, florid man, again dressed largely in black, marched across to the table opposite the bench, and a few yards distant from Farrell's. *That would be Smale, I guess.* He was interested to see him give Farrell a wide berth as he walked to his seat. Farrell stared at him as he crossed the floor. A look of real menace. He had been followed into the room by a young, slim, blonde girl, he guessed about mid-teenage. Even from here he could see her piercing blue eyes. She was already a beauty, although he could also see she was nervous. He watched as Farrell greeted her and then brought her towards the table.

He stood as they approached.

Farrell introduced them. "Sir William, this is Eliza Walker, the elder daughter of the late Samuel Walker." He smiled faintly. "Mistress Eliza is the letter writer…"

Brereton bowed briefly, and lightly shook Eliza's hand. "Mistress Walker. It is a pleasure to meet you. Your father was a good man and is surely now with God. Thank you for your correspondence. I am happy to be able to attend this… event… if it is of some service to you."

Eliza was flushed with embarrassment. Brereton doubted she had ever seriously thought that her letter would have had the effect that it did. "Sir William. I cannot tell you…" She stopped, clearly very nervous at meeting such a great man, and tried to regain her composure. "Sir William. I cannot tell you how honoured and grateful we are that you have come here today. My father held you in such high regard and your letter following his untimely death was of great comfort to me and my sister. I knew of no one else to turn to over this matter. We trust and hope that this unjust and ridiculous accusation can now be laid to rest."

Brereton chose his words carefully. "Mistress Walker, I am here to help Sir Edward," he indicated Savage, sitting to his left, "to reach the correct verdict. You are convinced of the innocence of your governess, Mistress Hume. I am sure your judgement is sound, but of course I must be guided by God and the evidence."

(13 July 1644)

He saw Eliza glance sideways at Farrell, a slightly worried look on her face. When she faced him again, her expression was one of quiet determination. "Then I am even more confident that justice will prevail. Thank you again, Sir William, for coming to our aid." She turned slightly and shook the hand offered by Savage, who now stood. As Elcock was deep in conversation with Smale, Eliza bowed slightly to both Brereton and Savage, and went to sit next to Brough, just behind the table where Farrell sat, going through various papers.

Brereton sat again, watching the room fill up with townsfolk. After a while, he noticed alderman, Captain Booth, sitting with the Minister; Stringer. He caught Booth's eye and nodded slightly. He must catch up with the man before the end of the day. On Booth's other side was a lady dressed in simple Puritan style, although her clothes were clearly of high quality. She kept her eyes to the floor, a picture of modesty. But Brereton knew, as only a handful of other people did, that this woman was one of his most effective agents. She had been visiting prominent Royalist supporters in Shropshire, and he was keen to hear her reports.

Through the doorway, he saw two of his bodyguard appear at the top of the stairs with the constable. This meant the main doors were now shut. *A prudent move.*

Elcock drifted back towards the main table, his conversation with Smale concluded. *No need to read the runes on which way Elcock will lean in his judgement.* He approached Savage, leaning on the edge of the table so he could speak just above a whisper. He seemed excited, his eyes shining with emotion.

"Sir Edward, Sir William. I have the most excellent news. Master Smale has informed me that we have the honour of the presence of the Maid of Rainow today. She arrived in the town yesterday evening, having made a barefoot pilgrimage from her hillside home. She is willing to attend the session and provide her testimony." He beamed at them both.

Savage looked sideways at Brereton, his face unreadable. "That is, erm, good news indeed, sir. She is, then, a witness to events surrounding the accused?"

Elcock looked slightly confused. "Well, er, no. I don't think so."

Savage smiled, helpfully. "So, perhaps a character witness? She knows the accused well?"

"I... I don't think so. No." His bafflement was increasing.

"Ah. I see. What then is her testimony regarding, sir?"

Elcock leaned in again, voice low but intense. "Sir. Respectfully. She is the Maid of Rainow. All around here know of her. She is the scourge of the unrighteous. She is our shield against those who bargain with Satan. With witches and their craft." He almost hissed the word 'witches'. "She asks God for his judgement on these wretches and He speaks to her. She has been a fierce and mighty warrior for God." He leaned in further still. *Any closer and he will touch noses with Savage*, Brereton thought. "Some say she is one of His angels on earth. If you had met her, you might say the same."

But Savage seemed unimpressed. "Sir. A care, please. I admire your passion, but we are trying Mistress Marleigh Hume for witchcraft today. I do not wish to invoke charges of blasphemy against others in the court."

Elcock stood back, shocked, his face paling. "I... Sir, I do not think you comprehend... My meaning was to..."

Savage held up a gnarly blue-veined hand. "Peace, Master Elcock. I am aware of the lady's reputation. The three of us will consider this question over lunch. First let us hear the earthly evidence and testimony afore we engage in alleged divine insights. Perhaps, in the face of what we will hear this

(13 July 1644)

morning, we need not bother the Maid, and she can return in peace to her home. For surely, miserable as we are, God will also direct us to a just decision? Are we agreed?"

Elcock bowed, resuming a more florid complexion. "Indeed, Sir Edward. A fine plan." As he moved away to negotiate the end of the long table, and to gain his seat, Savage turned to Brereton. "Our judgement will, I think, be based on the danger of a riot if we refuse this woman's testimony."

Brereton, who had seen Elcock's worried glance to Smale over Savage's shoulder, shrugged. "Let us discuss this later, sir. As you say." For himself, he was intrigued by the idea of hearing this Maid. His experiences and meetings in the Low Countries had rid him of some of the scepticism that Savage clearly held to. *Why not let the cards fall, and then we will see.*

With the level of noise in the hall rising in expectation, Savage looked to his left and right and nodded to his colleagues. He caught the eyes of both Farrell and Smale, nodded again, and then stood. He had a small wooden mallet, which he now banged three times on the table.

In the voice of one used to being heard and obeyed, Savage started the hearing. "Ladies and gentlemen, officers of the court and my fellow judges, we are gathered today to hear the truth of the most grievous accusation of witchcraft against a citizen of this town. Please hear me clearly. I am magistrate. This is my court. I will not tolerate abusive or foul language, intimidation, or riot. I will say this only once. I am very thankful to my two colleagues today for their assistance in trying this matter. As some of you may know, normally any case of witchcraft would be heard at the assizes in Chester but clearly, in the current situation, this is not possible. Therefore, to add weight to the judgement I have co-opted two prominent men of the North-West to support me in this task, to add their wisdom, insight and godliness to the proceedings. Are there any who object? If so, this is your only opportunity to do so."

Savage looked specifically from Smale to Farrell, but there was no response. As he went on to outline the process for the session, Brereton scanned the people in front of him. His eyes lighted upon a small, pinched-faced woman sitting almost immediately behind Smale. *Ah yes. The accuser.* He vaguely remembered this woman from the confrontation at the market in Wincle. She avoided his eye, but he knew she remembered him all too clearly. *An awkward day for her then,* he thought grimly.

Savage wrapped up and also surveyed the wash of faces in front of him. It was a scene of muted greys and blacks, with splashes of white from expensive lace collars and cuffs. White faces of townsfolk, and brown faces from those who laboured in the outdoors. All looked at Savage expectantly. He didn't disappoint them. He looked to the back of the hall where the constable stood by the second door. He banged down the mallet making more than a few jump in their seats. "Bring in the accused!"

The constable bowed and slipped out through the door with one of Brereton's soldiers. A moment later he was back. He stepped back through the door and then stood to one side to allow the accused to enter. As she did, he took her by one arm and started to lead her down the room between the two banks of seats, like a proud father leading his daughter down the aisle. The soldier followed.

Brereton's gut knotted again. He had expected to see her beaten down. Unkempt, dirty and ragged from her time in gaol. Weighed down with a few more hard years since he had last seen her. A sight to pity.

But as she reached her seat, in the gap between the tables occupied by Smale and Farrell, she looked up at the bench and immediately caught his eye. His heart raced in his chest and he thought he was going to be sick. Yes, she looked exhausted. Yes, her clothes were not exactly fresh. But in every other way, she was the Marleigh Hume he had met all those years ago as he exercised his dogs in the gloom of the Dane Valley. She still possessed that unearthliness that had grabbed his soul then. Her warm eyes and glowing skin, to him, seemed to hold some internal light. An impossible vigour radiated from her, and when their eyes met, he thought she looked right to the heart of him and his deepest thoughts. And yet, at the same time, he felt an immense depth within her as well. He couldn't make sense of it, but it was like looking back in time, across centuries. He felt dizzy and gripped the table.

He broke her gaze and looked down. It was only then that he realised that not everyone seemed as enraptured as he. There was a low sound from many of those present. A noise of fear and dread and hate. He saw that Marleigh's accuser could barely contain herself as her eyes flitted between the accused and Savage, almost pleading for permission to launch abuse.

Savage, still standing, again banged down his mallet, and the murmuring and muttering slowly subsided. He motioned the constable to step away and then addressed Marleigh.

"You stand before us accused of the horrific crime of witchcraft and of compact with Satan. You will receive a fair and just hearing from us today. You will have your chance, later in the proceedings, to speak on your own account, if you so wish. However, before we begin, would you please state your name and your normal place of residence for the records of the court."

Marleigh collected herself and brushed some wayward hair back under her coif. "If it pleases Your Honour, my name is Marleigh. Marleigh Farrell, recently of the Walker household in the Mill Street of this town."

There was silence.

Savage looked down at the paper in front of him, and then back to her. "Are you not mistaken? Your legal representative here…" he nodded towards Farrell, "…is named Farrell. Is your name not Hume? Marleigh Hume?"

She looked him in the eye and answered, "Aye. My name *was* Hume. But now I am wed, sir. I am married to Captain Farrell, just recently. I have taken his name, as is custom."

The guildhall erupted in noise. As Savage banged the mallet to little effect, Brereton's mind turned black.

*

Roger watched the commotion from the back of the hall with interest and no little amusement. He noted the look that swept across Brereton's face: first consternation and disbelief but then – and this was the interesting part – a black rage that he struggled to hide. He had gripped the table edge and stared first at Marleigh and then at Richard with a violent malevolence. Perhaps it had been a mistake not to tell Brereton of this turn of events – the man who always prided himself on his use of agents to gain intelligence for his planning and scheming. He guessed his professional pride had been wounded. Never mind. He would recover and see the wisdom of the move. He marked this to pass on to Richard later.

His amusement stemmed from watching Smale and Brassey absorbing this revelation. They both did passable impressions of fish, opening and closing their mouths, looking at each other helplessly. *First blood for the good people.* He reflected on seemingly finding himself on the good side, whatever that meant. Perhaps he had turned a corner himself. Then he thought about the events of the previous night and thought maybe he hadn't.

(13 July 1644)

He had known of the wedding, in fact he and Richard had discussed the merits of taking the step. For Richard, it had been a moral and emotional decision. He had discovered he had brought a child into the world, currently a very dangerous world, and above everything else he wanted to protect Eva.

Roger had also pointed out that Marleigh would have a better standing if she was married, particularly if she was wed to a war hero. Of course, he had also pointed out that perhaps Marleigh would not agree, and Richard had concurred that this was a distinct possibility. After all, he still knew very little about her. There was a sense that there was a past to her that he had not come close to exploring. He had no idea how she would take his proposal.

His friend clearly had ambiguous feelings about Marleigh. Roger was in the dark on this, as he had never seen the woman, let alone spoken to her or, you know, the other things… Richard's feelings for his daughter, and her safety, were entirely definite. Everything else was secondary and could be dealt with once the crisis had passed. Everything else obviously included what he would do about regaining the love of his life, Neelie, who he had previously betrayed through his jealousy and stupidity. *Hmm.*

Richard had approached the minister, Stringer, who had no reason to oppose performing a ceremony, despite his misgivings and dire warnings, and had accompanied Richard on the final visit to the gaol before the trial. Marleigh had warned Richard of the potential consequences for his reputation, but it was their shared concern for Eva that had persuaded her to the idea. The constable and his wife had stood as witnesses. Richard had given Roger the news on his return from his adventures to and fro over those bloody cold and wet Pennines.

Roger had seen the exchange with Brough before the magistrate had started proceedings and assumed this must be the completion of his formal adoption of Eva. So far, so good. He settled back in his chair to enjoy the show. Surely this would not take too long to resolve and then they could think about the next steps. For Richard, untangling the unholy mess he had made of his life. For Roger, well, pretty much the same. He had a family out there he needed to find and blight once more. Oh, yes. And of course there was an ongoing brutal civil war they had a part to play in. Mustn't forget that.

Savage had just about restored order and was now confirming Marleigh's statement with all those involved: Richard, the constable and the minister. Brereton's face was now impassive again, but Elcock was looking a little uncomfortable and kept shooting glances at Smale.

Savage then asked about Marleigh's daughter, and her whereabouts. "I have heard much of this, erm, child, you understand. There are certain accusations as to the provenance of the infant, especially given the fact your former, erm, husband has never been seen by anyone in this town."

Provenance, thought Roger. *Interesting way of putting it.* He could see most of the gathered people were trying to work out exactly what the magistrate had asked.

"Your Honour. As I have told a number of people," she turned to look at Smale, "my former husband, who hailed from Stafford-way, went to fight papists in the Low Countries. I have not seen him since he left, and that were nearly ten years ago. I have been a faithful wife to him, even to the extent of turning down offers of marriage from reputable local men." Now she turned and looked at Brassey. *If looks could kill*, thought Roger.

"But there came a point when I finally believed what many had said to me. So many men fighting in this war with the King are returned from the overseas wars that I was sure that, if he were still alive, my husband would have returned also. But

(13 July 1644)

he did not, sir. I am resolved that he is dead in some foreign country. To answer your question, Your Honour, I know my daughter to now have her true father as her guardian. Captain Farrell did... Well, he... Some years ago, Captain Farrell was in the town on business..." She was struggling to find acceptable words for the powerful men sitting in judgement.

Try 'provenance', thought Roger, who was amusing himself watching the back of Richard's neck turn scarlet.

She seemed to recall a particular fact. "In fact, I believe he was in the employ of Sir William Brereton at the time. While he was in town, we met, on a number of occasions."

"You met Sir William?"

"No! No, sir. Captain Farrell. I had resolved to move on with my life and accept my husband's death, and well, things went from there. It was Captain Farrell who secured the governess role for me with the Walker household."

Roger could see Eliza Walker nodding vigorously in ascent. Savage acknowledged her with a slight nod of his head.

"I see. Captain Farrell, can you confirm all of this?"

Richard stood, sweat beaded on his forehead. "I can, Your Honour. We became... close... during my time here. I was impressed with Mistress Farrell's accomplishments..."

"Sounds like it!" came a shout from the back of the hall, which raised some laughter, more noises of indignation, given the puritanical leanings of the gathering.

"Order!" shouted Savage, quelling the noise with a bang of his mallet.

"Sir, Mistress Farrell was formerly a governess, her father having been a teacher of repute. She seemed an ideal candidate for a vacancy that Master Samuel Walker had. And Master Walker agreed." He glared round at the rows behind him, and Roger noticed how the name of the dead man was more effective at dampening the mirth than Savage's lump of wood had been. "Your Honour, Sir William can confirm my duties were on his behalf and that the, ah, timing is correct. I am sure there may be one or two honourable gentlemen sitting here today, who can remember meeting with me at that time. We were to build an alliance of reputable men in support of Sir William and the Parliament. I spoke with the minister, and with Master Brough, the Walker family's lawyer, and both approved the wedding and my formal adoption of Mistress Farrell's daughter, Eva. Sir, I have tried to do the honourable thing, as prior to a few days ago, I was not aware of Eva's existence, or her, ah, provenance."

Oh bravo, smiled Roger.

"I see. Very well, Captain. You may sit. This casts altogether a different light on proceedings. Nevertheless, despite the change in your status…" Savage gave a thin-lipped, grim smile, "…we must hear the case in full and decide our judgement on the evidence. On the facts of the matter. Mistress Hume, erm, Farrell, please take your seat."

He looked up and addressed the gathering as a whole. "Now we will start that process. I call as first witness, Mistress Roe!"

Roger sat back and listened as the constable's wife went through a description of the task that she and the other goodwives had performed. There were some leers among the audience, but also many sympathetic faces and small cries of dismay from some of the women, as the details of the examination of Marleigh's body were laid out for the judges. Roger had to admit that this Marleigh Farrell seemed a remarkable woman. She did not flinch or change her expression as the description progressed, but sat straight-backed on her chair, eyes seemingly staring into the distance. She was an attractive woman and he would have been hard pressed to put an age to her.

(13 July 1644)

Sarah Roe finished her testimony, which was to conclude that they had found no suspicious marks, growths, tumours or other blemishes on her body.

Savage now asked Smale if he had any questions for the witness.

Smale rose and swung round to address his audience, turning his back on the three who were to judge the accusation. *Puffed-up, self-important prick*, concluded Roger. *I don't believe he cares about the verdict at all. This is all about looking the big man in front of the little people.*

"You say, Mistress Roe, that after your long and, may I say, very diligent examination..." he smiled greasily, "...you found no blemishes or marks of any kind on the witch?"

"Now, Master Smale, you know you cannot use that term until anything is proven. Please, mind your language and curb your enthusiasm, sir." Savage then nodded for Sarah Roe to respond.

"That is correct, sir. There was not a mark on her." She addressed her response to the bench, ignoring Smale.

"Mistress Roe, do you not think it unusual for a woman of her age, and background, to be so unmarked? Is it not suspicious to you? Surely, the granting of such a perfect, unblemished skin could be precisely the sort of gift that Satan would bestow on his servants!" His voice rose as he spoke, finishing with a flurry and a finger pointed to heaven. He was rewarded with a murmuring around the gathered people and he beamed, delighted at his own cleverness. Roger saw Elcock nodding along in agreement. Even Brereton made a note on the paper in front of him.

Sarah Roe, despite her nervousness when giving her evidence, was not daunted. "Well, sir, that may be so, or it may not, for I do not have experience of examining other women's skin in the way that we were required to here. Only my own, and my daughter's, when she was a young girl. Maybe you have more knowledge of this than me."

Smale's smugness vanished in an instant, and he flushed scarlet as the laughter built around him. Even Savage struggled to contain a grin. "I am a man of God, mistress. I rely on his wisdom to judge these matters." He drew himself up and attempted to quell the mirth with a stern glare around the room. "Nevertheless, it is quite plausible that this wit... the accused, could have drawn on demonic help to disguise her true form during the examination, and this should be borne in mind. What more would a woman desire from her master than the illusion of desirability?" He looked scornfully across at Richard. "At least desirability to some. To those that cannot use the grace of God to pierce the veil of evil to see the truth beneath."

Again, murmuring through the gathering. Sides were being taken. Opinions were being formed. *More note-taking for Brereton*, observed Roger.

As Smale sat down, self-importance re-establishing itself over embarrassment and indignation, Savage looked across at Richard. "Any questions from you, Captain?"

Richard stood. "Thank you, sir. Mistress Roe, thank you for your brave testimony. I have but two questions. Firstly, from Master Smale's statements, it would seem that if you had found marks or blemishes about Mistress Farrell's person it would mean she was a witch, but also, the lack of such marks and blemishes would also make her a witch. Would you agree that this does not make any sense?"

"To me, sir, it does not, but I am not as learned as Master Smale or those sitting in judgement."

"Thank you. I am also not learned, but I agree that there seems to be no sense in it. Secondly, Mistress Roe, during the examination, did Marleigh... I am sorry, the accused, protest or make any attempt to hinder your work or try to beguile you in any way?"

"No, sir, she did not. I would have hated to have to sit through what she did. Any person would. But she bore the indignity quietly and with politeness. In fact, she seemed more concerned for the women conducting the work than herself."

"Thank you, Mistress Roe." He looked across to Savage and nodded his head, sitting down.

Before Savage could release Sarah Roe, Smale said loudly, "Which just proves my point even more. 'Any normal person' would, she said. So, what does that make this woman?"

Savage banged his mallet and glared at Smale. "Sir. You will not make any statements to the gathering here without my permission. Is that understood?"

"Certainly, Your Honour. My apologies, Your Honour." But he looked anything except apologetic, leaning back in his chair and nodding slightly at Mary Brassey, who looked like the shock of the news of Marleigh's marriage had begun to wear off.

With each piece of evidence, or statement made, a pebble was dropped into the pond and Roger could sense the ripples running back and forth through those present.

Savage remained on his feet and addressed the hall, gesturing for silence. "The other part of the process of identifying a witch is the vigil. These steps have been outlined by our previous sovereign king, James the First, and we have heard of their use in trials of those accused of witchcraft up and down the land. Women accused of witchcraft are said to convene with Satan, or his demons, to conduct evil and malicious acts. In return for their, erm, compliance, they receive gifts of imps to help carry out their master's bidding. They are also said to, erm, lie with the Devil or his demons."

There were shocked looks around the room. Women blushed and some people prayed quietly. Wives gripped their husbands' hands. Some had come to witness the trial to see good prevail and God's good justice served, but many more had come to gawp and to stock up on tales to gossip with their friends about over the long winter nights around the fire. This talk of the Devil and his demons, from a man as learned and respected as the magistrate, had brought the accusation into more real and stark terms. Despite the growing warmth of the summer sun outside, the temperature in the room seemed to drop a few degrees.

"The vigil," continued Savage, "lasts for three days and three nights, and a watch is kept of the accused by three people. Should any unusual events occur, or should an imp or a demon appear in the room and convene with the accused, the watchers are to note this down as evidence. The vigil of Mistress Hume, I am sorry, Mistress Farrell, was completed in the last few days and I have here the notes made by the watchers, who worked in shifts so that they might rest."

He picked up a small pile of papers on the table in front of him. "These notes were passed directly to me by the constable as soon as the vigil was completed. My colleagues here have already seen them, and I will show them to you now."

One by one he held up pieces of paper, showing the gathering both sides. All of them were entirely blank. "It is clear from this that none of the watchers sighted anything unusual during the vigil and as a result, there is no evidence that the accused has had any consort with the Devil, or his demons. Master Smale, you were one of the watchers. Is there anything you would add?"

Smale shook his head.

"Captain Farrell. Is there anything you wish to say at this point?"

Roger watched Richard stand. "Your Honour. I would just like to say that, as you outlined yourself earlier, these two processes – the examination and the vigil – have not delivered any evidence against the accused. I would ask that the learned men sitting in judgement therefore consider dismissing the accusation now, saving the accused further distress, and saving the valuable time of yourself and your colleagues."

Immediately, Smale was on his feet. "I object most strenuously to this!" Again, the colour was rising in his florid face. "There are witnesses to call. Witnesses with convincing testimony to make before you." Savage was already making 'sit down' gestures with his palms down, but Smale continued. "And, Your Honour, above all, there is the testimony of the Maid of Rainow to consider. She is present in the town and willing to speak to us. There is nothing closer to the voice of God than her words. Surely you will hear her? I think all of the town wish to listen to her judgement!"

He turned, impassioned, to face the hall. "Do you not wish to hear her voice, good people?"

A growing muttering turned into something louder. Roger sensed that Smale had found the sweet spot. No one wanted to be short-changed when they had made the effort to attend. Some through a wish to see God-given justice, but more for the freakshow. And what bigger freak than the Maid of Rainow? Either you believed she was appointed by God, in which case, this was a chance to see divine intervention close up. Or, she was a fake, but great entertainment nonetheless. Who knew what sparks might fly and brighten up their dull lives? No matters of procedure were going to rob them of this spectacle!

Some shouts were heard, and some stamped their feet in protest. Some of the godly even flourished bibles in the air.

Savage waited for the noise to die down. "Master Smale. I admire your enthusiasm and your passion. We will hear witnesses. By this I mean actual witnesses, meaning those people who have actually witnessed something."

Smale turned again to the gathered goodfolk of the town, arms wide in supplication. The babble of voices, underpinned with a sense of outrage, again started to build. Now Savage banged his mallet down, making many jump in surprise.

"Master Smale! You will resume your seat, sir! On the matter of this Maid of Rainow, I will discuss this with my colleagues, over the lunchtime recess, but I will not be bullied into accepting her testimony. There is no evidence, no evidence, sir, that she speaks directly from God's will, and one does not have to go too far back in our history to see how those who have made such claims before have paid for it with their lives. At the stake, sir. A terrible end in fire. Now. No more of that matter until later in the day. If you have witnesses to call, sir, I suggest you call the first one."

Smale, now slumped in his seat, looked embarrassed and not a little crestfallen. Roger saw Richard turn in his seat and seek him out through the rows of heads. Their eyes met, and Richard asked the question with a raised eyebrow. He looked a little more confident and relaxed now, as Savage, the key man behind the judgement table, seemed to be losing patience with Smale. Roger just shrugged back at him.

Smale rallied, raising his impressive bulk up again and calling Mary Brassey as his first witness.

*

Marleigh straightened her stiffening back as she tried to remain upright on the chair. After the ordeal of the vigil, the lack of sleep and the cramping that afflicted her muscles from balancing on that small wooden stool were catching up with her. The respite of one good night's sleep was not enough. As she stretched, she could feel muscles and ligaments popping in protest, but the sensation was better than the slowly growing, gripping ache. She had been reaching out with her mind to Eva and was reassured to find her being cared for by Mistress Roe back in her cell. Eva gave off waves of concern for her mother but confirmed she was safe and looked after, sitting in the little patch of sunshine that slowly traversed the room.

The other thing adding to her exhaustion was the ebb and flow of her emotions. As the morning wore on, she felt, in turn, both elated and desperate. The evidence against her was pitiful, and all the while she gazed intently at Savage, trying to work out how each new piece of information affected his opinion. She watched expressions chasing across his face as clouds cast their shadows across the moors on a sunny, windy day.

The rambling, venomous tale that Brassey was weaving around her droned on. Seemingly every ill that had ever befallen her family could somehow be lain at her feet. From a wet harvest of winter feed for the sheep, to an ailing bullock with foot rot, to the suicide of her brother-in-law. She lowered her head as this part of the story played out. He had been a good enough man. Perhaps the only good man in that malevolent, petty, vengeful family. In the end, he had been weak, but she had mourned his passing. For him, and for the potential ruin it was bringing on herself and Eva.

She saw Brereton leaning in to whisper to Savage as the tale of the marriage proposal unfolded. Savage listened intently, his respect for Brereton written large, his demeanour one of rapt attention. He nodded thoughtfully and made a few scratches on the paper in front of him. She was confused by Brereton and his motivations. She always had been, and it would not have been her choice to write to him, but Eliza had taken that decision out of her hands. He was too complex, too unreadable. It was clear she had some kind of hold over him, but even that seemed nuanced. It was more than lust, or imagined love, but difficult to pin down. Like the silk of a spider web – strong and binding but with an unknown breaking point.

He stared at her as she focused on Savage. She tried to avoid looking, but whenever she glanced his way, his gaze was bent on her. Probing. Assessing. Judging. He would vote to acquit, she had no doubts, but she was less sure of his motivations for doing so. Now she was back in his orbit, what were his plans for her?

Elcock, on the other hand, was an open book. A similar creature to Smale, she judged. All piety and vanity. Here was a chance to make his mark. Here was a chance to impress the God-fearing locals with his godliness and wisdom. She was a stepping stone for him. Nothing more. When this was over, perhaps she would get a chance to meet both Elcock and Smale without such a crowd. She smiled grimly to herself. *Now wouldn't that be fun.*

Smale guided Brassey along, pausing for effect when he felt an important point had been made, until he led her to the recent events in the town marketplace. Here she painted a picture of evil-doing that Marleigh, grudgingly, had to admire. As Brassey had watched, the sky had appeared to grow dark and the very air had swirled around above the witch's head. She had heard both mother and devil-child reciting incantations, with their attention fully fixed on the egg-seller. She had definitely smelt a sulphurous odour, and moments later, the egg-seller, a godly and well-respected goodwife, had inexplicably thrown a tray of eggs into the air, frightening a horse and rider and causing mayhem.

It was at that point that Mary Brassey, after a plea to the Almighty, had plucked up the courage to make her accusation.

Marleigh had to admit, it was a strong performance. She imagined the hours Smale and Brassey had sat together

(13 July 1644)

rehearsing. She had heard the reactions from the good people of Macclesfield at every revelation. Muttering. Gasps of horror. Of fear. She hadn't turned around, but kept her back to them, focused entirely on those behind the table.

Smale stopped, and now he turned from his audience to face the three sitting in judgement. "Your Honour. A veritable tale of evil and malice. A tale never before told in a quiet, godly town such as this. A powerful testimony from a brave member of the community, I am sure you will agree."

Before Savage could speak, Elcock banged the table with his fist. "Indeed, sir. Thank you, Mistress Brassey, for your courage in coming here today. Surely God has given you the strength to speak in his name!"

Savage looked in frustration at his colleague. Brereton was writing his notes again. Marleigh risked a glance at Richard. Her new husband. Not something she was yet used to thinking. The strangeness of being bound in law to another person still felt so alien. He had his head down, thoughtfully rubbing the knuckles on his right hand. The knuckles that had so recently flattened Mary Brassey's husband in a Macclesfield street.

Savage raised a hand to quieten the room. "Captain Farrell, do you have any questions for the witness?"

"Indeed, sir. Thank you." Richard stood. "Mistress Brassey, would you look at me?" Brassey, who had had her eyes fixed on Smale looking for guidance, reluctantly turned to face him. The room was deathly quiet, wondering what was to come.

Suddenly, with no warning, Richard slammed the palm of his hand down on the table. Mary Brassey jumped in surprise, as did half those gathered. Her hand shot to her mouth, her eyes wide. Richard smiled, and turned to Savage. "Imagine what would have happened if she had a tray of eggs in her hands when she had heard an unexpected loud noise." He turned to the room. "As you all saw, the witness was looking right at me, and still she jumped in shock. How much more might she have reacted if she was startled by some noise or commotion behind her?" Marleigh noticed Savage nodding quietly.

"Mistress Brassey. I apologise for frightening you. No more tricks from me. Just questions that require honest answers, for, remember, you are under oath and your soul is in mortal peril. You know the consequences for those who would waste the time of the magistrate and his illustrious colleagues, particularly in a time of civil conflict."

Brassey's face was a contortion of fear and hate. Marleigh could hear she was breathing heavily and shot glances in turn at Smale, Richard and herself, radiating malevolence.

"Mistress Brassey, would you say the marketplace was busy on the day in question?"

"Aye, sir. 'Tis always busy when a market is on."

"And you say that you witnessed strange noises, strange signs in the air around the accused? You say that Mistress Farrell was summoning the Devil himself, or his demons, to afflict the poor egg-seller?"

"Aye, sir. It was a terrifying sight. It was what drew my attention to the witch in the first place as I was just goin' about my business."

"So, you are saying that the accused, in a busy marketplace, full of potential witnesses to her actions, attempted to summon the Devil, or one of his demons – a sight that you claim to have witnessed in broad daylight – in order to, what? Break a dozen eggs? A rather risky strategy for rather a poor return, wouldn't you say?"

There was some sniggering in the room, and Marleigh saw Savage actually roll his eyes.

Brassey, blushing scarlet, nonetheless stood her ground. "I

know what I saw!" She raised her voice to be heard over the restless audience.

There is no going back now is there, Mary?

"But no one else did, did they? In a crowded marketplace, you would think the appearance of Satan would raise a few eyebrows?" A burst of laughter from the back of the room. Marleigh half turned and recognised Richard's rather odd friend, clearly enjoying the exchange. "People drop things every day. I do not doubt that it is not the first time that our good friend the egg-seller has dropped a tray of eggs. I do not doubt that she did so because something unexpected surprised her. But it seems that only you saw some unnatural cause. In other words, it is only on your word that you would have these gentlemen kill this woman." He gestured to Marleigh who kept her face carefully blank, and eyes downcast.

"So, perhaps we need to look at why you might make such a claim, and this brings us back to the events at Wincle some years ago. A time when you say that this woman witched your brother-in-law so that he first proposed marriage and, when refused, she drove him to kill himself. Suicide is a heinous crime before God!"

"Aye, 'tis all true. He were a good man who deserved better. Twas her malice that drove him to it. Everyone knew she weren't truly married. There was no husband in the foreign wars. She used that to keep men at bay, but then she whored her way around the district to make a livin'!"

"Mistress Brassey, again you make accusation with no proof. No evidence. I, myself, served in the siege at Breda in the Low Countries. I was there when the walls were taken at great cost. I saw the number of English and Scottish men who died taking that town. Why is it so hard to believe that Mistress Farrell's husband was not one of them, or that he died in the countless other battles and skirmishes through those bloody wars? I have no doubt he died a hero of England, fighting against the papists in a just cause, and here are you, slandering his name and that of his loyal widow. Shame on you!"

Mary Brassey cringed and looked down. Emotion twisted her features into a mask of hatred she tried to hide from the room.

"But that is not all, is it?" Brassey looked up, eyes burning. Marleigh could see Smale sitting very still, looking down at his hands. "Because, Mistress Brassey, the whole reason for your brother-in-law's rash proposal to a woman who believed herself to yet be married, was not concern for him, but gain for yourself and your husband. You knew that you could only expand your tenancy of the neighbouring property if Samuel were to be the tenant. And for that he had to be married. And when your plan failed, and your greed thwarted, you lashed out in vengeance, and you have never stopped trying to bring down the good name of this woman since. You saw your chance, and you took it. But you have missed your mark. You offer nothing but bile and gossip and lies. Is that not the truth?"

Brassey said nothing. Her chest heaved and her hands gripped the arms of her chair with white knuckles. She gathered herself, and Marleigh had to admire how quickly she regained her composure. She was a formidable woman – a shame that talent had been directed against herself.

Brassey looked up and eyed the magistrate and his colleagues. Although she replied to Richard, her gaze remained fixed on those sitting behind the table in front of her. "All I have done is say what I have seen. I don't have the fancy words of the captain here. I don't have the looks of the witch…" Savage rolled his eyes, "…I am just an ordinary, God-fearing woman trying to do right. I place my trust in Him, and I wait for the

Maid of Rainow to confirm all the things I 'ave witnessed, here today." She paused. Marleigh saw Elcock nodding vigorously. Now, she addressed Savage directly. "May I go, sir?"

Savage nodded quietly, seemingly deep in thought. Brereton's face was unreadable.

It was as if the whole room exhaled together. Marleigh had not noticed until then how the tension had built during Mary Brassey's testimony. A pressure seemed to lift with her departure from the witness chair, and the people could breathe freely again. A wittering of subdued conversation slowly built, a background drone of noise. Opinions were being changed every few minutes as statements were made and questions asked. This had definitely been worth the effort of getting in early for a seat!

Smale, now seeming almost punch-drunk, called more witnesses. The egg-seller could add nothing helpful for him. Others present in the marketplace that day had clearly been rehearsed by Smale, but Richard reminding them of their oaths before God to tell the truth brought these God-fearing witnesses back to righteousness. They also added little to help Smale's case.

The morning started to drift after the earlier ferment. After an hour of meandering back and forth, Savage raised his hand for silence. "We have heard from all of the witnesses called by Master Smale. We have not yet heard from two people important to this trial. The Maid of Rainow – as Master Smale and my colleague, here, Master Elcock, keep reminding us – and from Mistress Farrell herself. I propose we hear from the Maid first, if she is present and is happy to provide her testimony. We will then take a break to rest and eat, and then resume to hear from the accused herself."

Something between a gasp and a cheer went around the room. Marleigh shot Richard a look of horror, but he seemed remarkably unconcerned by the turn of events. This was what she feared the most – a decision based on superstition and hysteria, not evidence and logic. How could people be taken in by this rubbish? Her dread had been building through the morning, and the atmosphere in the room now seemed close and suffocating. She glanced forward and saw Brereton watching her intently. Did he already know what had passed between the Maid and herself in the gaol? It didn't seem as if Savage knew.

Against her will, her thoughts were dragged back to the previous evening. Just minutes after Richard had left with the minister, Constable Roe had returned, a strange look on his face. "Mistress, I know you are exhausted, but you have more visitors. As it is a matter that may be important for the trial, I do not feel I can turn them away. I am sorry."

He had shown in two people, although she could sense and hear the noise of a small crowd outside in the street. She already knew who it would be. Eva sensed the coming presence too, and shrank back on the pallet. There was a muffled conversation outside her door and then a chill descended on her as a figure all in white seemed almost to float into the cell. A man stood behind her with Roe, both staying in the doorway.

"Mama. I don't like her," Eva had whispered. "Make her go away."

She had summoned all her remaining energy and focused on projecting calmness. "Quiet, Eva. I am sure the lady just wants to talk to us."

The pale face had smiled sweetly, but the smile did not touch the charcoal of her eyes. Marleigh felt like winter had come into her cell, cold and pitiless. The pale gold of her hair was like a promise of spring, but not for her. Not for Marleigh and Eva. She knelt on the floor, bringing her face close to Marleigh's, sitting on the edge of the pallet. She placed her palms on Marleigh's cheeks and stared into her eyes. But Marleigh had built a wall of blankness and she doubted that even the Maid of Rainow would penetrate that barrier.

The Maid had faltered slightly, a slight increase in the speed of her breathing, and a fractional raising of one eyebrow had indicated a measure of surprise. Marleigh felt Eva shuffle across the pallet, squeezing herself against her mother's back. Finally, the Maid had spoken. A soft, high voice, like a small girl. Marleigh had put her age at perhaps eighteen or nineteen, but she sounded ten years younger than that.

"Marleigh. Can I call you that? Let us pray, together. Let us speak to God and ask for his blessing."

That had been something she had not expected. A clever move. But she kept pace with the Maid's lilting words. She had, she hoped, portrayed herself successfully as a small-town governess. Familiar with common prayer, but also commanding a smattering of Latin.

But the Maid was also difficult to read. Always the smile, but always the cold calculation behind the eyes. Questions had followed. Why did Marleigh think she had been accused of these terrible crimes? What did she think about witches and witchcraft? With whom was Eva conceived? Could she name the father, and where was he now? Why were Eva's eyes different colours? What did she know of Satan and his demons? Had she ever travelled overseas? All the time, the Maid held Marleigh's wrists in her hands, and kept her face within inches of her own. The childlike voice whispering the questions. Dark gaze fixed on Marleigh's eyes – trying to see into her soul. Marleigh had no doubt that this process would have terrified someone less strong, less in control of their own body, less able to draw upon the long years of experience that she possessed, of hiding her true self, of constantly testing herself and being tested by others.

But still, she was terrified. Not because she feared the presence of the divine, but precisely the opposite. She saw through the Maid in minutes. These were circus tricks. Simple means of detecting lies and intimidating the weak. There was no knowledge or real learning. Just a few cheap tricks to fool the commonfolk. Oh, she was clever. Marleigh had to admire her for that. But this was a money-making venture. A very accomplished one, but nothing more.

She could see how this brother and sister combination had fooled the good people of Rainow. Terror and dread of witches would have been built up over weeks, or months. Accusations flying around. A sense of dark foreboding stoked and encouraged. And when the moment was right, here was a pure and angelic young girl who could release all that tension with an imprimatur of God Himself. Thank you, God, for our deliverance, and thank the Maid of Rainow. *That will be five shillings, please...* Marleigh knew this made things worse for her. Where was the spectacle in acquittal? Who was going to donate their hard-earned savings when the witch walked free? She had no doubt where this was headed, the only question would be whether the magistrate and his colleagues were also taken in.

But even more, she was frightened for Eva. The thought of this creature free to question, and to judge, her daughter filled her with horror and a deep loathing. She longed to lash out, physically and verbally. To rend and tear. To beat her down into the dirty floor of the cell. She had no right, this woman.

*

But the excitement in the room was building. Given the nature of the evidence so far, and the paucity of Smale's case against her, the testimony of the Maid seemed to be the last barrier to the accused's safety and freedom. Savage gestured to the guards by the door, and to Constable Roe, to find the Maid and to bring her to testify. The babble in the hall intensified.

Savage, sensing the rising drama, paused and looked to his colleagues for support. "And then, ladies and gentlemen, to the verdict."

As the soldiers left, Richard got to his feet and called across to Savage. "Sir, if I may?"

Savage nodded, resuming his seat.

"Sir, I object to the testimony to be given by the Maid. Why should we listen to one such as her? What power does she wield that we should bow to her judgement?"

"Well, Captain, I have not said we *would* bow to her judgement, just that we would hear her. We will weigh what she says in the balance. There is much respect for her in the community and I think we should allow the community to hear her view." He looked right and left at his colleagues. Brereton did not respond, but maintained his gaze on Marleigh. Elcock again nodded enthusiastically.

"I understand, sir, but my point is somewhat different. We are giving her respect because she claims to speak to God directly, on the matter of witches at least. She claims she is chaste and pure, and above the sins and debauched ways of the common folk. It is through this that she gains respect and people value her judgement, and take her at her word. Is that not the case? Or is there other proof of the credibility of her… visions?"

"Well, I, erm, yes, I suppose that is the case, Captain. I have not met the lady herself, but my colleague here tells me of an aura of goodness and purity that surrounds her, and that impresses itself on all who meet her. I think we should hear her, whilst reserving our judgement on the, erm, veracity of her testimony. Do you object to that, sir?"

Marleigh sensed Savage's underlying scepticism but also that he was not blind to the mood of the room. She saw Richard was trying to build this scepticism but had little hope he could block her appearance.

Richard had remained on his feet. "Well, sir. Before the Maid appears, if of course she is willing to testify, and we indulge in this... show, may I be allowed to call a witness first? I can pledge that it will be quick, and that it has a direct bearing on what would follow."

The room was growing impatient. Some started to shout for the Maid, determined not to be cheated of the promised entertainment. Some of the less godly, and more impatient, attendees aimed some ribald insults in Richard's direction. Savage looked irritated. "Very well, Captain. But please..." he gestured at the rows of chairs, stools and benches behind Richard, "...make it quick!"

"Thank you, sir. I will." He looked around. "I would like to call Master Thomas Manley to testify, Your Honour."

Savage looked bewildered, and Smale lifted his jowled chin from his hand in surprise. Marleigh looked at Richard in confusion. Who was this Manley? The only Thomas Manley she knew was the landlord at the Bate Hall tavern. What relevance did he have to this matter?

However, it seemed this was precisely who Richard had called to give witness. A rather embarrassed and awkward-looking Manley shuffled from the back of the room and made his way between the two banks of seating to the witness chair at the front. He held his hat scrunched in his fists and performed a slightly comical bow to those at the front. He nodded slightly to Richard and, when Savage gestured, sat down heavily. Marleigh managed a slight smile. Thomas Manley was not known for his manners and decorum; he was either drinking and singing along with his clientele or throwing them unceremoniously into the street when things got out of hand. He was in his Sunday best suit, and it looked like it had been thrown on in a hurry. It was fair to say this was not his natural environment.

Richard smiled at him encouragingly. "Master Manley. Sir. Can you please tell the magistrate what your occupation is?"

Manley looked across at Savage. "I am the landlord of the Bate Hall tavern, Your Honour. I have been for nigh on twenty years."

Savage nodded back to him, still looking confused. He raised an eyebrow at Richard. Brereton was staring at the table top, blank expression, listening intently with his head in his hands.

"Master Manley. Thomas, if I may? Amongst your current guests at the Bate Hall, can you tell me if you have any, what we might call… unusual?"

Manley looked back enquiringly. "Erm, what, sir?"

"Famous people, Thomas. People that might be known to those here in this court."

"Ah. Yes, sir. I do."

There was a pause and when Richard could see Manley was not going to fill it, he responded. "And who might those people be, Thomas? Can you please tell the magistrate and the court?"

"Aye, sir. I can do that."

Another pause.

Savage sighed with exasperation. "Captain Farrell, we really need to go a little quicker here. What is the point of this, erm, testimony, other than to try my patience?"

"I am sorry, sir. I will be more direct." He turned to Manley. "Now, Thomas, please tell Sir Edward who those people are."

Manley seemed to catch up with the mood of those behind the bench. He swallowed and said, "I have the

Maid o' Rainow, and her brother stayin' in the Bate. Your Honour."

Now Savage nodded. Brereton looked up and frowned at Manley. Elcock shot a glance at Smale, who shrugged faintly in response. Marleigh could sense the whole gathering taking a breath.

Richard, after a brief pause to let that sink in, resumed. "Thomas, when you left the tavern this morning to come to this court, where were the Maid and her brother?"

Manley looked awkward and addressed his reply to the wooden floor between his feet. "The Maid were still in her room. Her brother, I have no idea, sir. I have not seen him since I took a bottle to 'is room last evenin.'"

"And how do you know the Maid was still in her room, Thomas?"

"Well, 'cos I took her a tray of bread and jam, and one of the good apples, sir. I also took 'er a cup of wine, although I'm not sure maids are supposed to partake o' that."

"And you are sure it was her, Thomas? The Maid? There can be no mistake?"

Thomas sat up a little, to add dignity to his response. "O' course I am sure, Captain. You can 'ardly mistake her. It was her, alright. Although..." he looked at the floor again, "...she was not how I expected to find her."

A muttering spread through the people. *Whatever revelation is to be made, here it comes*, thought Marleigh, noticing how Elcock tried to keep his face impassive. Savage now looked mesmerised by the exchange, mouth even hanging slightly open.

Again, Richard let this sink in. "Thomas, and please remember you are under oath to tell the truth as clearly as you can, please tell the court how you found the Maid of Rainow." Marleigh could see that Richard was clearly enjoying this.

"Well, erm, Captain. She was, erm, in what you might say, a state of undress."

The muttering turned into a collective gasp of surprise.

"I see. But she was awake? The Holy Maid of Rainow, that is."

"Ah. No, Captain, sir. She were definitely not awake."

"I see. And Thomas, in your experience of twenty years as landlord of the tavern, how would you describe her condition? Would you say she was ill?"

"Well, in a manner o' speakin', Captain. Yes."

"Aha. She had a fever, you mean?"

"Erm, no Captain. In my opinion, she was sleepin' off a prolonged night o' drinkin.'"

More gasps. A few shouts of "No!" and, Marleigh noted, the beginnings of some mirth behind her in the rows of seats.

"I see, Thomas. Did you observe her drinking?"

"Well, I didn't actually see her drink, but it were a number of bottles that went up to 'er room over the course o' the evening."

"Ah. Thank you, Thomas. And, when you entered her room with breakfast this morning, did she wake and greet you, and, erm, cover her nakedness?"

Manley was warming to his role now. This was more like it. Just like telling one of his 'stories' to his customers, holding the whole room in thrall. "Well, sir…" and here he almost winked at Savage, but stopped himself just in time. "Well, sir… she didn't, but the gentleman with her covered her modesty for her. She didn't wake at all."

Uproar. Shouts of anger. Waves of laughter. Gasps of horror.

Richard let the sound roll around the room. Marleigh watched Savage's jaw almost connect with the linen covering the table. She even allowed herself a slight smile and, very briefly, caught Richard's eye. Her heart skipped. This was the first time they had really looked at each other since their wedding and it felt like a bolt of lightning across the narrow space between them.

Richard turned back to Thomas Manley, who was smiling broadly at the impact his story was having. "Finally, Thomas, can you describe the gentleman who was with the Maid, and can you perhaps guess what had transpired between them? Perhaps he was consulting her in relation to this case?"

Now Thomas smirked. "Ain't never heard it called that before, Captain. You are a military man, I am sure you can guess! From the stink in the room I'd say they were at it all night."

The noise level rose even further. Savage, seemingly woken from the spell of Manley's testimony, banged his mallet to try to regain order.

Manley continued, "...which I reckon were a good showing from the gentleman concerned, as he must have been well into his forties. A distinguished-looking fellow. I would say he too were military. Anyway, he paid up prompt, gave his apologies for the state of the room and went on his way. A real gentleman, that one."

"Thank you, Thomas. You really have been very helpful." He turned to Savage. "Thank you, Your Honour. That is all I have for this witness. Hopefully this has clarified a few things and the Maid can be located soon so we can hear from her directly."

Savage looked entirely lost, with the room in uproar. He looked to his colleagues for support, but both Brereton and Elcock seemed intent on examining the weave of the cloth in front of them. He banged his mallet, hard and repeatedly, until order was gradually regained. "Master Smale! Do you have any questions for this witness?"

(13 July 1644)

Smale just shook his head mutely. He, too, looked bewildered.

"Then we will adjourn! Myself and my colleagues need to consider this further. We will start again in one hour. Constable, please clear the room!"

When the room was largely empty, Marleigh rose and looked for the constable. It would be good to rest, even for an hour. Rest, and see Eva. To comfort her. And she needed to think, to plan. She could leave nothing to chance. She looked back over her shoulder at Richard as Roe led her away. He smiled encouragingly, and she returned his smile. She could tell he was trying to look confident for her. He had done an amazingly good job, given his lack of experience. Surely, with the Maid's testimony now seemingly worthless, there was no way Savage could convict? She could sense his intense frustration, his anger at being made to look a fool over such trivial nonsense. He wanted it finished. She started to allow herself to relax a little. She could handle her own testimony. She had rehearsed her answers over and over, examining them from all perspectives for anything incriminating. Anything that would raise doubts or suspicions. She knew she could handle Elcock, and even Savage. Sir William Brereton remained an enigma, but he wouldn't have come out of his way to the trial, at a time when he was sorely needed to confront Prince Rupert, if not to support the Walker girls. Clearly he felt some obligation to them.

Try as she might, she couldn't focus entirely on the trial. She still couldn't get used to the idea that she was married. That she and Richard Farrell had committed their lives to each other. She had not been in this position for so long. She had been alone in facing the world, in trying to understand the fundamental meaning of her purpose in that world. She had pursued ideas. Tested hypotheses. Read the works of the great philosophers. Always alone and risking everything for that knowledge. And yet now, just when it seemed the net had finally caught her and drawn her to some kind of reckoning, she found herself with two people tied to her in some way. Depending on her.

Loving her.

*

Richard watched Roe lead Marleigh away. He felt elated, but exhausted. He had never felt so exposed, even with Master Brough's crash course in how to behave in front of the magistrate. With the despatching of the Maid of Rainow, it seemed that they had overcome the final hurdle. With just Marleigh's testimony to come, they were home and dry. He could see it in Savage's face and in Smale's. The odious Smale had looked entirely crushed, his plans for deploying the Maid shredded, and his own reputation seemingly tied to this sorry affair.

Speaking of the Maid, he needed to find Roger. With the trial done, they needed to think ahead. They needed to think about the danger posed by Cobb and his men, about what he would do with Marleigh and Eva, about Roger's search for his family, and about how he could continue to serve the Parliament in the midst of this war.

He glanced up at the table as he headed for the door. Savage was still there, deep in an animated conversation with Elcock. He glimpsed Brereton at the bottom of the stairs, talking quietly with the town alderman, Captain Booth, and the mysterious lady who had accompanied him. Brereton looked up as Richard passed him, but made no effort to talk to him, his face unreadable.

Outside, the sun was blazing down and it felt beautifully warm. He looked around the north-western corner of the

(13 July 1644)

building and saw Roger leaning against the wall, in shadow, silhouetted against the sunlit Pennines, a blaze of green, away to the east. Paler green of the grass, darker shades for the copses of beech and oak, the bracken and yet-to-flower heather. A few white clouds floated slowly north, dragging their shadows across the slopes.

"So, how did it go?" Roger cocked an eyebrow. "Have they acquitted? It seems there was much excitement amongst the goodfolk of the town as they left the guildhall."

Richard grinned in response. "Well, not quite yet. But that must be the killing blow. They have nothing more. We should be done by mid-afternoon. I have to admit to quite enjoying the process. Perhaps I have found the career to pursue when my fighting days are over."

Roger laughed in return. "Ha! Well, maybe. You seem to do more damage with your tongue than you ever could with a blade."

Richard flexed his right arm. "That's certainly true at the moment," he conceded. "There is not so much pain now, but it is stiff to move. It needs exercise to loosen up the muscle, I think."

"Mayhap you will get that soon enough. If we are indeed to be done here this afternoon, we need to turn our thoughts to Cobb and his merry fellows. They are likely to be scouting around the town by now. Maybe there is even a chance they will try for Brereton if they know he is here. His guard is light and he would be a feather in Cobb's cap for certain."

Richard frowned. "You are right, of course." He felt his anger building. "This nonsense here is such a waste of time. Petty jealousies and small-town malice! I said I had learned to master my temper, but I can tell you, Roger, there have been times when I could have taken the edge of a sword to Smale."

"Richard. You have done remarkably well. Truly. I could not have done what you have done. You do have a talent for this. All jests aside."

Calming down, another thought occurred to Richard. "But, Roger. Your note was one thing, but tell me! How did you accomplish the dishonour of the Maid? You didn't have to… you know… actually hurt anyone, I hope."

"You mean kill them? No, Richard, nothing so extreme, although like you I was sorely tempted."

"And the brother? Where is he?"

"Ha! I tell you, friend, there is a story worth a week in this. As ever, things are not always what they seem. I have exhausted my ingenuity, and my balls, to achieve this result. I hope to be appropriately rewarded!"

"Not by God, I imagine."

Roger grinned. "No. I doubt that, although in some ways I may have gained his admiration, if not his full approval."

"I don't have a lot of time now. We restart in less than an hour. Can you give me the main thread?"

"Certainly. I hope that I can share the full epic saga with you and Marleigh, perhaps not Eva, around a campfire in the next days."

Richard, lost in the detail of the trial, had hardly focused on what would happen next with his new family, and it obviously showed on his face.

"What? Did you think she would go back to being governess to the Walker girls? Everyone would forgive and forget, and life would go on? She is your responsibility now. They both are. Welcome to fatherhood. Perhaps you get a sense of how it was for me trying to make a living in the wars and keep my own family happy."

Richard was starting to get that sense very clearly as reality slowly dawned in his mind. As this new realisation

(13 July 1644)

slowly seeped across his consciousness, Roger took up his story.

"It took a while, but I found your other lady-friend. You do mix with some strange types, I have to say. She took a little persuading that I was on the side of the righteous, but when she heard the plan, there was no holding her back. She offered me a philtre, although she also said she had hemlock, belladonna and some potion she'd concocted from foxgloves if I wanted to take things a little further."

"Ah." Richard was struggling to focus as his mind started to be enveloped in new worries and plans for his growing family. "You mean Alice?"

"That's the one. A bit, erm, fragrant and perhaps a bit long in the tooth – if she had any – for me, but no accounting for taste. Anyway, she hates the Maid of Rainow with a passion and fell over herself to help. Armed with the potion, I soon found out which room she was in from our friendly landlord and paid her a visit. They were taking her evening meal to her room, as she didn't want to sup with the ordinary sinful masses in the bar. Fortunately, the lad was happy to accept a small bribe – I said I was a big fan of the Holy One – and so I took it to her, adding a little spice to her wine on the way up."

"And the brother? Where was he?"

"Turns out he was supping with Smale and the Brassey woman. Couldn't have worked out better."

"So she drank her wine and you had your evil way with her?"

But here Roger's face clouded, the frivolity forgotten.

"No. I didn't. She took a little persuading that I was really part of the tavern staff, but she is an innocent thing, underneath it all. I tried to keep her talking to make sure she drank the wine. I have no idea what old Alice puts in her philtre, but the transformation was remarkable. She had been haughty, cold and distant when I entered, but now she couldn't stop talking. It was like she lost ten years of life and became again the child she really is. The potion didn't bring out unbridled passion, but she was like a different person. Rich, she really is just a child. Yes, the whole thing is an act. We probably knew that anyway, but the more she talked, the more I felt for her."

Richard raised an eyebrow. "Really? This child managed to get two women wrongly hanged not so long ago."

"I know. But it's not her. Not really. It's the brother. He controls her. He manipulates her. She showed me bruises, cuts, burns. Other… marks. All carefully hidden. She told me… she…" He swallowed. "She told me he made her sleep with him. Had done ever since their parents died. It's her own brother, Rich. He did it to punish her if she wouldn't play along. She thinks she is damned for murder and for incest. He deserved to die. He's a piece of shit, Rich. Her life is a hell."

Richard looked at him. "And did you? Did you kill him?"

Roger looked down. When he looked up, there was a coldness, a pure look of hatred that Richard had never seen before.

"I heard him coming back. Coming up the stairs to the room. I hid behind the door and told Ellen – that's her name, she does actually have a name – to pretend she was alone. By this time, she was quite willing to play along. I don't know how long it has been since she talked to someone other than her brother. Anyway, he marched in, saw the glass of wine and the food and, without a word, punched her hard in the stomach. I was out from behind that door like a shot from a cannon and caught him just as he turned. Nearly took the fucker's jaw right off. I've never hit a man that hard. He was out before he hit the ground."

"So how did you get rid of him?"

(13 July 1644)

"I had to calm Ellen down – she was hysterical. I suppose the effects of the potion and the shock of seeing her brother assaulted were too much – I think she is already on the edge of sanity. Her brother had told her it all added to her mystique. I told her he was a piece of shit and she wouldn't ever need to worry about him again. In the end, while we waited for dark to fall and the tavern to quieten, I ordered up some bottles of wine and slowly got her drunk until she passed out. I bribed more help from the serving lad, and we got him into a cart out the back of the tavern. I stuffed him into an empty cask. The carter was still in the bar, having a quiet ale before spending a night in the stable. I bribed him too. Told him I had put an extra barrel on his cart and he should deliver it to Master Oliver Cromwell in York. Paid him more than his cart was worth. I have no idea if he'll take it – I told him it was the general's favourite ale and he would be generously rewarded. He may just dump it and carry on his usual route. I've no idea and I don't care."

Richard looked at Roger with something like awe. "You've had a busy night."

"But, Roger, the tavernkeeper just testified that it was obvious that the room had been used for, erm, well, prolonged fornication. How could that be – more bribes?"

"Oh no. He was correct. I had a long and pleasure-filled night after that. Seems that stuffing someone in a barrel gets me feeling hot. I had prolonged fornication alright, it just didn't involve Ellen, the Maid o' Rainow. I spoke to the tavern lad – he did well out o' me last night, has probably retired by now – and he managed to procure me a companion for the small hours of the night. Slipped her out of the place before anyone awoke."

"And the Maid. Where is she now?"

"She is in the gaol. I left her with the constable's wife. I explained everything – well, not everything – to her. She is a good woman. Ellen should be safe there. She has a terrible headache from the wine, but will sleep most of the day, I guess. She will be fed and looked after. I will decide how to play things once Marleigh is free." He looked at Richard. "We all have a few things to decide then."

Richard nodded. His mind was scrambled. He didn't think he could take anything more in and not have his head explode. In a matter of days his entire life had been turned on its head. What was another waif and stray for their collection? He tried to focus.

"Roger. Look, I can never thank you enough for what you have done. Truly, my friend. But I have another request."

"Cobb?"

"Cobb. If we are to make our way from this town in safety after the trial, then we must know where he is. If not, we are out of the pan and right in the flames. Can you scout the country to the east? If we can get some idea of his movements, we can at least put some distance between us and his men. Then, if we can find somewhere to leave the women and children, maybe we can circle round and finish it for good. Will you do that?"

"Then I should leave now. In any case, it is probably best I make myself scarce until the verdict is in. Best if people like the tavernkeeper don't connect the two of us."

"Thank you." Richard felt enormous gratitude to have someone to help share his burden. He knew he was creaking under the load of his new responsibilities and the divided loyalties they brought. If he could lay just one part of it aside for a moment, that was a blessed relief. "Brereton will head for his headquarters at Nantwich after this finishes. I will meet you there in three days if I don't see you before then. I will take Ellen with us. If I can, and if she will come. We can think more clearly about the future then."

Roger nodded. "Thank you in return. I feel I owe her something, although I am not sure what that is. 'Til we meet again then."

Richard was pulled into a bearhug, and felt the furious emotion in it. He struggled to hold himself together. Finally, he slapped Roger on the back and pulled away. He saw his friend's eyes brimming with tears. They clasped hands and then Richard turned, going in search of Savage, and desperately trying to clear his mind.

*

Marleigh noticed that the numbers in the hall had reduced since the morning. Perhaps only three quarters of the seats were now taken. Clearly the demise of the Maid of Rainow had robbed the trial of some of its interest and drama. *Well, not for everyone*, she thought.

She had been overjoyed to see Eva again and she thanked Sarah Roe repeatedly for her kindness in looking after her. When the constable's wife then revealed her other charge, Marleigh had, for a moment, not known how to react. When she heard the tale that Roger had passed on to Sarah, she sensed the truth in it and she looked on the sleeping figure, curled under thick blankets in the neighbouring cell, with understanding and compassion. The constable took some persuading not to wake and question the girl, but in the end he was convinced to let things lie.

The hour of the recess seemed to fly by, and she had scarcely finished her bread than it seemed time to return to the guildhall. As Smale had not called her as a witness, the questioning fell to the three men sitting in judgement. In truth, the questions had been few and none too threatening. Sir Edward Savage, to her enormous relief, seemed to have already made up his mind about her and mainly probed again into the events of the marketplace and her previous encounter with Mary Brassey.

Elcock was the most awkward. He wanted to know more of her past. Where was she from originally? Where did her family originate from? What did her father do before his death? Ah, a teacher! Which school? Yes, I know of it. Which years was he there? Could she remember the names of any of the other teachers? How could she account for her considerable depth of knowledge of history, and of Latin? She seemed well versed in literature too and had excellent understanding of the natural world. Of God's broad creation. Was this all from her father? He must have been devoted to her to apply his time to her education. Why, she was more learned than most women of his acquaintance, women of far better stock than she. How could that be?

And then a question none had asked her to that point — how old was she? She faltered slightly. She was not entirely certain. She thought perhaps she was thirty-two? No one seemed shocked at her answer and she took further heart from that. Elcock picked and chipped at her story, trying to find gaps, weaknesses, inconsistencies. She remained humble, keeping her gaze lowered, trying to provide enough information to be helpful but not so much as to lay traps for herself. She did not try to extend any of her talent to try to touch the minds of these men. One slip along that line and it would be the end for her. Eventually he finished and sat back. She saw his slight shrug in Smale's direction.

When it came to Sir William's turn, she raised her head to look him in the eye. Without any efforts on her part, she nonetheless felt a slight jolt of connection. Whatever bond he felt existed between them, sparked those years ago on a darkening evening by the Dane Bridge, was still there. His dark eyes were intense. It was as if he had finally woken from his apparent detachment throughout the morning. Whatever he felt, she didn't want to prolong it, and she lowered her eyes to the floor again.

He questioned her on how she came to be in the Walker household. What had passed between her and Samuel Walker? What did her duties involve? How did she get on with his daughters? What was her relationship with Master Smale? How had she met Captain Farrell? What had persuaded her that she was now free of obligation to her husband? Did she believe she had sinned in conceiving a child out of wedlock and had she confessed her sin to God, and asked for His forgiveness?

She could see that Savage seemed to be increasingly uncomfortable with what seemed a rather personal and irrelevant line of questioning. After a period, as there was a pause in the to and fro, he asked Brereton if he were near the end of his questions. Brereton shot a final look at her, and nodded.

Savage then stood and addressed the room. "Ladies and gentlemen, there is nothing further to the proceedings. My colleagues and I have heard the witnesses. We have heard of the vigil and the examination. We have questioned the accused ourselves. I am satisfied we have heard the available evidence, such as it is. Now, is there anyone in the room who wishes to speak before we retire to consider our verdicts?" He looked around the guildhall at the faces turned towards him.

"Very well then. We will return in an hour and announce the verdict. Gentlemen..." he turned to his colleagues, "...is one hour sufficient?"

Brereton looked up at him. "For my part, Sir Edward, I do not need to deliberate. Do we need to retire, or can we proceed now?"

Savage smiled back at him. "I see. We are of a mind. Certainly, I have reached a conclusion. However, we must not deprive Master Elcock of time to deliberate. Sir?"

But Elcock too seemed content to finish the trial. "No, sir. Thank you for your thought, but I too am ready to provide my verdict."

Marleigh drew a deep breath. She had hoped to have some time to prepare herself for the moment in private. To marshal her thoughts and finalise her plans. *Here it is.*

She glanced to her left; Richard was on his feet. Balled fists on the table. He managed a thin smile, and a slight nod of his head. To her right, she saw Smale also standing. She turned to him, but he would not meet her eye. Since the dismissal of the Maid of Rainow and her evidence, she had sensed the fight go out of him.

"Very well." Sir Edward sat again. He looked to his left. "Master Elcock, do you find the accused, Marleigh Farrell, guilty or not guilty of the charge of witchcraft?"

"Sir Edward, first let me say what an honour it has been to serve on this panel of judgement. Whilst we give our verdicts here, truly, the only true verdict comes from God Himself. I hope and pray that we do His bidding. I would also like to say that we are beset on all sides by peril. The real and immediate peril of war, where brave men such as Sir William, and indeed Captain Farrell, do battle against the evils of popery and the misguided men and women who have led our King astray. But we are also assailed by perils to our mortal souls, and all too often weak men and women fall prey to the Evil One. We hear that this curse, this scourge of good and honest folk, of witchcraft most heinous and damaging, is on the rise. Equally brave men are fighting this enemy across our country, and victories are being had in counties across the realm. We, sirs, must also play our part in this battle. I am a humble man and honoured to sit in judgement with such illustrious pillars of our land and of the godly cause. I have to say that I find myself compelled to believe the witnesses that Master Smale has brought forth. I find their testimony credible."

"Master Elcock. Just for the benefit of those present, can you please clearly state if you find the accused guilty, or not?"

"I find her guilty, Sir Edward. God have mercy upon her."

Although Marleigh had been expecting this, Elcock's verdict still hit like a hammer. A low murmuring filled the guildhall.

Now Savage addressed the room. "For my part, I cannot agree with Master Elcock's reading of the evidence, although I thank him for his diligence." He nodded and smiled at Elcock, who didn't seem in the least surprised by Savage's disagreement. "I find the accused, Marleigh Farrell, innocent of the charge of witchcraft."

He then turned to his right. "And Sir William, please can you also provide your verdict to the court?"

Brereton looked up. "Certainly, Sir Edward. I too find the accused guilty of the charge." He stared straight into Marleigh's eyes. "Marleigh Farrell is a witch. May God have mercy on her."

There was silence for a moment, and he gathered his papers together, then a storm of noise rocked the room.

*

He sat back in his chair. In a glance to his left he could see Savage staring down at him, open-mouthed and eyes wide in disbelief. Elcock was leaning round, equally shocked.

Savage spoke. "Sir William. Did I... did I hear you correctly? Did you pronounce a guilty verdict?"

Now he looked up, only just able to hear the magistrate over the shouting. "Yes, Sir Edward. Yes, you heard me correctly. I find her guilty." In front of him, perched on her small chair between the tables occupied by Smale and Farrell, Marleigh sat like she was carved from marble. Her eyes were fixed on him, but he could not read the expression on her face. The track of a single tear was visible against the accumulated grime of long days in a gaol cell. As he gazed at her, the noise in the room faded into the background. "In fact," he said, "I have seldom been more sure in a decision."

Farrell was staring at him incredulously while Smale, having got over the shock of the clearly unexpected decision, was grinning from ear to ear, slapping the palm of his hand on the table in triumph. People were on their feet, yelling abuse at Marleigh. Farrell had left his seat and was kneeling next to her, talking urgently into her ear. But her expression never changed and her eyes never left his. Now Farrell was marching over to him. Standing over him. Hands on the table, face screwed up in fury. Asking, "Why, why?"

Savage was trying to regain order, banging his mallet on the table and waving for the soldiers to seat people. Gradually the room was quietening. Savage urged Farrell back to his seat. A soldier placed a firm hand on his shoulder, but it was shrugged off. A hate-filled look over his shoulder and Farrell walked back to his desk.

Brereton knew why. He had known why since receiving Farrell's letter outside York. Oh, this trial had been a farce. The evidence presented was pitiful and he was not in the least surprised that Savage had found her not guilty. But there were things that Savage did not know. Nor Farrell, or Elcock. And that pompous, jumped-up joke of a prosecutor, Smale? Ridiculous man! How could he count himself amongst the godly? He was a disgrace. It would have been interesting to see the Maid of Rainow, but that possibility had been thwarted. He suspected Farrell's involvement in that. Farrell and his

(13 July 1644)

odious colleague. He smelt of many things – corruption and low cunning.

But none of them knew what he knew. Of the long nights, bereft of sleep, haunted by her face. Not his dead wife's face. Or the face of his new wife, Cecily, or his son, Thomas. Not dreams of his home, walking in his garden among the roses in the warm sunshine. Not dreams of glory in battle, of carrying his flag over the ramparts of Chester in triumph, his troops following behind and cheering his name. No. He dreamt of Marleigh. Years after their two fleeting meetings and brief conversations. He dreamt of her.

How could this be? He had committed himself to the service of God and had seen his life blessed. He had risen through the ranks of Parliament to be a trusted commander and soldier of the Lord. He had sponsored godly preachers throughout the North-West and within his regiments. Every day he strived to win God's favour and reflect His Glory in his deeds and thoughts. So why did this woman, this mysterious woman, Marleigh Hume, no, Marleigh Farrell – *ha!* – exert such a poisonous unrelenting hold over him? So seemingly innocent. A victim of circumstances not of her creation. Alone and adrift in the world, without resources. She had never asked him for anything. Even his summons to the trial had been by the Walker girl. Marleigh had not even known the letter had been written, according to Farrell.

There could only be one explanation. The realisation that had come to him and it had unlocked the mystery. This trial had not been a trial of Marleigh Farrell. It had been a trial of Sir William Brereton. As Jesus was tempted by the Devil, so he was being tested too. How could it be otherwise? Neither fate nor coincidence had set the events in motion that led him to this room, in this town, at this time. It was a test of his faith, and he had passed it! Against common sense and against the apparent evidence presented, he had seen through it all and found the truth. By being strong in his faith, through prayer and reflection, he had been presented with this... this *opportunity* to prove his worth, and he had taken it. She was a witch. She had bewitched him. Now he was free.

He reflected that he had probably also saved Farrell. Perhaps sensing her danger, she had latched on to Farrell and bewitched him too. He doubted Farrell's godliness, but he took him for an honourable man. Whatever her nature – witch, demon or some other evil tool of Satan – and whether the child was his or not, she had clearly bound him to her, playing on honour and obligation. Well, now Farrell too would be free of her, although only God knew what would become of the child. He would not think on that. It was not his responsibility.

With this verdict, everything fell into place. He banished her from a dream to a memory. He safeguarded his marriage. He freed himself to pursue urgent military goals in the service of the cause and, above all, he strengthened his faith in God through a conscience cleared of her evil taint and a temptation resisted. As he had said to Savage, he had never been more certain of a decision.

Attention had shifted from him to Savage, who had remained standing. Sir Edward held up his hand for attention, but the room was now quiet.

"We have our verdict," he said. "Marleigh Hume, I am sorry, Marleigh Farrell, will you please rise?"

She did. She rose from the small stool with no shaking and no more tears. She looked strong, determined, resolute. She looked beautiful. At that moment perhaps more beautiful than anything he could recall seeing in his life. And tomorrow she would be gone. He forced a rising emotion back into its prison and slammed the door. Look forward, not back. Look

(13 JULY 1644)

to the light of an optimistic future, and not the darkness of his past, tortured soul.

*

After the shock of Brereton's verdict, Richard fought hard to control himself. His first instinct, like Savage's, had been that Brereton had made a mistake. There was no way on this earth that the evidence pointed to conviction. Only corruption, personal ambition or madness could lead to that conclusion, and Richard couldn't see how this applied to Brereton. But then it came to him. Why would Brereton commit his time to this trial? What was the real story behind his link to Marleigh; the mysterious previous meetings and the lingering connection that seemed to bind him to her? Now he saw it so clearly, because it was so simple. The bastard had sentenced his wife to death through jealousy. His twisted puritanism had kept him in thrall to Marleigh but unable to act on his feelings. This must have been a torment to him over the years and now, to find that she had given herself to him, and had his child? It must have driven him over the edge. For who was Richard Farrell? A minor son of a minor country gentleman farmer – and yet she had chosen him. And now Brereton had his revenge.

The tension of the last few days had been denied the outcome he had expected, and before he knew it, the pressure released as his rage erupted. He was out of his seat and striding across the hall to stand over Brereton, yelling in his face. He did not even know what he was shouting and he fought to keep his hand from the grip of his sword, but finally Savage's words penetrated his bitter fury and he felt a strong hand pulling him back from the table. He shook it off, and as he did so, he caught sight of Marleigh. While he raged, she sat quiet and controlled. Their eyes met and he could feel her pleading with him, almost as if she were in his head, to sit. To be calm. To wait.

Not for the first time he was astounded at his selfishness. Like a flood of cold water, shame put out the fire of his temper. Had he truly learnt nothing from the events of the last years? He slumped back into his seat as Savage fought to regain quiet. He looked across at Marleigh and marvelled at her stoicism. If he had ever wondered about his feelings for her, in the moment that she rose to meet Savage's words, he knew that he would die for her in an instant. His rage turned to an icy fear and that cleared his mind. He had to stay calm for her. He had to plan. There would be some way to free her. He just had to think!

He heard Savage pass sentence. The old man had clearly been thrown off balance too and he was struggling through it. But at the end, the only important words were the ones which condemned her to hang, the following day. Behind him, came uncontrollable, inconsolable sobbing. He knew, without looking around, that this was Eliza Walker, weeping for Marleigh, and weeping for the fate awaiting herself and Maggie with Smale triumphant.

As Savage motioned for Constable Roe to take her back to the gaol, Marleigh's voice cut through the rising noise in the hall. Clear and controlled, not the voice of someone who had just learned they were to die in a matter of hours.

"Sir Edward. If I am to die, may I speak? There are words I would say."

*

She watched the indecision flash across his face as he turned to look at Brereton and Elcock. She saw Elcock urging him

(13 July 1644)

to deny her the chance. Clearly, he thought she might use her Devil-derived powers to enchant them or turn them all into toads. *What imbeciles these people are.*

Brereton offered little by way of opinion. His motivation was to be gone. Anything to be out of this room and on his way back to his army. Perhaps she should just take the decision out of the magistrate's hands.

"Sir. I will be quick. I cannot, and will not try to, change your minds. By what twisted thought you have arrived at your verdict, I do not know," here she looked directly at Brereton, "but let me allay your fears. I am no witch. I have not conspired with the Prince of Darkness. I will not, Master Elcock, turn you into some creature of the mud and slime. You would expect me to say this, I know. But I am no witch."

She paused. Her three judges seemed captivated. Like rabbits held in the gaze of a hunting weasel. No such enchantment held those behind her. Smale, always the loudest voice in the room, bellowed that she blasphemed. She should be taken down and hanged immediately. She heard Richard trying to shout him down. She shut it all out. She just wanted to say her words and then she would go. She was not done yet – they truly had no idea. And as she continued, silence again fell on the room.

"Kill me tomorrow, but know that I will go on. This story does not end tomorrow, with my ending. No. I am something far more dangerous to you. Me, and those who will follow after. So much more of a threat to you than the curse of 'witch' you place on poor, widowed, starving women who scrape an existence from the earth. Women who are so far beneath you that they can be treated as lower than the beasts that you farm. Women who cling on in hovels which others want to possess. Women who look ugly, or who beg, or who dare to stand up for themselves against local gentlefolk. What an opportune form of revenge. What an easy accusation. Like felling ancient trees to clear a field for the plough. Let us fell these inconvenient old hags so our lives can continue in the good grace of God.

"You call me a witch, but I am not one of those poor women. I am that most dangerous of things to you. I am an intelligent woman who holds herself as at least your equal. I know Latin and Greek. I speak French, Castilian and Italian. I have read the great philosophers and mathematicians, and I know more about the world than you will ever do in your lifetimes. I have travelled further and experienced more. I am dangerous to you because I am the future. I am the change that will come and sweep away the privileges of sex and lineage and property.

"I reject your judgement because, after all, who are you to judge me? I reject your authority as I rejected your religion long ago as meaningless worship of magic and superstition, presided over by ignorant and wicked men who line their pockets on the backs of the pitiful poor. There is no God, there is only the world. The earth, the sky, the air. The water and the soil and the sun that bring life to all things and to which we will all return. This is what matters. Sacrifice me to feed your twisted, bitter fantasies, but know that it changes nothing."

That did it. That broke the spell. Elcock was on his feet, yelling and waving his bible at her. Even the so-far mild-mannered Savage was red with rage. And behind her, Smale shouted, over and over, *"Burn her!"*

"Now," she said. "Now, Sir Edward. You can summon the constable because Marleigh Farrell is ready to die."

She turned, and without waiting for Roe, walked towards the door. She looked at Richard, who stood motionless, stunned, watching her go. The noise in the hall was intense – red faces, staring eyes, open mouths filling the air with hate and fury. She shouted to him to be heard. "Come and see me.

You must come to me!" And behind him she met the gaze of Eliza, red eyes brimming with tears. But eyes also full of pride, of confusion, of... what? Fear?

"And bring Eliza! Please, Richard, you must bring her too!" She stood her ground, easily holding off Roe at arm's length, until she saw Richard nod in acknowledgement. Then she relaxed and let herself be led away, the two of them surrounded by Brereton's soldiers to protect them from the mob.

*

Brereton spurred his horse west.

He had left two of his men with Constable Roe to help protect the gaol; the other four followed him along the road to Nantwich. The sun was setting in front of them as they kicked up dust along what passed for the road to his headquarters and his waiting army. He tried to focus on what lay ahead of him. He tried to concentrate on the intelligence he had received on Rupert's movements as he tried to stitch together the ragtag of units scattered after the battle outside York, and what that meant for the orders he would give to his commanders. He tried to weigh in his mind the arguments he had had with the victuallers in Macclesfield and what they meant for the money and resources he could deploy. *Never enough.* He tried to bring the faces of his wife and son into his head. The next moment he could possibly escape his military responsibilities, he would be back home to visit.

But above all, he contemplated his immortal soul and what the last few hours meant for his relationship with God. *He had been so sure.* Even more so when Marleigh let slip her mask of downtrodden, abandoned but virtuous woman. She had cursed God and the cause – all religion in fact – and portrayed herself as some kind of pagan! A disciple to the old superstitions that still haunted forgotten corners of the world. He had a sudden vision of a stone circle, high on the lonely moor, with the sun rising and casting shadows across the heather and yellow grass. He had not expected that! He had been convinced she was a tool of the Devil, but now he was not so sure. Had she not turned her back on all religion? That was not the action of one who worshipped at the feet of the fallen one.

He shook his head angrily. Nevertheless, she had blasphemed terribly. She had sealed her fate. He had watched silently as Elcock and Smale made the case to Savage for a burning, not a hanging. The old man had seemed exhausted and defeated. Confused and betrayed by his own emotions, and his own failure to recognise the guilt of this singular woman. The evidence had shown nothing to convict her on, but she was guilty despite it, not because of it. *Surely*, Brereton thought, *only God could have brought us to this truth. Not the truth I anticipated, but a truth nonetheless.*

In the end, his intervention had carried the debate. Burning was a horrendous fate. He had seen the aftermath during his journey to the Low Countries and heard stories of the mass burnings in some of the German states. No. Hanging was a sufficient punishment. Performed skilfully, the drop would mean a quick death. Perhaps he owed her that at least. After all, it was not clear to him she had actually caused any real harm. He had left clear instructions with the constable before he had left.

They had also discussed the fate of Marleigh's child. While Smale and Elcock cautioned letting the girl go free, he saw no law by which they could keep her imprisoned. Savage had concurred. For better or worse, she was now Farrell's problem. *Good luck with that!* He had no time to witness the execution,

(13 July 1644)

nor any desire to see her ending. He had other duties and responsibilities. With a prayer for a final release from Marleigh Farrell, he kicked his horse into a gallop.

*

The cell was nearly dark. The last of the sun was fading and precious little light found its way through the street-level opening. He called again for the constable to bring a lamp, but since Marleigh's speech, or whatever you would call it, after her sentence, Roe had been decidedly less friendly. A moral woman wrongly accused was one thing, a blaspheming unbeliever was quite another. Nevertheless, Richard persisted, and finally a lamp was brought.

In fairness, Richard thought, Roe was now under intense pressure. After Marleigh had been led away, some of the crowd had decided it was time to have a good few drinks and celebrate the death of a self-confessed heathen around the town. Although hangings were not uncommon, putting to death a good-looking druid bitch was not something you got to see every day. A few even held out hope that that stalwart of the community, Jeremiah Smale, might get his way and they could have a burning. No town in the whole of the North had seen a burning in many a long year. It would really put them on the map!

Inevitably, a few drinks led to several more, and then the fighting started. As a consequence, the two cells of the small town gaol were now precious space. One cell was crowded with drunken, puking, fighting local men. The other cell held Marleigh and Eva and, to Richard's surprise, Ellen, formerly known as the Maid of Rainow.

Ellen was still all in her white, but now looking grubby and unkempt. Her pale hair hung drab and lifeless off the side of the pallet where she lay stretched out with her back to the other occupants, Marleigh, Eva, Richard and Eliza.

"She still sleeps," Marleigh said quietly. "She could barely walk through from the other cell, and lay down to sleep immediately. Somehow I think she lost more than just her reputation last night. She seems entirely broken. Truly her brother deserves death for what he did to her."

Eliza seemed surprised. "You bear her no ill will? After what she intended to do? I am not sure I could be so forgiving!" Her eyes were still red-rimmed and her face deathly pale, but she had rallied since the trial finished. Richard could see again the streak of fierce independence that she had displayed at their previous meetings. She sat with Eva on her lap, playing with her hair. Eva looked up at her adoringly.

The dim light of the lamp showed Marleigh too was tired. He had seldom seen her so. *Tired, but not defeated*, he thought. Selfishly he wondered at her request – no, demand – that Eliza should come too. Having outlaid a significant amount of coin to the constable to get this opportunity, he had thought he and Marleigh might spend a few hours together to somehow say goodbye. Marleigh clearly had other things in mind. She seemed to be concentrating ferociously on Eva and Eliza, as if trying to memorise every detail of them. A few times he had thought to start conversation, but she silenced him with a look before he could even open his mouth.

Finally, she broke the silence. "Eliza. You must listen to me. Carefully."

Eliza looked up from her game with Eva.

"Eliza, you must know, Smale will make your life hell from this point on. For you and Maggie. Your friendship with me, over and above whatever schemes he has regarding your estate, will mark you as a figure of hate to be dealt with. One way or another he will see you disgraced, banished or dead. I cannot have that on my conscience."

"Have no fear, Marleigh. I will take care of Maggie. With Mr Brough's help we can…"

"No. I am sorry, Eliza. You have many qualities. You will make a fine, strong woman, but your name is tainted now and you do not have the guile or cunning to keep one such as Smale at arm's length. Believe it or not, he is now the hero of the town. The man who laid the witch low and saved the godly from the clutch of Satan! You would lose such a battle, Eliza, and I do not want you to lose everything."

Eliza looked down. Richard smiled to himself to see that she was preparing to defy Marleigh. She was indeed a strong woman. But Marleigh was right in this. "Eliza. Please listen to her. She has the right of it. Smale can bring to bear the law, the Church and good burgesses of the town to damn you for your association, and he will still be seen as saving you. You cannot win this."

And yet all the time, Richard himself was wondering about what Marleigh had said. Of course she was no witch, but to deny God and the Church? He may have his own doubts. He always had, but to stand and openly proclaim it in public? In court? And what was all that about trees and soil and the sun? He knew Marleigh was different. Unlike any other woman, any person, he had met. But he realised now he didn't really know her at all. What did that mean for them? What did his marriage mean? Did he still love her? Of course, he knew he did. That hadn't changed. But he was desperately confused, and beyond the fact that Eva would become his responsibility, he didn't know what he would do after tomorrow.

He had wanted to discuss escape. Lay plans and set strategies. Surely with his horse and his blade he could scare the shit out of these soft townsfolk long enough to grab her off the back of the cart and they could make a run for it. But not with Eva, and they couldn't leave her behind. And Marleigh seemed so resigned to it all. Although she was icy calm, she didn't seem to even entertain the idea of avoiding her fate. He was missing something, but he couldn't understand what.

"Eliza, will you come to... to the... will you come tomorrow? Please?"

Eliza looked horrified. Eyes wide in shock as if she hadn't even contemplated it. Hadn't allow herself to picture how things would go.

"Please. It would mean everything to me if you were there. With Richard, you and Maggie are the only friends I have in this town. I would look on a friendly face when... we have to say goodbye. Will you do that?"

Eliza set her jaw and swallowed hard, tears starting again in her eyes. "Of course. Of course, if that is what you wish. But... but I can't bring Maggie. She is too young and the Smale would not allow it."

"Of course. I am sure Maggie will stay with Mistress Smale. Jeremiah will not want to miss this for the world, and so if you wait for him to leave the house, I have no doubts you can make your own way out and to the marketplace."

Eliza nodded.

"And then, after... it is done, you must leave with Captain Farrell." She looked at him. "He will protect you. You must both go, and take Maggie too, and leave the town with Eva. Even if one day you come back. You must protect your inheritance via Brough. But keep clear of Smale's grasp. If I can help in that in any way tomorrow, I will. But it is up to you and Captain Farrell to save the other two. Will you do that?"

The question was addressed to Eliza, but he knew it was also meant for him.

(13 July 1644)

"You must be brave, Eliza. I know you can do this, and it is the only way to save Maggie and yourself."

Eliza stood, gently placing Eva back on the pallet.

She stepped forward and threw her arms around Marleigh. "After my father's passing, you were the only one who showed Maggie and me any real love. I do not pretend to understand everything you said in the guildhall. I don't think... no, I cannot deny God, as you have. I wish you could have explained it all to me. I love you, Marleigh, and I know Maggie does too. And Eva. She is another sister to us. We will not let any harm come to her. Of course I will come tomorrow." She had held her emotion for so long, but now she sobbed into Marleigh's neck, shoulders shaking.

Richard saw that Eva was getting distressed and scooped her up and held her to him. She put out a small hand and placed it on Eliza's hair. "Don't worry, Eliza," she said in a small voice. "It is not the end. We will be together."

Eliza surfaced, and regained her composure. You took Eva's hand and kissed it. Richard found himself wiping a tear from his eye and saw Marleigh, the cool, calm Marleigh, doing the same. "Tomorrow," she said, "Eva will stay here. She will be upstairs with Sarah Roe, the constable's wife. Although she is no longer of goodwill towards me, she holds no grudge with Eva. She has promised to look after her until... after. When it is over, Richard, you must come for her. Eliza, you must do what you must, but think on what I have said."

Eliza nodded.

"Then I shall see you in the morning. Be brave, and you will come through all that you must witness. Know that I love you even if you may doubt it in the time to come. Now, please, would you mind waiting a while outside so I can speak with Captain Farrell? Perhaps you can take Eva too. We will not keep you for long."

Richard watched the two of them step outside. The cell needed no guarding. The only way out was up the stairs and through the room occupied by the constable and the two soldiers Brereton had left behind.

"I do not know how she can sleep through all of this." Richard nodded at the figure on the pallet. Marleigh just shrugged.

"What has she to live for now?" She looked him in the eye and, taking a step forward, threw her arms around him. "Richard. I owe you both an apology and explanation. I had hoped that, with time, neither would be necessary, but it seems Marleigh's time has run out. She cannot leave you with no word."

Richard disentangled himself and held her at arm's length. He wanted to be able to see her. *Needed* to see her. "I never thought it would come to this." He shook his head. "How could they... Brereton... I mean, how could he come to that decision? What did I miss? Was it just jealousy? Was it Eva, and our marriage? I don't understand..."

She cut him off with a hand to his mouth. "That is gone now. We cannot turn time back. I am not sure myself, but I think it tortured him to do it. Let it go. We must concentrate on now. I owe you an apology because you came to me a free man and I leave you with the cares of the world on your shoulders. No, listen to me. Richard Farrell, at first, I used you shamelessly. I confess it. I could see you had the talent. We have spoken of it. The power you feel when someone dies. You feel that energy surge through you. Well, I too have that. Only what I have is stronger, and deeper, more practised and... older."

She held up her hand again as he started to speak. "No, Richard, please. We don't have long and I must say this. Maybe you must try to understand it later. I needed to have a child,

(13 July 1644)

and I needed to have that child with someone else who had the talent. Eva is a miracle. Well, not a miracle, as this is not some supernatural visitation, but she will amaze you. You will see this as you watch her grow. You must look after Eva as if she is the most precious thing in the world, because, probably, she is."

Richard could feel an anger growing inside him, but this was still masked by a deeper confusion. "Marleigh. She is my daughter, isn't she? Do you think I would not cherish her, even if to you I was no more than a means to an end? Please do not insult me with that. I love her. Perhaps even more so because I could have gone a lifetime and not known she existed." The anger continued to build. "And anyway, I don't think I have the… talent… or whatever you call it any longer. I lost it after Marston Moor. Funny. I saw it as a curse, not a talent! But I am glad it was useful to you."

"You are right." Her face was anguished. Not an expression he had seen before. Always she was so assured and confident. Now, though, it seemed like he was seeing through to a different person. "You are right. I treated you poorly. I thought that for you it would be a night of some pleasure and you would be on your way without a backward thought. Then you sought me out for the position at the Walker household and I came to see there was more to you than I had thought. When we met again, I realised that I had feelings for you. Feelings I had not felt for so long that it took me some time to recognise them for what they were. When you offered marriage, I did not accept purely for Eva's safety. I accepted also for myself. Richard, I realise that I think I feel love for you. A feeling that is mixed with gratefulness and respect. I genuinely wanted to be with you and now that is being taken away. I weep for what could have been, for what we might have grown between us in a life together. I am sorry."

He found he couldn't maintain his anger. He stepped forward again and this time he took her in his arms. "When I asked you to marry me, I admit that I too was not sure of my feelings. I have to admit that I am also just a little afraid of you."

She pulled back and looked at him with an eyebrow raised in enquiry.

"Well. You are so... beautiful. So... I don't know. So different, so fey and strange. And under that, there is a power that I feel but don't understand. I suppose it is this *talent* that you talk about. And your words at the trial? Like Eliza, I don't understand. But somehow that is all put to one side because within all of that mystery and confusion there is a person called Marleigh, whom I love. And she has a daughter whom I love. I don't need anything more. Not now."

She leant forward and kissed him. Not a kiss of passion but one of love and tenderness.

"My gallant captain. You must go now. Take Eliza home, and when it is done take her, Maggie and Eva and get as far away from here as you can, as quickly as you can. I fear for the girls, but most of all I fear for Eva. I do not expect Smale and Mary Brassey will suffer her to live now she is marked as a witch's child."

"Of course. Marleigh, even though it has been brief, and perhaps we did not start in the way lovers usually do, know that I have treasured my time with you. Look for us in the crowd. We will not desert you at the end, but be at peace knowing Eva will be safe. I did not get the chance to say goodbye to my sister or my brother before they were murdered. I did not get chance to say goodbye to the woman I wronged. My first love. Now I have the chance, I am not sure if it is better or worse. But... I love you, Marleigh, or whoever you really are. Goodbye."

23

AN EXECUTION

(14 July 1644)

She was awake well before dawn. Sounds in the street – shouting, jeering and other abuse filtering through the narrow ceiling-high opening – had kept her awake until late. With a full cell next door, Constable Roe seemed disinterested in trying to move anyone away. She had spent the time talking quietly with Eva. Sometimes with spoken word, sometimes through their minds. Eva was worried but calm, understanding what would happen in the morning, and what this would mean for her. Marleigh was already reassured that Eva trusted Richard, and that there was a growing love for this man she had learned was her father.

No sound came from Ellen. It was as if she wasn't even there. Just a lump under the thin blanket that Marleigh had pulled up to cover her. She had woken in the night, sobbing quietly to herself, but soon after had become limply unconscious again. Marleigh pitied her.

At least she didn't have to endure the sound of a scaffold being built. Like many towns, there was already a gibbet in the marketplace. It just required a cart to be drawn underneath the rope that would be provided, and a push in the back to oblivion. She had had no food the previous evening, Roe deciding it was not worth wasting his time with a heathen. He felt betrayed by her and she would receive no kindness from him now.

She had managed just a few hours' sleep but had willed herself awake so she could prepare herself. She had accomplished nearly everything she had hoped. With luck, she had secured Eva's future, at least in the short term. She had, finally, gained an understanding of her life, of all life, and its meaning. Of course, there were things she didn't know, maybe they were just unknowable, but she felt justified. All of the things she had done in her long quest for understanding had been worth it. She hoped the casualties along the way would feel so too, although she doubted it. She herself had no regrets, just sadness.

But she found it difficult to maintain a focus. Eva and Richard dominated her thoughts. In many ways this was what she had always tried to avoid. The human entanglements that stood in the way of her journey to understanding. Now that she had achieved her goal, and opened the door to emotion, she realised that the two were not exclusive.

As the first light started to filter in through the narrow window, she sensed it would be a glorious day. *That is fitting. Its last day on earth and my body will feel the warmth of the sun. The sun that makes all of life possible.*

She picked up the white pottery jug that held the water for washing and drinking. *Washing first*, she thought, *then I have other tasks to complete.*

*

He led his horse by the halter, trying to find faint paths through the alder and birch stands, in the pre-dawn light. Water oozed up around his already sodden boots as he squelched his way

(14 July 1644)

through the mire. Somewhere ahead of him were Cobb and his men. He was sure of it. He had found traces of a company of horsemen the previous dusk and followed the tracks long enough to gauge their direction before darkness halted his progress. He had slept fitfully, not daring a fire. He felt cold and it would be hours before the sun was high enough to warm his bones.

He came to the edge of the trees. Stunted and skinny as they were, they had provided some cover, but they could not grow in the morass ahead of him. Cotton grass, moss and coarse rushes held sway around a small pool, and he saw the ghostly shape of a heron wading through the dark water and the thin strands of mist that hung over the surface. He could see the trees continued to his right and left, and could see them start again on the far side of what was a large clearing. He could also see that the tracks split, and seemingly equal quantities of men and horses were going off in different directions. He had to make a decision which way to go.

A heaving coughing fit seized him, and he buried his face in the sodden cloth he was carrying in his free hand, desperately trying to muffle the sound. He waited, straining to hear if there was any reaction ahead of him. The sound of waking birds was filling the air, echoing back and forth across the otherwise still clearing. He turned right and followed the set of tracks that turned south-west. *They will expect him to be with Brereton. Heading for Nantwich. They will lie close to the road and hope for ambush.*

Trying to avoid the worst of the marsh, he made his way around the fringe of trees. As the sun rose, he remounted, kicking the animal into a trot. Soft light spread slowly across the open space, long shadows of trees reaching over the mire towards the hunting heron. Roger knew he had to make up time on the group ahead, but he had to remain undetected. He swigged the last of his water to wash the blood from his mouth, spitting down into the moss. He hoped there would be a more wholesome source than this black marsh water up ahead.

*

It seemed like the whole population of the town and most of the surrounding countryside stood in the marketplace. Richard was at the top of the short flight of steps up to the churchyard, elevated enough above the heads of the crowd to have a view across the open space. As the sun climbed into the clear blue sky, the smell of the good townspeople drifted up. He was no better. He had not slept but had spent the night planning and organising. Trying to think of all eventualities. Trying to keep a cool and clear mind when all he wanted to do was break down the door of the gaol, lay out Constable Roe and ride off with Marleigh and Eva. And he was pretty sure he could do it, but where did that leave Eliza and Maggie?

With the crush in the marketplace, he knew that any rescue was now virtually impossible. He doubted he could drive his horse through the crowd to get to her, and even if he did, all his escape routes were clogged with bodies. They would be sitting ducks for any competent musketeer. And he couldn't understand why Marleigh was so intent on helping the girls. Of course, she was fond of them, but to pass up the chance of escape? To sacrifice herself and risk Eva's care to him? He knew her priority was Eva's safety. Maybe she calculated this was the best chance for her daughter. He trusted her judgement, but with all of his heart wished there were a better way.

He could see Eliza standing to his right, on the bottom step. She had found him earlier, but he had counselled her to stand away from him, to lessen the chance that Smale might see her. When the proceedings started, and Smale was

(14 July 1644)

distracted by his triumph, then she could try to pick her way forward so that Marleigh might see her before the end.

He had told her the plan, such as it was. He had two horses, saddled and provisioned, with his pack, pistols and sword stowed, waiting in the yard of Brough's townhouse. One horse was his, the other he had loaned from Brough. *A good man*, he thought. *Once he had thought it through, he had seen the rightness of taking Eliza and Maggie out of Smale's clutches. At least for a while.* He hoped none of this would backfire on the lawyer, but he seemed as respected in the town as Walker had been.

After the end, as the crowd dispersed to their homes or the taverns, he would lead the horses round to the gaol and collect Eva. He had already called there and spoken to a hostile Sarah Roe. The child would come to no harm from her, but still she wanted her gone. Richard had little trouble in convincing her that this was his own wish. He saw no trouble there.

Eliza would return home and retire to her room to mourn. Nothing suspicious in that. Then she and Maggie would slip out of a rear window where Richard would be waiting with Eva and the horses. All being well, with the whole town distracted or drunk, they could slip away, hopefully picking up Roger on the southern edge of the town. He intended to head back to his home, such as it was. Once there, he would lodge the three girls with Lionel; God only knew what he would have to say about that, but Richard would not give him an option. Then he and Roger would head back to find Cobb and finish things, if Roger was still of a mind to help him. Being closer to London, he might want a reunion of his own but, either way, Richard knew none of them was safe until Cobb was in the ground.

In the meantime, he had to watch his wife, his love, be lawfully murdered in front of a baying mob. If he couldn't save her life, he could be with her as it ended. Somehow, that didn't give him any comfort. He put his hand on the pommel of his Toledo rapier and thought about how he would use it on Smale, Brereton and, when the time came, Cobb.

There was commotion in the square as a cart was pulled slowly through the crowds towards the gibbet. It was drawn by an enormous Shire, its coat gleaming black, muscles rippling, throwing its head about in nervousness at the noisy crowd. Cheers went up as more and more people spotted it. Its handler looked as nervous as the horse as he fought with the halter and tried to keep the animal calm. Behind the cart walked Brereton's remaining two soldiers, flanking Sir Edward Savage, Elcock and Smale.

He could see Eliza craning her neck to try to catch sight of Marleigh. She started to pick her way through the crowd to get closer to the gibbet. He could only imagine her distress, struggling to get close to the thing she most dreaded seeing. Marleigh had been her inspiration, her mentor, and her friend and protector. Now she was going and had begged Eliza to stand witness. What could she do? Anyone else shoving the good townsfolk who had bagged their ringside seats early would probably have received a fist or a volley of abuse, but not the eldest daughter of deceased Samuel Walker. They made way for her; helped her to make progress through the throng until he saw her stop, no more than ten paces from where the cart had come to rest, its rear positioned under the gently swaying rope. Wooden steps were found and the three men of the law climbed unsteadily on to the cart. Elcock stern and serious, Savage casting a worried look up at the noose as he slid past it, and Smale like a puffed-up cock pheasant, surveying the expectant up-turned faces of the crowd. He hadn't seen Eliza. Richard could see her looking down at her feet and shuffling behind a large man with a broad hat.

(14 July 1644)

Suddenly Richard sensed that eyes were on him. He couldn't say how he knew, but he was sure. He cast around the square. All faces were turned to the figures on the cart. There! On the far side of the marketplace, under the eaves of an old timbered shop. Partly in shadow, partly lit by the strengthening sun, he saw the pair who had drawn his attention at the trial. The alderman, Captain Booth, and his female companion. It was she who was gazing over at him. Her features were largely shaded and hidden under a bonnet, but she caught his eye. She smiled slightly and nodded. Who was this woman? He knew Brereton kept a network of spies, and they had been in close conversation in the short time he had been here in the town. But a woman as a spy? And why the interest in him?

Now the noise in the marketplace grew again and he swung back in time to see the crowd part again. Arms were raised and fists were shaken. A few vegetables and stones were thrown, although these seemed to hit other members of the crowd rather than the small party that wound its way in from the far corner, making a slow passage from the gaol on Dog Lane. Although he was some distance from the gibbet, his slightly elevated position allowed him to glimpse Constable Roe leading Marleigh by a short rope which held her wrists together. Six members of some local militia company flanked them. Richard had little doubt he could take all six; they looked like the dregs left behind for town guarding duty while the trained and battle-hardened troops were in the field. He longed to do so, but fighting his way to the cart would be like wading through quicksand, and Brereton's guards would be a different proposition. It was too late for heroics of that kind.

Marleigh was dressed in her black, and a coif contained her long red-brown hair, exposing her sun-browned neck. Easier for placing the noose. There was no tension in the rope between her and Roe. She walked in step, calm and serene.

Richard could now see, and sense, the energy and power she radiated. Perhaps only those with the talent, as she called it, could see this, but she seemed almost lit up with an inner light. The people closest to her fell silent. Perhaps they did sense something about her. Those further away continued to hurl insults or prayed devoutly to keep the evil at bay. Rumours of her testimony at the trial had been embellished to the extent that most believed at best she was some naive sun worshipper or at worst she was a scion of Satan himself.

She looked about her as she walked and all that met her gaze fell silent. It was the strangest thing to watch, and the strangeness now seemed to take hold of the whole marketplace as the people ceased all their shouting and a tense stillness took the place of the bedlam. The party reached the steps and Roe mounted the steps uncertainly, trying to keep his footing while gripping tightly onto the rope. Marleigh was up close behind him, flowing like a dancer. The militiamen arranged themselves at the foot of the steps, failing to look competent or menacing.

On the cart, now high above the townsfolk, Richard could see her searching the faces below her. He saw her relax fractionally as she found Eliza and a smile lit up her face. A smile that said, *Thank you*. A smile that said, *Do not worry*. For a moment he imagined that smile on the face of Jesus as he said farewell to his disciples. He saw Eliza sobbing into her handkerchief, shoulders shaking. The large man who had shielded her from Smale's sight turned and placed a meaty hand on her shoulder. His wife, Richard assumed, came around and took one of Eliza's hands in hers.

Now Marleigh looked up. Looked straight at him on the steps, no searching around the crowd. She knew where he was. The same smile engulfed him and he felt strong. He felt powerful. He felt like the warmth of the sun was focused on him alone. He sensed – because how could he see from that distance? – her eyes brim with tears. She held his gaze for a moment then nodded, seemingly content, and turned back to the others on the cart.

Throughout those moments, Elcock had been intoning from his bible while Roe fussed with the noose, checking the knot and the height. He spoke urgently with the carter who seemed to have his horse under better control. There was now no way that Smale could have failed to see Eliza. He strode to the edge of the cart, a face like thunder. Richard could see him gesticulating to her. Pointing in the direction of the house on the Mill Street. Eliza merely shook her head and folded her arms across her chest. Defiance replacing sadness. Savage placed a hand on Smale's shoulder and pulled him away. Richard hoped they would avoid the confrontation that Smale clearly had in mind for Eliza once the hanging was done.

Marleigh now stood next to Roe, her bound wrists at her waist, as Elcock finished his reading and Savage stood at the edge of the cart and addressed the crowd. He summarised the accusation against her, the verdict of the three judges, and reiterated the sentence to be carried out. His voice could be clearly heard over the low murmuring of the expectant crowd. More than ever, he looked like he wanted to be anywhere except on this cart in Macclesfield marketplace.

Roe carefully placed the noose over Marleigh's head and tightened the knot. Richard saw her lean towards Roe and whisper something to him. Roe looked surprised and made some reply, but Marleigh shook her head. She gestured with her bound wrists towards Smale. Still holding the rope that bound her, he let go of the noose and approached the three men. There was some discussion. *What's going on?*

He could see Savage again place a hand on Smale, this time gently pushing him towards Marleigh.

*

She followed Roe's broad back up the steps on to the broad flatbed of the cart. He was sweating in his coat in the morning sun, although she imagined it was the tension of the day, rather than the weather, that was the root cause. She saw the militiamen fan out behind her, their motley collection of uniforms, helmets and weapons impressing no one. The three good men of the law were waiting, already on the cart. She smiled to herself as she saw they kept a healthy distance from her.

The energy flowing through the marketplace from so many people threatened to overwhelm her. It had been many years since she had been in such a gathering and, with her new vision, she struggled to keep her mind from being overloaded. She needed to focus! She concentrated on the Shire horse. She reached out with her thoughts and found and touched its mind. It was angry and confused. It too was unused to such crowds. *Let us help each other. I will calm you and you can calm me.* She shut out the crowd and concentrated on soothing the animal's brain. She reminded it of its strength and felt its assurance grow. Now she too regained her control and composure, retuning and adjusting her senses.

Now she looked for Eliza, hearing Elcock start droning his sermon for the guilty. There! *My good and faithful girl!* She poured her thanks straight into Eliza's mind, amazed at how straightforward she found this now that she had attuned herself. *Too much!* She saw Eliza suddenly overcome with emotion and pulled back. *Gently now...*

She could sense Richard as well, somewhere across the marketplace. His own talent was rudimentary, but it still marked him out to her immediately. She had sensed it vaguely when she first met him, but now... now Eva had enhanced her perceptions to this degree, she could pinpoint him quickly. At the top of the steps, his face unreadable, but his mind accessible to her. She felt his emotion, barely controlled, and the strength of his feeling for her, and it tugged at her heart. *So many things must end today...* She felt tears forming and let them well in her eyes.

Elcock was finishing his oration and Savage was now addressing the gathering. Roe stepped awkwardly towards her with the noose. *Poor man. Murdering innocent women cannot be how he saw his vocation.* The coarse fibres of the rope itched her neck as Roe tightened the knot. He whispered to her, "I have left some slack in it. When the cart moves, jump, and the drop will make it quick." He paused, looking at his feet. "I know not what ye are, mistress, but God have mercy on yer."

"Thank you, Daniel. Truly. And thank you for looking after Eva. It has been a blessing. I would ask one more thing of you, while I have time?"

He managed a weak smile. "I am not sure there is time, mistress."

"There is for this. I would like to confess to Master Smale before... the end."

"You mean to Master Elcock? He is the minister here."

"No, Daniel. It should be Master Smale. I have blighted his life and he fears I have corrupted his nieces. I would make amends with him and God before I depart. Can you make it so?"

Roe looked at her doubtfully but stepped towards the group of three men, who were looking on impatiently. After a brief discussion, which she couldn't fully hear, Savage seemed to be urging the reluctant Smale to 'Get it done, man.' Clearly Savage wanted this to be done and the crowd dispersed.

She took a deep breath. In the space of a moment, she took in the blaze of life around her. The slow thoughts of the horse, scratching its flank against the wagon shaft. She could glimpse the sunbathed hillsides to the east, as they marched away to the north. Far above her, a kite circled, enjoying the lift from the warming air. She closed her eyes and drank in the glory of it all.

When she opened them, the men were filing down the steps. Roe made his way to the front of the cart to speak with the carter. Smale, however, stood in front of her, his features cycling through looks of hate, fear and triumph. "Well, whore? Say your piece and let's be done with this. I have my nieces to deal with after I have done with you."

Marleigh looked him in the eye, and smiled.

*

Sarah Roe was getting increasingly agitated. She had known hangings before in the town, but never had she witnessed such feverish excitement about the death of a prisoner. And never had she had to babysit the daughter of the prisoner during her execution. And never had she encountered a child such as the one who now sat in front of her on the rough oak table in what passed as the office of the gaol.

Eva smiled at her like a little angel. *Or a little demon!* Those strange eyes! Not just the mismatched colours but the depths behind them. It was like looking into the past – the knowledge of lifetimes in the eyes of an infant. When she had felt genuine sympathy for the Hume woman – *no, the Farrell woman* – she had felt a real fondness for the cheeky little girl, but now her mother had damned herself from her own mouth she just felt an incredible unease around the child. Not that some of what the woman had said was wrong, as it had been reported to her. She was no London radical, but Sarah Roe was no fool. She knew the way the cards were dealt between men and women

(14 July 1644)

and, if arguments over prayer books and stained glass could start a war and turn the world upside down, then maybe a few other matters could be put right! Perhaps it was time all these great men realised who did all the work in the country and that they too deserved a better lot in life!

But to turn your back on God. That was... that was damnation for eternity! And for what? Communing with the trees? Not even a pact with the Devil and the earthly rewards that could bring, albeit with a terrible, terrible price. She didn't understand, and she felt a sadness and an anger about the inheritance the mother had left for the daughter. Did she think the dashing captain would take on a little girl? *Not so dashing*, she thought. That battered face gave him a look she couldn't quite trust. Fair or foul – depending on which side you saw. Trouble followed that one around. And it did, because she had seen the ruffian company he kept. That grey-haired and grey-bearded old rogue would not welcome the baggage of a youngster in tow. It would all end badly for little Eva. How could the estimable Samuel Walker have been taken in by the likes of these? She would never understand. She despised Jeremiah Smale, but at least he had seen through them all. Now he had his little triumph. There would be no hearing the last of it around town.

She fidgeted, not wanting to let Eva out of her sight, but needing to be doing something to take her mind off all this... complication. There was a soft knock at the door and her friend Constance Holland leaned around the frame. "Just thought you'd want to know. They are about it now. She's on the cart and the end is coming." It was then she saw Eva on the table and her eyes went wide in horror and guilt. She put her hand to her mouth. "Oh Lord. I did not see her there. Do you think she understood?"

"Oh, she understands alright. But don't fret yourself, love, she seems unconcerned by the whole thing. In a little world all of her own, I think. She is an odd child, but I can't bring myself to hate her for her mother's sins."

A thought occurred to her. "Constance? Could you do me a favour?"

"Well, I had thought to go and watch the…" she glanced at Eva, "…you know."

"I know, and I'm sorry, but I will go mad if I sit here with her any longer. Can you just watch her a moment while I go and check on our other resident? That Maid o' Rainow, or whatever she calls herself now, hasn't stirred all morning and I want to clean out the cell as best I can now that at least one of them has gone." She too shot a glance at Eva, but the child just smiled back at her as if she hadn't a care. "Please, just a few minutes?"

Her friend nodded and sat down at the table warily, eventually forcing a thin smile in Eva's direction.

Sarah swung round with relief and headed down the dark, narrow steps to the basement cells. The one on the left was now empty; the drunks and brawlers of the previous night had been kicked out. That cell would need a deep cleansing, but she would leave that for later. She wanted to check on this Ellen girl and remove all the items that had been touched by Marleigh Farrell. Just in case…

The door was not locked. This girl had not committed any crime she was aware of. There she lay. Curled up with her back to the door, her increasingly grimy white dress barely covering her modesty. The soles of her feet were black with dirt and, if anything, her skin seemed even paler than ever. On the floor the white water jug lay shattered into several pieces. A wave of irritation hit her. Was this a last piece of petty revenge from Marleigh? Didn't she know that the Roes had to cover these things from her husband's meagre wage? It was a kindness that they kept the cells in good order and provided the means for washing. Many gaols were no more than pigsties, but they took a pride in their work.

She set to gathering up the pieces, and she winced as she cut a finger on the edge of one of the shards. That would need extra careful washing. Who knew what it was tainted with? Some witch poison, no doubt. She peered into the darkness below where the sleeping girl lay, in search of further pieces of the pottery.

She got to her feet and moved around the mattress. She shook the shoulder of the Maid of Rainow. She felt cold, and there was no movement. No reaction. She grasped her shoulder and rolled her onto her back. Even with the strength of the morning sun the cell was only dimly lit, but it was enough. A lifeless eye stared back at her. The other was black with crusted blood. Ellen, Maid of Rainow, had vacated the cell some time ago.

Frantic, Sarah Roe grabbed one of the pieces of gleaming pottery and flew up the stairs. Without a word to the wide-eyed Constance, she hitched up her skirts and ran as fast as she could along Dog Lane and towards the marketplace.

*

I am sorry, Ellen. Truly I am. But what life did you have in front of you? You were virtually dead, but you could still help me. You could help me to help Eva. And you could help Eliza and Maggie. I have your power in me now. Watch how I use it!

Slicing the bond with the edge of the pottery shard was the work of an instant, and she held the severed ends between her palms. In a sea of people, she was alone on the deck of the cart with Smale. A gloating, leering Smale who leaned in to give her the benefit of his sour breath.

She sensed a commotion start in the corner of the

marketplace. From the corner of her eye, she saw Sarah Roe forcing her way through the crowd. But the constable hadn't yet seen her. Smale hadn't seen her. He had his back to them.

"Go on then. Let me hear your whining apology and feeble confession. You are on your way to hell, woman. Tell them I sent you there!"

"You think you have caught yourself a witch, Master Smale. You are wrong. For I am much, much worse. You have no conception of what I am. Tell them in hell who sent me? Why, Master Smale, tell them yourself!"

With all the strength she could muster, her own and the power borrowed from Ellen, she brought up her hands, driving the gleaming white shard into his overhanging belly, ripping upwards as she felt it penetrate clothing, skin and fat. He stared at her for a moment, eyes wide in horror, and then down at the bloody cascade that ran down his thighs. He doubled over, grabbing at the terrible wound, as horrified screams went up from those nearby in the crowd. As his head lowered, she whipped a loop of the noose rope around his neck. As the constable reached the top step, she gave him a smile, grabbed the collar of Smale's coat and stepped back off the cart, dragging him with her.

*

Richard stood frozen to the spot. He saw, and felt, the power flow in Marleigh as the upwards thrust nearly lifted Smale off his feet. He couldn't see what weapon she wielded, but the impact was tremendous and a shower of blood splashed heavily onto the boards of the cart. The horse reared in terror as the carter fought with its halter and, just as the constable reached the pair, he saw Marleigh seemingly fall backwards, wrapping a hand, and the rope, around Smale's neck as she went.

(14 July 1644)

It seemed as if the whole marketplace held its breath. Everything seemed to move in slow motion. First there was a sickening crunch as the weight of the two bodies was taken first by the loop of rope around Jeremiah Smale's neck. Then, as the frightened horse shrugged off its handler and pulled the cart away, scattering the crowd, he saw Marleigh. No contorted, purpling face, no dancing limbs, no frantic rolling eyes. Just the same calmness he always saw in her. With a familiar heightened sense returning to him, he saw, he felt, Smale's life essence flow into Marleigh, channelled by her.

She just hung there, for what seemed like seconds, staring calmly into the crowd in front of her. Then she closed her eyes and he sensed a wave of power building within her, even at the distance he was from the slowly swinging rope. It was like a noise growing in his skull, rising to a silent scream of release. Higher and higher until suddenly Marleigh, Smale and the rope itself were engulfed in a thin tower of flame. It rose fully ten feet above the height of the gibbet before there was a thump of bodies hitting the dirt of the marketplace and the fire abruptly ceased.

He sank to his knees. The crowd was scattering, running to leave the marketplace by any means possible. The Shire horse, maddened by the fire, the smell of blood and the noise of screaming people, picked up speed and thundered across the open space towards the top of the Mill Street. Richard saw Constable Roe hanging on to the back of the swaying cart for dear life. After just a few seconds, it seemed only a few figures were left. Elcock was helping Sir Edward Savage back to his feet, both of them pale, shocked and slightly singed. Sarah Roe was doing her best to follow her husband's perilous traverse. And there, just yards from where the rope had hung, where two blackened lumps lay in a pile of ash and dirty fluid, Richard could see the shape of Eliza Walker, apparently out cold. Or worse.

He tried to gather his shattered mind together. Now he could understand what Marleigh had achieved. The main threat to the Walker girls was gone and she had created chaos. The best opportunity for Richard to escape with Eva and the girls. He couldn't let the time she had bought go to waste!

Cajoling his wobbling limbs into action, trying to blank out the unbelievable scene he had just witnessed, he made his way round to the back of the church and re-emerged with the horses. He jogged across to where Elcock was now kneeling next to the fallen Eliza, Savage peering over his shoulder and chasing some smouldering remnant of the hanging rope off his coat.

"Out of my way!" Richard snarled at him. "She is in my care now." He shoved him away and, taking off his leather glove, felt for Eliza's breath. She was cold to his touch but was breathing. *Thank God!*

He slipped his arms under her shoulders and behind her knees, and strained to lift her off the packed dirt. Even though she was lighter than he expected he still struggled to unceremoniously dump her across the saddle of his horse. He then quickly led both away, heading towards the Dog Lane and the gaol. He glanced back over his shoulder. Savage and Elcock just watched him go. Neither seemed to have yet processed what they had just witnessed, and while they hadn't fled with the rest of the mob, they seemed incapable of taking any action. Even to speak.

Having seen Sarah Roe chase after the disappearing cart, he had no idea where Eva would be. As he burst into the office, it took him a few moments to see a woman he didn't recognise crouching in the far corner, trying to shield Eva from whatever horrors she imagined were outside. Seeing an armed man, apparently fully in control of his wits, she jumped up. "Oh, sir! Thank God you have come. I don't know what I should

(14 July 1644)

have d…" She then recognised who she was speaking to and faltered. The infamous husband of the proven witch who had just provoked the mayhem that had been passing by outside the gaol.

Richard had no time or inclination for violence. Mustering all his self-control he managed to calm his voice. "Mistress. I mean you no harm." He held up both hands, palms outwards. "I am merely here to collect my daughter from you. Nothing more. Stand aside now, and let her come to me."

Constance had no intention of exposing herself to harm to protect a witch's child and hastily stepped back, pressing herself into the wall to be as far away from him as she could.

"Eva. Come, love. We must go now. Like Mama said to you. It is time for us to leave now and we must go quickly." He expected a frightened little girl, near hysterical with grief and anger at the loss of her mother. Instead, Eva just calmly nodded at him and toddled around the table to take his hand. She even smiled up at him, and he felt a faint warmth spread through his mind, clearing his thoughts. Outside, he swung into the saddle and cradled her against his chest with one arm, while grabbing the reins and again leading the horses. She reached out a tiny hand and rested it for a moment on Eliza's blonde curls. At the touch, the figure seemed to stir slightly, and there was faint moaning.

"I'm sorry, Eliza. We must keep moving. We have to get Maggie. Then we can get out of the town and find somewhere to hide and rest."

There was no response, but he was heartened that she seemed to be waking. He headed back across the marketplace and towards the Walker house.

*

It was evening and they had left the road somewhere around the village of Sutton. He aimed to head for Leek and then south-east towards Derby, and on for Huntingdon.

It had been a bitter day and he was exhausted. He led the two horses on a rough, narrow track through a copse of beech, oak and elm. He had seen an old stone barn earlier, from a rise in the ground a mile or so back, and he hoped to spend the night there. It would be sheltered from eyes watching the road and might provide more comfort for the girls than being out in the open, although doubtless they would be experiencing that soon enough.

In the end, his plan had been thwarted. He had arrived in sight of the Walker home to find that Savage and the constable had not been idle. A small crowd had formed outside the property, including the ragtag of militiamen. Maybe alone he could have intimidated them to giving him entry, but not with Eva in his arms and Eliza still slumped across the back of his horse. He had slunk away, playing cat and mouse with those brave enough to follow him until a pistol shot had been sufficient to drive off the last of his rather half-hearted pursuers.

The path through the trees took them through a small break in the stone wall, and out into a broad pasture. There were no grazing animals as far as he could see in the dimming light; the gaps in the wall suggested it was not in use. The war had stripped the countryside of livestock and farmers, and there was no telling when both would return. The barn was to his left, built as part of the wall, and it had a tall entrance, wide enough for a pair of horses and a cart to enter. There was a window opening on either side of the door, and narrower slits above suggested a hayloft. It was a substantial building to be sitting empty and abandoned, but he gave thanks for it. Double doors of thick oak stood half open and the barn

(14 July 1644)

looked across a gradually rising green pasture to an opposite wall and beyond, where a scrub of gorse, heather and bilberry started among small outcrops of gritstone. A line of low hills was visible over the nearer ridge.

In the centre of the field stood a solitary oak. Richard marvelled at it. It was the mother and father of oaks – ancient and huge. It was not an old rotting mass, clinging on and shedding decaying branches. Despite its obvious age, it seemed in its prime, a picture of vigour and health, lush with foliage, and alive with the sound of birds settling to roost. As tall as it was, its lower branches were so long and thick that they touched the ground, before curving up again. It was like a venerable old drinker leaning on the bar. Leafy hands open and awaiting the next mug of ale. He smiled to himself despite his weariness. *Have one for me, friend!*

The last rays of the sun barely clipped the leaves on the topmost branches and all the colours below were becoming muted, but the tree seemed to radiate the energy of life. It seemed to exert an almost magical effect on Eva.

She was sitting on Richard's shoulders having ridden in front of him in the saddle since leaving the town, held within a loop of rope to make sure she wouldn't slide off if he had to move the animal quickly. Eliza was now sitting vertically on the horse but still seemed to be deeply shocked by what she had witnessed. Her eyes seemingly vacant and sitting on the horse like an automaton. Despite this, he had seen her maintain and recover her balance several times when they had needed some speed, or had to negotiate slopes and winding paths if they had left the road.

The presence of the oak seemed to energise Eva, who sat up from her slump and curled her little fingers into his shoulder-length hair. Again, he felt a warm glow spread through his mind, like slipping into a hot bath. *When was* the last time I had one of those! There was something else too. It was like an insistent tapping – something trying to get his attention. Like something you see out of the corner of your eye, but when you turn your head, you sense movement and whatever was there is gone. Except this was inside his mind.

He felt Eva's fingers knot themselves deeper and try to turn his head around. She was trying to steer him like a horse! He obliged her and looked round. He saw Eliza's eyes were open, and she too seemed transfixed by the scene. She still looked drunk, her lids heavy, and she swayed in the saddle. But she was awake. Eva's little voice came from behind him. "She needs to rest now, Papa."

"I know, love. Can you just sit here on the horse for a moment? I want to check the barn is safe for us." She nodded in reply and for the first time in their travels, she too looked tired.

He walked quietly along the pasture side of the wall, and keeping close to the barn wall, edged around to the front of the building. Despite being abandoned, the stonework was excellent, and the whole structure spoke of strength and durability. He inched around towards the partially open door nearest to him and ducked inside. In the fading light it was gloomy, particularly as it had its solid back to the west and the setting sun. There was rotting straw on the floor, but there was little smell of cattle or horses. Abundant dry straw had been pushed into the corners and he could see further piles of it in the hayloft. A ladder led up to the platform which extended round the back of the structure, connecting the larger space at either end under the timbered roof. At the rear of the hayloft, a small opening with waist-high double doors suggested it might have been used for pushing hay out at some time. There was a small clearing below, connecting to the path they had approached on, although that had become a little overgrown,

(14 July 1644)

which was perhaps why he had missed it on the way in. Satisfied they had it to themselves, he tried shifting the doors and, after some protest from the hinges, and his own joints, he got them closed, leaving just enough space for the horses to enter.

He rejoined the girls in better spirits. "Our first piece of luck today. We could not wish for better lodgings outside of a warm tavern. With a few bats and some harvest mice, I think the company will be more pleasant than even that."

Eva gave him a tired but weary smile and reached out her arms to him. He could not believe that this child had lost her mother today, a mother she so clearly adored. He hugged her to his chest and led the two horses behind him into the dimly lit space. Eliza just stared blankly at him. "We are out of sight of the road so I will risk a fire, I think, even with all of this…" He gestured at the dry straw. "We all need some warmth and a little cheer at the end of this day."

He set Eva down and reached up to Eliza, grasping her slim waist and half lifting, half sliding her off the saddle. Her legs held up as she reached the earthen floor of the barn, but she just stood perfectly still. Like a stone statue. He led her over to a bale of hay against the eastern wall, near one of the windows onto the meadow, and she sat. Leaning against the stonework, she closed her eyes again. He had seen reactions like this in war. A total and deep shock at witnessing some horrific event, rendering the person insensible to the outside world. He had seen some recover their full wits. He had seen many who didn't, and he was deeply concerned for her.

"Sit with her, Eva. Hold her hand or something. I will be with you both when I have seen to the horses." Food was no issue, but he needed to find them water before darkness fell completely. He needed some firewood too. *No rest for the wicked…*

When he returned, Eva was sitting next to Eliza on the bale. She was holding her hand and she too had her eyes closed. They seemed like sisters, listening to some story being read to them by a parent at bedtime. Trying to concentrate on the words, but already dozing. He closed the barn doors, wedging them shut with stones and bits of wood. Clearing straw from a patch of the earthen floor, he managed to get a small fire going. Laying out blankets, he carried the girls over to the flames in turn and laid them down. He settled himself near one of the windows, trying to arrange himself so he could see out into the darkness but his silhouette would not show to anyone attracted by the dim glow of the fire. He didn't know how long he could stay awake, but he figured that, by a few hours after sunset, no one would be moving around. Roger must be out there somewhere. *At least it's not raining on him this time.*

He thought about Maggie, the missing sister, and how she was faring that night. With Smale dead, perhaps her lot would not be too bad. Smale's wife was, apparently, a very different proposition and more likely to treat Maggie with kindness. So he hoped, but losing her husband in such circumstances? Who knew how that might affect her and her thoughts towards her niece? In any case, as soon as he had settled Eva and Eliza with brother Lionel, he would return for her.

He could feel himself drifting towards sleep. He tried to fight it, but he was exhausted. He thought of Marleigh. He hadn't really stopped. The scene on the cart playing and replaying in his head. He could glimpse, sense perhaps, what she had done. From his own experience of the talent – he didn't know what else to call it now – he had a vague thought of how she might have achieved it, but clearly her abilities to channel and control that energy far surpassed his. He couldn't describe how he felt. Sadness. Anger. Always anger lurking.

(14 July 1644)

He couldn't help but compare Marleigh's ending with that of Gabriel, the carpenter from York. Violent revenge with peaceful forgiveness. Desperation to buy time and safety for her loved ones, with the serene acceptance of reunion in a life to come. What did that mean? Why was he thinking this?

*

He woke before dawn. His back was stiff from slumping against the stonework at an awkward angle and he badly needed a piss. When he returned to the barn, the sky was lightening slightly but the clouds felt low, and there had been light rain in the night. But the air felt altogether fresher. *Like a new start.* He had had a few of those recently, but he always seemed to end up at the same shitty ending. And it seemed to involve losing someone he loved.

He climbed up into the hayloft and settled himself at one of the slitted windows. The cool air squeezed through, carrying the smell of wet grass into the slightly stuffy atmosphere of old, dried-out straw. *We'll wait 'til after the sun's up.* That way he could get a good look at the land to the east before they set off. He could also scout back up the road for a while to check tracks and see if anyone was following them.

Suddenly, he felt a light pressure on his shoulder. He jumped like a startled animal and swung around. His shoulder connected with another body and his trailing leg swept into a pair of ankles. Eliza crashed down into the straw beside him. "Oh God! I'm sorry! I'm sorry! Are you hurt?" He bent and offered her his hand.

She looked a little startled herself but quickly regained her composure. She took his hand and he pulled her up. "No, sir. 'Tis my own fault. I am sorry to have surprised you so." She looked at him, a faint smile on her lips. "I am also amazed to have crept up on such an experienced fighting man. Perhaps you were asleep?"

He felt very confused. How *had* she managed to surprise him? Last night she had seemed lost in the deepest shock. This morning she was lucid and obviously in full control of herself again.

"Is Eva asleep? Did you leave her below?" He looked behind her for sight of the little girl.

"Yes. She is still sleeping. I think she is exhausted from yesterday, despite the brave face she shows to the world. But we will depart this place soon? I am anxious to put miles between us and the men who did that to Marleigh." As she spoke, her face twitched slightly, as if the memory of it all threatened her newly rediscovered composure.

"Yes, Eliza. We should go soon. But are you well? Well enough to travel? You still seem a little…"

"A little what…" she paused, as if in a momentary dilemma, "…Captain Farrell?"

"I don't know. Yesterday was such a shock. Such a… I don't know. I am still not sure what I saw. I am struggling to understand it all myself. For you? So close to her when… it… happened. I don't know if that was her plan all along, or she just saw a chance to remove Smale from your life. From Maggie's life. I don't know. I don't understand…" he repeated, trailing off. He looked at her again. "I do understand that you need to rest. You need time, I think, to try to make sense of this." He laughed, despite the blackness of the conversation. "And perhaps you can explain it to me when you do!"

"Yes. I am sure you are right. Perhaps, soon, we can talk about it." Eliza, though, seemed entirely distracted. On edge. "But we should go. Soon." Again, a wave of some emotion passed over her, as if she were fighting down an impulse to speak. He saw her jaw muscles clench, her earlier composure deserting her.

(14 JULY 1644)

"Please, Eliza. Sit down. Please." She shook her head. Grim determination behind her eyes.

"No. Thank you, sir. But we must go. We cannot stay near... that town. Those people."

"I do not think any will follow us. After all, 'twas Marleigh who killed Smale, not us, before... before whatever it was happened. With the fire." He shrugged. He repeated, "I don't understand..." It was not some pursuit from the townsfolk that bothered him so much. It was Cobb and his men that concerned him. A further danger of which Eliza was entirely oblivious. He too wanted to get on the road, but if she was still unwell, it might be more dangerous than staying where they were for another day.

"At least let us rest a while longer? You could wake Eva and find some food from the bags? I will scout the road and the area and check that we are safe."

She looked at him uncertainly. Anxious. As if she were fighting some inner demon. Abruptly she looked down. Defeated. "I will follow your advice, sir. After all, I owe so much to you. But please, let us not tarry longer than needed."

"We will not. Just try to relax, Eliza. And try to keep Eva calm when she wakes. I will not be gone long."

He saddled his horse and watered it. He jogged it back up the road north for a mile or so. He saw no one. It was like the countryside had emptied. A fox was making its way home in the dawn light, sliding under the glittering hedgerow, the sun catching last night's raindrops on the hawthorn leaves and the dew caught in lacy spiderwebs. He struck east, keeping to the edges of fields, and any cover he could find. He was aiming for the ridge he could see from the barn doors. It would be good to know if anything, or anyone, was loitering there out of sight.

As he reached the grassy ridge, he dismounted and left his horse tied to a rowan. He didn't want to be highlighted on the exposed ground in the rising sunshine. He squinted into the sun and saw more hills, gradually rising to form the southern end of the Pennines. There was no one. There was plenty of cover. Woods, rocks, ditches and lanes. He lingered some minutes; nothing was moving. Nothing on horseback at any rate.

He remounted and walked down the slope, back towards the barn. He found a gap in the stone wall and steered through, gathering pace down the hill and looping around the monumental oak. There was no sign of their presence in the building. The doors were closed except for a narrow gap, and the other animal, the girls and their baggage were hidden from view. *Good.* He hoped Eliza was feeling better and they could get on their way. He tied up his horse with the other, around the back of the barn.

He had decided he had to tell her about the plan to link up with Roger. And he couldn't avoid the subject of Cobb. He couldn't lead Eva and her out into the daylight and not have them prepared for flight. He slipped inside.

*

He crested the low ridge, the rising sun casting his shadow far out ahead of him, lost in the hazy distance. The low cloud of pre-dawn had broken up and patches of blue-grey were starting to appear, just faintly, in the hesitant light. He pushed on quickly, not wanting to linger on the high ground. The scrubby gorse, rowan and rocky outcrops provided good cover, but he didn't want to be silhouetted against that sun.

As he made his way into a small stand of alder trees, a noise in the distance caught his attention. The dawn birdsong was not of the same extent as earlier in the year, but he thought at first it was just some feathery conversation greeting the day.

(14 July 1644)

But no. There it was again – definitely human voices. Not close, but close enough. If this were Cobb and his men, they may have outriders, checking for just such people as himself. That is what he would have done. He suspected Cobb was no less careful. He halted and dismounted. He crept forward to the edge of the copse.

The slope ahead of him was littered with rocks and more scrub, but then the land flattened and rose again to another ridge. Maybe a couple of miles away? Just at the bottom of the next upward slope was a line of men on horseback. He counted seven. Leather jerkins, one or two with steel cuirasses, a couple more helmets. All armed. All comfortable on horses. He saw more movement over to the left. Perhaps a hundred paces out. And… yes! There on the right too. He had no doubt a further rider trailed the main group, looking over his shoulder. Looking for ambushes. Looking for parliamentary soldiers. Looking for opportunities to loot.

This was them. He had found them, and now to follow them without becoming the followed. The captured. The dead. He buried a cough in the crook of his elbow. *That won't help my cause.*

He went back for his horse and waited, watching the horsemen reach the top of the next ridge and pass over. From here the land beyond looked flatter as the waves of Pennine foothills met the long Cheshire plain that ran to the Irish Sea. As he watched, a final, single rider appeared on the horizon. The mount paused as the rider turned in his saddle and then turned his mount through a full circle. He imagined the man squinting directly into the low sun. Roger was well hidden, but he waited a few moments more before he trotted his horse down the slope, through the camp Cobb's men had made the previous evening, and then ascended. He could close the distance while he was shielded by the ridge and then could think about maybe getting around their flank to find Richard and to make their escape.

*

The sun's light was just appearing over the rise opposite, just catching the top of the oak, mirroring the light of the sunset the previous evening. It grazed the top of the barn, highlighting the wooden shingles. The inside of the barn was still only dimly lit, but there were Eliza and Eva, sitting together on the straw bale they had occupied the evening before. There was some evidence that they had eaten, but now Eliza was again sitting with eyes shut. Eva held her hand and seemed to be concentrating hard, staring at Eliza with a real intensity. A look that seemed so odd in such a young child.

"You are ready? Eva? Have you eaten?"

Eva spoke without turning from Eliza. "Yes, Papa. We had bread. And an apple." He still couldn't quite get used to 'Papa'. "We have left some for you. It is wrapped in the cloth, in case you wanted to eat as we travel."

"And Eliza? How is she? Is she not well again?" But even as he spoke, she opened her eyes again. She blinked hard, swallowed, and rose to her feet. Eva kept her grip on her hand. She seemed serene again. As she had been when they spoke in the hayloft. She picked up her bag.

"Thank you, Captain, but I am quite well now. I can travel. Please, eat first. I am sorry for my impatience earlier."

"It is fine. As I said, I too am anxious to be gone and on the road to my home. Such as it is. And please, whilst it is just the three of us, you may call me Richard. In other company, I think it best you call me Captain Farrell, or Master Farrell."

She looked mortified. "Oh no! I couldn't! It would be rude

and presumptuous. My father would be ashamed of me. He would regret his trust in me."

He approached her and placed a hand on her shoulder. "Eliza, I know that I am, in truth, not a great deal older than you are. I cannot be your father. I would say, see me as your uncle, but that brings up too many unfortunate memories." She hadn't mentioned her uncle's bloody ending and he did not know if she felt horror or relief, but either way, perhaps best not to dwell on it. "So please, treat me as your friend. Can you do that?"

She wiped a small tear. "Yes, Richard. I can do that, if you are sure? And Captain Farrell in company."

"Well, Eliza, and you too, Eva, speaking of friends, before we set out, I must tell you of a friend of mine whom I hope you will soon meet. He will help to keep you safe on the journey. There are, however, a few things you should know about him. Also, there is another man. He is not so friendly. In fact, he wants me dead. Whilst I hope to avoid him, it may be we run into him too. If we do, things could get… let's say it could get exciting. I need to tell you about these things now, as there may be no opportunity later."

The two girls sat again, a mixture of apprehension and curiosity. He told them, as quickly as he could, about Roger and the plan to meet up on the road south. He left out details, but just warned them to speak to Roger as little as possible as he was not, not remotely, a godly man. His tone changed when he talked about Cobb and why their stories were entwined. There were gasps as he described the ill-fated duel, and tears when he told of the destruction of his home and family. Both girls were determined to continue the journey, and both seemed strangely interested to meet Roger DeLacey. *If only they knew…*

He glanced out of the window and realised his story had taken a lot longer than he had anticipated. The sun was climbing well above the line of the ridge; they needed to be on the move. He turned again. "I must just eat a mouthful before we start. Are you sure you have all your things? Eliza? Did you help Eva?"

She nodded and gave him a small smile. "We are all ready. But yes, you must eat something. You need your strength for what we may encounter."

"Please understand. If we encounter Cobb and his men, there will be no heroic fight. We will turn tail and run. We will try to hide. If we cannot accomplish that, then we ride for our lives and hope for divine intervention, or to find a friendly village or soldiers on the march."

Again, she nodded. "I understand. You do this for me and Eva. I do not doubt your bravery – I have seen your battle scars." She glanced down to his thigh, a hint of a smile reaching the corner of her mouth. Then, in an instant, her face froze, and she whirled away, bending to her bag as if rechecking the contents.

Richard stared at her back. And stared as the silence went on. Eliza continued to rummage through her few belongings. Eva also stared in silence, first at Richard, then at Eliza.

He found his voice. "How… how could you know that?" It was hardly more than a whisper.

Without turning round, she answered, "Know what? I don't know what you mean."

He grabbed her arm and pulled her to face him. "How do you know about my scars?" He too glanced down. "That scar. Only two people know of that. Have seen that." His voice was firmer, louder now. Anger and confusion overwhelming any embarrassment.

She kept looking down at his boots. "I… I think Marleigh must have told me. She told us everything really." She glanced quickly into his face, and then down again.

(14 JULY 1644)

His grip tightened. "Eliza! Look at me. I don't believe you. How do you know of this? Look at me!" He felt his world turning upside down. Surely Marleigh would not have discussed this with Eliza? He just couldn't imagine that conversation with such a young and innocent girl. What was happening? Why was she lying to him?

She struggled to keep her eyes on his, her earlier composure melting away under his gaze. Suddenly she collapsed, as he had seen her faint in the marketplace, and crumpled to the floor. But instead of unconsciousness, her whole body writhed and twitched, her teeth clenched, her eyes closed, as if in the grip of some terrible nightmare or possession.

*

She didn't know if she could hold on any longer.

This had been more difficult than she could ever have imagined. More difficult than any time before. She had thought it would have been easier, with her enhanced powers and her familiarity with Eliza, and with the added surge of energy she had harvested from that fat pig Smale. Revenge had been a sweet moment, but all the sweeter as it fuelled her transition from the body of Marleigh to that of Eliza Walker. Faithful, loving Eliza who had fought her way through the crowds to stand exactly where she was needed.

Attuned to her mind over months, the pathway was clear and, although a matter of seconds only, she had swept across and taken possession more quickly and smoothly than she could have dreamt of. She had even had enough in reserve for the fiery ending. She had not been able to resist that. It was pride, she knew that. *Burn the witch?* She had given the townsfolk a burning they wouldn't forget in a hurry. Perhaps they would think twice about persecuting women like old Alice.

Under the cover of fainting, a natural enough response to the unfolding events, she had consolidated. She was only dimly aware of what was happening to the body; she had to trust Richard to deliver the plan. Her plan – only she knew all of the components. She and Eva. It had to be that way.

But then, after such a promising start, things had started to go badly wrong. More than at any other time before she had encountered resistance. This was expected. After the sheer horror and confusion of having your mind invaded by another, there was always a fight back. That or a quick descent into madness. She had always been able to overcome it. To pummel and push and squeeze the host into accepting her control. To close off the pathways of command to the other. To force the flesh to accept a new identity. A new reality. Oh, the same name, the same appearance, but to identify itself to itself, differently. A new intelligence taking control.

New memories had to settle into the caverns of the mind, transported from the old. Different reactions and muscle combinations learnt by the physical elements. It was like moving into a new house. You kept the doors locked and the shutters closed while you rearranged the furniture and painted the inside. You knocked down some internal walls and you built others. You made it into *your* home. And the walls and the furniture, the stairs, the ceilings, the ornaments soon came to identify themselves as yours. As you. A new, happy, harmonious household. Then, when you were satisfied with the outcome, you could open up and let the light flood back in.

And when the light returned, the previous occupant was already locked away in the basement.

She had long rejected the concept that this was the work of her soul. Her soul capturing the shell of a physical body occupied by the soul of another. That was not her experience.

(14 July 1644)

That was not how it worked and her connection with Eva had simply confirmed this.

The body, and by this she knew it was largely the brain in her skull, was shaped by the mind because it demanded to be so. The body needed to know what it was, who it was, and how it should interact with the world, in order to function. It needed to understand itself. It needed to know how a bag of muscle, bone, water and blood could be conscious, and most importantly, have a consciousness separate from the rest of humankind. From the rest of nature. And it did so; it ordered this chaos by creating its mind and becoming a person, not a mound of inanimate tissue. It led its own separate existence, at least for a while, but was still part of the whole.

She had long felt this to be true, but the enlightenment that Eva had brought, watching and sensing her form in her womb and sharing her growth, physically and mentally... this had confirmed it all. She had learnt to *see* the flows of energy that bound the world together, rather than just sense or imagine them. She had come to actually understand the process that she had discovered long ago. The process of prolonging *her* individual existence. The process to impose her identity, her reality, on to other individuals. To break down the existing structures that the new body had erected, through her ability to harness the energy released by a death.

At first, she had merely sensed it. Then she had learnt to use it, just a little, as Richard could do. But there had been no *understanding*. That was when her long journey started. She knew there was something fundamental to *all* life here, bigger, far bigger, than herself, and she had to understand it. She learnt to channel it, to hold on to it, before it faded back into nature. This was her promise to herself.

She likened it to a watermill. Each person, each animal or plant, was powered by an energy like the wheel of the watermill was powered by the force of water. The wheel turned the millstones or other wheels and machinery, carrying out important tasks. The water was held in a millpond, which was gradually and continually replenished by rain, in the same way that a person's energy was replenished by food, water and sleep. Water drove the wheel in a constant way, running the actions needed by the body, including running the mind. These were the flows she could now see. As a person aged, or took ill, the level in the millpond lowered, until it was no longer replenished and eventually the wheel stopped turning. Water leaked out of the pond as it was no longer repaired, and this gradually drained away. These slow, gradual leaks of energy were not something she could use. She could not grasp them, not channel them to herself and her own needs. At least not yet. The volume of the flow was not enough, it just seeped through her fingers, like water from tiny streams slowly finding its way back to the sea.

But as warriors had found over the millennia, as the Aztec priests had found at the top of their blood-soaked temples, if the dam of the mill pond is broken suddenly and violently, then there is a cascade, a powerful torrent. Throughout history, some had discovered this and had learnt to use it, but not like she could. She could divert this flow into her millpond. She could hold it there longer than those berserker warriors. She could feed it through her waterwheel with precision. She could control it. She could use it not just for moments of spectacular physical effort, but she could use it to bridge between bodies. To subjugate others and to prolong her life seemingly forever, recreating her identity in the bodies of others. And the longer she was successful in prolonging her existence, the more accomplished and confident she became. With Eva to help her gain understanding as well as competence, who knew what they could achieve together.

(14 July 1644)

With how much she had grown as Marleigh Hume, and the life she had helped create as Eva, she couldn't understand why it was proving so hard to subdue the identity of Eliza Walker. Young, innocent, caring Eliza, who had so looked up to Marleigh.

She battled to gain control, but every time she seemed to have the battle won, every time she seemed to be gaining composure, her grip was loosened; the foundations of her identity in this new body were undermined. She could push Eliza down the steps to the basement, but she couldn't lock the door. This distraction, this fight, distracted her, and she was making mistakes. She had struggled to maintain consciousness and now... now she had blundered badly. She sensed Eva's shock in her mind. She could even vaguely sense the turmoil in Richard's. He was a fool if he thought he had lost the talent. You never lose it.

She was at the height of her powers, why was she struggling so? She had tried to analyse it, using rational, logical enquiry and not flailing panic. Eliza was fighting, but they all fought. In that respect, there was nothing different. But if it wasn't something different about Eliza, then it must be something different in her. As she wrestled with this question, her distracted mind couldn't focus properly on events outside in the world. It was like trying to complete some complex tapestry with one hand while holding a snarling dog from her throat with the other. She was making mistakes. She had made a mistake.

Her weakness meant that it was not just Eliza shoving at the door of her control. Other identities, long since purged from her mind, threatened to reappear. Lost women, with memories and emotions threaded through her long existence, suddenly sensing an opportunity to regain a grip on the real world. To inhabit flesh. To sense the world around them.

The warmth of the sun, the breeze on their face, the touch of another's skin. They kicked towards the surface. They came to overwhelm her.

She had collapsed then. All the effort, all the concentration needed to fight back and to stem this tide of insanity meant she had no resources left to respond to Richard. He would have to wait. She gave herself to the struggle. The women from the distant past were little problem to her. It had been so long since they had experienced any control or manifestation in flesh that they had no idea how to oppose her. She pushed them down with ease, slamming the lid, turning the key again. She focused now on Eliza.

This was a battle she was no longer certain of winning. Her confidence was shot; she had no strength left. She was failing. She would be lost and her grip on the world gone forever. She felt the fingers of her own mind, her own identity, losing their grasp. She was sliding down the slope again, just as she had when Eva had entered her consciousness. The abyss slid closer, not black and empty but wild, uncontrolled, never-ending chaos. She would never emerge from that! The body that had belonged to Eliza would remain an incoherent, twitching, drooling wreck. Lost, until the flesh died and decayed, and all the identities contained in the contested mind seeped back into the whole.

But what was that thought! *Just like when Eva came to me. Eva!* She searched for her daughter through a howling wind of confusion. It was so hard to concentrate. So hard to see anything now. But then she did see her, like a hand reaching down into the whirlpool. Still and strong in the raging current. She reached and grasped. Eva's mind grabbed hers like a vice. Where does she get such strength! *Mama. Stay calm. Hold on to me. I will pull you out. Don't look at them! Don't listen to them! Hold on to me, Mama.*

(14 July 1644)

And suddenly she was free of them. They dropped away and all of the heat and frenzy were gone. She opened her eyes and saw Eva crouching by her head, smiling at her, her little cool hand on her forehead. Behind her, Richard also kneeled, face white, eyes wide. A look of horror on his face, turmoil behind his eyes. Now her mind was calm and composed. Her eyes were clear. She had to tell him the truth. Now, while she had some semblance of control.

*

He couldn't understand it. Not really. He sat with his back to the barn wall. She sat in front of him on a bale of straw. Eva was on tiptoe, watching the world through one of the windows, balanced on a low wooden box.

He couldn't understand that he was looking into the eyes of Eliza Walker but hearing the voice of Marleigh. Not even that! It was Eliza's voice, but not Eliza speaking to him. How could that be? She had convinced him that it was indeed Marleigh. She knew things about him, what they had done together, that only she could know. Wasn't that how she had given herself away? Things that made him blush hotly, but of which the young, innocent face of Eliza showed no embarrassment. But *how* had she done it? How had she taken possession of Eliza?

She was trying to explain the *how*. He remembered some of their previous conversations. It was true, she had spoken to him of what she called the *talent*. He could not deny he had experienced this. Had he not cursed it and thought himself rid of it after the battle at Marston field? But she was so far beyond his experience. He had seen it with his own eyes. The tower of flame in the marketplace in Macclesfield and the charred bodies. But this? This was so much more. It was hard enough understanding how she had invaded Eliza's body and taken it from her. But that was only the surface, it seemed.

"I am old, Richard. Not in the sense that you see in people around you. The person that is me, not Marleigh, or Eliza, or any of the others, the real me, is older than you could imagine." She seemed almost sad as she said this. It was true that he could sense, perhaps always had sensed somehow, the depths behind her eyes. The feyness. The faerie quality. He knew others had seen it in her too. Like that old crone Alice. Some people could sense a *difference*.

He didn't want to know, but he asked anyway. He felt little choice but to continue down this path. "How old, Marleigh?"

"I am not really Marleigh, as I am not really Eliza." She sighed, but held his gaze. "But I will come to that. I will try to explain. I am old. I was born to the north of here, in land that had been called many things over the years. It has been ruled by the Norsemen, the Romans, the great Abbey of Furness. It is a wild country of mountains, rivers and lakes." Her eyes seemed unfocused, remembering. "I was born outside the Roman fort of Galava, at the head of the longest lake in England. My father was a centurion there. My mother was of Norse descent. She was the daughter of a farmer and wool merchant. Her family had settled there a long time before."

He shook his head. "This is... this cannot be! How can your father be Roman? Are you making fun of me? Do you think I am stupid?"

"Well, he was not Roman in the sense that he was from Rome. He was Illyrian, but his family had been soldiers of Rome for generations. He was a citizen."

"That's not what I meant! That is... I don't know... hundreds of years ago. It cannot be!"

She placed her hands on either side of his face. "Richard, it is not hundreds of years, it is more than a thousand years ago. I told you. I am trying to explain. I am old."

She must be mad. The shock of all this... whatever *this* was, must have collapsed her mind. He couldn't speak, just took her hands away and stared at her.

"As I have said, this is not the first time I have done this. Not the first time I have extended my existence in this way. I have lost count of how many times I have done it. The bodies I have inhabited. I lost count centuries ago. I have seen the world change more than you can imagine. I am, perhaps, the oldest living thing you have ever met and may ever meet. I could tell you the things I have seen. Try to convince you of the truth in this, but I don't think you can understand. Not this quickly. It will take time. I am sorry."

He swallowed hard, trying to stay calm in the face of madness. His, or hers. Maybe both. He could see that Eva was still gazing out of the window but knew she was listening. Perhaps feeling his eyes on her, she turned and gave him an encouraging smile. Such a strange expression on a child so young. Nothing was right anymore. He was lost.

He closed his eyes and sighed, shaking his head. "Alright. I must take what you have said and think on it. But you have not given me the answer to the bigger question. Why, Marleigh? Why have you done this? How could you do this to yourself, and to others?"

"Richard, I am not Marleigh. Better you call me Eliza now."

Again, he shook his head. "I can't do that."

She nodded and looked down. She seemed to be collecting her thoughts and arranging the words in her head. "At first, when I discovered I had such power, I did it because I could. Who would not want to remain young and live on to experience the world? When I was young, truly young, I was driven by selfish motivation. I loved the wild nature around me and I wanted to be a part of it, forever. At first, I could use the talent to make changes to my own body, to help it last longer, to stay free of pain and disease. But after a while, this power started to fade, or at least I couldn't keep up with the speed of my body's decaying. Quite by accident, being close to the violent death that goes with living near the largest Roman garrison in the area, I found I could affect not just my body, I could reach to others. It seemed a miracle. I suppose, in some way, it was a miracle. I could abandon my ageing, dying flesh and wear that of another, younger woman.

"But as time passed, there started to be suspicions about me, or rather about the bodies I controlled. You saw yesterday how those suspicions can quickly turn into a noose, or a stake and a pile of dry wood.

"I had to move away from what I had called home for several lifetimes, and I found that this afforded me more freedom and opportunity. If I was not known in an area, as long as I could provide a good story, none would know, or be interested in, my past. People have other cares. If I was cautious and did not draw attention to myself, I could blend in. And all the time I was getting better at controlling this… talent. With the right opportunity, it became easier to cross the bridge from one body to another. For many, many years, I used this to travel across the world. I have visited places you have never heard of. I have met people you could scarce imagine. All the time improving my skill and acquiring the knowledge and wisdom of other, different, times and cultures. I enjoyed life, loved life too much to consider death an option."

She glanced across at Eva. "But then, I couldn't fight it any longer. It had been gnawing away at my mind and I couldn't escape the need anymore. I had to understand. Really understand. What was this ability that I had? How did it work? I was playing with the very essence of life and being – if

I was so close to it, and so in control, could I not extend myself a little further and understand life itself? How it all works and how it fits together?

"Now I had a purpose beyond the aimless wandering and I made a sacred promise to myself. I would not leave this world without first understanding it. I would do whatever it took to survive, to learn, and finally understand. My life became a serious endeavour, and I became even more cautious. I travelled back to England, and I studied. Always I felt close to gaining the truth. I would get glimpses, feel like I was standing on the edge of real knowledge. But I could never open the final door. I could not unlock the box which held the secret."

She smiled at him. "It was you, Richard Farrell, that provided me with the key. Captain Richard Farrell. After all these long years, you gave me Eva, and Eva opened the box. In ways I still do not understand, it is almost as if she is the box and the contents. She already has a power and insight beyond mine, I think. She is like a distillation of all life into one body. For me, I came close to the answer through hard work, study and perseverance. For Eva, it is just a part of her. She feels it and sees it rather than knows it. You have glimpsed this power, but for Eva it is always there, I think. She does not need death's release to harness the energy of the living world. She can just draw on it from all the life around her. Borrow it, shape it and return it. Do you understand?"

Richard shook his head numbly. He was still trying to marry this stream of words with the fact they were coming from Eliza Walker's mouth. That Marleigh, who was not Marleigh, was some kind of spirit able to flit from person to person over what... centuries? He was so far from understanding any of this.

He tried another approach, drawing on an emotion *he* was all too familiar with.

"And what of all of the people that you have killed to achieve this? What of all of the bodies you have possessed? Do you feel no guilt? You lived with Eliza. You taught her. You even said to me she was like a child or younger sister to you. Did you not betray her sacred trust? How can you live with yourself?"

"But, Richard, can't you see what I am saying?" She sounded exasperated. "I think I have finally understood the basis of all of life. Of everything. Not just observed and catalogued it. Not just killed it and dissected it and drawn the pieces on some roll of parchment. I understand it. Against that, what are a thousand lives? Ten thousand? Do you know how many people died in the war you fought in the Low Countries? In the war you are fighting now? For what? The King risks the break-up of his petty short-lived kingdom, and the massacre of not just some thousands of soldiers, but poor, hard-working men, women and children across the land, for some words in a prayer book? Innocent lives, people who could hardly scrape a living. The harshest of existences. Condemned to starving, looting and the diseases that war brings. And the only valuable thing they would ever possess, their own brief lives, the miracle of nature made conscious in human beings, snuffed out forever, to answer a question about how to worship a god? A god that does not exist! What I have discovered, with your help, and through Eva, is the fundamental flow of nature, and how this animates life in the world. Surely you can see – that is worth a million lives!"

Richard looked at his hands. Looked at her. Motes of dust from the straw in the barn hung and drifted in the morning light now streaming through the windows and the gap in the double oak doors. The soft light lit Eva's face as she peered over the stone sill. The most beautiful and precious thing he had ever created. That was the closest he would ever come to witnessing a miracle, whether she had all the powers Marleigh claimed or not.

"In all of this you have not mentioned love. You said that you felt love for me. I can see that you feel love for Eva. It is in your eyes. Her eyes. Marleigh's eyes. Was that you, whoever or whatever you are, or was that some remnant of Marleigh Hume saying those words, and feeling those feelings? Or is it just a lie through which to fulfil your promise? Where is love in all of this? How does love fit in to your watermills and machines and your books and learning, and..." he threw his hands up, "...all those things you talk about. *Do* you love Eva, or is she just some kind of key, as you called her? Did you feel love for Eliza before you took her life, or being so wise, are you incapable of feeling it?" He did not feel anger. Just a kind of sadness.

She stared back at him. She opened her mouth to speak and closed it again. For the first time since he had known Marleigh... Eliza – God in heaven, what must he call her now! – she seemed uncertain. She opened her mouth again to speak but was interrupted by Eva.

"Mama. Papa. Someone is coming. Lots of people, I think, coming over the hill."

*

He gave Eliza a look and pushed past her to get to Eva and the window. He squinted into the low sun but couldn't see any movement except a few circling birds, certainly not any group of people. "Eva, there is no one there. Just a few crows." He put a gentle hand on her hair and she looked up at him, her face crinkled in a frown. "Why do you think there are people coming?"

"I can... feel them. Can't you?" She glanced at Eliza. "And the crows. They are warning." She seemed to be concentrating.

Listening. "More birds are talking now. I think we will see them soon. What shall we do?"

Eliza stared at Eva. "You can hear them? The crows? You can... understand them?"

"I feel them. They are upset at being disturbed. It is not words, Mama." She rolled her eyes in a very adult way, almost making Richard laugh despite the tension. "I can feel their... energy. They are cross, like you get sometimes."

"Whether Eva is right or not, we need to think about leaving. We must talk about... what you have told me, later. Now, we must leave and find Roger, or all of this will be meaningless."

Eliza nodded and started to gather their few things.

"No. They are here. Look." Eva pointed out of the window. "Told you so." A statement of fact, not the smugness of a child proven correct.

"Shit!" Richard lifted her down from the bale and peered out, trying not to show himself, painfully aware that the front of the barn would be bathed in the clear light of early morning sun. On the horizon, a single mounted figure stood. It was soon joined by a second. It was difficult to tell against the light how they were dressed, but he could see they were moving their arms, pointing, he thought, at the road that ran behind the barn and the small copse that surrounded it on three sides. They would have a good view of it from the high ground.

"Shit!" He put his back to the wall, next to the window. "I don't know if it is them or not. Cobb and his men. I can't tell from this distance."

"Shouldn't we go anyway? Even if it is not this man Cobb, it is not to say they will be friendly. Who knows, these days? It could be anyone."

"If we move from here, they will see us in a moment. There is no way out of the back. Doors and windows all face east.

(14 July 1644)

Whoever it is, they are headed for the road, I think. Hopefully they will pass us by. It is early in the day and so they are not looking for a camp. They will pass by. We just need to keep quiet and keep hidden." He looked out again.

"You are probably right. But if they do come to the barn, then we are trapped in here. Outside we can at least run?" She was worried. Far more worried than he had seen her before, in the trial, even on the way to the noose.

He groaned. "I think it is Cobb. At least it is someone from the military." A single horseman was threading his way down the slope through the rocks and gorse bushes, and more had joined their companion on the skyline. He counted nine in total.

"They are sending a scout ahead. It is what I would do. They mean to check out the barn and the wood before they pass through. They are being very cautious, which suggests they fight for the King, this being Parliament country. Who else would it be but Cobb?"

He turned to Eliza who was now holding tight to Eva's hand. "If we run, on the two horses, I can't protect you. They will catch us very quickly. I think that is the bigger risk. If we hide in here..." he glanced round, "...up the ladder in the hayloft, maybe they will just look in and move on. If they can see there is no one here, why would they search further?"

"If not?"

"If not, then we kill enough of them to persuade the others that it is not worth their lives to capture a barn. They cannot want a pitched battle. It would attract too much attention." He looked carefully round the frame of the window. The scout was through the gap in the stone wall and halfway to the oak tree.

"Eliza, quick! Take Eva up the ladder and into the darkest corner of the loft. Cover yourselves with the straw as best you can. I will be close by. If we are lucky, he will just stick his head into the barn and move on."

"Then let us hope we are lucky. Do you have a knife, something I can use if it gets to that stage?" She glanced down at Eva, back to him. He took her meaning. He nodded. "I can do better. Here, take one of the pistols. You know how to use it?" She nodded, and took it from him, holding it barrel up. He could see she did indeed know to use it. "And this." He took the dagger from his belt and passed it pommel first. He thought of the savagery with which she gutted Jeremiah Smale. "I know you can use a sharp edge."

She was climbing awkwardly up the ladder, half helping Eva, half carrying her new arsenal of weapons. He risked a last look out of the window and followed her up. The scout was walking his horse straight at the barn doors. He was only twenty-five paces away. As quietly as he could, he settled himself next to one of the upstairs windows and shifted some bales to mask his position from the top of the ladder.

His heart thudded in his chest. He thought about his long bloody search to find John Cobb. Now, here he was, coming straight to his door. But he was in no position to take revenge, not with the need to protect Eva. His thoughts about Eliza were harder to understand. He could not forget the love he had found with her, but he could not forget her confessions. Truly he could not look at this innocent teenage girl and believe it was the same person he had shared a bed with. Made a child with. He thought he might be going mad.

Now he heard the sound of the hooves slowly approaching. Cautious indeed. They stopped, and the creak of saddle leather and a slight thud told of the man dismounting.

And it was only then that the sizeable hole in his plan announced itself to him. He was aware the plan already had holes like a fishing net, but this was a fucking huge hole with two heads and eight legs, and was tethered around the back of the barn in the trees. How could he have forgotten the horses? How? He prayed that the animals would make no noise. Please God, just let him take a quick look through the barn doors and then ride on. *Is that too much to ask?*

The barn door creaked open slightly and a little more of the early morning sunlight lanced in. Through a small gap in the planks beneath him, he saw a long shadow project across the dusty earth below him. He tried to breathe as slowly and quietly as possible and fought the urge to peer out of the window. All the eyes of Cobb's men would be on the barn. The slightest movement would be spotted.

No sound of movement came from below. He was light on his feet, he had to give him that. Then came a slight creaking sound again as the man remounted. He called out, "It's clear!" An accent he was not familiar with.

But then it came, maybe by chance, maybe because the scout called out. A loud whinny and snort came from behind the barn. Even Cobb and his men waiting near the oak tree would have heard that. There was no shout from outside but again, the sound of the scout getting down from his horse. Through the window he heard quiet, cautious footsteps heading for the corner of the barn. They couldn't afford to lose their horses.

He got to his feet, taking care to avoid being seen from the front window, and as quickly and quietly as he could made his way through the ankle-deep straw to the small double-door opening at the rear of the hayloft. He prayed, for the second time that day, that the hinges would not creak, and gently pushed one of the wooden doors open. It swung quietly open and immediately below him he saw Cobb's scout reaching to grab the reins of their horses. The movement of the door must have caught the man's eye as he leaned back to look upwards. As their eyes met, Richard was already hurtling downwards. He bent his knees to cushion the impact, but his boot heels landed, one on each shoulder, and drove the man to the ground. He had the impression of eyes wider than dinner plates staring in disbelief just before they collapsed together in a heap, Richard trying to roll free. The man had completely broken his fall and he was on his feet in a flash, carbine raised to stove in the man's head. But he felt the old power flow through his body. A power he thought he had lost, and he knew what it meant. The scout's head lolled at an angle which had never been intended for his neck, and his eyes continued to stare at the sky.

Richard had no idea how much noise they had made, but he had no doubt Cobb would soon send more of his men to investigate. He snatched the scout's carbine from his dead hand and tried to quieten the horses. There was no way he could get back up into the barn from here, the opening was way out of his reach. He would have to use the wall and the trees as cover now, and at least he was no longer trapped in the building. He would just have to try to thin them out enough for them to cut their losses and move on.

With one weapon in his hand and the other over his shoulder, he crept to the rear corner of the barn and crawled into the thicket of hazel and birch that stretched away on that side. He inched forward until he could see the group of waiting men. The scout's horse still stood patiently just yards from the barn doors. As he watched, he noticed one of the men had remained up the slope near the wall that enclosed the upper edge of the pasture. Although he was watching events at the barn he kept casting a glance behind him, to the scrub and rocks and the low ridge.

As the mounted men moved around in their group, he noticed one remove his steel helmet and rest it on the pommel of his saddle. He rubbed his gloved hands vigorously across a shaven head and Richard got a clear view of his face above a coarse, greying beard. If he had had any doubts to this point, they vanished. There was Cobb. A slimmer, more weather-beaten version of the man he had met in London, but it was him. The man responsible for the killing of his brother in cold blood. The man responsible for the rape and murder of his sister. The man responsible for burning to death several of the tenants and leaving his home a smoking heap. He was leaning in his saddle to speak to one of the other men, and a chill ran down Richard's spine as he recognised the mysterious companion of the King's agent, Montague. There could be no mistake. This was the same man he had seen with Montague in the Blue Boar, at the house after his father's funeral, and on the road across the Pennines. Here was his proof. Montague was in league with Cobb. Had been all the time. No doubt it was he who pulled Cobb's strings. No doubt it was he who ultimately bore responsibility for his loss. This one, he would not kill. This one, he needed to question. All he had to do was kill another eight men and avoid death himself. He smiled grimly to himself. The cold-hearted killer of Marston Moor was back and he couldn't say he was sorry to welcome him.

  He lined up the carbine on Cobb and judged the shot. Difficult, but not impossible. But if he missed, or hit, what would Cobb's men do? Scatter once their leader was down, or reap torture and murder on his killer? And on the killer's defenceless companions. He needed no reminder what type of creatures these were. As he weighed the options, the bead of the carbine following Cobb's head as his horse slowly turned, the decision was taken from him. Cobb seemingly lost his patience and three of his men – three of eight Richard counted – dismounted, grabbed pistols from saddle holsters and started in the direction of the barn. One headed directly towards him, one for the barn door, and one to flank the far side of the building.

His priority was the one in the middle; he would worry about the others after. He couldn't let him get inside the barn and at the girls. A knife held to a throat, and he would have no option but to surrender. He had to delay that possibility for as long as he could. He felt calm now. He was committed. There were no moral dilemmas. No uncertainties. He had a simple job.

He carefully rose into a kneeling crouch, still hidden in the bushes, and swung the carbine from Cobb to the man approaching the barn. It had to be now before the angle became too acute. He lined the sight to his torso, the largest target, and led the walking man by a fraction. The carbine crashed, kicking his shoulder, and he heard the body fall heavily. He moved quickly into the shadow of the barn wall, so only the man heading for that corner of the building would be able to see him. He dropped the discharged carbine, and swung his own down and around. The second man was rooted to the spot, trying to see through the smoke and scrub to find Richard, but also looking to his left at his fallen comrade.

Too slow, friend. Another crash, but he had rushed the shot and just clipped the second man's shoulder, spinning him around and knocking him to the ground, but not finishing him. Still, no action from that one for a while. He knew he had to get back into the barn to protect the girls. He couldn't risk trying to lead them away. It would only take one man to make it inside. The thought of what might happen to Eva gave him strength and he peered out around the corner, ready to make a dash for the nearest window.

As he looked out, two lead balls smacked into the stonework by his head. A moment later he heard the roar of the muskets. Splinters exploded and a small shard tore through his scalp.

(14 July 1644)

He didn't feel any pain, that would come soon enough, but he felt a wet stickiness start to drip down his forehead. He had no choice, he had to make the run, and he had to do it now while at least two of them were reloading. As he braced himself for the run, he heard another shot, further away up the slope, followed by shouts from Cobb and his remaining men. He risked peering round the corner again. Now they were faced away from him, and beyond them he could see the man guarding their rear was down. They were milling around in indecision and the churn of their horses was raising dust in the shadow of the great tree.

In the distance, racing down the far slope was a single horseman. He slowed slightly and took the stone wall in an enormous leap. Like an arrow, he headed straight for Cobb's group. *Oh, fuck me!* It was Roger. It had to be. Pistol raised in one hand, he was doing his best to keep low in the saddle. Richard knew that even a skilled veteran like Roger couldn't take down five battle-hardened men. He needed help. Grabbing his pistol from his belt, and sweeping out his heavy cavalry sabre, he set off at a run up the slope, screaming as loud as he could. Anything he could do to distract them.

Now they really were in a panic. As the comet that was Roger DeLacey bore down on them, one man opted to run, and hauled his horse around and set off across the pasture. Richard panted and sweated his way through the knee-high yellowing grass and saw a puff of smoke from Roger's pistol, the sound reaching him moments later. Ever the pragmatist, Roger had gone for the biggest target he could, and one of the horses screamed and collapsed to the ground. It pinned its rider, who jerked and pulled to get free.

He would have to wait. Roger's sword was out now and he was almost on the first of the remaining three men. They had achieved some semblance of order and the other two now turned towards Richard, seemingly to try to ride him down. Richard was always happy to take a lesson from Roger, and he stopped, aimed his pistol at the nearest rider and shot the horse in the chest. The ball must have smashed through its heart, as without a sound it went down in a crash of limbs and dust. The rider sailed over his mount's head and landed not ten yards from Richard. He hit the ground face first, the steel helmet driving his head back and Richard knew immediately that he was dead before the rest of his body hit the ground.

Again, the energy flowed into him, and he embraced it. Gloried in it. Because he knew that second rider must be Cobb. Slowed by the fate of his companion, Cobb fought his horse to keep control and lost the fight. He slid off sideways but managed to land on his feet as his horse bolted.

As he swung around to face Richard, he realised who it was his band of guerrillas had found. His mouth dropped open, and he stared wide-eyed. The surprise lasted only a moment. John Cobb may have been many things, but he was not slow-witted. He smiled as Richard advanced towards him.

"Seems kind of appropriate. Just you and me. One murderer to another." He raised his sword and gestured at the carnage around him. "It is worth it, all this, to have you here in front of me at last. It will be a pleasure to finish you as I finished your sis…"

The object of Richard's cold-blooded campaign for revenge stood right in front of him. All the daydreams and nightmares in which he had imagined this moment. It all came down to this. But now, when he had the opportunity to immerse himself in a climax of bloody justice, he just didn't have the time for a grand gesture. Cobb didn't even see the blow coming. Grimacing through the blood now freely running across one eye and down the side of his face, Richard summoned all of his strength, and that of Cobb's dead companions, and swung.

(14 July 1644)

The speed of the blade through the air and the force of the impact tore Cobb's head from his shoulders to land yards away. What remained of his body fell forwards into the grass, staining the pasture crimson.

Richard whirled around looking for Roger. His fight was also over, riderless horse quietly eating the grass as his friend wiped his blade on the dead man's back. He looked up at Richard and grinned.

"Where the fuck have you been! Had your feet up in some tavern again?"

"Well, you seemed to be doing alright and you know I like to make an entrance." He nodded at the headless body of Cobb. "That him?"

Richard nodded. And then Richard remembered. There was another one left. The third man who had headed for the barn. "Fuck! Roger, you deal with that one…" he nodded at the man trapped under his horse, "…I must get back to the girls." He hoped that the third man had run like his companion, but he couldn't be sure. He wiped blood from his forehead and turned to run back to the barn. He shouted over his shoulder, "I think he is Montague's man. Don't kill him, I need to question…"

He was interrupted by the loud crack of a pistol. He whirled. "Christ, Roger! I said…" He stopped. Roger was draped face down across the dead horse. Powder smoke was drifting across him. He saw the head of the pinned man frantically jerking as he tried vainly to free himself. He took two steps and leapt the horse, landing next to Roger. He could see a large wet, red hole halfway up his back on his right side. Amazingly, he could see his back slowly rising and falling with his breathing. He stepped around him and held his sword to the pinned man's throat. He kicked the spent pistol out of his reach.

"You have one chance. I have to go to the barn. When I get back, if he is alive, you will live too. My word on it. If not, then it will go badly for you before I kill you." He gently rolled Roger over and slid him down the flank of the horse until he was propped next to the other man. His eyes were slitted and he was only breathing with difficulty. He had left a smear of blood six inches wide across the horse's hide. His hands were over the stomach wound but couldn't stop the slow pulse of blood welling up between his fingers.

"I will be back as soon as I can. Don't go anywhere." He tried to smile. He failed.

Roger's words were slow and strained. "Save the girls, you bastard. I'll just sit and chat to my friend here."

Richard nodded, spun on his boot heel and sprinted down the slope to the barn.

*

She was back to sitting on the hay bale, her back against the rough stonework. Her hands were over the stomach wound, but she couldn't stop the slow pulse of blood welling up between her fingers. She heard shots outside the barn, the sounds of horses, living and dying, and the sounds of men, living and dying. She couldn't get up to go as far as the window or the door, so she had no idea if Richard were dead or not, or if she would soon be receiving more visitors.

The last one lay at the foot of the hayloft ladder, a shaft of sunlight from the open door slicing across his torso and face. His left eye was in ruins, his right eye closed. Blood seeped from the back of his head, forming little meanders and oxbow lakes on the dusty earthen floor. Eva, bloody dagger still clutched in her hand, stood at the top of the ladder, her little legs too short to enable her descent. She had her eyes closed, and swayed slightly, disconcertingly, as she concentrated on keeping her mother alive.

When the violence had started, the person who had been Marleigh had been in an agony of doubt as to what to do. At approximately the same time as Richard, she had remembered the horses. She had risked a look out of the hayloft slit and seen bodies, dead and injured, in the grass, and watched as Richard charged up the slope to help Roger. She had decided to make a run for the horses, to bring them to the front of the barn so she and Eva could run if they had to. If things went badly.

She was halfway down the ladder when she sensed the man standing in the doorway. She had turned and looked down the barrel of his pistol, looked up to see the unpleasant grin on his face.

"Down you come, lovely," he had said. "Don't want to hurt you by pulling on those young legs." He had motioned with his pistol for her to continue climbing down. She had done so, with her back turned to him. As she had reached the ground, she had swung round, pulling her own pistol out from her waistband and pulling the trigger in his surprised face.

But it had misfired. As her assailant had fallen backward, desperately trying to avoid having his head blown off, he had fired in return, blowing her off her feet and into the straw. Thinking her done for, he had looked up to see Eva watching horrified from above. Recovering from his lucky escape, he had shouted at her to come down, and when she said she couldn't, and wouldn't, had started up the rungs to drag her down. At the top, instead of a hysterical child, he had been met with six inches of German steel, which she had punched into his eye. He was dead before his fingers left the ladder.

She had managed to drag herself towards the door but now could go no further. In normal times, she could have used the energy she had harvested from the fallen man to heal her wound, but she was weakened by her internal conflict. Eliza was fighting her harder than ever and it was taking all her strength to keep her at bay. She pleaded and argued with the other. *If you don't let me heal the body, we will both die.* But it seemed that Eliza preferred death to imprisonment in her own flesh. She could understand that.

In fact, that was the surprising thing. She couldn't bring herself to hate Eliza. She had had time to reflect on what Richard had said to her. About love. About her feelings for those around her. For those who had cared about her and sought to protect her. All down the centuries she had brushed such feelings aside. It was not important. It did not affect her studies, her knowledge. Had she not survived this long because she had ignored this? Had avoided it? What had changed now?

A voice in her ears and in her head at the same time. "I changed it, Mama. You and I together changed it. You gave a piece of yourself to me, as Papa did, and it changed everything. But you are stronger now, not weaker. You know what you need to do to save yourself, and now you know that you can. Because of me." She looked up at Eva who now had her bright mismatched eyes open and focused upon her. Eva, the sweetest, prettiest, cleverest child. A child who had just killed a man by stabbing him in the face. A tear balanced on her cheek, defying gravity. There were no certainties anymore.

She heard pounding footsteps getting louder and the door was suddenly shoved wider, spilling more light in to the gloomy interior. Richard staggered in, drying blood obscuring one side of his face. He was deathly pale and on the edge of collapse.

Her labouring heart leapt to see him alive. She wanted to take him in her arms and sob into his shoulder, but she knew that could spell the end for her. She was balanced on the point of a needle and the slightest slip could lead to madness and to her death. She, who had lived for more than a millennium, looked into the abyss.

"Are you hurt badly? Is it over?"

He was on his knees in front of her, eyes wide with concern. She carefully lifted a hand to wipe some of the blood from his eye but only succeeded in smearing an additional layer of her own.

He looked across at Cobb's man at the foot of the ladder, and up to where Eva stood, holding the top. "Yes, it is over. I think so." He looked into her eyes. "Is it bad? Can you move?"

"I am at my limit, I think." She laughed softly, but immediately groaned at the stress this placed on her abdomen and the tearing wound. "For all my cleverness, for all my new understanding, I am at an impasse. I know not what to do." Her laughter had turned to tears, and she was incredulous. Never in her memory had she cried with sadness for herself.

Richard gently moved her hand from her wound and looked at the pulsing mess of flesh. He looked her in the eyes and kissed her gently on the forehead. "Can you not use your powers to heal yourself of this wound now?"

Inside her, the turmoil raged on. It took all that she had to clamp down the rebellion that threatened to overwhelm her. She grimaced at the effort. "Are there any wounded outside? One of Cobb's men that still breathes?"

She saw him consider for a moment. "Yes, there is one just outside. His shoulder is shattered, I think. He just sits there. He watched me pass as I came to you. There is... another." She saw him swallow hard. "Trapped under his horse. I think... I think he has killed Roger, although he was still alive when I left him to come to you."

"Oh, Richard. I am truly sorry. I know little of Roger, but I know he was your friend. Not something I have known." She grimaced as pain lashed through her. She felt the blood welling again beneath her fingers. She swallowed hard. "Perhaps with the first one? If you can drag him nearer to me, I could draw on him as dies, and maybe with that strength I can save this body and imprison Eliza again."

He looked at her. "Is that what you wish? Even if I could get him here, he may take hours, days, to die."

"You would have to finish him. You would have to kill him here. Beside me."

He stared at her. "You want me to… sacrifice him for you? I don't know if…" He trembled slightly but held her gaze. "I have killed many, but in battle, but this would be murder. I have never…" He paused and seemed to look inward for a moment. "Alright. I would do it, to save you."

What was she asking him to do? It wasn't fair to ask it. Again, she felt astonishment. *When has fairness ever guided me?* She looked up again at Eva. The look of compassion, of support, of love. She understood now. She finally understood it all. And Eva would be what she had not been able to be.

Richard took it as an instruction and dropped her hand, quickly climbing the ladder until he could reach Eva. He knelt in front of her again, Eva balanced on his thigh. She took her tiny hand, the other clamped on her wound. Then she laid it on Richard's head. Eliza's slender fingers, her unblemished skin, tangling in his dirty blood-soaked hair.

"Don't worry, my love. It was wrong to ask it. It was wrong… to think it." Her voice was light, she felt herself weakening. "I think I have solved my… dilemma. Rather, you and Eva have solved it." She smiled again, and this time her smile was full of warmth for him, for the world. He looked at her uncertainly.

"I can heal the wound, Richard. It will take all I have, but I will do it. I must do it. It means that I will leave you, but the flesh, this body, will survive with the right care." He opened his mouth to speak, but she motioned him to silence. "Please. Just for a moment more." She paused, summoning the will. "I will release Eliza. She will return to her body again. She will be frightened, confused, angry, exhausted. You must care for her." She glanced up at Eva. "Both of you must take the best care of her while she recovers. Will you do that?"

She couldn't quite believe what she was going to do. So many times she had cheated this moment through cunning and the sheer power of her need to survive. This was different. Now there was Eva, and she would go on. Eva would carry her knowledge and her talent to new challenges, and she would do so much better than her. Tears ran down her face, and his. She touched his cheek, her finger leaving a faint bloody trace across his broken cheekbone. "Goodbye, Captain Farrell. You were right. For all my knowledge, it was you and Eva who were wisest. None of this means anything without love. Without love, what is the point of understanding? Why else are we given this chance of life? Figures built from earth and air and water, and the fire of our energy. This brief moment in the sun – a separation from the whole. I was so intent on the *how*, I mislaid the *why*. And now I know. Now I understand. You and Eva have helped me to understand."

She gazed at him for the last time. She was calm now. She had finished and she felt complete.

"You will be the best father. Trust me in this. Take care of her, for she is the most precious thing in all the world."

Before he could speak, she closed her eyes and started to shut herself off. She could not allow any words he might have to sway her now. She had looked at herself, and what she had become, and Eva had allowed her to escape a terrible future. Even now, she was there in her mind, helping her, holding her up, as she focused her remaining energy towards the terrible wound the metal ball had made. Joining, folding, cleansing. As she approached the end of her work, she paused and reached out with her remaining consciousness for Eliza. She touched her mind and calmed it, reassured it. She asked for forgiveness. With Eva's help she led Eliza back to the centre, back into the house that had once been hers, and they boarded up the cellar door.

And then there was nothing else left to do but to go. For the last time as an individual, conscious being, she felt the flows of energy all around her. She *felt* the world, but this time, instead of observing and studying, she let herself *rejoin* it. Slowly fading into the whole like a glass of water poured into a slow-flowing river.

*

He felt a small hand on his cheek. Mismatched eyes smiled at him. "Papa. I can help her to finish this. There is nothing you can do." For a small child she had already seemed impossibly mature, but now, it was almost like speaking with a grown woman. He blinked. Not for the first time that day, he felt he was losing his mind.

"Papa, go. Go to Roger. You can help him. You can do nothing here now. When Eliza is awake, she will need you, but now, your friend needs you more."

And of course, she was right. He placed her on the bale, next to the unconscious Eliza. Eva closed her eyes then, her brow furrowed in concentration, in a look far beyond her years. He wiped his eyes, his hands moist with tears, snot and blood, and he tried unsuccessfully to clean them on his breeches. He felt that he too was at the end of his strength, but he couldn't rest yet. He hauled himself to his feet using the edge of the barn door and staggered out into the sunlight. A light breeze had risen and the yellowing grass of the pasture was swaying gently, a few late summer wildflowers adding sparks of blue, magenta and yellow. As the sun continued its climb into a blue sky, fluffy white clouds were forming. Its warm light picked out the purple of the heather on the ridge in the distance, carpeting the spaces between the rocks and the gorse bushes.

If you ignored the dead and dying men and horses that littered the foreground, it was truly a beautiful scene.

He stepped around Cobb's headless body, almost invisible in the long grass, and the pool of blood that continued to grow and soak into the earth. The first flies were already starting to line up along the tidemark. Here and there observant crows had found the waiting feast. High above him he heard the whistle of a kite. He shaded his eyes and picked out the circling dot. His fellows would join him soon enough and then the party could really get started.

Still shielding his eyes, he could see ahead the motionless bulk of the horse where he had left Roger. Even in his physically and emotionally exhausted state, he could see that things were not as he had left them. Cobb's man had somehow managed to extricate himself from the wreckage of his mount and was now sitting, leaning against his saddle, feet towards Richard. Roger was slumped against him, his head tilted back slightly where it lay against the man's shoulder. His eyes were closed, and he looked peaceful, but his shirt was soaked in blood. The younger man's head was down, as if asleep, his long brown hair a curtain for his features.

Slowly Richard walked towards the two men. He glanced to his left where the man with the shattered shoulder sat. He was rocking back and forward, clutching the wound. Richard gave him an even chance of surviving at best. He was no danger now. Halfway to where Roger lay, he suddenly realised he was not armed. He had left his sabre on the floor of the barn. His pistols were spent and discarded. All he had was a knife in his belt. He took it out and made his way as quietly as he could.

He was within ten paces when the man heard him and looked up. As his head came up, so did his right hand, and Richard looked into the black hole of the cavalry pistol's muzzle. This mysterious man. This face that he felt was so familiar, and yet he couldn't place. This man whose identity had gnawed at his mind since his encounter with Montague, in the Blue Boar. It wasn't the pistol that made him stop dead in his tracks, because now he had his answer. And now, he had no words.

But the man with the pistol did.

"Yes," said Benedict DeLacey. "Just when you think things can't go any worse, God has one more fuckin' joke to play." His face was ashen and his eyes red raw.

Richard sank slowly to his knees. "Is he…?"

"Yes. I had thought him already dead. My mother told me he was dead. Now he is dead again. But by my hand." He looked at Richard. "What do you intend to do now?"

But Richard's mind had given up. He could take no more. The world span and went black, and he collapsed face first in the grass, at the feet of Benedict and Roger DeLacey.

*

He felt a faint tugging. He was in the dark. It was quiet. He felt warm. He liked it where he was.

Tug, tug, tug.

He tried to ignore it. It didn't feel like someone was pulling at his body. He concluded it was just in his mind. *Go away!*

He was in a courtyard, a familiar space. It was hot, but he was sitting in the shade. In fact, he was lying, and his head was resting on something soft and warm. As he opened his eyes, a

(14 July 1644)

face was looking down at him. Blue eyes, black ringlets curling around a young, pretty face. A smile. A beautiful smile not spoiled but enhanced by a slight gap between the two front teeth. The mouth closed, but still smiling, the lips came down towards his.

Now he was being pushed. He set his heels, but the pressure was too much, and he felt he was moving inexorably towards... what? *Go away! Please...* He didn't want to find out what he was being pushed towards. *Leave me alone!*

But he was accelerating now. Rushing upwards. The courtyard was gone and all was darkness. The darkness becoming dimness. Now he was racing along, each push adding to his speed. He was going to hit a ceiling, a roof. He was going to smash into something solid. He had to stop. *Stop!* He called out soundlessly. He couldn't hear himself.

Only one way to stop, but he was torn between that choice and the fear of the motion. When he could bear it no longer, he opened his eyes. Really opened his eyes. He screamed. Really screamed. He heard that.

Even with his eyes open it wasn't much brighter. There was still something moving in his head, but now it was calming, soothing, stroking his consciousness. Something moved in his peripheral vision, and he tried to move his head slightly towards it. He saw Eva looking down on him. Beyond her dimly visible head were wooden rafters. Packed earth under his back, grating on his palms. Back in the barn?

Another face appeared opposite Eva. A young face with blonde hair. Wisps of it, framing a worried, earnest expression. Eliza Walker. *Marleigh?* And now, as he saw her more clearly, he could see the mind behind the eyes was Eliza's too. Not some fey strangeness. No. Not Marleigh anymore. *Jesus! What is happening to the world?* He couldn't separate dream from reality. It was all a horror to him. Over her shoulder he could see Roger. *Roger?* No. Not Roger. A younger version of Roger, because Roger was lying dead in the meadow. *Was anyone real or what they seemed?* He felt himself losing control and spiralling down again into the darkness, but a small, cool hand was placed on his forehead, and he sensed a small, cool presence in his mind, holding him up.

Eva was crouching next to him now. Eyes closed and her brow furrowed in that look of concentration again. He could hear her in his head. *It's alright, Papa. It's alright. Sleep now. We will wake you soon, though, because we must leave here. But sleep now.*

And he let himself float with her voice. Calmer now. Not mad. Not panicked. Just exhausted.

When he woke again it was still dark. A blanket had been thrown over him and he felt a throbbing at his temple. He reached up and felt the crusty scab of dried blood over his eye. He tried to sit up and managed to raise himself onto his elbow. He was in the barn, and faint silvery light slanted in through the windows and the partly opened door. A figure was sitting on a hay bale, at the nearest window, what looked like a carbine lying across his lap, the metal of the barrel glinting slightly. He heard movement from behind him and the seated figure turned toward him, alerted by the sound of soft footsteps coming towards him.

"You're awake." Eliza Walker knelt next to him and put her hand on his forehead. "How are you feeling now, Captain Farrell?" She radiated concern.

Benedict DeLacey rose from his watch by the window and came over. The resemblance to his father was uncanny. His long hair and neat beard had none of the grey that had overtaken Roger, but there was little doubt in Richard's mind that this was what Roger would have looked like thirty years ago. He put Benedict at a similar age to himself. Perhaps a year or two older.

His face was careworn, and he too seemed close to exhaustion. He also noticed a slight limp as he approached, and the usual scrapes, bruises and scars of a soldier on campaign.

"Can you ride, Farrell?" His voice was lighter than Roger's but not dissimilar, and he wondered how he had not seen the resemblance before. What had blinded him to the truth? He cast back in his mind to the times he had seen him previously and realised that Roger had never been with him. Couldn't have been. His head felt clearer than when he had woken previously, although now he was more aware of the various hurts he had suffered during the fight.

"Yes." His throat was so dry. "Yes. I can ride. Ride where?"

It was Eliza that answered him. "We must return to the town, Captain. We must find Maggie and bring her with us. I cannot leave her. Who knows what might happen to her."

"Yes. Clearly, she has been in far more danger being looked after by her aunt than travelling safely with us."

Laughter from Benedict at that, but he saw the hurt and tears welling up in Eliza's eyes. "I am sorry, Eliza. I am so sorry. That was hurtful. I am not… I am not yet myself, I think." He studied her again. "You, though, you do indeed seem to be yourself again. Are you…? I mean, has she…? Forgive me. I don't know what the right words are…" He faltered and took her hand in his.

Her expression hardened. "Neither do I, Captain. I am not entirely clear what has happened to me. It seemed like a bad dream, a nightmare from which I have only just awakened. Eva has tried to explain that it was not a dream but was real, but I can make little sense of it. I will need time, I think, to understand it better."

"On that we are agreed, Eliza."

"If you can ride, Farrell, we must go. We are sitting on the edge of a skirmish. Shots were fired. Someone will surely come along and discover us next to this field of death. We must move, whether 'tis to Macclesfield or in some other direction, but we must move from here." He offered his hand to pull Eliza to her feet.

Richard levered himself up, swaying slightly as he felt a rush of pain to his head.

"I tried to clean it a little, but I am no physician." Eliza stood on tiptoe and looked at his wound. "I think it will be alright, but it really needs some brandy or hot wine to clean it properly."

He felt himself coming together, getting a grip on reality again. But, my God, there were so many questions he needed answering. Something to do first, though. He looked at DeLacey and looked pointedly at the carbine which was currently leaning on the man's shoulder, pointed at the ceiling. "And what do you intend to do? It seems I have been rather at your mercy, yet I am still alive, and you are still here."

The carbine swung down. Benedict locked eyes with him. "I spoke to my father before he died. Here." He thrust the stock of the weapon towards Richard. "I have no desire to have your blood on my hands too. I am done with this."

A wave of shame washed over Richard. "I... I am sorry. Forgive me. It seems I can do nothing but trample on people's feelings. I am so sorry about Roger. About your father. He was my friend. Probably my only friend really. He was a good man, although I am not sure he saw it that way. He saved my life many times. Without him, I would probably be dead in a ditch in Flanders somewhere."

"He told me to look after you. Ha! Seems I cannot look after myself, let alone another. I am sorry I never knew that love in my life. He was never around, always following wars around the continent. And then Ma told us he was dead. I guess she had enough, and I cannot blame her. He thought we were all dead too, but you told him the truth. He told me he was coming to find us. When he had finished this…" he waved his arm around the barn and shrugged slightly, "…he was coming to find Mother, me and my sister. I couldn't tell him that Bess had died. Really died this time. Coughing sickness."

Richard felt a dizziness again and he swayed. "He truly believed you had all died of plague. It was only chance that a friend told me he had met your mother." Richard paused as a thought struck him. "You asked me if I could ride as if you were coming with us. Is that what you intend to do?"

Benedict shrugged again. "My assignment is done. It seems you killed them all or scared them off between you." He gestured towards the barn doors. "I must head back to Oxford for fresh orders, but I will take a few days to help you first." He glanced across at Eliza, who was carefully picking up a sleepy Eva. "I think perhaps you might need help protecting Miss Eliza. And your daughter of course. I would be happy to do so."

Richard could not help but notice the way he looked at Eliza. There was an edge to his response. "She has been through much in the last few days. And Royalists killed her father in battle. Tread carefully."

"I am only offering to help you, Farrell, before I head south again. No more."

As Richard continued to clear his mind, and his aching head, unwelcome memories flooded back in. And questions, harsh questions, came with them. "I am not sure it is so easy just to pick things up in such a way. It is not but a few hours ago you were trying to kill me!"

"I was trying to kill Roundheads. We are on opposite sides in a war. And I didn't know it was you firing on us." He paused and looked down at his boots. "Just as I didn't know it was my father until I had holed him." He now looked up defiantly.

"And how many have you killed in the last years? Quite a tally, I believe. Are you so blameless?"

A warm tide of anger rose within him. The barrel of the carbine moved again, this time as Richard centred it on DeLacey's chest. "I would not want to kill Roger's kin, but I will if your answers do not satisfy me."

"In cold blood, sir?"

"It wouldn't be the first time." *No, it wouldn't. As the carpenter from York could testify.* "You are Montague's man. Don't deny it! I have seen you with him. More than once."

"Why would I deny it? Master Montague is a loyal agent of the King. None more loyal. I think loyalty is an honourable quality, although you may not agree." His voice softened. "Nor would my father, I think. Not so long ago he was fighting for the King at Marston Moor."

"Montague is a vindictive, evil man."

"How so? What has he done other than fight for his King? For his country? He has used all his strength, intelligence and cunning, which are considerable, in His Majesty's service. I didn't take you for a Puritan zealot, Farrell. How are you the moral man in all of this?"

Richard blinked. His certainty, not for the first time, was being undermined. "I am fair game. Roger… your father… was fair game. But your honourable Montague set that murderous bastard Cobb on to my family. He primed him, aimed him and let him go like any other weapon. My brother, innocent tenants… murdered and burned alive…" His voice cracked. "My… my sister. Raped and slain. It was…" His voice cracked with emotion.

"…unspeakably evil. I know."

The wavering barrel of the carbine swung upwards again. A chill coldness in his voice masked the burning rage in his soul. He had thought this anger dissipated with Cobb's death. He had not had time to think on this, to dwell on the accomplishment of his revenge. Now he was starting to realise his revenge may not be complete. He saw Eliza backing off into a dark corner of the barn, Eva in her arms.

"How do you know? I suppose Montague told you of his cleverness. Using Cobb to do his dirty work so he could keep his hands clean. Is that the cunning you were referring to? How else would Cobb know where my family lived?"

Anguish replaced anger on Benedict's face. "Montague didn't tell Cobb. He didn't."

"You lie." He cocked the carbine and took a step back to give himself some room if DeLacey rushed him.

"I do not lie." He sighed. "I know Montague didn't tell him. Because I did."

There was a short silence.

Benedict held up his hand. "Wait! Listen to me!" It wasn't fear on his face. More an urgency. "Cobb tricked me. Of course, I knew where your family lived. I was with Montague after your father's funeral, wasn't I? When Montague started to work with Cobb, Cobb found out that Montague had had dealings with you. He tried to get information from him. Tried to get Montague to give him an official order to raid the place. But Montague wouldn't do it. I told you, he is an honourable man and he knew full well what kind of a man Cobb was."

"So you told him?"

"As I said. He tricked me. I knew nothing of all this at the time, of your dealings with Cobb and his son. Cobb sought me out. I knew he was working with Montague, so what was the problem? He flattered. He bought me drinks. Many drinks. He made out that Montague *had* given him the order. I didn't know. He asked me where you lived. And I told him. I didn't know. I am sorry."

"So sorry that you were riding with him? This doesn't wash up clean, boy."

"That… that was my penance. Montague was devastated when he heard what happened. You know, he actually liked you, Farrell. He called you stupid and naïve, lacking in all purpose and direction. But he saw something in you. Ha! He said that the best thing for you was to be rid of the malign influence of Roger DeLacey. It was only then that I found out my father still lived. Montague thought that a great joke."

Richard was even further taken aback. This man he had demonised for all these years had actually protected him from Cobb?

"He was devastated. Partly because of the hurt to you but, I won't lie, mostly because he felt his own honour had been tarnished. He was furious with me. And with Cobb. As I said, my penance was to ride with Cobb. To try to keep his worst urges under control, and to report back intelligence on a regular basis. That was really what Montague wanted from Cobb. Cobb was just a thug, but his raids provided us with vital information, and I relayed that back to Montague."

Richard lowered the barrel. He turned and walked across to the barn wall, slumping down onto a bale. No grand conspiracy. No cold hand playing pieces against him. Just an accident. A simple mistake.

"Fuck." He said it quietly to himself and put his head in his hands. Of course, Montague was right. Stupid and naïve. Lacking in purpose. Quick to anger, slow to think. He had wronged Neelie with his stupidity and his anger. He had wronged Montague himself. Roger was dead because he had followed Richard on his naïve quests. Maybe Eliza had suffered permanent damage at Marleigh's hands because his desire for her had driven him to make the introduction to Samuel Walker. A trail of death and misery through his stupidity and lack of self-control. A wave of misery and self-pity crashed over him.

Something touched his knee. He looked up. Eva had her hand on his leg. She smiled up at him. Not the expression of a child, but a kind, encouraging smile. She said nothing, but a voice in his head said, *Papa. I love you. I need you. Eliza needs you. We must rescue Maggie. Will you help us?*

Perhaps not everything he had done had been wrong. Eva's eyes glistened with hope and love, willing him to be her father.

He crouched down beside her, and now she pressed her small hand against his cheek. The cheek where her mother's blood still marked him. He stared into her eyes, reaching for her soul. This strange, strange little girl was indeed the most precious thing in the world. Perhaps for the first time in his life he had something certain.

"I will always be your father, if you will have me, after all you have heard. That is my promise."

She smiled and stood on tiptoes to kiss him on the forehead.

He stood and looked around at them, all of them heavy with loss and pain. "Let us bury Roger. We cannot leave him for the crows. Then we ride to rescue Maggie. And after that," he shrugged, and for a moment the blue eyes of his dream returned to him, "let us see what fate brings."

EPILOGUE

Richard leant back against the brick, next to the front door, and tilted his head back. The crispness of the autumn evening was battling with London's miasma for control of his senses. He had grown to hate the stink and closeness of the city after months of travelling through the countryside, but at least this was a safe place. A Parliamentarian stronghold which felt a long way from the continuing skirmishes of the war.

He felt content, at least for the moment. Here was both a joyful reunion and a weight of responsibility lifted from his shoulders. He had spent a few happy hours with Will and his wife, Sarah. 'Beauty and the Beast', according to Will. She was certainly a formidable woman, and she was also a beauty. And in Sarah, Eliza and Maggie Walker had found the perfect role model. Eliza had been overjoyed to learn of Richard's plan. He was depositing her and her sister right into the centre of the most strong, passionate and articulate group of women in the country. With views that chimed with her own. Here she could debate, challenge, discuss and grow. Neither she, nor Richard, had any doubts that she could hold her own, and that Maggie too would prosper.

Epilouge

Meeting Will again had felt a little like coming home. His own home was in ruins, although he had called on the most senior of the tenants on his way south to London and asked them to formulate plans for rebuilding for him to review on his return. He had found he could not walk away, not when others were depending on him. He found that this was a feeling he was encountering more and more and, he had to admit, it was not something that felt a burden. More like an opportunity. It was confusing; perhaps it felt like some kind of redemption. Will had been delighted to help with the Walker girls. London was awash with orphans and other flotsam of the war, and many families found themselves helping with this tide where they could. With Will's rank, he and Sarah were comfortable, at least when wages were paid on time, and with money that Richard could send, financing two extra mouths would not be a struggle. Two extra mouths were soon to be three as Sarah was far gone with child. Sarah did not want to see her political work decrease and could see advantages in kindly and doting lodgers helping with the new baby.

Pushing off from the wall he turned and headed in the direction of the guildhall, just a few streets away, where his horse was stabled. He turned the corner and stopped abruptly. Ten paces ahead a figure stepped out of a doorway, broad hat pulled down to shield the face. Despite that, Richard knew instantly who this was, and his right hand reached under his long coat for the pommel of his Toledo blade.

"You won't need that, Farrell." Montague's voice was low and calm. He pushed his hat back slightly so that Richard could see his face more clearly. He was tired and seemed to have aged ten years since Richard had last seen him. He raised one hand, palm towards Richard. "Please. I just want a few words, and then I am gone." With his other hand he pulled his own jacket open. Richard could see no weapon but did not doubt a man like Montague would have several hidden away. Still, in a Parliamentarian city, a Royalist agent, perhaps the top Royalist agent, would have need of caution. This emboldened Richard. He tried to keep his face unreadable but brought both his own hands into view.

"Speak then. Why are you trailing me?"

Montague smiled, a little sadly. "Don't flatter yourself, Richard. I may call you that? I was in London on other business, and I saw you ride past. I was on my way back to Oxford but, well, there were things I wanted to say to you, so I thought standing for two hours in a cold doorway was not too great a price to pay. My, what an interesting life you lead."

"How so?"

"How is an accomplished, experienced soldier such as yourself not on the frontline serving his generals? Why is he no longer on the staff of the renowned Sir William Brereton? Why is he escorting two young ladies of the county of Cheshire to the address of known radicals and firebrands in London? How did he escape the shame of his marriage to a convicted and executed witch?"

Richard felt his unease returning, along with a rising anger. His sword hand twitched involuntarily.

Montague chuckled, and this time it looked like the mirth was genuine. "Don't worry, Richard. The truth of it is that I care very little about these things. Brereton is capable, but overcautious. He will never take Chester, at least not any time soon. As to your personal life, well, I know something of the details and the motivations. That is really why I wanted to speak to you."

He paused, a more serious look coming to his face. "I wanted to thank you for returning young DeLacey to me. Thank you for sparing him when you could have finished him. I know you loved his father, but Benedict has the chance to be

Epilouge

more than his father was. I have invested in him. I did not want to lose him. He will be valuable to His Majesty." He shrugged. "And maybe after. Who can say how all this will end? Anyway. Thank you."

"I... I did not expect that. From you. I did not feel like killing any more that day. I still don't. We have all done too much of that, and anyway he was just too much like Roger for me to leave a lead ball in his head, even if he had been trying to kill me." He paused. "He also told me I had been wrong about you. I had thought you behind the murder of my sister. My brother. I hated Cobb for it, but I think I hated you more. Benedict explained what happened."

"Yes. That was... unfortunate. I am sorry. Truly. It is not how I work except in utmost need. We have all lost those we love in this war and, it seems, not always through malice or righteous rage but through accident and unforeseen consequences. I think for every soldier who dies on the battlefield, ten innocents are taken by disease, or famine, or ignorant acts."

Richard could not disagree and somehow found that surprising. He nodded slowly. "And you, sir?"

Montague sighed. "My business here today. I am not spying, or assassinating. I am here to visit my wife. She lies yonder in the cold earth." He nodded to the church of Saint Lawrence. "I was trying to get her out of London to join me in Oxford. She ran into a mob of 'prentices, out rioting and looting. Just an accident. The wrong place at the wrong time. I seldom get the opportunity to visit her."

"I am sorry. Truly."

There was a silence that stretched out into minutes as both were lost in thoughts of loss. Abruptly, Montague swept off his hat and bowed from the waist. "My compliments, sir. I wish you well. I am for Oxford. No rest for the righteous agents of the King." He smiled. A genuine smile of friendship, it seemed. And then a thought appeared to occur to him. "Your friend, the radical. William Fletcher? A word of warning, Richard. He is a marked man. Not just by the King's men – his reputation for military success and nonconforming views are well known amongst us, but on his own side too. Not all on the Parliamentarian side are as progressive in their thinking as he and his friends, like Lilburne. No, sir, there are many that secretly would welcome the return of His Majesty, albeit on a leash to them as wealthy winners of this conflict. They have no interest in levelling. No interest in turning the world of privilege upside down. You would do him a favour by telling him so."

"Thank you, sir. And again, I find I am in agreement with you. But I think it easier to hold back the tide than to silence him. I think he has eyes on a new world for us all."

"So be it. But I must be gone." He smiled again. "I am not a popular man here in the city. Farewell, Richard."

An hour later, he was riding north-east out of London. Heading back to his home, and the smile of his daughter. Already he had a faint echo of her voice in his head. Wishing him a safe journey and reminding him to get her some sugar sweets along the way. And beneath her childish tone, there was a deeper note. At the edge of his mind, something far, far older circled slowly. Not a feeling of threat but of comfort and companionship. Not cold darkness but warmth and wisdom. He knew he was sensing it through Eva, and that she had a name. And that she would always be there.

AUTHOR'S NOTE AND ACKNOWLEDGEMENTS

This is a period of history that entirely escaped me in my school days. Apart from a few basics such as the beheading of Charles I, and the rise of Oliver Cromwell, I knew very little. Now I know a little more about it, I am amazed that it is not more widely taught, because there is so much happening in terms of social, political and religious ideas, and how these mobilised large parts of the population to actions previously unheard of in England, or indeed large parts of the world.

Starting to read about the period led me to some fascinating sources that helped to provide the historical context for my story. I want to pay tribute to some of the more prominent sources of information for the novels in this series.

My starting point was the excellent overview provided by Trevor Royle's *Civil War: The Wars of the Three Kingdoms, 1638–1660*. This, combined with the fabulous resource of the British Civil Wars, Commonwealth and Protectorate website (http://bcw-project.org/about), gave me a roadmap of the times, but also so much valuable detail. Antonia Fraser's

Cromwell: Our Chief of Men also provided great insight into the political minds of the day, and Cromwell's in particular.

I set much of the narrative of the first two books around my hometown of Macclesfield – not the setting for many novels, I think! Here, C.S. Davies' excellent *A History of Macclesfield* was extremely helpful, along with an archaeological assessment of the town published by Cheshire County Council and English Heritage. My own original research included a few drinks in the historic Bate Hall pub in Chestergate, where the friendly barman told me of sightings of its famous ghosts.

As the character of Sir William Brereton became more important to the story, I discovered a wealth of information about his life and career. Much of this is from books authored by Andrew Abram, John Barratt, R.N. Dore and Joseph McKenna, but also from some of his own diaries, which are held in the British Library and describe his colourful journeys through the Low Countries, Scotland and Ireland in his youth.

Dealing in Death: The Arms Trade and the British Civil Wars, 1638–52 is an incredibly detailed piece of work by Peter Edwards, which was absolutely fascinating, and essential, to describe the business that Richard Farrell finds himself engaged in. The radical political debates and confrontations of the time are beautifully captured in John Rees's wonderful book *The Leveller Revolution*, where the revolutionary passion and commitment of freeborn John Lilburne and his heroic wife, Elizabeth, are immortalised. *Witchfinders* by Malcolm Gaskill is an equally detailed and vital source for my attempts to weave this important thread of the period through the story. Peter Newman's *The Battle of Marston Moor, 1644* was also invaluable for describing the battle, and the build-up to it.

However, *At the Edge of Promises* is not a scholarly work but the fictional stories of certain people trying to find purpose for their lives in this tumultuous period of change. I think

Author's Note and Acknowledgements

it is important to emphasise that most of the 'point of view' characters in these stories are entirely fictional. Richard Farrell, Marleigh Hume, Will Fletcher, Roger DeLacey, Montague, John Cobb and the Walker family are all fictional characters. Sir William Brereton is the only real historical character who has a 'point of view' role in the books, but all of his interactions with the fictional characters are, by definition, fictional. From the research into Sir William, I have tried to guess at his character, and how he might react in the circumstances where I have placed him, but the main arc of his story in these books, albeit constructed around the real events he was very much part of, is entirely made up.

Finally, I wanted to pay tribute to the support provided my key critics and advisers, my sons, Michael and Joe, but particularly my wife, Sarah, who has had to endure my periods of excitement and depression as my confidence in what I have written waxed and waned. Thank you.

My thanks as well to Adrian Shuker and Dr Michael Tate for their commitment in reading the drafts of the books and for their kind words of encouragement. Thank you both.